WILLOW TREE BEND

Cover Design and Interior Format

Willow Tree Bend

KAYE DOBBIE

ALSO BY KAYE DOBBIE

The Glass House
The Bond
The Dark Dream
When Shadows Fall
Whispers from the Past
Footsteps in an Empty Room
Colours of Gold
Sweet Wattle Creek
Mackenzie Crossing
Willow Tree Bend
The Road to Ironbark

**Also books previously written as
Deborah Miles**

A Passing Fancy
Sweet Mary Anne

To Sandy Curtis, friend and fellow author. Many thanks for our conversation over dinner on a chilly Melbourne evening, when the idea for Willow Tree Bend *was born.*

I

HOPE

Saturday 8 January 2000, New York

SHE'D FALLEN INTO bed after midnight. People were still caught up in the idea of the new millennium, still coming down from the high of Times Square at midnight and the fireworks displays shown in their televised glory from around the world. Once everyone realised their computers weren't about to go awry when the clocks safely ticked over from 1999, they were more than happy to party.

Last night Hope had had dinner with some of her closer friends and colleagues—mainly those like herself, with families far away or non-existent. It was a bon voyage dinner, because she was going home to Australia to work on a program there and she didn't know when she would be back. They'd drunk far too many glasses of red wine, bemoaning the state of a film industry that catered to young men rather than thinking adults, and she had soaked up their sympathy over her recent disastrous effort. It was late when she'd waved them goodbye and set out for her apartment on the Upper West Side.

Even before she'd climbed into the cab, she'd had an uncomfortable sensation deep inside, but it had taken the entire ride home to understand what it was. A mixture of excitement and terror. She was going home. She was about to face her past in a way she hadn't done for years.

Once inside her apartment, Hope had had the strong urge to ring her older sister, Faith. They were only separated in age by a year, and as children they had been very close. But as they grew older they'd drifted apart—it was difficult not to when they lived on different continents. Hope reminded herself that she would be seeing Faith in a few days anyway. All of the arrangements had been made. Right now, it would be afternoon in Australia, but Faith would probably be busy as usual. How strange that their lives had turned out like this, so far away from each other.

Between thinking of the past and still deciding whether or not to make the international call, she'd fallen asleep.

The sound of the ringing phone shocked her into wakefulness. At first, she didn't know whether it was real or just a dream and she almost let it ring out, but then she reminded herself that it could be more than someone wanting her to read another dreadful script. It could be important. So she reached for the handset by the bed, at the same time slipping on her glasses.

The illuminated clock told her it was almost

two am as she said, 'Hello?'

There was a sound like waves crashing on a beach. Just static, she told herself, and then she heard Faith's voice.

'Hope?'

Despite having forty-six years to become familiar with it, the idea of sisters called Faith and Hope still made her groan inwardly.

Faith didn't wait for her answer before launching into a jumble of words. 'There was a photo in the newspaper, that one of all of us. You, me, Mum and Sam. Taken ages ago. When you first went to America and Golden Gully came out to send you off. Do you remember? They've just reprinted it because you're coming home. It's everywhere. I never thought … never imagined … All these years.'

Hope pulled herself up against her pillows and switched on the bedside light. That was better, she was feeling more awake now.

'What is it?' she asked. 'Has something happened to Joe? To Samantha? Is Mum all right?'

Faith made a sound that could have been a laugh, or a sob. 'Do you know you're the only one who calls her that? *Samantha*. She's always been Sam to us.'

'Faith,' Hope paused, knowing it was important to sound calm despite her heart rattling about in her chest. 'You haven't rung me for ages and now it's the middle of the night, and you're telling me that I'm the only one who calls your daughter by her full name?'

That silence again, or rather the sound of the

waves of static crashing over the distance between them. Hope tried to picture Faith's house. She hadn't been home for nearly ten years and then only briefly, but she remembered the little nook off the lounge, where the phone was situated. It would be summer there, afternoon, and outside the summer sun would be blazing. The house would be closed up to keep out the heat, shades drawn and the light muted.

'What is it?' she said again. 'Tell me what's wrong. Faith?'

'I was remembering the Angel. I still think about it you know.'

'The Angel? Faith, what—'

'I had to go.' Her sister's words ran into each other. 'You see that, don't you? I *had* to go. It's up to me to fix this.'

'Fix what?'

But by then the call was disconnected.

Hope sat and stared at the shadowy corners of her bedroom, and then slowly returned the handset to the cradle. She waited a little while, in case her sister rang back and explained it was all a mistake and she was sorry to have frightened her. Because Hope *was* frightened.

Suddenly she was cold to her very core.

Shivering, she climbed out of bed and found her address book and then she tapped in Faith Cantani's number.

It rang for some time before finally someone answered.

'Joe?' She spoke quickly as soon as she heard his familiar voice.

'Joe, it's Hope.'

He drew a breath. 'Hope?'

'Faith just rang me. Can you put her back on please? I—I don't quite understand what she wanted.'

There was a pause. 'I'm sorry,' he said, and she could hear the break in his voice. 'Faith left yesterday and I haven't seen her since.'

'Left? What do you mean, Joe? She was just on the phone!'

'Well, she wasn't ringing from here.'

Hope took off her glasses. 'Where is she, then? I need to call her back.'

'I don't know her number.'

He seemed to be unable to explain himself. He sounded very tired. Through further questioning, Hope managed to discover the sequence of events. Faith had been preoccupied. 'The new range of Cantani Desserts she has coming out this month. You know about that?'

Hope did know. Faith had sent her a sample, which had caused endless issues with US Customs. She'd agreed, if her schedule allowed, to be at the unveiling.

'And then with you coming home … well, she was busy redecorating.'

'What happened yesterday before she left?'

'Hope … she'll be back before you get here, I know she will. Just leave it, please. Whatever it is … Everything will be okay.'

'What happened, Joe?'

He sighed, and at first she didn't think he was going to answer. 'She took an interstate phone call at the shop and the girls said she looked upset.'

He was upset.

'Who was the call from?'

'It was a man. She didn't mention his name.'

She waited a beat, trying to understand and not understanding at all. 'And then …?' She wanted him to elaborate on Faith's mood, but instead he went sideways.

'There was a dinner we were meant to attend. Best local business awards. We were nominated. I don't even know who won.' He took a moment; she could hear him breathing. 'I, uh, I went to get my suit from the dry cleaners and when I got back she was gone.'

'Just … gone?'

'She left a note. It was a bit of a scrawl. I was away twenty minutes.' Hope waited and eventually he told her what the note said.

'*Sorry. I need to go and fix this. Hope you can understand. Forgive me.*'

Hope tried to imagine her sister frantically throwing clothes into a bag, grabbing her purse and running from the house. All to avoid Joe so she could 'fix this'? Why couldn't she tell him? Had something happened between them that prevented her from telling her husband of thirty years where she was going and why?

'Did you argue?'

'No, we didn't bloody argue.' For the first time he sounded angry. And yet it was a reasonable question. Faith and Joe had been known to argue now and again, but they always made up. Joe was such an ocean of calm that even Faith, with her set ideas on how things should be handled, eventually gave way.

'After she'd gone I tried to ring her mobile, until I discovered she'd left it behind at the shop. She'd taken her car so I drove around, nowhere in particular, because I didn't know what else to do.'

'Joe, I don't understand. Explain to me what is going on.'

'Don't you think I would if I could?' There was a bleakness in his voice that was frightening. Then, abruptly, 'What did she say to you? Just now, on the phone? What did she say?'

Hope tried to gather her thoughts, which were jumping about all over the place. 'She mentioned the Angel. The nightclub she worked at all those years ago.'

'The Angel.' It was a whisper, a breath. A curse.

'When she came back home she wasn't the same, Joe. I remember that much. Something happened to her.'

The truth was Hope hadn't been in any state to find out the details of whatever secrets her sister was keeping from her. She'd had her own secrets.

Joe was still waiting on the other end of the phone.

'I'm coming over,' Hope said.

'I know. That television show you're making.'

'*Looking Back.*' It was an Australian program focusing on wellknown people in the public eye, exploring both the nature and nurture that had moulded them into who they were. Or at least that was the premise. As an Australian actress who'd done well overseas, Hope Taylor fitted the bill. She had agreed to it because: one, she needed the money, and two, she was anticipating it would bring her more work. Until now, number three, visiting Australia and seeing her family, had seemed a long way down the list. Strange how a family crisis changed your perspective.

And if *Looking Back*, a little like some of the sleazier gossip magazines, had a habit of shocking its viewers with previously undisclosed information, at least their researchers were professionals. They would hardly sully the program's reputation by telling lies. Hope already had a few ideas for her own 'revelations'. Harmless stuff really. She told herself she was comfortable that they wouldn't dig up anything on her she didn't want aired. Mainly because all of her secrets were too deeply buried and they wouldn't know where to start digging.

'I'm flying in to Melbourne on the twelfth, yes, but I can come now, Joe. Or as soon as I can get a flight and organise what I need to.'

She waited for him to protest. It took him longer than she'd expected.

'No, don't change your plans. Faith will be back by then. To— to explain. Everything will be back to normal.' He said it as if he wanted to believe it.

'Joe …?'

'Faith knows you're coming, and then there's the unveiling …

It'll sort itself out. It has to.'

She promised to let him know when she was on her way, and he promised to ring her if he heard any news.

By the time she hung up Hope was wide awake. She sat a moment, abruptly aware of the chilly atmosphere of her apartment—the furnace in the basement had broken down again. She should have asked Joe more questions, but it was all so strange she hadn't known what to ask. And what on earth was that note about? Maybe Joe knew what was going on and maybe he didn't. He was so intensely loyal to his wife that it was difficult for Hope to tell.

She tried to remember all that Faith had said, going over the words and the pauses between them, wondering if she'd forgotten anything crucial. Her sister had mentioned a photograph, taken years ago, reprinted because Hope was coming home.

She told herself it made no sense, but she knew that somehow it did. *The Angel.* Something had happened while Faith was there, just as something had happened to Hope that hot January afternoon thirty years ago in Willow Tree Bend.

2

FAITH

June 1969, Willow Tree Bend

THE CAR HAD reached the turn in the road that ran along the creek and Faith really didn't want to look back. Not when she was starting out on her new and exciting life. In those circumstances, looking back wasn't the cool thing to do.

But she did. She couldn't seem to help it. The old cottage sitting on the hill exerted a pull on her that was quite suddenly irresistible.

The windows reflected the colours of the winter sunset, while the shadows were shortening in the evening light. Just as she'd feared, her mother was standing and watching, huddled into her old tweed coat, as Joe's car faded from sight. Her heart sank when she realised what that stony gaze meant—her mother was trying not to cry.

With a groan, Faith turned to face the front.

'What?' Joe asked, looking at her as if he thought she'd changed her mind. Or maybe he was hoping she had.

Faith felt like crying herself. Why was everyone making it so difficult for her to do what she had her heart set on doing? First her mother, who acted as if life in Melbourne resembled Sodom and Gomorrah, and then Hope with her accusing glances and trembling lip. But she refused to let them spoil it for her, and perhaps that more than anything was keeping her from caving in.

'Did they give you a hard time?' Joe said quietly.

Straight away she felt he was on her side and there was comfort in that. She managed a smile and a shrug. 'Sort of.'

Faith had been working in Joe's mother's milk bar since she left school a year ago, and while she decided what she wanted to do with her life. She liked it because it made her feel as if she was in the centre of things. Everyone dropped into the milk bar at some point during their day, and when Mrs Cantani wasn't there, Joe made sure the radio was tuned to the latest hits.

Joe, his older brother, Pete, and his mother had run the place since Mr Cantani died last year, and she'd noticed how much Joe had grown up. She supposed he'd had to. He used to go out with Faith a bit, to the pool or the church socials, just as friends, but now he hardly ever did.

Mrs Cantani had been disappointed when she heard that Faith was leaving. She didn't like flighty girls and she'd shaken her head as if she didn't remember what it was like to be seventeen and frightened that this was all your life was ever going to be. Joe understood though. He was nineteen, and while he seemed happy enough with the status quo, he'd offered Faith a sympathetic ear on the couple of occasions she had expressed her feelings to him.

'Mum wants me to bake the best scones and win first prize at the Golden Gully show, just so she can lord it over those old biddies in the CWA. She wants me to go to church every Sunday and marry a man she approves of. She wants to be proud of me, but only if I do what she says and never upset her. But that life wouldn't be my life, would it? I feel as if the air is being sucked out of me by this place.

I need to breathe, Joe!'

'Wait until you're twenty-one,' had been Joe's advice. 'Stick around until then and you can do whatever you like.'

'But that's four years away!' Faith had wailed. 'I can't wait that long, Joe.'

He'd smiled and looked at her as if he was so much older and wiser, and then he'd surprised her by offering her a lift to Melbourne.

'I have to pick up some stuff from my uncle. He lives in Coburg. Where are you staying?'

Faith was staying with her cousin Kitty, at least for now. She'd been to Kitty's twenty-first birthday party, which was what had started this whole yearning to get away from Willow Tree Bend. Faith's mother, Lily, was so bound up in this small town and her small life that she couldn't understand anyone wanting something different. Now her words replayed in Faith's head like an LP from her favourite band, the Allnights.

'It was that weekend you spent down in Melbourne for Kitty's party, wasn't it? Some no-hoper you met put ideas into your head. I knew I shouldn't have let you go!'

Lily had been red-faced, her fair hair scraped up on top of her head, dressed in her old shirt and trousers. She'd been feeding the few animals left on the farm. Most of their land was leased out for agistment. Since Faith's father had walked out on them eleven years ago, everything had been down to her. And Lily, once a city girl who had married a country boy, had learned fast. She'd had to.

'It wasn't like that,' Faith had said, trying not to sound desperate. 'No one's put ideas into my head. They're my own ideas, Mum.' But the party *had* opened her eyes to what she was missing. People who spoke her language, who understood how she felt and what she wanted, and who related to her in a way her mother never could. And worst of all was the thought that one day she might end up here, at the cottage, in her mother's shoes.

'What did Hope say? About you leaving?' Joe's voice interrupted her thoughts, rising above the hum of his VC Valiant. He'd bought the car a few months ago and it was his pride and joy.

'Why, what has she said to you?'

Her sister, Hope, was still at school, but she often hung out at the milk bar, or the fish and chip shop next door. Faith suspected that it was Pete who was the attraction, although whenever she warned her sister about Pete's flirtatious ways, she became irritatingly coy.

Hope had been so upset when Faith told her she was leaving that she'd run off down to the old willow tree by the bend in the creek.

The willow had always been the sisters' special place. Somewhere to brood when life wasn't going the way they wanted it to, or to share their secrets or current concerns, or just have a good laugh. This time it was Hope who sat alone within the winter-bare curtain of branches, looking miserable. Faith hadn't followed her. Because what could she say? She wasn't going to change her mind no matter how much Hope wanted her to. This was her chance to break free of her stifling life, and all of the dreams and expectations that Faith realised were not hers and that she did not want to fulfil.

Joe replied in his measured way. 'Your sister didn't say much. I told her you'd probably be back in a couple of weeks.'

Faith narrowed her eyes at him. The thing about Joe was that he was always so charmingly laidback, you couldn't be angry with him for long. So instead of sulking, she said, 'Hope's in the high school play this year, did you know? She's the star and it's a big deal for her. I've told her I'll try to get back to see it, but …'

'But?'

'I probably won't want to.'

Joe lifted an eyebrow in a way that always made her laugh. He had dark hair and blue eyes, which Faith didn't think of as very Italian, but according to him that was because his grandparents had come from the north of the country, up near the

Swiss border. He had a nice smile, too, and a few times she'd felt that if she gave him just a bit more encouragement he might ask her out.

Yes, he was nice. Good-looking, dependable and, according to her mother, of the 'right' religion—her mother had always been a churchgoer. Knowing that Lily approved of Joe had the opposite effect on Faith. She'd choose to go out with any number of losers rather than him. Anyway, right now she was focused on her future. Melbourne, the Big Smoke. She was heading into the open arms of the city, and she didn't want anything or anyone holding her back.

She'd wanted to leave for quite some time now. The party had just brought it all to a head. There were days when she felt as if this place was slowly strangling her, and, as she'd tried to tell Joe, making it harder and harder to breathe. She might die if she stayed a moment longer, or worse, be so weighed down by the minutia of her life in this small country town that even if she had the opportunity to escape, she would no longer have the strength.

Joe turned on the radio and a song from the Beatles' *White Album* filled the car. Faith closed her eyes as the world slipped by outside the window. The familiar bushland and paddocks, the narrow road changing to asphalt, and then the highway. She listened to the music and didn't want to talk anymore; her choice had been made.

A slow curl of excitement began to unfurl in the pit of her stomach. Even remembering Hope's teary rejection earlier today, and her mother's sad face, couldn't dampen it. Tomorrow she would wake up in Kitty's room, and when she looked out of the window she wouldn't see the slope running down to the creek and the old willow tree with its pendulous branches whispering in the breeze. She'd see busy streets with cars rushing past, and people moving forward with purpose.

Her life was going to be very different from now on, and Faith couldn't wait.

3

SAMANTHA

Monday 10 January 2000, Golden Gully, Victoria

I STRAIGHTENED UP AS some corellas flew squawking overhead. My back might ache but I was smiling. Surely nothing was better than this? There before me was laid out my hard day's work in the form of the newly planted front garden of a newly built house on the outskirts of town.

The owners had heard of me through the local grapevine—Suzy, who managed the local supermarket, was good for getting the word out. We'd been to school together back in the dark ages and now she was married with four kids, unlike single, childless me.

After she'd regaled my most recent client with stories of my brilliant garden designs, they'd requested I draw up some plans. Sometimes when I set out my vision of a client's garden it was rejected or, worse, fell into a black hole. With the latter, I rarely found out what it was about my plans they disliked, which was frustrating, especially when I'd poured my heart and soul into them. In this case the client loved my ideas and, I hoped, my friendly professionalism. So much so that they had no hesitation in contracting me to put my plans into action.

And, I smiled to myself again, they'd be pleased with the result, too. I'd been at pains to explain that you had to wait, and in these times of instant gratification, waiting could be a difficult ask. Give it a year or two and their garden would be just as they imagined it—a retreat from the hurry of their weekly lives in the city, and an idyll to escape to on the weekends.

More and more people who'd moved into the Golden Gully district were weekenders, nine-to-fivers who were hoping to eventually retire full-time to the country. Green-changers, some of the locals called them.

They were my bread and butter, and without the green-change movement Green Dreams, my fledgling garden design and landscaping business would have foundered long ago. Particularly during the hot, dry months of summer and the frosty cold winters. It had taken me a long time, and a lot of false turns, to discover my true calling, and I was determined to make it a success.

A car horn tooted and I looked up as a dusty four-wheel drive came to a stop. My father was here, right on time. He really was the most reliable man I knew. I reminded myself that whatever had caused the ruction between him and my mother was none of my business. Faith could be difficult, it was true, but she was never intentionally unkind, and for her to go off like that, with all that was happening …

I'd heard about middle-aged women unexpectedly wanting a complete life makeover, it's just I never thought she'd be one of them.

Of course I had asked Dad about it. Or tried to. Apart from him telling me it was Mum's business and to leave it, I didn't get much joy. Mum had rung me a couple of days ago, so I knew she was fine. I kept telling myself there was nothing to worry about and I would have believed it, if it hadn't been for my increasing sense of misgiving.

'Where are you?'

'North Queensland,' she said, after a hesitation, which made me wonder whether she was even going to tell me. Then, before I could ask her where in North Queensland, 'I'm okay, everything is okay, don't worry.'

'But what about Hope? Will you be back in time? Dad's freaking out—' I broke off, not wanting to be disloyal to my father, and anyway, she must know how worried he was.

'Things are difficult here, but I'll try.'

I attempted to get my head around that one. Faith, who always liked to be in control, wasn't bothered by her sister arriving from the US and her not being there to boss everyone around? Not to mention her new line of desserts, which she had been working on for months and months, and were due to be released any day now.

'Mum, what is it? You know you can tell me. Is something … has Dad …?'

'This is nothing to do with your father, Sam. He hasn't done anything wrong. It's just something I have to do. Something from the past that I need to sort out.

I'll explain it when I see you.'

'Explain what?'

'Sam,' she took a breath, 'when you were born I held you in my arms and I felt as if I'd been handed a miracle. I still feel that.'

My family didn't say things like this. We loved each other, but we rarely spoke about how we felt. To hear these words from my mother was far more shocking than her telling me she was in North Queensland.

'I don't understand,' I whispered.

And then I heard the waves in the background. Was she on a beach somewhere sipping a pina colada? The image flashed before my eyes: my mother in a bikini—she still had the figure for it—a flower in her blonde hair and a sun-bronzed surfie at her side. Suddenly I was angry and frightened, and as usual the combination brought out the worst in me.

'You know this is so selfish,' I said in a tight little voice. 'Maybe you shouldn't bother coming home after all.' That was when I hung up.

Afterwards, I'd reminded myself that my parents were both adults, and whatever it was that had sent Mum off on this secret mission, well it was up to them to sort it out. Despite her odd words she had sounded fine, not as if she was having a breakdown or anything. No, the very idea was ludicrous. The only times I had seen her overwrought were when she was angry with me and my life choices. She'd wanted me to join her in the Cantani Desserts business, and when I refused it was as if I'd started World War III. Since then things had settled down and she'd come to accept that I wasn't her and never would be.

I had to make my own way in life, and therefore my own mistakes.

Collecting together my tools, I walked towards the four-wheel drive. Dad got out to help me load them into the back. His blue eyes were narrowed, deepening the wrinkles in his lean, sun-browned face, and his short dark hair was sprinkled with grey. My father was a handsome man and I didn't think I was biased in thinking so. It was a bit of a shame that when I looked into the mirror I always thought I resembled the Taylor side of the family, although I'd inherited his blue eyes.

'Good day?' he said, but it wasn't really a question. Evidently, he could tell by the look of me that it had been.

'Yes, thanks.' I smiled at him. 'And thanks for picking me up, Dad. The garage rang to tell me my rust bucket should be ready by tomorrow, so I'm hoping you won't need to come to my rescue again. Not for a while anyway.'

The old ute had been giving me more grief than usual, but it ran on an oily rag, and as long as it was fixable I figured it was cheaper than spending money I didn't have on buying something new and pretty.

'You must have enough to do as it is,' I added, as we climbed into the cabin. I meant *with Mum not here*, therefore giving him an opportunity to vent, but as usual my father kept his thoughts buried deep beneath his stoic exterior.

'I'm managing.'

I glanced at him, seeing the strain and the sleepless nights, and wondered about that. Had he and

Mum ever been apart? I had a feeling they never had, not since their wedding day thirty years ago. Their love for each other was something I had taken for granted for so long it was a shock to imagine it might be starting to unravel.

He backed down the driveway, twisting around to see where he was going. My gaze fell on his tanned wrist, and I noted with a sense of relief that he was still wearing the Rolex watch. I wasn't sure why I'd been worried he might have taken it off, only that seeing it there as usual was comforting.

Mum had given him the Rolex on their twenty-fifth wedding anniversary, and according to her, she had saved up for months because she wanted it to be special. A gift he could keep. As Dad told it, he'd been totally blown away. He'd even shed a couple of tears, and seeing them together, smiling into each other's eyes, I had never doubted their marriage was still as strong as ever.

So, what was going on?

I glanced sideways at him as we set off down the road. When Hope arrived with her camera crew in tow, would it be just me and Dad bearing the brunt? Hope would want us to play happy families, when the truth was she hadn't been home in ten years. Did Dad find all of this as awkward as I did? Usually my father took things in his stride, but his sister-in-law's imminent arrival, as well as Mum running away up north, had brought a haunted look to his eyes.

It was true that a couple of times recently I'd interrupted words between my parents. As soon as they noticed me they'd gone into 'cover-up mode', as I called it, pretending everything was peachy. They should have been ASIO operatives, or actors like Hope. I'd shrugged it off because I had worries of my own. I was twenty-nine, for God's sake. I had my own life, such as it was. And yet the idea of my parents' marriage imploding left me wanting to squirm about in my seat like a little girl.

Right now, Hope's impending visit seemed like something we could really do without.

My aunt was pretty much a stranger, to me anyway, and I'd never thought she and my mother were all that close. Not the clingy sort of sisterly love I'd seen displayed by other families. There was a wariness about them, a sense of things that had been left unspoken for so long that now they were unmentionable.

I could count on the fingers of one hand the number of times during the year my mother spoke to Hope on the phone. When she had a new movie or was making an appearance on television, we made the effort to see it. There was never the sort of sibling envy one might have expected. My mother smiled and took it all in her stride, giving the impression that she wasn't jealous in the slightest. And it wasn't an act— Mum honestly didn't want to change places with her famous sister. She was happy in her own skin.

Or at least she had been until she set off for the Sunshine State.

I turned my mind back to the last time Hope came to visit. It had been a whirlwind trip, and I was eighteen and it hadn't gone well. I'd still been going through my rebellious stage—yes, I was a late bloomer. I was standing there in my old torn jeans and dusty boots and halter top, and out of the blue in had walked Hope in a cloud of Shalimar. She had brought a suitcase full of designer clothes from the US, which she presented to me with a smug little smile. She'd expected me to be ecstatic, but I wasn't that sort of girl. She must have wondered what was wrong with me. My boyfriend at the time had been more impressed by my glamorous and famous aunty than I had been.

I admitted now that I'd been insensitive and ignorant and judgemental. At the time, Mum was furious with me, but she'd begun to see glimmers of maturity, as if I might finally be turning from a grungy caterpillar into a butterfly, so for that reason she hadn't made too big a deal of it. Hope had no children of her own and didn't understand, and although she'd pretended to laugh away my rejection, I knew I'd hurt her feelings. The memory still made me uncomfortable. I hadn't lost my complete disdain for the high end of fashion, but if it happened today I'd accept the clothes and sell them on eBay. I needed the money after all.

'How long will Hope be staying?' I asked my father.

'I'm not sure,' he said. 'You should ask Faith.' And then he stopped and took a sharp breath, almost as if someone had struck him.

I felt my worry ramping up by leaps and bounds. Maybe I was wrong and the situation was worse than I'd imagined! Why oh why had I told my mother not to come home?

'Dad …?'

'She said she'd like to take some time to catch up with us after the filming.' His voice was measured, back to normal, but he wouldn't meet my eyes.

'The program's *Looking Back*, right?' I kept my gaze on him, and I noticed he had returned to cover-up mode.

'*Looking Back*, yeah. Not something I would have thought Hope did all that often.'

I was wondering what he meant, until his next words chased all those questions from my mind.

'You know her plane is arriving day after tomorrow?'

'So soon! It seemed weeks away.'

'Don't worry, she's being collected. She'll see us when she gets here. No doubt we'll receive our instructions.' He half smiled to show he wasn't really having a dig at Hope's high-handed manner.

'The town will go crazy.'

It already had. People I knew, and those I didn't, were asking me questions, eager to see her.

'Yeah. Local girl returns to her humble roots. I can imagine the TV news headlines. Don't be too hard on her, Sam, she is a pretty good actress.'

'Is she still linked to that Hollywood director?' I tapped my fingers on my knee. 'What was his name?'

'I forget his name, too. Someone famous. You'll have to ask her.'

Definitely not. I wasn't going to pry into my aunt's personal life. Although I was grateful to her.

When my grandmother, Lily Taylor, had decided it was too much for her living alone at the Willow Tree Bend property, she, Faith and Hope had put their heads together to decide what to do about it. Lily probably would have liked one of her daughters to carry on there, but Hope had her life overseas, and Faith was married to Joe and her business. Neither of them had ever expressed any desire to move back into the cottage.

I didn't know my grandfather, Rex Taylor. He'd walked out when Mum was little. They'd all lived in the cottage on the hill, and although in later years we'd visited often, Rex was never mentioned. It was as if Gran had wiped him from her memory. Mum said that was fine by her, he wasn't a nice person, but she didn't say much more than that. I did get the sense, though, that he'd been one of those men who couldn't see a woman without trying to sleep with her.

Dad's large extended family was a different matter. When I was little we'd had many happy holidays with the Cantanis. Although Joe and Peter had been the only children of their parents, there were plenty of great uncles and aunts, as well as a matriarchal great grandmother, and I'd sometimes found myself with more cousins than I knew what to do with. The original Cantani settlers lived further to the south, where most of the older descendants remained, but as time went on, and family members died or their children grew up and left home, they began to scatter and lose touch.

When it came to my relatives, I was probably closer to my mother's side, and in particular my grandmother. I was sorry when Lily, Faith and Hope sold off Willow Tree Bend, and the property was subdivided. Mind you, the sale made more than enough money for them to be able to move Lily into a unit in Golden Gully, which was the service town for a wide district that included farming properties and smaller settlements and protected bushland. Unbeknownst to me, there had been a chunk of the Willow Tree Bend property kept aside—I later learned that was Hope's idea. When I turned twenty-one, and was considered mature enough to appreciate it, they told me it was mine.

It was the kind of start many girls could only dream of. Now the memory of my good fortune, and my behaviour towards Hope, made me ashamed all over again.

'Sorry,' I said, with a glance at my father. 'I'm being difficult. I'll make Hope so welcome she won't even notice Mum isn't here.'

'I hope so, love.' He hesitated, and I thought he was going to say something else, but then he changed his mind. He lifted his chin to indicate something in front of us.

I narrowed my eyes against the glare on the dusty windscreen and took in my driveway and gate and, set back behind a fenced-in yard, the low silhouette of my house. There, waiting by the gate, was a diminutive figure in a floral frock.

Lily Taylor had come for a visit.

'Did you tell her?' I asked my father, not taking my eyes off my elderly grandmother. She had an overstuffed bag, and I thought that was ominous. She was also wearing her best shady hat. 'About Mum, I mean?'

'She knew already,' he replied, slowing the car.

'The octogenarian grapevine.' It was a well-known fact that the elderly ladies of Golden Gully knew what was going on before the rest of us.

Dad's mouth curled into a proper smile. 'She's got Pompom with her.'

Pompom was a mixed breed and had been called the ugliest dog in the world, but not in front of my grandmother. She loved Pompom and never left him alone for longer than a couple of hours.

That she'd brought her pet with her didn't bode well.

'Great,' I muttered as I climbed out of the four-wheel drive. Pompom ran towards me and I tried to fend him off as best I could, while plastering a welcoming expression on my face.

'Sam, there you are!' my grandmother said, managing to sound simultaneously pleased and critical.

'Gran, what are you doing here? It's nearly forty degrees!'

Something in her eyes shifted, as if she had an answer but had no intention of sharing it with me. 'Pompom and I have come to stay,' she said grandly, and stood back while I opened the gate.

4

HOPE

Monday 10 January 2000, New York

TONIGHT WAS HER last night in the tiny apartment on the Upper West Side, and the air was only marginally warmer than it had been a couple of nights ago. The furnace was supposed to have been fixed, but Hope had her doubts. She'd lived here for five years and she couldn't remember a time when it wasn't going to be 'fixed'.

Sometimes the apartment had been nothing more than somewhere to drop into exhausted sleep after a long working day, especially over the past two years, with all the stresses of *The Document*. No, she wouldn't miss this place.

For the first time in a very long time, her work horizon stretched before her like a lonely country road, with only one stopping-off point. And let's face it, even if it could, *Looking Back* wasn't going to win her an Oscar. But that wasn't her reason for making the program. Australians were always interested in those of their fellow countrymen who had made a success of their lives overseas, no matter how nebulous that success might be. There would be interviews with newspapers and magazines, television and radio. Not just for *Looking Back*—they'd arranged their own publicity—but stuff she could do on her own. She'd also been tossing up the idea of writing a book about her life and career, but she wasn't certain. It was one thing to play the part of Hope Taylor, small-town girl made good, but another to deliberately lie on paper.

No, not lie. She refused to think of it like that. She was simply airbrushing some of the wrinkles.

Most of her personal belongings had been packed up in boxes and placed in storage until she decided what she was going to do with them. The apartment was to be let and eventually sold, and as for her future …

It was as if she was drifting, at the mercy of whatever the gods decided for her, and that wasn't a comfortable place for Hope to be. She'd tended to micromanage things—every detail had to be looked at and then looked at again.

With a shiver, Hope pulled on the sweater Faith had sent her for her last birthday—emblazoned with a picture of Prince telling her to party like it was 1999—and climbed into bed. Propped up with several pillows, she reached for her book. She was attempting to read James Joyce's *Ulysses* because someone had said everyone should try at least once, but not surprisingly found her mind wandering.

Faith had gone AWOL.

Why did that cause this squirm of guilt? As if Faith's irrational behaviour was in some way her fault. As if her coming home and digging up the past had set Faith off and running.

What was Hope supposed to have done? Refuse the offer? The truth was, *Looking Back* was the only offer she'd had since *The Document* came out.

And flopped.

The Document. Even the title sounded dull— but at the time she'd thought it had a gravitas that couldn't fail to win over the thinking public. Her career, which to be honest had been pretty lightweight, could only benefit from a role that showed off her acting chops.

Had she been deluded? Maybe. And yet the story itself was sound. It had seemed the perfect vehicle for Hope—the role for a mature actress wanting to lift her career to a new level. The younger crowd mightn't be interested, but the serious film-goers and critics were sure to love it.

Despite her belief in the project, and her certainty in her own ability to carry off the starring role, she had struggled to find investors. They didn't see big box-office appeal even though she explained that wasn't the audience she was aiming for. Eventually she'd ended up putting her own money into it, scraping together her savings and calling in favours from friends. Against everyone's expectations, apart from her own, the filming went well. There were excellent reviews from the early showings. The film was launched into the smaller boutique and art-house cinemas, and it was looking good.

And then it all went wrong.

She learned that someone else had made a movie with the same storyline—small-town girl takes on a giant corporation in a David-and-Goliath situation—but the actress in this movie was a Hollywood sweetheart. It didn't matter that *The Document* was well made and, according to the reviews, Hope was the best thing in it. Her film was never going to be able to compete. She lost a lot of money, and although she made enough to be able to repay her backers, everything else was gone.

At one point, there was even a rumour going around that she was dead.

And in that moment Hope had wished she was.

'Come home,' was Faith's solution to the problem.

'My life is here,' Hope had protested.

'But your family is here,' her sister had argued.

Then *Looking Back* had come along and Hope hadn't hesitated. Not for a second. It was only later that she began to wonder if she'd jumped from the frying pan into the fire.

Faith must know she was going to keep to the script—in other words, the story of Hope's life in Willow Tree Bend as it appeared in the public domain. Surely she didn't have to spell it out? Surely Faith would realise she had everything under control, micromanaged as usual. Well, maybe in hindsight she should have discussed it with her sister before she'd signed the contracts, but it hadn't occurred to her that she needed to.

All she'd thought about was that the program was the perfect solution to her problems.

No, Hope couldn't believe her decision was the reason for Faith's sudden departure. It must have been something else. This was simply a coincidence.

It'll be all right, she tried to reassure herself again. The only possible glitch was her mother, but she'd told *Looking Back* that Lily was frail and elderly and mustn't be bothered. Admittedly, she'd made it sound as if she was in the advanced stages of Alzheimer's disease, but the important thing was that they'd agreed.

Hope glanced at the clock and then put aside James Joyce with some relief. She had a plane to catch in the morning. She just hoped Faith would be home by the time her cavalcade rolled into town.

Rearranging her bed, she removed her glasses and switched off the light, and tried to still her mind in preparation for sleep. But her mind wouldn't be stilled. Why was it that the knowledge that she needed a good night's rest seemed to sabotage her every time?

Restlessly, she turned over. The linen was freshly laundered and she breathed in the sweet scent, knowing this was one of the things she would genuinely miss about the apartment. Clean sheets every night—what a luxury! Perhaps because it went against everything she'd been brought up to believe in by her mother. Frugality, making do, humility. Lily's religion—always a big part of her life—had almost become a mania after their father had walked out. Hope didn't remember it in detail—Faith, being that little bit older, remembered more.

The endless prayers, the fervent longing to reach a level of perfection that would make her worthy in the eyes of God. Occasionally their father would drop in, but never for more than a day or two, and there was a cruelty in that. It had given Lily a sense of hope, when he would have been kinder to have stayed away. In later years, Faith used to speculate that their mother believed if she was good enough then their father would have to stay. He never did.

And then one day he turned up and there was a tremendous argument. Hope didn't know what was said, because they had been sent outside to wait it out. She still remembered huddling with Faith on the verandah while the angry shouting had turned to quieter resignation, and then watching his car driving away.

They'd expected their mother to fall to pieces, but instead she'd come out to watch him go. White-faced, shaky, but with her green eyes hard as ice. 'Good riddance,' she'd said.

After that she'd changed. She wasn't interested in trying to please everyone else. She grew strong and stubborn and mouthy—people crossed the street when they saw her coming. The long prayers stopped. God wasn't quite as infallible as he had been, and although she still went to church she no longer expected miracles.

Lily worked hard and slept deeply, which was handy, because her daughters liked to stay awake long into the night. Hope remembered she and Faith lying in their beds, whispering in the darkness, as dreams were expressed and ambitions shared. She wanted to be a famous actress and Faith wanted to travel. There was a poster of London on the wall and even before it was fashionable Faith had a bucket list of the places she wanted to see. But the sisters had always planned to leave together. Hope still remembered the day her sister drove off in Joe's car without her, and how upset she'd been. Faith was leaving *her* behind, and it took her a long time to forgive her for it.

Of course, later on Faith had returned and it had been Hope who had spread her wings and set off into the big wide world. Yes, there was satisfaction in that, and in knowing she had achieved the goals she had set herself. But Hope admitted that there would have been more satisfaction if Faith had shown, even for a moment, that she was the teeniest bit jealous.

Her mind began to drift to what else she would miss about living here in New York. Central Park in the spring, and the shops along Fifth Avenue. The opera at the Lincoln Center, and the ballet, things she enjoyed dressing up to be seen at. Clichés, she realised, but it was true, she had always loved the obvious about this city.

God forbid, perhaps at heart she was still a wide-eyed girl from country Australia!

A good line for the program. She must remember it.

The producers were going to take her 'home' to Willow Tree Bend. They wanted to film her as she wandered misty-eyed through the old cottage, and reminisced about the past.

Was it still the same?

Samantha would know; she lived nearby. She could even see it from her property. When Sam had learned about her windfall, she had written to Hope. It was a very nice letter, but it was the sort of letter you might write to a distant relative. Stilted. One stranger to another.

Well, she *was* a stranger, wasn't she? Ten years ago, when Hope had last been home, she had looked forward to some sort of connection between herself and Samantha. Instead, she had found her niece very like the person Faith had become—same stubborn pride, same take-me-or-leave-me attitude. In that regard Faith had turned into Lily, and it seemed as if Samantha was turning into Faith.

Hope began to drift into sleep at last.

And then, as if a switch had been flicked, she found herself back on that hot summer afternoon in January, the road stretching before her …

Everything seemed to waver, the heat rising from the earth, and the smell of dust and eucalyptus. Cicadas were humming, their song rising and falling, but there was no other sound. A narrow strip of bitumen ran down the centre of the road, but it was soft, melting, so they walked to the side, his hand in hers. He was laughing at something she'd said and his breath reminded her of the Fanta they'd shared beneath the willow tree. Afterwards.

In the dream, the landscape was a washed-out gold and brown, while the sky was an amazing, eye-aching blue. She could feel the heat through the thin soles of her sandals, and the burn of the sun on her bare shoulders. She was already tanned, the deeper shade of her skin a striking contrast to her fair hair and green eyes. He told her she was beautiful.

And then they heard the car.

They both looked up and watched it coming towards them. A big black old-fashioned machine. Hope half recognised it, and she shaded her eyes to watch its approach. He rested a hand on her shoulder and said something that made her smile.

Dust drifted towards them in the still air, and they moved sideways onto the dry crackly grass to get out of the way. Around here people weren't often in this much of a hurry, and even when they were they'd always stop to chat and say gidday. So, it didn't seem strange when the vehicle began to slow down.

Hope's gaze lingered on the shiny chrome bumper bar and the protruding headlamps. The car was like something her father might have driven when he was younger. Or maybe not. There was too much solid respectability about this car for her father, who had always preferred flashy. Like the women Faith said she'd seen him with in town, before he left for good.

The car stopped beside them and she could smell the heat from the engine, and then the window slid down. That was when she saw the driver's face and remembered who the car belonged to.

'Can I give you a lift into town?' He looked from her to the boy beside her, and back again. 'A bit hot to be walking, isn't it?'

They exchanged a glance. Hope knew they were going to say 'yes', just for an excuse to ride in the car

. . .

In the New York apartment Hope stirred restlessly in her bed, trying to wake herself. She knew she wouldn't be able to. She always had to follow the dream through until the very end. Every excruciating moment.

She was climbing into the car, enjoying the sensation of the soft leather seat against her bare legs, when a sound woke her. Not the telephone this time, but someone outside singing loudly, followed by several complaints voiced by the neighbours.

Hope sat up, trying to breathe deeply, as her heart gradually slowed its rapid beat. Despite the chill in the apartment her skin was hot, and as she listened to the insults drifting back and forth, she knew she wouldn't be able to sleep again, not for a long while. Maybe not at all.

She reminded herself that the road incident had happened thirty years ago. There was no need to be afraid that *Looking Back* would find out. And yet she *was* afraid. Frankly, she was terrified. Despite all of her careful planning and expressions of confidence, Hope knew there was always a possibility that her foray into her past could go very, very wrong.

5

FAITH

July 1969, St Kilda, Melbourne

THIS IS THE first day of my new life.

Faith kept repeating the words to herself, over and over again, as she walked at a brisk pace down the street. It was busier now than it had been earlier in the day because people in this part of Melbourne didn't get up until after noon. She knew that come nightfall things would really start jumping, especially around the Angel.

She wasn't sure when the Angel had been built, but Kitty said it was in the 1920s, when gangsters had roamed these same streets and prostitutes had plied their trade on every corner. It was a night-club with a tarnished history; still, that didn't stop famous people from flocking there.

Faith was just so glad things had turned out okay. She hadn't expected to find work so soon and had been prepared to horde her savings. Eke them out a cent at a time. Now she had a job and it would give her the sort of freedom she'd never had at home. She might have worked at the milk bar for the past year, but her pay packet—such as it was—had never been her own, not when she had to hand over half of it to her mother.

At first Melbourne hadn't seemed welcoming at all. Kitty wasn't waiting to greet her when she arrived, and Faith's aunt, uncle and other cousins were busy with their own concerns and uninterested in hers. She had the suspicion that Lily had already been on the phone expressing her displeasure, and they all thought it would be for the best if Faith turned around and went home.

Well, she wasn't going to let them beat her.

So, determined, she went out the next day on her own and caught a tram, then wandered along the streets, looking into the shop windows and trying to ignore the rain. The day after she spent inside, helping her aunt bake cakes for a school stall. It was almost like being back at Willow Tree Bend—comfortable, that was the word, and because of that, vaguely unsettling.

'Kitty's working all hours,' her aunt warned her. 'We hardly ever see her.'

After another sleepless night, and another, she was so desperate she went out on Saturday night and rang Joe from a public telephone box. He'd left her his home phone number scribbled on the back of a petrol receipt—as if she didn't already know it by heart! As he'd handed it over, he'd said, 'If you need anything, or just to talk, okay?' She'd felt his eyes on her as she'd bent her head, pretending to read it and not wanting him to know how touched she was.

'So, how's it going?' he asked her when his

mother grudgingly fetched him to take the call. She could hear the sound of the television in the background—the *Graham Kennedy Show*—interspersed with Pete's laughter.

'All right.'

There was a pause as he tried to interpret her tone of voice. 'Faith, you know you only have to say and I'll come and get you. There's no shame in that. If you try a thing and don't like it at least you've tried.'

Faith gripped the handset tightly, staring through the grimy glass as two girls walked towards her along the street, their skintight jeans and bright jumpers proclaiming them as Sharpies. Kitty had told her that Sharpies and Mods were the two foremost gangs in Melbourne and that they hated each other. The girls stopped under a street lamp to light their cigarettes, and they were laughing about something. In that moment her heart ached for Hope.

'Faith? Do you want me to come and get you?'

She told herself she was being pathetic. She'd only been here a week! If she chickened out then that would be it as far as her mother was concerned, and she wouldn't be allowed to leave home again until she was twenty-one. No, she had to wait a bit longer. Things would get better, they had to.

'Okay,' Joe said, when she told him she was staying. 'I'll be down in a few weeks anyway. I'll drop in to see you then.'

Faith finished the call, hoping that by then she wouldn't have this terrible urge to cling to him.

The week dragged by. It was the weekend again, and Kitty arrived like a breath of fresh air in her bright-yellow dress and diamond patterned stockings. She took in the situation with one glance and promptly packed up Faith's things, scoffing at her mother's dire warnings, and bundled her off to her digs in St Kilda. It was a two storey house, narrow and creaky and old, and very untidy, but that was only to be expected with three other girls sharing. Because it reminded her of the often messy room that she had shared with Hope, Faith felt instantly at home.

'You can have the spare bed in here with me—I'm out a lot of the time anyway. We can split the rent. You'll have to find a job.' Her cousin stubbed out the inevitable cigarette. Faith's eyes were already stinging.

'What sort of job?'

'I'll think of something,' Kitty muttered, before making herself a cosy nest in her blankets and falling asleep instantly.

That night Faith lay awake again, worrying about her future, and what would happen if the hoped-for job didn't eventuate. There was no one to talk to because after Kitty went to work, she didn't come home again, and the other girls kept to their rooms.

But when Kitty arrived with the dawn, she brought good news. 'Jared says he'll take a look at you and see if you're suitable for the Cocktail Lounge. Should be okay.' She took in Faith's tangled hair and baggy pyjamas. 'Have you got some clothes to wear to the interview? Not that little-girl stuff you had on yesterday.' And seeing Faith's blank expression, she sighed. 'Go to Circe in Charnwood Crescent and ask for Leanne. Tell her you'll be working at the Angel and she'll know what you need.'

Faith tried not to feel hurt. She and Hope had spent hours poring over teen fashion magazines and trying to copy the newest looks. She'd always felt she was up to the mark. Hope had even said that if she cut her hair short and lost weight, she could be Twiggy. Their mother had overheard and given them a long lecture on the importance of accepting yourself as you were, with a longer one on the starving children in Africa.

'You need to think about what looks good on you,' Kitty was enlightening her. 'Make the best of what you've got. Look at me.

I'm not beautiful—'

'You are!'

Kitty's mouth quirked, but she shook her head, suddenly serious. 'No, I'm not. I've learned how to draw attention to my best features. Be yourself, Faith, that's the trick. Play up your good points and play down the bad. You just need a bit of practice. Your hair is lovely, and your eyes. You have a nice figure, not much of you, but men like petite women. Makes them feel big and strong. Jared's always on the lookout for girls who can bring in the customers.'

So, was this all for Jared? she wondered resentfully. And then she remembered it was Jared who would be deciding whether or not to give her a job, and buttoned her lip.

Faith headed off to Charnwood Crescent, fuelled by Kitty's encouragement and her own determination to give it her best shot.

Charnwood looped between two busier streets, and was lined with older-style houses and businesses that had seen better days. According to Kitty, the pop-music newspaper *Go-Set* was produced from one of these buildings, and that made her feel as if she was really in the beating heart, and certainly a long way from Willow Tree Bend.

Circe was a boutique, and situated in a small, front room in what looked like an old butcher's shop, if the hooks in the ceiling were any indication. Leanne was older than she'd expected, and when Faith explained why she was there, she stood back and assessed her with a practised air.

'You're young for the Angel,' she said. 'If anyone asks say you're eighteen.'

'I *am* eighteen,' Faith lied.

'Hmm.' Leanne gave her a knowing look.

They got down to business. Faith tried on outfit after outfit. Leanne called for another staff member, who appeared from the back of the store, and turned out to be more Faith's age. Together the women began to discuss her size and shape just as if she was one of the shop mannequins.

Under their guidance, she bought a fitted woollen mini-dress that buttoned up at the front, and some white boots, several short skirts and tight-fitting tops, as well as a gorgeous fake fur coat and a more practical one in black wool that tied around her waist.

When she mentioned the Twiggy similarity,

Leanne gave her a once-over. 'Maybe,' she said doubtfully.

'Twiggy?' the other girl spoke up. 'Nah. You're Petula Clark.

Don't Sleep in the Subway, babe!' They all had a good laugh about that.

By the time she struggled home with her new gear, Faith was beginning to worry she'd overspent. Kitty's unstinting approval helped to soothe her worries, as did her announcement that Faith was now ready to meet with Jared at the Angel that very night.

The nightclub was bigger than she'd expected— four storeys high—and the windows were all lit up. To Faith's disappointment, Kitty didn't take her in through the front entrance, and instead used a side door. She could hear voices though, as if a party was going on somewhere, and music, too.

'This is it,' Kitty said, leading her up a short flight of stairs to the office. She ran her gaze over her cousin. 'Ready?' And then, before she could answer, she knocked and opened the door.

Jared turned out to be about forty but pretending to be younger. His camel-coloured leather jacket was open over his black shirt and trousers, and his beard was trimmed to his jaw. His eyes widened when he first saw Faith, and he shot a look at Kitty.

Kitty shrugged and he turned back, eyes squinting against the smoke from the cigarette in his mouth, his stare lingering on her short skirt and pale stockings.

'You eighteen?' It wasn't a question. He just wanted her to say 'yes' because eighteen was the lawful age for entering any establishment that sold alcohol.

'Yes, of course,' she said.

Jared nodded. 'Rightio, then. Tomorrow Kitty will show you the ropes. You can start at four.' Then, as they were leaving, she heard him say to her cousin, 'Better keep her away from Dalzell. For the present anyway.'

Kitty didn't reply, hustling her from the room.

'Who's Dalzell?' Faith asked her, when they were out of earshot.

But Kitty didn't answer her either.

That had happened yesterday, and now here she was in her new mini-dress and white boots, snuggled into her black coat, and heading to her job.

'This is the first day of—'

'Hey, luv!'

A dark-haired young man was calling to her. At first she thought he must have heard what she'd said and felt her cheeks heat with embarrassment.

'Luv, is this the way to the Angel nightclub?' he asked. He had the sound of Liverpool, and the Beatles, in his voice.

Faith looked hard but no, he wasn't Paul, John or George, not even Ringo. This was a stranger, with the skinny pale look of someone who spent too much time inside, but with such an obvious raw sex appeal she felt her heart ratchet up a notch. His hair was cut to his shoulders, freshly washed and shiny, and he *looked* like he was a member of a band. If he was asking about the

Angel then he probably was. Kitty had said they had some top acts performing there, and Faith wondered if she'd heard him on the wireless in the milk bar.

'I'm going that way,' she replied, copying Kitty's confident smile.

'Okey-dokey, then.' He swaggered along beside her. His dark grey suit was the height of fashion and he had pointy-toed boots with heels. This close to him she could see he wasn't quite perfect because he had a shaving nick on his chin, while his eyes were hidden behind the darkest glasses she'd ever seen.

'You a singer, then?' He was turned in her direction, and she noticed the pale blur of her face reflected back, with her dark eye makeup and honey-blonde hair like a smooth cap flicked up at the ends. 'Should I recognise you, luv?'

It was on the tip of her tongue to tell him she was Petula Clark. Faith grinned and then stopped, aware of how it made her cheeks look pudgy and her eyes squinty. 'I work there,' she said instead, in Kitty's offhand voice. 'This is my first day.'

'Well, 'ow about that!' he said, wrapping an arm around her shoulders, giving her a squeeze and filling her head with the scent of his aftershave. 'Mine, too! What's your name again?'

She knew she was blushing even more now, but she didn't care. This was sheer bliss. 'Faith Taylor,' she said, with her newly borrowed self-assurance.

'I'm Ray Bartel,' her companion said, and all thought left her head.

She *did* know him! In fact, she was amazed she

hadn't recognised him from his photo in *Go-Set*, although he hadn't been wearing sunglasses then.

Ray Bartel and his band the Allnights had put a hit song out last year. True, they'd been proclaimed a bit of a one-hit wonder, but it had been her favourite. Still was. Ray was part of her life, part of the reason she was here, and he didn't even know it.

'What you laughing about?' he demanded. But he didn't seem insulted, he was smiling too, and she thought she might tell him.

'Faith, you're late.'

Kitty was standing in the staff entrance, cigarette butts, lolly wrappers and other detritus at her feet. She was looking anxious, and then she noticed Ray and her face turned sly. She grabbed Faith's arm. 'Come on,' she said with a tight smile. 'I need to show you the ropes before we open.'

Faith went with her, looking back over her shoulder to where Ray was lighting a cigarette and seemed to have forgotten she existed.

Inside, the air stank of smoke and beer, and her shoes stuck to the linoleum floor as she followed Kitty along a narrow corridor and into the big ground-floor room that was the Cocktail Lounge. Round tables with accompanying chairs were scattered throughout the space, and there was a stage with a brightly wallpapered wall and a bar opposite. In daylight the place looked tired, with none of the glitz she'd imagined.

She tried to keep her spirits up, but she could tell Kitty suddenly seemed less than enthusiastic about her cousin working with her. Or maybe she was reading too much into the other girl's expression. Maybe Kitty was just tired from her shift last night. Faith hadn't heard her come in till all hours, and now there were shadows under her green eyes and her blonde hair looked greasy despite all the comb-teasing Kitty had given it.

She tried to pay attention while Kitty explained to her what was expected of a Cocktail Lounge waitress. Serving drinks and keeping the customers happy seemed to be the main requirements. Patrons could order meals or snacks if they didn't want to be bothered making their way up to the dining room on the Mezzanine floor. There was also a Friday-and Saturday-night show in the Cocktail Lounge. Modern stuff, Kitty said, as opposed to the more traditional—and more expensive—acts in the entertainment area that was part of the dining room on the Mezzanine.

'We get lots of clients in here from the high end of town,' Kitty said with a wink. 'They tip well. Some of them find it more comfortable. Informal. The captain up on the Mezzanine runs a tight ship.' She chuckled, as if it was a joke. 'You don't need to worry about the Mezzanine though, or anything that happens up on the fourth floor. The Penthouse, we call it. Next stop heaven.'

Faith looked up at the ceiling in a bewildered fashion, and Kitty laughed, herself again. 'Come on,' she said, grabbing hold of Faith's hand. 'Let's go and have one of Gaz's breakfasts.'

'Breakfast? Isn't it a bit late for that?'

'Not at the Angel. Gaz is the cook and he'll want to be introduced.'

The kitchen was enormous, although mostly empty of staff at this hour. Faith was to learn that it was always quieter early in the week and it wasn't until Thursday that things started jumping at the Angel.

Gaz turned out to be in his fifties, a burly man with a bald head and unshaven face, and tattoos snaking down his arms. His paunch filled out his white tee-shirt and overflowed over his trouser belt. But his eyes twinkled and his smile was warm and welcoming.

'Faith, eh?' he drawled in a way that reminded her of the country. Of home. 'Where's Hope and Charity?'

Faith opened her mouth to tell him where Hope was at least, but her cousin cut her off.

'Don't tease her. She'll get enough of that from the other girls.' Kitty was already filling her plate with sausage and egg and bacon. Obviously she wasn't hung over.

'I'm not teasing her,' Gaz replied, nodding Faith to a chair and filling her plate himself until it looked as if it would need several of her to finish it. 'Don't you think she looks a bit like Mela—?'

'Shut up, Gaz. We don't talk about you-know-who.'

'Right. Sorry.' He caught Faith's puzzled look and smiled. 'I like your name. Old-fashioned, dependable. Honest,' he added with a meaningful glance at Kitty.

'As usual you don't know what you're talking about,' she muttered around a mouthful of egg.

'I know when someone is tip-toeing along a

balcony five storeys up,' Gaz said flatly.

Kitty didn't reply, but she didn't stay long either. Finishing her breakfast, she got up abruptly, reminding Faith she'd see her when her shift started. 'Don't be late,' she warned. 'Jared sacks girls who are late.'

When she'd gone, Gaz sat down opposite her with an enormous mug filled with milky tea. He was silent, which made Faith anxious. When she pushed her plate away, too full to eat another bite, she saw that he wasn't staring at her; his faraway gaze was fixed on the shelves behind her, which were weighed down with crockery.

'I'd better go,' she said with a smile. 'Thanks for breakfast, Gaz.'

He watched as she pushed her chair back and got to her feet. 'Be careful, Faith,' he said, nodding as if to enhance the warning. 'You tread carefully, sweetheart, even if Kitty won't.'

Something in his kindness, and maybe his country accent, caused tears to spring to her eyes, but she refused to let them fall. This was her brand-new life, she reminded herself. New and exciting. And she did not intend to tread carefully, however well-meaning Gaz's advice. Faith intended to jump straight in, white boots and all.

6

SAMANTHA

12 January 2000, Willow Tree Bend

THE OLD UTE rattled to a halt outside the gate to my property and I sat a while with the engine idling, deep in thought. I'd picked up the aptly named 'rust bucket' yesterday and it seemed to be back in working order. I told myself I should be able to put off buying a newer model for a bit longer.

At least until I could afford it.

Work-wise, things were going as okay as expected with this long hot summer. Unless they had no choice, most people weren't thinking about creating new gardens. Sensibly, they were waiting until the weather cooled and there was more chance of rain.

And I knew the rains always came.

Eventually.

For now, I had enough work to last another month, but there was always that niggling worry about the future. One question in particular seemed to pop into my head several times a day, try as I might to keep it out.

Can my business survive?

On the plus side, the new primary school was keeping me busy, and the staff were just as enthusiastic as the kids about their new veggie garden and bird-friendly landscaping. It was quite avant-garde, but I was a great believer in sustainability. Recently, I'd been asked for a few quotes for new gardens and it was encouraging to know they were out there, floating about, and might bear fruit. One in particular had taken my fancy.

A restaurant was opening on the outskirts of town and the owner was a well-known Melbourne chef. His restaurant served French-Australian fusion, which seemed a bit odd to me but was a big hit with the patrons, so what did I know? If he chose me to create his kitchen garden and he was happy with it, and then he raved to his friends and customers … That would certainly bring in the clients.

Of course I knew that everything would have to go extremely right for that to happen. And if it didn't? There were so many hungry mouths depending on me that sometimes I felt overwhelmed.

Positive thoughts.

I opened the ute's creaky door and dropped my booted foot down onto the dusty ground. Immediately, a cacophony of sound greeted me, and I smiled as I opened the gate, my anxieties slipping once more below the surface in the face of so much adoration.

The two donkeys, Chocolate and Fudge, were

calling to me in their usual noisy fashion, and the two horses, Sundae and Caramel, were not far behind them in their race to reach the side paddock fence. I smiled. I thought animals were great, which explained my ever-expanding brood. They didn't ask for much back—well, food and water and medical care when they were sick, all accompanied by hugs and pats. But I couldn't complain because they gave me so much love in return.

I'd had two serious boyfriends since I left school and in my opinion neither of them was worth a fraction of one of my animal friends. After the last one walked out on me because I wouldn't just drop everything and head off with him for a weekend of hot- rodding, I'd sworn off men. Maybe not forever. Perhaps in eleven years' time, when I was forty, I'd re-evaluate the situation.

My property at Willow Tree Bend had been part of the land holding on which the Taylor family had lived for generations. I even had some creek frontage, although this summer the water was little more than shallow pools.

At the time I'd inherited, I had cautiously eval-uated my good fortune and decided I couldn't look after the whole twenty hectares I'd been given. So I'd sold off all but four, which were the best four naturally, and using the money, built a typical country house with a verandah all the way around, and breezy, open-plan rooms. I'd also put up fences and sheds, and dug a dam.

It was all mine. I owned it lock, stock and barrel. Or at least I had before I'd taken out a mortgage to finance Green Dreams. The alternative was to give up my ambitions and work for my parents, and I couldn't imagine Mum and I surviving that for more than a day. We were too much alike.

Mitch the kelpie crept up to me, wagging his tail so hard he threatened to turn himself inside out. I knelt down on one knee to say a proper hello. The ground felt hard and rocky. Dry. There'd been no good rain for months now. Recently, I'd had to resort to carting in feed for the animals, and the dam was so low I was beginning to wonder where the water ended and the mud began.

If things got much worse, and if my teetering business tipped over, I'd lose everything. It would break my heart, I knew that, but I kept telling myself that I'd just have to deal with it. Dad and Mum would back me up, of course they would, though I would insist on standing on my own two feet. It was a matter of pride with me that I do that—like following in the family tradition. Mum had made a success of her business through guts and sheer hard work, and Dad had taken on the role of chief provider for his family after his father died. The Cantanis and the Taylors were go-getters who didn't let anything stop them from achieving their goals.

Speaking of Taylors … I couldn't see any sign of Lily near the house. Or Pompom, who should have been going crazy by now if he couldn't get outside to say hello.

I gave Mitch another pat. He looked a little relieved. He and the ugly little dog didn't get on, but at least they didn't come to fisticuffs. They just ignored each other with a dignified silence.

Was my grandmother taking a nap? She probably needed one. Since she'd arrived for her unannounced and unexpected visit, she'd cleaned every inch of my place and I was too browbeaten to protest. She didn't have to say anything, just run her finger across a surface and show me the result, and I'd find myself stammering out excuses like I was back in primary school and the headmaster had called me into his office.

If Mum was here I'd be on the phone in an instant begging her to intervene, but she wasn't. I still didn't understand the reason for her absence, and when I'd asked my grandmother all she did was quote me a Bible reference.

'"Forget those things that are behind and reach forth to those things that are before".'

I must have given her a blank look. 'Philippians 3:13. Look it up.' I thought I'd pass on that.

'Will you be coming to the cottage with us to see Hope?' I asked her instead. 'You might be on television, Gran.'

'Haven't been asked.' She gave me a piercing look from eyes that were that same light green that Mum and Hope had inherited. There was something very fey about those eyes, as if they could read minds, and I was sure, in Gran's case, she could. 'Oh come on, Hope would love to see you there.'

Gran gave me a smile that seemed to suggest otherwise.

Why wouldn't Hope want her mother to take part in the big homecoming scene? There were things going on here that I didn't understand, like a dangerous undertow beneath a calm surface, and yet how *could* I understand when no one was talking?

A few weeks ago, I was over at my parents' house in Golden Gully. We'd heard Hope was going to appear in *Looking Back* and we wanted to watch a video of an older episode. I suppose we were keen to know exactly what we were in for. The program was well made—I could see how it would have wide appeal—and I'd found myself fascinated by the minutia. The star in this episode was a comedian and because he was so famous I'd presumed I knew everything about him, but that didn't turn out to be the case. I discovered things that completely amazed me, and there were even tears at the end, when a long-lost relative unexpectedly reappeared.

Hope, I'd thought, would revel in it. All that attention! I'd said so aloud, turning to my parents, only to be startled by how uncomfortable they both looked. And how worried.

'What?' I asked, trying to read their faces. 'Don't you want to be on national tellie?' Then, with a laugh, 'We can say no. It's not like we're going to be the main focus. Maybe you could ask them to take a long-range shot of us, far into the distance.'

'Over the border,' Dad quipped, and he seemed to be trying to return my smile, but it was an effort.

'As long as we're not expected to perform any re-enactments of your younger days,' I joked. 'You know how I hate dressing up.'

They looked at each other as if I'd said the worst thing in the world. My mother had an expression on her face … *ravaged* sprang to mind. Of course I tried to get them to tell me what was going on, but they shrugged it off. Changed the subject. That was when I really started to get worried.

Later on, when I'd done the dishes and spent some time checking out my mother's new range of desserts—they really were classy and tasted even better than they looked—I'd overheard them talking. They were in the lounge, their voices low. I admit I was eavesdropping, but they were acting so oddly.

'She hasn't thought it through,' Mum said, her voice a little high, which meant she was upset. 'When I told her to come home I didn't mean this. She could pick up plenty of work without baring her soul.'

'You don't know she's going to do that,' Dad responded, trying to pour oil on troubled waters, just as he always did. 'Hope knows how far she can push it.'

'I really want you to be right.'

'She doesn't know about the Angel, does she? Did you ever tell her about—?'

'Of course not. That's over and done with, Joe. In the past. Let's leave it there.'

I hadn't thought my family had any secrets. But now …

I gave Mitch one last pat and smiled into his brown doggy eyes. 'Come on, mate,' I said gently. 'Let's go do some work.'

The fact that I'd already done a day's work

didn't faze me. I enjoyed my time around the farm—although Dad told me it was really too small to be called a farm. This was my domain, and as I rounded the side of the shed and saw my new garden beds, all neatly laid out, I couldn't help feeling a wave of pleasure and pride.

I'd been experimenting with some new ideas and despite the lack of water everything was doing well. I'd chosen drought-hardy species, and the fleshy greys and reds stood out nicely. The idea was to interest some of my new clients in the concept of a dry garden.

If I got any new clients.

Inside, the house was indeed empty. Lily seemed to have vanished in a puff of Mr Sheen. Maybe she considered her work was done—the house certainly looked spick and span. I switched on a fan to stir the air, and then I poured myself a tall glass of cold water with ice. The mail I'd collected earlier from town was in my bag and I tipped it out.

Bills, mostly. A request for help from a charity, and a price list from the local pizza joint. Pity that according to them I was too far out of town to get a delivery or tonight was the night I might have taken them up on the offer.

Impatiently I pushed the envelopes aside. Where was Hope going to stay during the filming? Staying with my parents had been the original plan, but now that Mum was gone it occurred to me that she might want to come here. I glanced about, relieved that, thanks to Gran, things were clean and tidy now. All the same, I wasn't all that keen on having my famous aunt casting a super-cilious eye over my tatty second-hand table and chairs, and my other eclectic odds and ends. By the time I'd paid for the house I didn't have any money left over to buy new furnishings, and any-way what was wrong with retro?

Selfish perhaps, but I liked my peace and quiet, and the thought of Hope arriving with her cam-era crew trailing behind her wasn't something I was looking forward to. I could grit my teeth and get through it—I'd have to. However, there was one particular aspect of the visit that made me want to cringe. Or leave town.

The day after tomorrow we were all supposed to rendezvous at the old Willow Tree Bend cot-tage.

I could see the cottage from my verandah, if I tilted my head to the side and squinted in the right direction. You could only physically reach it by turning off the Golden Gully road, and then down a long, unsealed driveway. If you had a horse, then it was possible to ride along the creek and get there that way.

Not that I'd done either of those things for many months now, and for a very good reason.

When the cottage was first sold, the new own-ers used to rent it out, and a couple of times there was trouble with the tenants. Once I had moved into my own newly built home, I'd felt obliged to keep an eye on the place—this was because of my family connection rather than a sense of civic duty. My mother's stories of my grandfather's forebears, migrating from England to Victoria in the 1860s, as well as the large family they'd raised, were tales I loved listening to. This was my story, too, and it made me feel even more a part of this country.

I belonged.

During one unforgettable year, a couple renting the cottage grew and sold drugs, which was disappointing in all sorts of ways. The police dealt with them, and the place had been sold again—at a knock-down price—in the first half of last year.

The buyer was a man named Lincoln Nash.

In 1987, when I was sixteen, I had a terrible crush on Lincoln Nash. I wasn't alone—so did most of the teenage girls in Australia. He'd fronted a band called Black Crow, a sort of cross between INXS and Icehouse. Lincoln had been a Michael Hutchence/Iva Davies type of character—charismatic, talented and fascinating to the eye. He was also dangerous in a break-your-heart sort of way, and according to the gossip magazines he did break hearts and lots of them. When the band fell apart after their one successful overseas tour, Lincoln had walked away. He'd vanished from the public eye for years and it was only lately that he had re-emerged.

He was now my next-door neighbour.

But this Lincoln was a very different character from the one I remembered. Now he sang ballads, dark angsty tunes that weren't my thing at all, and were probably aimed at an older crowd—he was thirty-five by my calculations. And most disturbing of all, he wore glasses with dark frames like Elvis Costello, whose lyrics always drove me insane. So, when he had moved into the cottage at Willow Tree Bend, apart from a momentary starry-eyed gasp, I'd shrugged my shoulders and dismissed him.

Until that spur-of-the-moment encounter six months ago.

Why had I done it? I wasn't sure, but I still squirmed at the memory. I'd been in Golden Gully and ducked into the hardware store to get something—later I couldn't even remember what it was. I recognised him as soon as I saw him, despite the short hair and restless stare. If I'd been thinking straight I would have realised he didn't want to talk. That he just wanted to be left alone.

But that morning I had received a phone call notifying me of my successful bid for the garden I was currently finishing. I was riding high, feeling bulletproof, which was probably why all of my natural caution had gone out the window.

He was standing by a pallet full of seedlings, some of them way past their best, and it was my intention to tell him he could do better at the nursery on the road out of town. That was where I did my business. I might even have planned to mention that the old cottage he now lived in was my family home. Sometimes, in the mornings, when I cricked my neck, I could see him pottering around in the garden. Did he want some help with that? And, by the way, I'd been a big fan of his music once upon a time.

I took a step towards him, just as a couple of giggling adolescent girls went by, casting him little glances. He didn't look up at them until they'd passed, and when he did he was frowning.

I watched him reach into his pocket and slip on some dark glasses. That seemed a bit pretentious; after all, he hadn't been a star for fifteen years, and it was only people my age and older who still remembered him. But in my exultant state I was prepared to give him the benefit of the doubt.

My friendly 'Good morning' elicited another frowning glance. His head tilted as the dark gaze behind the lenses flicked down my tee-shirt-and-jean-clad body and reached my mud-caked boots, pausing there, as if they were far more interesting than the rest of me.

'Is it?' he'd said, and walked away.

Surprised, appalled, I stood and stared after him. I knew my face was as hot with embarrassment as it felt, but I could deal with that. It was his indifference, complete and utter indifference … I wasn't used to men being indifferent to me.

Was that an arrogant admission? Maybe. I was a reasonably attractive woman, and my body was toned and strong from my physical job. Men tended to smile back at me. Yet it was more than that. Maybe I was being contrary, but he'd been my idol throughout my formative teenage years and his behaviour had felt like a betrayal.

It was after that encounter I swore to myself that there would be no neighbourliness from my side of the fence, not while Mr Nash was in residence.

But that was before Hope made her announcement, and now we would all be trooping up to the cottage tomorrow whether we liked it nor not.

I wondered what Lincoln Nash would think of that. I was shallow enough to want him to hate the intrusion. Maybe he'd lock the door and refuse to let my famous aunt inside? I pictured Hope tapping on the windows, pressing her face to the glass, while Lincoln glared at her.

That made me smile.

Maybe, I thought, it would be fun after all.

7

HOPE

12 January 2000, Melbourne

*H*OME. DID SHE really still consider Australia, and in particular Willow Tree Bend, home? After all this time? She'd been unable to get away and 'spread her wings' quickly enough, and when, from a distance, she had thought of the cottage, she'd certainly never imagined it through rose-coloured glasses. Like most performers, her past had become a mish-mash of real and make-believe, bits of which she trotted out, depending upon which questions she was asked.

Never quite the entire truth.

Hope was under no illusions about the aim of a program like *Looking Back*, which was to astonish its audience and, if possible, drop a few bombshells along the way. The meagre details of her life, which she had sent to the producers as part of her contract, were never going to be enough for them. So, she'd made herself a backup plan. There was her romance with the Hollywood director, she could expand on that, and her early struggles in the Melbourne theatre scene, some of them particularly dire. She'd known real poverty during those months before her career began to take off. Surely that would satisfy them? She'd also had an intense fling with a man who was now an Australian celebrity and she was expecting them to discover that. Maybe it could make a nice little denouement right at the end of the show?

Looking Back had assigned her a personal assistant, or was she in fact a spy? The PA's name was Prue and she was as skinny as a whip with pink hair, but her smile was warm and admiring as they shook hands. 'I love your work,' she'd said, as if she really meant it. Another thing in her favour, as far as Hope was concerned, was that she dealt competently with the luggage and then drove them calmly through the heavy rush-hour traffic into the city.

'We thought you'd be more private and comfortable here,' she'd explained, when they ended up in the foyer of a boutique hotel just off Bourke Street. 'It's rather quirky. Used to be a homeless people's dosshouse,' Prue added with a grin, as if a past history like that was something to be pleased about.

Hope tried not to shudder.

'You'll meet with everyone in the morning,' Prue was explaining to her. 'In the meantime, if you need anything, do let me know. We've lined up some media interviews when the filming is done, but I don't think you'll be bothered before that.'

The unspoken statement was that she wasn't famous enough to need special security for the hordes of fans not hanging around on the street outside.

The girl meant well, but it was a relief to be alone again.

Hope went to the window and looked down into the narrow thoroughfare. There were trendy little shops there, and busy cafes. She thought about changing her clothes and setting off to enjoy the ambience, but suddenly the effort seemed too great. What she really wanted to do—and it was the strangest sensation, one she hadn't felt in many years—was to curl up into a ball under the cover on her bed and squeeze her eyes closed.

Something about being home—that word again—was affecting her in ways she had never imagined. The very thought of travelling to Willow Tree Bend ... the tightness in her chest made her feel breathless and slightly nauseous.

Don't be ridiculous!

She had meticulously planned all of this in her usual OCD fashion. She knew what she was doing. She couldn't afford to fall apart. Tomorrow she had the meeting with the show's director to get through, and the filming schedule to sort out. After that she could concentrate on Faith. Lily, too—the thought of seeing her mother face to face, of looking into those eyes so like her own ... What would she see there? Love and regret? Fear and condemnation? Or would the shutters be down just as they had been the last time they'd parted?

A plate of sandwiches had been prepared for her, and her favourite brand of tea, and she nibbled and sipped, before jet lag kicked in and she decided she was too tired to bother finishing.

Perhaps, despite her promises to her family, her stay in Australia might be briefer than she had intended. After all, she had things to do back in New York, like finding somewhere else to live, and trying to whip up some interest in her stalled career. She could make excuses, tell lies. She was good at telling lies.

She lay down onto the comfortable bed and drew the cover over her. It might be summer, but the air conditioning was making her feel cold. Snuggling up, she sighed and closed her eyes, and almost immediately her body grew heavy and sleep claimed her.

This dream was different to the last one. She wasn't back in the past, she was seeing the past as it was now—or as she imagined it to be …

The house, which she remembered with such clarity from that January day, was on the verge of falling down. She looked behind her, but the black car that had brought her here was gone, and she was quite alone. She didn't want to go inside, and yet inexorably her feet were taking her there.

The brick walls were crumbling, the windows smashed, and when she pushed the door open it dragged on the ruined floor. Dust swam in the gloom, and the hall was like a tunnel, leading her through to the rear of the house. She knew the garden was out there and she didn't want to see it, but somehow she couldn't make her feet stop. A moment later she was stepping over some fallen masonry into the sunlight.

The perfume drifted to her, at first subtle and sweet, and then stronger. Still compelled by something unseen, she moved forward, towards the structure almost entirely clothed by the old rosebush. Bees clambered over the pale-gold blossoms, their humming monotonous. Hypnotic. As she stood watching them she felt someone behind her, standing so close that the hairs on the back of her neck stood straight up.

He was there.

She didn't turn around. She couldn't. She was too afraid of what she'd see …

Hope woke with a soft cry and sat up. It was still light outside. Though only just. The room was silent apart from the whisper of the air conditioner. And there was a scent in the air, subtle and teasing, a scent that brought with it memories.

Slipping from the bed, she padded across the thick carpet to the table and reached for the small vase of flowers that had come with the sandwiches.

And that was when she noticed the old-fashioned roses. She didn't know the name of the pale-gold one, she never had, but she recognised it. Carrying the vase as if it was a dangerous explosive, she opened the door and put it outside.

Prue arrived to collect her just after nine, full of confidence and enthusiasm, and they made the slow journey through the city. The sky was a smoggy blue, and Hope watched the trams go by, covered in colourful advertising. Above the city streets she could see the construction work that seemed, all over the world, to be never-ending.

She knew it was paranoid and ridiculous, but when she woke that morning it had occurred to her that somehow the show's producers *knew*. That the roses were put in her room to see how she would react, and now they were going to drag up that particular horror from her past and present it to her, all wrapped up in pretty paper and a bow.

Hope was doing her best to be charming as she listened to Prue talk about how much she was looking forward to working with her, but the suspicion wouldn't be dismissed. It clung like one of the burrs that grew along the roads of her childhood, thorns digging deep enough to puncture the tyres of her bike.

The headquarters of *Looking Back* was an apricot-painted building, set in a leafy street in the inner-city suburb of South Yarra. It looked as if it had once been a large private residence.

She was greeted warmly by the production staff and taken into a cosy meeting area. They were young and casually dressed and very earnest. Hope felt old and overdone in her Prada suit, and knowing she'd needed enough concealer to fill the San Andreas Fault, just to hide the circles under eyes, didn't help.

Over tea and biscuits, she learned that tomorrow morning she, Prue and their cameraman, Ken, were setting off for Willow Tree Bend.

Her heart gave a little jump, but she reminded herself that it was too late to back out now. She'd signed the contracts. There *was* the possibility of her refusing permission for them to transmit anything too invasive, but it had been made clear to her that the program was proud of its no-holds-barred approach. In some of the episodes she'd watched, the shocks had come thick and fast, from tears to laughter and back again, and she had the impression that was exactly what they were looking for from Hope Taylor.

'My life is an open book,' she said.

There were exchanged glances. 'Well, the thing is, we prefer to air information that isn't widely known,' one of the team ventured.

'We'll be doing our own research.'

'I'm sure you will.'

'Your sister, for instance. We'd love to speak to her and her family.'

Faith isn't here. She's run away and I don't know where to find her.

She almost said it aloud but stopped herself in time. Better if they found out for themselves and then she could pretend ignorance. 'Of course,' she said.

'We've arranged for your sister to be present at Willow Tree Bend tomorrow at eleven. To walk with you around the cottage.'

'Lovely,' she said with a smile. 'Looking forward to it.'

'You're close to your sister, then?' There were more exchanged glances. The air of expectation was making it hard to breathe.

'Very. We live on different continents, but apart from that … She *is* my only sibling.'

'We did hope to speak with your mother …?'

'No. I explained. She isn't well. I don't want her involved.'

She sounded anxious and was annoyed with herself, knowing it would prick their curiosity. *And* she'd heard a strong hint of an Australian accent creeping into her usually crisp pronunciation. Time and hard work had tidied up her country-girl drawl, and she knew the only reason she was reverting to it now was stress.

'We did agree that my mother wouldn't be part of the program,' she added more mildly.

'Hmm.'

Deciding that she needed to get out before she unravelled completely, Hope rose to her elegantly shod feet.

At once Prue seemed to understand what was required and took the lead. 'Thank you, I think we've covered all bases,' she said smoothly.

Someone gushed about how much they were looking forward to working with her, which was followed by other versions of the same thing, and then finally Hope was free. She had a medical appointment in two hours' time—the show insisted on a medical check-up before they got stuck in. A formality, they said, and Hope had no problem with it—she was as fit as a fiddle—but the last thing she wanted was for Prue to be trailing after her.

And there was something else she wanted to do. It was an idea she had been tossing up ever since Faith's phone call, and last night, just as she finally fell asleep, she'd decided to go ahead. It meant sneaking off on her own, which was rather exciting, like that school excursion to the Melbourne museum, which she'd found so boring she'd gone missing for a couple of hours. She'd sat alone in a cinema and devoured popcorn and the film *Georgy Girl*. The teacher had been frantic, but it had been worth it.

'I'm going to do some shopping,' she said to Prue, glancing at her watch. 'There's a friend I want to catch up with tonight. What time will you be here to pick me up tomorrow?'

Prue gave her a look. Hope could see the cogs turning as the girl considered whether or not to make a fuss, but she was also clever enough and experienced enough to know when to let it go.

'Seven should do it.' She gave her friendly smile. 'We'll need plenty of time to spend at the cottage. We have permission to film inside, but the guy who owns it hasn't been very accommodating.' She waved a dismissive hand, as if she could handle him. 'Then we'll head into Golden Gully and get you walking about and so on. If we finish all of that tomorrow, it'll give you a few days to spend with your family. After that, we'll need you back here to do some more filming. Your early career and so on. We have some surprise reunions lined up.'

Hope kept her smile in place. 'That sounds exciting. Any clues?'

Prue shook her head. 'My lips are sealed,' she said airily. She hesitated, as if she knew her next words weren't welcome. 'There was mention of dinner, Miss Taylor. To meet some of our backers.

It might be nice for them. Do you think …?'

But Hope pleaded a headache in a tone too definite to be argued with, and that was that. She also insisted she would take a taxi to the medical appointment, and was glad to close the door on Prue's slightly suspicious expression. Quickly, she changed into jeans and a blouse, put on a hat and sunglasses, and then waited impatiently for half an hour—just in case Prue was lurking outside— before she set out from the hotel.

There was a taxi rank at the end of the lane— she'd noticed it earlier—and she gave the address to the driver, instructing him to wait for her once they reached their destination. Then she leaned back in the shiny plastic seat that smelled faintly of antiseptic, and wondered again why this was such a good idea. She would never have thought of it if Faith hadn't mentioned the name during that bizarre phone call.

The Angel.

Hope didn't remember where Faith had lived during the time she worked at the infamous nightclub. She thought her sister might have been staying at her aunt's house, but she'd soon moved out. Hope had memories of their mother being furious about the whole thing, although typically she'd refused to discuss it with her younger daughter. Faith hadn't written, apart from sending a parcel containing some groovy clothes for Hope's birthday—she'd worn the miniskirt a few times, despite it barely covering her bum.

Lily had fallen out with her sister—she was dead now—and Hope hadn't kept up with her cousins. She'd never been as close to them as Faith was. The only thing she knew for certain was that Faith had been a cocktail waitress at the Angel, and something had happened to send her running for home. And when she got there she was a different girl from the one who'd left.

The taxi turned off St Kilda Road, and after a couple more turns, slowed to a halt. Hope leaned forward to stare up at the ruined facade against the pitiless summer sky. Her first thought was that, for an angel, it had seen better days. The windows at street level were boarded up, although she noticed that hadn't stopped the vandals from smashing them in several places and covering anything left in graffiti.

'Please wait,' she told the driver, ignoring his dubious glance. 'I won't be long.'

The footpath was grubby and refuse had blown up against the frontage. There was a homeless man who'd set up shop, sitting on his rolled-up bed and surrounded by a selection of plastic bags containing his worldly goods. A metal bowl was set in front of him for receiving donations. She found a twenty-dollar note in her purse and tucked it in amongst the sparse selection of coins.

The orange-coloured bill caused him to sit up a little straighter, and he squinted at her as if wondering what she wanted in return.

Hope walked past him, over to one of the boarded-up windows, and leaned forward to peer through a narrow gap in the hording. Inside there was only darkness.

'Condemned.' Her new friend called out to her

in a gravelly voice. 'They're tearing it down to build apartments. There's been a fair bit of protest about that. Wonder you haven't heard about it.'

The place was empty and forgotten. She remembered some vague story, from the early days of her acting career in Melbourne, about it being closed down for a time and then reopening again under new management. Well that hadn't lasted.

The homeless man was still watching her with interest and she went back to him. Pointing a finger at the building, and unable to hide her disgust, she asked, 'Why would they want to save it?'

He laughed, showing more than a few missing teeth. 'That's a change! Usually I get the bleeding hearts. They say it's a part of our heritage. Just so happens it's a part not many of the people who were there wanna remember.'

Now that she was closer to him, she saw that he was about sixty, although he could be younger and living rough had taken its inevitable toll.

'That bad?' she said.

'Worse than bad. I've heard it called the *Fallen Angel*.' 'Did *you* call it the Fallen Angel?' She smiled.

The smile did it; he opened up. 'Used to work there.' He grinned back at her.

It seemed almost too good to be true, and she had to ask. She even crouched down in front of him, and then got a whiff of his unwashed body and last night's drinking session and wished she hadn't. 'Did you know someone called Faith Taylor? She was here in nineteen sixty-nine.'

'What, in the Penthouse?'

'In the cocktail bar, I think. Something like that. She was a waitress.'

'Lot of girls worked here,' he said flatly, 'and Jared always put the prettiest ones in the Cocktail Lounge. Was this Faith Taylor pretty?' Hope thought of the young Faith, with her blonde hair and big green eyes. Her sister had been beautiful in a way that Hope had never quite achieved, and it didn't hurt to admit it now.

'Yes. She was.'

Maybe she'd taken too long to answer because he was eyeing her curiously. Or maybe it was more than that—maybe he remembered Faith. She *was* memorable.

'Then she would have worked in the Cocktail Lounge for sure,' he said, and cracked his knuckles, but at the same time she could see his mind working. 'What is she to you?'

'You don't remember her?'

'Nah. Too many drugs, too much booze. I hardly remember my own name, love.'

He was lying. Being an actor herself she had learned to read the signs.

Behind her the waiting taxi driver tooted his horn. Glancing over, she saw that a van was wanting to get into his parking space, edging impatiently closer. When she turned back to the vagrant, she realised he had pocketed the money and was now packing up his gear.

'Can you tell me anything? Did something happen?' She knew she sounded desperate and thought that if he did know something then he would use it as leverage for more money.

'You could try Jared Shaw,' he said, to her surprise. 'He's in a nursing home now, the one over in Acland Street. Still making trouble from what I've heard. He might remember this girl. If you get him on a good day. Yeah, you could do worse than try him.'

'Thank you.'

He gave a strange half-bow, and she wondered again who he was, or who he had been. No time to ask though—a glance at her watch told her it was getting close to her medical appointment—and the taxi driver called out for her to hurry up. Briefly, she considered cancelling and going to the nursing home instead, so that she could question this Jared Shaw, but it was impossible. The show's crew would wonder why she'd changed her mind, and she didn't want to do anything to encourage their suspicions.

It could also be a pointless exercise.

What did she think Jared would know about her sister, and even if he did, how could it be relevant to events happening now? She needed to focus on the here and now, on the program, and doing her job.

On keeping her own life under control.

8

FAITH

July 1969, St Kilda

FAITH FELT AS if she was really settling into her new life and new job. The Angel was an exciting place, especially at night, with the lights blazing and the dance floor heaving to the thump of the music. Everything sparkled and everyone had a good time. But there was also an edginess to the place, as if danger lurked in the shadows, and it was better not to look too hard in case you saw something you'd rather not.

Apart from the Cocktail Lounge on the ground floor, there was the Mezzanine dining room and entertainment area, and a small private room called the Lounge Bar, which seemed empty most of the time. There was an intense rivalry between them all, although according to Kitty, the Cocktail Lounge was the hands-down winner. Faith was certainly kept busy.

The music on Fridays and Saturdays was aimed at a younger audience, but Faith noticed a lot of older men turning up, as well as the inevitable prostitutes at the table near the door. Kitty said they liked it there because they could hurry any clients away to their digs, before they had a chance to change their minds. Women selling sex weren't permitted in the Angel, well that was the rule, but Kitty said rules were meant to be broken. Faith had seen her take money from the girls in return for allowing them to stay, but she was also just as likely to demand they leave if there was any trouble.

Most of the staff at the Angel wore uniforms, except the girls in the Cocktail Lounge. They were allowed to dress in their own clothes—it was thought it made the place more 'hip'—which was why Kitty had insisted Faith go to Circe. Kitty had brought that innovation in, as well as the music, and both seemed to be working. She was the person in charge and known as the captain, although no one called her that—it seemed an archaic term to Faith.

In the beginning, when Kitty was in one of her moods, Faith had called her Captain Kitty and raised a laugh from her, but the second time she did it Kitty told her to shut up. There was a different captain for the Mezzanine floor. The two captains were always arguing about who ran the best bar or had the best music. Kitty said the Mezzanine was outdated and the service slow, and anyone who was under thirty wouldn't be seen dead there.

Faith had heard from one of the other waitresses that before Kitty there had been someone else employed as captain, but when Kitty came along, Jared had sacked him and given her the job. A number of staff hadn't been happy about it at the time, but Jared was the manager and he could do what he liked.

Faith's shift ran from four until ten o'clock, but on Fridays and Saturdays the Angel remained open until three am, ostensibly as a cabaret venue. Alcohol could be served to the tables with food and refreshments, but even so Faith was aware that Kitty often stretched the letter of the law if it suited her. According to her, Jared had the police in his pocket. Sometimes Faith stayed on until closing time, which could be four in the morning.

Sometimes, too, the party moved up to the Penthouse, but Faith had never been invited there. It was a private area and, according to Kitty, required a different type of employee altogether. Faith wondered about that, because she'd seen Kitty murmuring to the girls near the door, and later seen them trooping up the back stairs in their high heels and tight black dresses. But she didn't think about it too much; she was too busy enjoying her own life.

Used to rising early at home, Faith was strangely proud that these days she barely opened an eye before midday.

She'd begun to make some tentative friendships with a couple of the other waitresses, too, and several of them had gone to a Monday session at the cinema to see *Age of Consent*. Kitty didn't go with them, although Faith had asked her. She'd just laughed, as if the idea was childish.

Sometimes Faith was puzzled by her cousin's attitude, and her moodiness. One minute they might be giggling together like the children they used to be, and the next Kitty would look at her with contempt, as if she was so much older and wiser.

Gaz's warning had stayed with her, although she couldn't see how Kitty was walking some sort of dangerous tightrope. It was true that Kitty was secretive. More often than not, when Faith finished work and went home, Kitty stayed on, and then she wouldn't see her until well into the next day.

Once, when Kitty didn't get home until the following afternoon, Faith had been worried enough to ask her where she'd been. Kitty had been furious. 'Mind your own bloody business,' she'd hissed. 'Just because you don't know how to have fun doesn't mean everyone's like you. And don't go gossiping either. I used to be a waitress, I know how it is. Just keep your head down and do your job.'

Some of the Angel's customers were high profile and wealthy, and it had been known for employees to take bribes from newspaper reporters to let them know when certain names would be attending the venue. If they were found out, those employees were sacked. So Faith took Kitty's advice and kept her head down and her smile on, and minded her own business.

Probably the highlight of her new life was Ray.

Ray and his band, the Allnights, had performed the evening after she'd first met him. Kitty told her that Ray had been trying to get into some of the top Melbourne venues for a while now, but no one would take him seriously enough to give him a chance. Until Jared. Ray was very grateful. The two men seemed to have become firm friends, and she'd often see them talking, heads together over their drinks.

As he'd played, Faith had watched on, riveted by the power of his songs. She'd struggled to keep the drinks orders straight in her head, with the music blasting over her, and the bass guitar echoing her heartbeat. After his only hit single, Ray had dropped out of the music scene, but now here he was, determined to claw his way back, and she hoped he'd make it, she really did. If the crowds who came to see him were anything to go by then he was on his way.

At the moment Jared was financing an Allnights tour of the provincial cities, building on their rise in popularity, but when Ray was at the Angel he always made a point of singling Faith out. The first time he'd stopped her for a chat, he'd offered her a cigarette, and she was flattered enough to take one of his Craven As. She'd soon decided smoking wasn't for her. Anyway, she asked herself, why did anyone need to smoke when the rooms were so thick with the stuff you could get your nicotine hit just by breathing in?

Before Ray left for his tour, he'd come over to her while she was waiting at the bar for a customer's order. 'Take care of yourself, luv,' he'd said, and kissed her cheek as if she was his little sister. Faith didn't want to be his sister, but the other girls were so jealous she'd swallowed her disappointment.

When she'd told Kitty about it—the words tripping off her tongue in her excitement—her cousin was unimpressed by her 'schoolgirl crush' as she called it.

'You know he puts on that accent,' she'd sneered, flicking ash towards the saucer on the kitchen table. 'He's from Auckland not Liverpool, but he thinks if he sounds like one of the Beatles he'll get more gigs.'

'I like it,' Faith had said loyally.

'You're not a virgin, are you?' Kitty's eyes had narrowed through the smoke. Then, when Faith didn't answer, 'Please don't tell me you're saving yourself for Mr Right?'

Her voice was so savage it had taken Faith by surprise. She'd walked away without answering, and although Kitty didn't raise the subject again, sometimes Faith would catch her watching with a look that was cool and speculative, and made her strangely uneasy.

After that she didn't feel quite the same about her cousin. She had idolised her since she was a little girl, thinking she was perfect and wanting to be her. Now that the lustre was starting to dim, Faith began to pay more attention to Kitty's faults. For instance, there were only a couple of people Kitty was friendly with and one of them was Lenny the door man.

He was a broad-shouldered bear of a man with short hair like a Sharpie and suspicious dark eyes. He seemed to enjoy his job, and once when there was a fight, she'd seen him twist a drunken man's arm behind his back until he screamed. Lenny and Kitty often took their break together, their heads bent close in conversation. One time, in the early days, when Faith had tried to join them, she'd known at once that she wasn't welcome. Feelings hurt, she'd wondered what Kitty could share with Lenny that she couldn't share with her.

Lenny might be Kitty's confidante, but he wasn't the one she was in love with. Faith was pretty certain of that, and she wasn't the only one who noticed that the man Kitty was angling after was Jared Shaw. Once, when they didn't realise anyone was watching, she'd seen Kitty stretch up on her toes and kiss his lips, only to wriggle away, laughing, when he tried to grab her. Jared wasn't the sort of man Faith found attractive—like the Angel, there was something dangerous about him, but maybe that was what Kitty liked. When Jared spoke to Kitty his voice changed, and when he watched her walking across a room … He looked like he wanted to eat her up.

Now Kitty's late nights made sense.

Faith realised how much of an innocent she'd been before she left Willow Tree Bend. She'd thought she knew all about love and sex, even though she'd never had a proper boyfriend—most of the boys she'd known, like Joe, had been neighbours and friends. It was difficult to be intimate with someone when all your relatives were watching, but that was the reality of life in a small town.

It had been drummed into her since she was little that there were only two sorts of girls—good and bad. Bad girls slept around before marriage, good girls waited. Her mother believed marriage was the only way a girl could sleep with a boy and continue to be valued. Cherished. Despite her own unhappy experience, Lily refused to contemplate anything else.

'Men get nearly everything they want,' she'd say bitterly. 'Our bodies are something we can bargain with to get what *we* want.'

Of course Faith had rebelled against such old-fashioned values, laughing with her friends, but deep inside she must have believed them. Now that she was away from home and working at the Angel, she could see that not everyone went along with her mother's rigorous stance of no sex before marriage. Women made their own choices for different reasons. The need to be loved and to belong could see them being coerced into pleasing a man by sleeping with him, despite their own doubts. And then there was money—using sex as a way of making a living. Faith could see that Lily was right, in that sex could be a powerful bargaining tool, but it was also something that could be given freely, equally, by both sides.

One evening, Faith had finished her shift and was fetching her coat from the staff cloak room, which was on the landing near the staff door into the Mezzanine. She caught the unmistakeable sound of Kitty's breathless laugh. Peeping around the corner, she could see up the two flights of stairs ending in the Penthouse. She'd heard there was a private party going on up there—Kitty had told her some American celebrity had been brought in by the company that was sponsoring his Australian appearances, and Jared was told to give him a good time.

'Jared is the man to come to for that,' her cousin had said proudly. 'People all over the world know about the Angel.'

Now here she was with Jared, and he had his arm around her waist, and her head was on his shoulder. He was holding her up, Faith realised with a shock, rather than cuddling her as she'd first thought. As they started up the final set of stairs, she moved so that she could see them through the banisters. The door to the Penthouse was closed, but Jared knocked and it opened with a loud burst of noise, which was muted as it was closed again behind them.

Faith was still pondering over what she'd seen when she reached her house.

'Faith!'

She turned and her mind went blank. Joe Cantani was getting out of his car, and he seemed so out of place. It was as if she'd already left all of that behind, and now suddenly the Golden Gully milk bar had popped up in the middle of St Kilda Road.

'Joe.' She pulled herself together, hoping he hadn't noticed her dismay and confusion, and went to kiss his cheek.

'Hello, Faith.' He held her tight, and for a moment the feel of his strong arms, even the scent of his aftershave, was twisting something deep inside her. A strange sort of ache she thought might be homesickness.

He's like a brother, she told herself, *and part of me misses him. That's all.*

Once inside she made him a cup of tea and found some biscuits that were still okay, and sat him down in the cluttered kitchen at the green formica table. At first it felt a little awkward—she could hear herself talking too much—but then the electricity went off. She was used to that happening now, but Joe started up, concerned, asking about fuse boxes.

'Don't worry, it happens all the time,' she reassured him.

Faith found candles to light, setting them around the room in vegemite jars. Joe made some comment and they laughed, and just like that everything was okay again. As they chatted her housemates came and went, which was mostly, she suspected, to get a closer look at Joe. But she didn't mind that. She was rather proud of his good looks, and that it was *her* he was interested in and not them.

'How's Hope?' she asked, nibbling on a chocolate Golliwog biscuit.

'Haven't you spoken to her?' he replied, surprised. Of course he was surprised, Faith thought with friendly scorn. The Cantanis couldn't go without a family get-together for longer than five minutes.

'I'm sending her a birthday present.'

'She misses you, I think.' He gave her a quizzical smile.

'And your mother? And Pete?'

'Mum's good. Pete is starting to worry about

being called up.

He's turned twenty and his name is in for the next lottery draw.'

'They won't pick him, why should they?' Faith retorted.

Twice a year there was a lottery, where men who had turned twenty could be chosen to be conscripted into the army. It seemed inconceivable that Pete Cantani, with his charming smile that had been the downfall of many a Golden Gully girl, should be called up for National Service and sent to Vietnam.

'I saw a protest the other day. People with placards, calling for us to get out of this war. Maybe the government will decide not to send any more soldiers over there.'

Joe shrugged, but she could see he was unconvinced.

'What about you? One of your friends—' he nodded towards the dark doorway and the rest of the house—'said you were working at a nightclub.'

He made it sound like she was halfway to hell. Faith giggled at the thought, and then couldn't stop. He smiled back at her, not taking it personally, and eventually she managed to control herself.

'Sorry. It was the way you said it. I'm a ... I'm a waitress. At the Angel. Serving, uh, food.' She'd been going to say drinks, but maybe that wasn't such a good idea. If her mother heard about it, she'd probably arrive to take her home on the grounds that she was underage and being morally corrupted. She imagined Lily storming into the Cocktail Lounge in her old tweed coat and wellington boots, and it nearly set her off again.

'And what sort of, uh, food, do you serve?'

His eyes were warm, full of candlelight, and there was laughter in them. She realised then that he knew. Of course he did. Joe was no fool.

'Don't tell on me, will you?' she begged him. 'I'd hate to have to go home. Not yet, anyway,' she added, when she caught his surprised look.

'But you will come home eventually?' he said, his head bent as he turned a teaspoon over and over on his saucer.

''Course I will.'

Later, when he left for his uncle's place in Coburg, she gave him another hug goodbye and watched, shivering in the cold night air, as he drove off in his Valiant. It had been nice to see Joe. He knew her and she didn't have to pretend and put on an act, or watch herself as she did now with Kitty.

But all the same he was just Joe Cantani from home.

Next week Ray would be back.

9

SAMANTHA

14 January 2000, Willow Tree Bend

'WHEN ARE YOU meeting Hope at the cottage?'

My grandmother was watching me over her teacup. She knew very well what time. I wasn't sure why she kept asking, unless it was to make me feel guilty because Hope hadn't invited her. 'Gran, you can come if you want to. I'll take you with me.' 'I haven't been asked,' she retorted.

I opened my mouth to remind her that had never stopped her before, and what about the time she'd gate-crashed the local Country Women's Scone Morning, after they cold-shouldered her over some comment she'd made about their president? But she got to her feet and moved to the sink to clean some non-existent speck of dirt. Pompom was lying on the floor, catching the breeze from the open glass doors that led out to the back deck. He looked like a dirty dish mop with ears.

'I have a few things to do before I go,' I said with

a note of desperation. 'I'll see you later, okay?'

'Of course you will. Where else would I be?'

It was already getting hot outside, but I busied myself around the property, watering and feeding my animals, making sure everything was done to my satisfaction. I'd created more shade in the chook house, and now I made sure the girls weren't feeling too stressed. Gobble the turkey had his own area—I wasn't sure whether it would be a good idea for him to hang out with the girls. I'd have to ask Estelle. The activity kept me from thinking, and by organising these things, I had the sense I was in control of at least a part of my life.

Mitch the kelpie stuck to my heels—probably because he refused to be in the house when Pompom was in residence. I'd had him ever since he was a pup, and he wasn't the only stray I'd accumulated. I wasn't sure when my property had become a refuge for abandoned animals, perhaps when that first box of puppies got dumped inside my gate. I had arrived home and found their frightened, appealing little faces gazing up at me, and knew I wouldn't be turning them in to the local pound unless I was sure they'd find a home. The next day I spent time I didn't really have taking them to the vet, feeding them the recommended foods, and then finally picking up the telephone to bully my friends and acquaintances into becoming adopters. By evening I'd found a place for all of them but one, and the relief and satisfaction gave me an incredible high.

Mitch was the one I kept for myself.

After the puppies there had been a few similar incidents— coincidence I thought at first, but then people started dropping in with their unwanted animals, saying they'd heard I was opening a shelter. They didn't want to get their pets put down, but it seemed that, for whatever reason, they didn't want to keep them either.

I don't know how I would have managed if it hadn't been for Estelle.

Estelle and her husband, Doug, ran a shelter for what she called 'animals in need'—which basically meant anything she wanted it to. She lived nearly forty miles to the south, so I rang her, not sure what to expect, but it certainly wasn't the breezy, calm character Estelle turned out to be. She admitted she was swamped most of the time, and ran the place on a shoestring budget, but she was happy to help out when she could, and to offer me advice when she couldn't.

We struck up an enduring friendship.

It was an eye-opening moment. I realised how blissfully ignorant I had been about animal welfare. There were a lot of neglectful people out there, some of them downright horrible, but there were also a lot of fantastic ones like Estelle and her volunteers. My latest guest was Gobble, who had been found abandoned in a rubbish bin. I hadn't had much to do with turkeys before, apart from Christmas dinner, and after making the acquaintance of Gobble, I wasn't sure I could see myself sitting down to eat his relatives in the near future.

'See how you go,' Estelle had said, as she handed

the bird over. 'You might like a few more hens, too. That chicken farm I was telling you about closed, so I have plenty. They're not very pretty to look at, but they're the sweetest-natured girls.'

I had five already so I said I'd think about it and told myself there was no reason to feel guilty.

My grandmother was unimpressed with Gobble. The last night I had caught her eyeing him as if she was imagining him in a baking dish surrounded by vegetables.

After her cleaning frenzy I'd thought she'd gone home, but it turned out there had been a bus trip booked and she was off for the day enjoying herself with her friends. Now she was back at my house and, when I'd tentatively asked her why, she'd just smiled serenely.

'You really don't have to stay, Gran. I'm used to being on my own.'

She'd given me one of her looks. 'I'm on my own, too, Sam. That's why we should keep each other company.'

I wasn't sure what to say to that, apart from thank you, and then return her hug. Which was in itself rather disconcerting because Gran was not normally the hugging kind.

I wished I knew what was going on, and I was sure that Gran did know—she just wasn't going to tell me.

Hope would be at the Willow Tree Bend cottage at eleven o'clock this morning—that was where Dad and I were meeting her. She'd have the film crew with her, all ready to film us as we welcomed her home.

I frowned every time I thought of that—after I'd snorted in amusement. What did they want? Tears? I was looking forward to seeing my aunt, or at least I thought I was, but I resented being asked to perform for the camera. I'd wanted to say no, that I was too busy, but I couldn't do that to my father. And then there was the question of my mother. Had Hope bothered to tell the show that her sister had taken off for Queensland? I knew Dad hadn't said a word.

It was going to be awkward but, really, it wasn't my problem. They'd just have to sort it out between themselves.

My smile turned slightly malicious. *Lincoln Nash.* How on earth had they managed to get him to agree to them using his place for their program? They must have offered him a wad of cash.

My father had offered to pick me up and take me, but I'd said no, that I had things to do and would make my own way and meet him there. It wasn't strictly true, but I figured that at least it would give me an escape if, after five minutes, I'd had enough.

I glanced again at my watch and saw with annoyance that it was barely nine o'clock. I really couldn't sit around waiting for the next two hours. Then I remembered I had been planning to put some seedlings into the garden at the front of the school, and I thought I may as well do it now as hang about. As long as I left enough time to come back and change into clean clothes, everything should be fine.

I called out to Gran to tell her where I was going.

'Make sure you put on a bra when you get back,' she said, giving me the sort of look that made me want to cross my arms. 'Why aren't you wearing one now?'

'It's too hot.'

Gran was a strong woman with a will of her own, but she wasn't liberated when it came to underwear. We'd had this conversation before.

I went to collect my work tools and stacked them in the back of the ute, and Mitch hopped in, too. I had thought he might stay home, despite Pompom's presence. My grandmother had cooked a large pan of lasagne last night and there were plenty of leftovers, and she had been known to cave in to Mitch's doggy pleading. Lasagne usually tipped the balance for Mitch so I tried to call him out, but he sat down and wouldn't budge, and I didn't have the heart to refuse him. I told myself I could bring him home when I changed. There'd be plenty of time.

But in the end there wasn't plenty of time.

Planting the seedlings took longer than I'd expected because some kids who should have been enjoying their holidays turned up and wanted to help. Their parents thought it was a good learning experience, so I couldn't really get all grumpy and say no. They were very enthusiastic—it was sweet really—but they weren't quick. By the time I'd finished it was well after ten-thirty and there was no time to go home and shower, despite my sweaty state. Oh well, I thought with a grimace, too bad. What did it matter anyway? No one would be looking at me.

I wiped my grubby palms down the legs of my jeans and climbed into the ute.

'She'll just have to take me as she finds me,' I excused myself to the kelpie. 'I don't care if I'm not in the show.' In fact, I wondered if, subconsciously, that had been my plan all along.

Mitch wagged his tail in response.

'You don't mind how grubby I am, do you, boy?' The kelpie agreed he didn't.

I wondered if Lincoln Nash would notice my boots this time. I promised myself that if he stared I would do a little tap dance, just for him.

The old cottage at Willow Tree Bend sat on a rise at the end of a long dusty road. The elevation gave it an advantage when it came to cooling breezes, and a view over the surrounding countryside, including the winding creek and the old willow tree.

I was always surprised how small it appeared from the outside, especially as my mother and Hope had shared the front bedroom. They must have been treading on each other's toes the whole time.

As an only child I'd never had to share. I could remember going through a stage where I'd longed for a sibling, had begged my parents to have another child so that I wouldn't be alone.

'Not gonna happen,' had been Faith's response. 'We had enough trouble getting you.'

But being the only child had its advantages. I might have been lonely sometimes, and being the sole focus of my parents' attention could be exhausting, but I couldn't complain too much about my upbringing. Mum and Dad had been loving but strict, although I could always try to persuade them to my point of view, and sometimes I succeeded. Dad was the softy, but Mum made up for that with her strict guidelines and the lists of chores I had to finish before she would hand over my weekly pocket money.

Yes, my mother was a strong person, not prone to sentiment, but the odd thing was that, occasionally, if I happened to look up when she wasn't expecting it … she would be staring at me as if she couldn't believe her luck.

I slowed the ute on the unsealed road with its centre strip of old bitumen. Either side was bush, consisting mainly of the hardy stuff that seemed to proliferate in the gold-rush country around here. Trees which, with their thin, weedy trunks and grey, drooping foliage, gave the impression that they were only just hanging on until the next rains. It wasn't true. In actual fact, the indigenous vegetation was very hardy—it had to be.

As I pulled up I saw to my dismay that the film crew had already arrived. That shiny grey four-wheel drive must be theirs. They'd parked in the patchy shade of one of the gum trees, and the vehicle was empty. They must already be in the cottage.

No sign of Dad yet.

Damn! My stomach knotted and my hands tightened on the steering wheel. I'd been hoping he would be here, then at least there would be two of us to face Hope and her entourage.

I turned off the engine and took a deep breath, slipping my keys into my pocket. There was a smudge of dirt on my arm, and I rubbed it off as best I could. A quick look in the rear-view mirror showed my face was flushed and my fair hair was flattened on the crown by the hat I'd been wearing to protect myself from the sun. Half-heartedly I tried to fluff it up, then abandoned the attempt and tucked the lank strands behind my ears.

Was it too late to change my mind? But I knew I couldn't, not if I wanted to get this over and done with. Otherwise Hope and her crew would probably pursue me all over the countryside. And what did it matter how I looked or what they thought? Surely the worse I looked the better my famous aunt would appear in comparison?

Still feeling optimistic, I climbed out of the ute and Mitch joined me. I grabbed his leash and called him to my side as we started up the worn track towards the gate. I could hear voices coming from outside the cottage, and one of them was definitely the carefully modulated tones of Hope Taylor.

'Are you going to be good, Mitch?' I asked my dog.

It was a rhetorical question. He was usually well behaved in company.

I stood there and, whether it was the sound of Hope's voice, or this being the place where the sisters had grown up, I suddenly missed my mother. Here I had been resenting her absence and all of the complications it had caused, when really I was missing her terribly.

She was the unflappable one, the one who would have taken charge and refused to allow us to be talked into doing anything we didn't want to do. Without her … well, I was very much afraid that anything could happen.

IO

HOPE

14 January 2000, Willow Tree Bend

PRUE HAD ARRIVED to collect her on the dot of seven, just as she'd promised, and the journey out of Melbourne had been reasonably smooth. Ken, the camera operator, was young and scruffily dressed—or maybe that was just his idea of fashion. After Prue's cool introduction—'Remember Ken?'—he didn't seem keen to chat and spent the time reading a book and frowning, although Hope noticed he wasn't turning many pages. Perhaps he was a slow reader, but she thought, if the strained atmosphere between him and Prue was anything to go by, it was more likely they had had a tiff.

Which suited Hope because it meant she could sit in silence and relax. Or at least try to. She hadn't slept well. After her visit to the Angel, and her medical—which she'd flown through—she'd gone out to dinner with a couple of old friends.

She'd expected to enjoy reminiscing, but by nine she'd pleaded jet lag and had returned to her hotel. As she'd walked past the eclectic collection of photographs in the lobby, those wane and hopeless faces, she'd wondered again about the homeless man and what he knew of Faith. Funny, but she'd thought her sister, if not quite an open book, wasn't really that complicated. How wrong she had been!

There were shadows in Faith's past. How had it happened that they had never talked about what had made Faith so sad after she came back from Melbourne? It was true that when Faith went away, Hope had found it difficult to forgive her. Did it really all stem from something as childish as that? Could a festering resentment have turned them into strangers? Only, she told herself, they weren't strangers, because Faith had rung her that night in New York to tell her … something. She had reached out to her sister, and Hope was damned if she was going to let her down.

The only problem was *Looking Back*. She didn't want them poking about into the past—especially, frustratingly, in Faith's case—because she didn't know what they might find.

Her dinner friends had been quite vocal when it came to the program, telling her some worrying stories about their style of investigative journalism. Evidently one 'guest' had tried to sue them, but it was all hushed up—no doubt payments were made to ensure silence. To change the topic to something less disquieting, Hope had asked them about the state of the local film industry—they ran a small production company, so she thought they should know. They were upbeat and the situation sounded more encouraging than she'd imagined.

They'd thought she was sussing them out because she was planning to relocate. It occurred to her that she could find work here in Australia, carve out a niche for herself, as other expatriate actors had done over the years. Until she remembered the reasons she had left in the first place.

On the journey they stopped for takeaway coffee, and Hope sipped hers in silence, pretending to be engrossed in the scenery because she didn't want to go over the schedule yet again. Prue was speaking to Ken, their voices too low to make out the words, but the tone was plain enough. They'd definitely had a tiff, and Hope was beginning to think it was personal. She could give them a lecture on the perils of mixing work and pleasure, but she doubted they'd want to hear it.

The sun kept ducking behind clouds, so it wasn't nearly as hot as it could be this time of year. Prue had told her it was forecast to be around thirty degrees in Golden Gully and Hope thought her outfit—dark slacks and a cream-coloured silk blouse—would be perfect, but she had a jacket, just in case. The idea was to look smart but not intimidating.

Looking Back wanted it raw and real, but that didn't mean one couldn't look one's best. Over the years, she'd modelled her appearance on a quote made by *Vogue* when her career in the US was just taking off. 'Hope Taylor has the cool, blonde good looks of a Grace Kelly, only more approachable.'

When they reached Golden Gully Prue drove straight through. It happened so quickly that Hope barely got more than a glimpse of Faith's new Cantani Desserts shop. She did notice the old milk bar though, and the pub, and the park where the teenage kids had hung out, the boys eyeing off the girls, and vice versa. Not that Faith had ever done that. She'd preferred to set her sights on the city and the future she was planning, which was amusing really when it had been Hope who had set off to find fame and fortune, and Faith who had crept home and made do with Joe and a life in the country.

That was unfair.

One didn't simply *make do* with the Cantani men. Hope found her gaze blurring and blinked hastily, several times, until the tears had gone. This wasn't the time or the place to let her emotions escape the tight control she had on them. She glanced surreptitiously at Prue, to see if she'd noticed, but her PA was too busy shooting black looks at Ken.

Willow Tree Bend cottage was around five miles from the centre of Golden Gully, but these days there were plenty of new houses trying to fill the gap. When they turned into the long driveway and the old cottage was finally in sight, Hope found herself remembering bits and pieces of the past as if it was yesterday, and with a clarity that astounded her. The day she decided she wanted to be an actress and her mother had said that was vanity, and she had some verses from the Bible to back it up. The day Faith left in Joe's car, and without her the room they'd shared all their lives had seemed so big, so empty. The hot afternoon the big black car had stopped and the man behind the wheel had offered her a lift.

'Here we are!'

Prue's voice made her jump. Hope managed a smile, telling herself once again this wasn't the time to lose focus.

'Tell us about the cottage,' Prue suggested as they slowed, and Hope realised Ken had his camera trained on her face, waiting to capture whatever emotions might be fermenting inside her.

She was too much of a professional to freeze up or turn away. Instead, she began to speak in a slightly breathless voice, as if she was a little overcome by the moment.

'Well … I'll try.' Hope pretended to gather her thoughts, but in reality this was a speech she'd had prepared for some time. 'The cottage was actually a two-room kit home. It arrived by ship from England around eighteen sixty, and was put together on site. Kind of like old-world Ikea. The Taylors, my father's great-grandparents, were a family of seven by then, so I imagine it was extremely crowded in those two rooms. Later on they added another two rooms, with the sleep-out at the back. The kitchen used to be separated from the main house in the early days, in case of fire.'

Prue smiled at her, looking inordinately pleased, so she carried on, talking about when she was a child and how she used to imagine those five

Taylor children from the early days.

'And did you ever see any ghosts?' Prue asked, a twinkle in her eye.

Hope lost her thread. She opened her mouth to answer, but unexpectedly she couldn't think of anything to say. It was as if the synapses between her brain and her mouth had been cut, and there was a moment of total and complete panic, before yet again her training came to her rescue.

'I think when a place has been in your family for so long, with that much history, it's easy to imagine all those people still living there, along with you.'

Prue opened her mouth to ask more, and there was a searching look on her face, as if she was aware that Hope was holding back, but luckily she was distracted by Ken.

While they murmured together, Hope narrowed her eyes against the sun's glare. There was the window of the bedroom she had shared with Faith. Occasionally, when they were reduced to it by their mother's strict rules, they had climbed out of that window and gone off to meet friends. Sometimes they climbed out just so they could sit on the creek bank, under the willow tree, and enjoy the cool night air.

The willow was still there, older and more gnarled. If only those branches could talk, what tales they could tell.

Prue had slowed right down. 'Nice garden,' she said. 'Was it like that when you were here?'

Hope tried to picture the garden, but she found it a blur. She was fairly certain it wasn't as well tended and pretty as this. Lincoln Nash, the current occupant, must have a green thumb. There were a number of ornamental metal sculptures set among the shrubs—she noticed the silhouette of a crow that rocked gently on the breeze and would no doubt spin with a stronger gust of wind.

She'd been told that Lincoln Nash was a musician, one of those flash-in-the-pan ones. Evidently the band had imploded, as so often happened with young men thrown together day and night, touring, tired and probably high on alcohol or drugs. They'd gone their separate ways.

According to Prue, Lincoln was trying to resurrect his career, and had only agreed to allow them inside to film if they played one of his songs over the end credits. Hope had never heard of him, but she had no problem with that. To her mind, it showed entrepreneurial acumen and she had always admired someone who knew how to strike a good deal. She'd done it herself once or twice when pushed into a tight corner.

Outside the car, the air felt warm and dry, and somehow … she recognised it. Those hot days of her childhood, she and Faith sitting under the pendulous branches of the willow, throwing pebbles into the creek, and talking. What had they talked about? She couldn't remember exactly. Silly stuff mostly, dreams and their future, and which boy they were interested in this week. And then the day Faith had told her she was leaving. Hope hadn't believed her at first, because they were supposed to be leaving together, but Faith was in earnest. She remembered jumping up and running back to the cottage, and her sister letting her go, not trying to stop her or comfort her. When Joe came to pick Faith up in his car, Hope had stayed away, refusing to say goodbye, she'd been so hurt and upset, so angry.

But now wasn't the time to be thinking of her past. She must stay focused—the camera was on her.

She shaded her eyes and gazed up the slight slope at the cottage within its garden. Another of the sculptures, a wind-direction finder with a guitar instead of a pointer, turned a little and stopped.

The gate creaked as Prue swung it open.

Hope went to follow and then paused. She didn't want to but she couldn't help it. Slowly she turned, looking behind her at the road stretching back, completely empty. No black car with a chrome bumper bar. Nothing to say that anything bad had ever happened when she was sixteen and in love and life was just beginning to be so good.

She shut down the memories before they could take hold. Not because the camera would pick up on her emotions—she was too much of a professional for that—but because what she was feeling was her own private business.

'Miss Taylor? Can you walk up onto the verandah?'

Where were Samantha and Joe? If they didn't turn up soon she'd look like a fool, and worse, she'd feel like one. Well, too late now. She stiff ened her back and lifted her chin and moved towards her childhood home as if she was perfectly at ease.

There was a screen door blocking their way. From inside she could hear the sound of a radio, and then a cat approached and stared at them through the mesh. Its fur was a mixture of pale orange and cream and brown, which caught the light and had the appearance of a frothy cappuccino.

'Mr Nash?' Prue knocked and waited. She and Ken exchanged a glance, and then she knocked again.

And that was when they heard the vehicle coming up the road behind them. 'It must be Mrs Cantani,' Prue said with a hint of relief.

Joe, thought Hope, but then her heart sank.

It was Samantha and she was driving an appallingly disreputable ute. Dull patches of rust speckled the dirty white exterior and the door groaned ominously when she opened it. There was even a dog in there with her. Such a cliché! And when she stepped out ... Hope's heart sank even further at the sight of her niece's dirty jeans, singlet top and dusty boots.

Last time she'd seen Samantha she had been barely an adult, edgy and difficult, her character still forming. Now she was a woman. The pointed chin and neat features, along with her fair, shoulder-length hair, reminded Hope of Faith, while her slim figure and height reminded Hope of herself.

And even from here she could see that her eyes were that clear, remarkable blue. Cantani eyes.

Her father's eyes.

II

FAITH

August 1969, St Kilda

THE POLICE RAID happened shortly after midnight, just when the Angel was really jumping. At first Faith didn't even notice the police rushing in through a side door, not until there was a yell from one of the patrons, and then the uniformed cops seemed to be everywhere. Shouts of *Don't move!* rang out above the din, but no one took any notice as they stampeded for the street. Her tray of glasses crashed to the floor before she could get out of the way.

As Faith knelt to gather up the jagged glass, a man in a rumpled grey suit nearly stepped on her. His face, from the brief glimpse she got of him before he turned his back, seemed just as rumpled. And grey—he didn't look well. He was busy directing the uniforms, eyes everywhere, and she heard him say, 'Right, get up to the top floor. No, don't take the lift, but put a man on it in case anyone tries to leave. Now go, go!'

Moments later she could hear them pounding

up the stairs to the Mezzanine, and then higher still. Doors slammed open so hard it was like a bomb going off. Earlier Faith had been up to the Mezzanine herself, looking for Kitty, and she'd heard a song drifting down from above—'Touch Me' by the Doors, being played over and over again.

Kneeling, Faith stayed where she was, too shocked to notice her stockings soaking up spilled cocktails and beer. She was in an alcove area usually reserved for those who wanted a bit of privacy, and no one seemed to be taking any notice of her. Rumpled Suit had disappeared, and she was thinking about leaving too when someone started shouting.

It was one of the prostitutes at the table by the door. She'd been too drunk to move let alone run, and no one had thought to help her. Now she was on her feet, swearing, as a couple of the uniforms attempted to grapple with her. Finally they managed to restrain her, and half walked, half dragged her out of the room. Her angry swearing faded and it was only then that Faith realised the lounge was empty. Apart from her.

She got to her feet, ignoring the crunch of glass under the soles of her boots. All the action seemed to be taking place above her head and she was too curious to stop herself as she made her way out of the Cocktail Lounge, along the dingy corridor and up the stairs that were the staff's route to the Mezzanine. She peered into the big dining room and entertainment area and found them empty, too. Jared's office, reached by a short staircase near the staff cloakroom, was also empty, the door swinging wide. His desk was a mess, as if the cops had been going through his paperwork.

Again she was distracted by the noise coming from the Penthouse. What had Kitty said about the upper floor of the Angel? Next stop heaven?

Standing on the landing, her hand tight on the balustrade, she listened as Jim Morrison's voice was cut off abruptly, mid-sentence. A moment later another male voice filled the silence, demanding to be allowed to leave at once, while a woman's sobbing punctuated his furious outbursts.

Was that Kitty? Her heart began to bump harder. If it was Kitty … well, for Kitty to cry then things must be very bad.

According to her cousin, the cops turned a blind eye when it came to the Angel. She'd said Jared and his bosses were in contact with the right people and paid them well enough to escape any official attention. They wouldn't dare, she'd said.

Well tonight they had dared.

Faith knew she had to go up there and make certain Kitty was safe. Only a coward would sneak off home. The elevator went all the way from the Cocktail Lounge, via the Mezzanine, to the Penthouse, but unless there was a party going on the door was locked at the very top, preventing it from opening. Even then some of the customers preferred to use the stairs so that they wouldn't be seen by anyone who might tell tales. But she remembered she couldn't use the elevator anyway, not with the police in charge of it.

Slowly Faith began to climb.

The third floor was used for storage, and there were a couple of rooms where the staff could stay over if necessary, or some of the customers if they'd drunk too much and needed to sleep it off. The fourth floor was another matter. Jared held his private parties up there, with the emphasis on 'private'. Girls came and went, and sometimes a band played, but mostly it was music from the record player. If food and drink were needed then Kitty handled it. Faith had yet to be asked to waitress up there, and she had a feeling her cousin might have something to do with that. Kitty could be surprisingly protective when the mood took her.

She thought Faith didn't notice what was going on, but Faith was no fool. She knew about the prostitutes Kitty paid and took upstairs, she knew about the illegal drugs Lenny handed out—the little pills she'd guessed were LSD, among other things. She knew a great deal. It was only that she chose to pretend she didn't.

Faith could see that the door at the top was slightly ajar, and as she drew closer the smells of cigarette smoke and booze drifted out. The sobbing grew louder and, overcome with relief, Faith leaned on the handrail. It *wasn't* Kitty. And then she reminded herself that Kitty was still up there and she needed to see for herself that her cousin was okay. Cautiously, she reached for the door and pushed it further inward, just enough so that she could see inside without being seen herself.

The walls were painted in psychedelic colours and the furniture was minimal. There was a large silver statue in one corner that could have been an archangel … or a devil. A colourful sea of cushions spilled onto a thick pile rug in the middle of the floor, and Faith noticed the scattered remains of food and drink. Discarded clothing lay about—there was a tie just inside the door, as if whoever had arrived last had simply stripped off and dived in.

By now there weren't that many people in the room, despite the noise they were making. She could hear the elevator operating, taking a few of them at a time downstairs to whatever fate awaited them. One man stood closest to the door, looking as if he wished he could disappear, his belly hanging over his Y-fronts. The man who was doing all of the shouting had no clothes on at all, although a frustrated cop was trying to persuade him to get dressed. Faith recognised him from the Cocktail Lounge—his face at least, and his loud voice. He owned a real estate business in town and was always boasting to the girls how much money he made.

The rest were women. She recognised three of them; they were from the group who sat on the table by the door, and she'd seen Kitty leading them upstairs on previous occasions. Right now they were busy pulling on their clothing. A hiccup caught her attention. It was the woman who'd been crying, except she was more of a girl. She'd made an attempt to look older, caking on the makeup, but Faith—who had the same problem herself—could see past that.

She was huddled in a chair, wearing a grey

woollen coat that looked like it was once part of her school uniform, and her eye makeup was running in black streaks down her face. 'The money was good,' she mumbled, her mouth sullen, like a child's. 'So why not?'

'Because you're under age, love. Can you explain what—'

'How was I to know she was only fifteen?'

The interruption came from Kitty. She stepped into view and Faith was so relieved she must have made a movement. She might have thrown caution to the winds and gone to her cousin's side, but Kitty saw her.

Her green eyes flared, and Faith saw shock and anger and concern, all rolled into one, and then she took a couple of paces to the side, taking the attention of the cop with her, and away from the door. Quickly Faith moved back again, out of sight, but not before she'd noted with relief that Kitty was fully dressed.

'You could have asked her,' the policeman was saying in a disbelieving voice.

Kitty put her hands on her hips. 'Didn't think I had to. I expect people to tell me the truth.' He snorted.

Kitty ignored him. 'Where have you taken Jared?' She lit a cigarette, and Faith wondered if anyone else noticed her hands shaking.

She hadn't looked Faith's way again.

'Your boss is helping us by answering a few questions.'

'I need him here to sort out this mess.'

'The sooner you cooperate the sooner—'

'Who's *your* boss? Someone is going to be in big trouble over this, you know that? Jared has friends, important friends, and when they hear what's happened tonight … Well, I wouldn't want to be you. So why don't you just *go!*'

The last word seemed to be aimed at her, and as Kitty obviously didn't need her help, Faith decided to do just that. She shuffled away from the door. She was thinking about getting her coat as she turned to hurry down the stairs, planning her way out of here before anybody noticed her.

But there was someone standing behind her.

She gave a strangled gasp and almost fell. A hand fastened on her arm, steadying her. It was the tall man in the crumpled suit, the plainclothes detective. He put a finger to his lips to hush her, and then shot a glance over her head, into the room.

He was middle-aged—late forties or older—with deep, weary lines bracketing his mouth, and a hard-eyed stare. His face had a grey tinge to it, due to tiredness or ill-health, or maybe both. He listened to the questioning, but he didn't seem to want to join in, and after a moment he reached out and shut the door with a firm click before turning back to her.

He was looking at her properly for the first time and whatever he saw seemed to startle him. He stiffened, shaggy brows coming down over his hazel eyes. Confused, Faith wondered what it was he was seeing, but before she could ask he'd shaken off whatever was troubling him and was speaking to her in a low, gravelly voice.

'What are you doing up here? Who are you?'

'Faith Taylor.'

She wondered in hindsight if she should have lied. Kitty would call her naive and stupid. But— she glanced at him sideways—she had a feeling he would have known at once if she hadn't told him the truth.

'What are you doing here?'

'I work in the Cocktail Lounge. I was downstairs when the cops … you arrived. I heard the commotion up here and wondered …' Her voice trailed off.

His mouth quirked into what might have passed for a smile if his gaze wasn't so humourless.

Behind the door there was a crash as something—or someone— went flying, and then more shouting erupted.

The detective gave a weary sigh, as if he had seen it all before. 'Come on,' he said, taking her arm again, and began to lead her down the stairs.

She tried to shake him off. 'I need to go home. You've no reason to keep me. I haven't done anything wrong.'

'You can go home in a moment, but I want to talk to you first.'

They'd reached the third-floor landing and he looked along the gloomy corridor with its single light bulb. 'Is there somewhere here we can talk, Faith?'

'Are you arresting me?'

He smiled properly this time, and his whole face changed, so that he looked much more approachable. 'No, I'm not arresting you.'

Faith hesitated, but it was obvious she wasn't

going home until he'd had his talk to her, so she led him along the corridor to the first door.

It looked like Gaz used this room for his tinned food supplies, but it had also been a spot for some staff member to skiv off work, going by the overflowing ashtray on a table by the window. The detective walked over and pushed up the sash. The sounds of the street flooded in, along with the wet smell of the bay a few blocks away.

'Sit down,' he ordered, without looking at her.

There was a cheap moulded plastic chair opposite the table, so she sat in it. Just for a heartbeat Faith considered making a run for it, but there didn't seem much point. She'd told him her name, and even if he couldn't catch her, he'd find her. Besides, why should she run? She'd done nothing wrong. And then she remembered she was still seventeen and actually he could charge her with being in licensed premises and under age. Probably charge Kitty, too, for employing her.

Nervously, Faith clenched her hands in her lap and tried to compose her face into what she hoped was the same hard-as-nails expression her cousin had just been wearing.

He'd turned, his gaze flicking over her, and she saw a gleam in his eyes. Evidently her play-acting was amusing him. He reached into his jacket pocket and brought out some cigarettes, offering them to her. When Faith shook her head he lit one for himself, taking his time.

'How long have you worked here?' he said.

'A while.'

'Where did Jared find you?'

'He didn't find me anywhere. I needed a job and a friend suggested the Angel,' she explained grudgingly.

'A friend? Does that friend have a name?'

He couldn't know that Kitty was her cousin, and she certainly wasn't about to enlighten him.

'What does it matter? You don't know her.'

He'd been leaning back against the windowsill, narrowed eyes on her face, but as she spoke the last word he seemed to relax. As if she'd relieved his mind of some unease.

'You obviously didn't know what was going on up there, did you?' he asked, with a jerk of his head towards the ceiling. 'Don't pretend you did. I saw your face.'

'No. I didn't.'

Her answer seemed to please him. 'Right, well, there might come a time when they ask you if you want to earn some extra cash. If they do you'll know what to expect. After tonight, do you think you'll say yes?'

Faith shook her head jerkily. She felt sick at the thought, but she hardened her expression again, not wanting him to know how shocked she really was. Kitty had accused her of being an innocent little miss, and it seemed she was right.

'You're a clever girl, Faith. I bet you see things, hear things. You know what goes on here, don't you?' 'I do my job,' she said woodenly.

He nodded, but he wasn't really listening to her, he was working out what to say and she straight away understood what he was about. He was going to ask her for something, and he was working up to it by frightening her.

Faith relaxed a little. Whatever it was he wanted she would say no.

'Some men like to be entertained with booze and drugs and women. They pay well for it. The people who run the Angel, they use Jared as a front because they're criminals, Faith, underworld names you've probably never heard of, but they have their fingers in a lot of pies. There's money to be made and where there's money then there's always the chance someone will get hurt.'

'Hurt?' She heard herself say it even though she didn't want to. Curiosity again.

'Killed. Hurt or killed,' he said in a matter-of-fact way, but he was watching her, reading her conflicting emotions, drawing her in.

By now Faith had forgotten all about pretending to be like Kitty. 'Killed?'

He nodded. 'There was a girl …' He hesitated again, choosing his words. 'She was young, like that girl upstairs, but her hair was fair. Like yours.' The hazel eyes fixed on hers and she couldn't look away. 'She looked very much like you, Faith. When I saw you just now it was the first thing I thought. *Melanie.* That was her name. She worked in the Cocktail Lounge, too, but then Jared offered her more money to work upstairs. Serving drinks, he said. But it was more than that. She'd caught someone's eye and this someone is an important man. He gets what he wants.'

Faith blinked. She was feeling very uncomfortable. Melanie. Was that the name Jared was going to blurt out when he first saw her? And Gaz?

She'd never asked, and perhaps that was because she knew the answer wasn't going to be something she wanted to hear.

She told herself she wasn't going to ask this time either. She wasn't, she wasn't, she wasn't …

'What happened to Melanie?'

'She went missing.' He looked down at the cigarette as if he could no longer meet her eyes. Despite his even tone, she could hear a note in his voice that made her think this mattered to him. He cared.

'She was from the country and her parents hadn't heard from her in a while. They were worried. I led the investigation, and without much help, because who cares when a young girl goes a bit wild and runs away? Eventually, the trail led us to the Angel and, according to Jared, she'd walked out one night and was never seen again. We found her a fortnight later, crammed into a packing case in a warehouse in Port Melbourne. She'd been strangled. She was still wearing her high heels.'

Faith sat up straighter. 'You don't know it had anything to do with—'

'No, I don't. But she told me things, so I can make an educated guess. One thing I do know, Faith. She wasn't planning on dying.'

She tried to think clearly, but instead a voice in her head was asking: *Was Kitty involved?* Suddenly, she had an intense longing to go home to Willow Tree Bend. She wanted her room, and her mother, and Hope. She wanted Joe.

She looked up at him. 'Why are you telling me

this?'

He reached over and mashed out his cigarette in the already full ashtray, but she thought it was to give himself time.

'I want you to bring me information, Faith. We've established you're the sort of girl people confide in. You know things, or you can find them out. There'd be money in it. You could walk away from the Angel and start again somewhere else.'

Faith stood up, her legs trembling. She forced anger past the fear in her voice. 'You're crazy. They were saying upstairs that whoever is in charge of this raid will get into big trouble. The Angel *never* gets raided.'

His face hardened again and he made a sound of disgust. 'The Angel! Girls like you are chewed up and spat out here at the Angel. Don't you know that?'

'I serve drinks, that's all. I don't know anything about Melanie and I don't intend to ask.'

He sighed, and the spark that had seemed to possess him while he told her about the dead girl drained away. Now he just looked tired. 'I'm not going away, not for a while anyway, so if you change your mind then come and see me in Bowen Street. Ask for Detective Inspector Avery.'

He stared at her as the seconds ticked by and she found she couldn't look away. She was just beginning to think she might have to sit down again when he spoke.

'How old are you anyway?'

She made herself shrug indifferently. 'Twenty-two,' she said.

He nodded slowly, but she could see he didn't believe her. He was going to find out she was seventeen. He was going to come back. She cleared her throat and, to distract him, but also because she wanted to know, asked, 'That girl?' She wouldn't say her name. 'The one in the crate. Did you pay her for information?'

The truth was there in his face before he could hide it.

'She died and now you're asking me to do the same thing she did,' she accused him. 'What sort of man does that make you, Detective Inspector Avery?'

His laugh was rough, as if he didn't use it much. 'Desperate,' he said in a flat voice. 'I'm retiring at the end of the year and I want this case put to bed. I've got nothing to lose, Faith.'

Why was he telling her this? But she knew why. He was just like Sydney Poitier in *The Heat of the Night*. She'd gone with Hope to see that film because they both loved *To Sir, With Love*. At first she'd found it confronting—Hope hated it—but by the end she'd loved it, too. Probably because the good guy had won, but also because he defined many of her own moral principles—particularly her sense of rightness. Maybe she was tired, with her emotions jangling, but Avery had swiftly taken on the role of the policeman on a mission.

He reached inside his jacket and took out a photograph. Carefully, deliberately, he put it down in front of her.

It was glossy and in colour, a bit blurred. At first, she wondered what she was looking at and then she realised. Naked limbs entwined, bodies moulded together, a seething mass of humanity engaged in the pursuit of pleasure. It was a snapshot of an orgy.

One face stared out at her. A girl with blonde hair, her pale eyes wide as she stared into the camera. There was a man on top of her and another one under her, and yet somehow you had the sense that she had distanced herself from what was happening to her.

'That's Melanie,' Avery's voice seemed to come from a long way away.

It wasn't until the door closed that she knew he was gone. Faith sat and waited while his footsteps faded before she tried to move. He'd taken the photograph away with him, but she could still see it. Her legs were shaking and her stomach felt queasy. She told herself it was probably all lies, just so that he could get what he wanted.

Well, she wasn't going to let him manipulate her. She had no intention of being an informer for Detective Inspector Avery, just as she had no intention of letting herself be drawn into the murky world she'd caught a glimpse of tonight. No, she would just carry on as usual, looking the other way.

12

SAMANTHA

14 January 2000, Willow Tree Bend

DRY LEAVES CRACKLED under the thick soles of my work boots as I made my way to the gate. It was already open and I paused with my hand on it, noticing that it wasn't your ordinary metal gate. Within the framework I could see crows, large and small, some of them dancing on crescent moons, others flying among the stars.

Black Crow. His band.

Unexpectedly it made me smile. Maybe Lincoln Nash had a sense of humour after all, or at least I hoped he did, and that this wasn't meant to be taken seriously.

I looked up. The three people on the verandah were all watching me intently, two women and a man. Reluctantly I released my sweaty grip on the gate, horribly aware of my worn jeans with the stains on the knees, and my singlet that used to be blue but had faded to a shade between mauve and white. I wished I could turn and run, but I wasn't a coward, so I gritted my teeth and began to walk up the path towards them.

Even though it had been a while since I'd seen my aunt, there was no mistaking her. She'd always had a certain style, a pizzazz that I couldn't emulate, even if I'd wanted to. She'd lost weight, but maybe that was just the way actresses were supposed to look. From this distance she looked younger than I knew her to be, but as I got closer I could see that her face was actually quite drawn, and even her skilful use of makeup had failed to cover up the shadows under her eyes.

Our harsh summer glare was a bugger when it came to looking your best.

Hope was watching me, too, a little smile playing around her lips, and I wondered what she was thinking. But everything went out of my head when I realised the man had a camera balanced on his shoulder and he was filming. Hope moved forward to meet me, and the camera followed her every step. Whatever I had been expecting it wasn't to be thrust into the spotlight so soon, and I felt a little freaked out.

'Samantha!'

'Uh, Hope.'

I paused as she held out her arms, remembering how mucky I was, and wondering if she really wanted me to walk into her pristine embrace.

And then Mitch took the decision out of my hands.

He bowled right past me and sprang up onto Hope, paws on her silk blouse, so he could give her an exuberant lick on the cheek.

It wasn't something he did very often. Just

occasionally he took a liking to someone and his enthusiasm overcame his training. Or maybe he mistook my aunt for my mother, whom he loved. Now he had his dirty paws all over Hope's cream blouse, and she stumbled back with a startled, 'Oh!'

Too late I lunged forward to grasp the furiously wriggling body. Mitch already sensed he'd over-stepped the mark, sitting immediately upon my command, although the look he was giving me from his wounded doggy eyes seemed to be asking what he'd done that was so terrible. It wasn't funny, not at all, and I felt my face heating with embarrassment, but at the same time I was struggling with a terrible urge to burst out laughing.

I took a breath, tamping down my hysteria. 'I'm so sorry,' I said in a stifled voice. 'He's normally well behaved.'

Hope finished brushing at her blouse. The marks were dry, so the damage wasn't too serious. 'Of course he is,' she said with a slightly wry note. She took a breath, planted on her professional smile, and tried again. 'Hello, Samantha.'

This time I found myself locked in her embrace, arms tight about me, her soft cheek against mine. Well, her favourite scent was still Shalimar, I thought, trying not to look as shell-shocked as I felt.

'You could have dressed up a little for the occasion,' Hope murmured for my ears alone.

Before I could think of an answer she'd stepped back, smile still in place, perfectly posed.

'Ah … excuse the work gear,' I said, forcing out

my own smile. 'Emergency.'

I could sense what Hope was longing to say: *An emergency garden conversion? Do tell?* But thankfully, being in front of the camera meant I was spared from having to hear what she really thought.

Just then the screen door to the cottage creaked open behind us. We all turned. A tall, dark, handsome man stood there, but that was where the clichés ended.

Joy oh joy, I thought, could things get any better? It was Lincoln Nash, Mr Charm himself.

He was dressed casually in faded blue jeans and a black tee-shirt. His feet were bare. He was looking from me to Hope, and something in the creases around his eyes made me think that he, too, found the situation unexpectedly amusing.

'Hope Taylor.' My aunt stepped forward and held out a manicured hand. 'Thank you so much for allowing us to invade your cottage, Mr Nash.'

'My pleasure. And I believe it's historically your cottage. Or was.' I had to admit he did have a nice voice. 'Come in.' He stepped back so that we could enter, or at least we would have been able to if his tortoiseshell cat hadn't been sitting in the middle of the doorstep blocking the way. After an awkward moment, when it didn't seem about to move, he reached down and picked it up. The feline tucked itself into his arms as if this was its proper and rightful position, and glared at the guests—particularly Mitch—with baleful yellow eyes.

The kelpie gave one bark, realised the error of his ways, and then flopped down onto the verandah, head on his paws. But this time I wasn't taking any chances. I slid the dog leash from my pocket and clicked it onto his collar, as I should have done in the first place, and then wrapped it securely around one of the verandah posts.

'Be good,' I warned him in a low voice, and he gave me his *What me?* look in response.

The others had already vanished inside, but Lincoln Nash was still politely holding the door ajar, waiting for me. No chance of avoiding him, then. With a muttered, 'Thank you,' I slid past him. I didn't mean to glance up, but somehow I did, and found myself looking into his eyes.

They were grey with a darker circle at the outer edge of the iris. And yes, there *was* an amused gleam in them. Perhaps he had a refined sense of the ridiculous. So much easier, I told myself darkly, to find things amusing when you weren't directly involved in them.

Hope was wandering down the central corridor, gazing about her, as the camera followed closely behind. She seemed engrossed in her surroundings, yet I doubted that was true. I may have been cynical where my aunt was concerned, but I thought it more likely Hope was following a script.

'This room was the dining room and kitchen,' she was saying aloud, in a dreamy sort of voice. 'I remember the wallpaper being cream with green flowers.'

And so it went on. I remembered the cottage, too, but obviously not in as much detail as Hope did. My grandmother had spoken about it now and again; however, typically, she stuck to the very early days and not her own time here. Nor did she express regret at leaving and moving into town, or not to me anyway. It abruptly occurred to me that my grandmother never spoke much about those days at all. I knew my grandfather had left her and times had been tough for them. Was that why she didn't speak about it, because she had the ability to lock away anything she didn't find palatable? Was Hope able to do that, too? And my mother? The family I had always thought free of secrets could be riddled with them, like a termite-infested fence post, and I wouldn't know.

'Shouldn't we be following?'

I'd been deep in thought, and I'd forgotten Lincoln Nash was behind me. I know, hard to imagine, but I had. I gave him a glance, not quite meeting his eyes this time. 'I suppose so,' I said, and began to trail reluctantly after Hope and her cameraman.

The girl with the pink hair—she said her name was Prue— dropped back to ask me where my parents were, but the camera guy gave her a glare, pointing to the microphone, and she fell silent again. As I'd suspected, Hope hadn't told her what was going on.

Well, I wasn't going to be the one to break the bad news.

Ahead of me Hope continued with her dissertation. I half listened as I began to take in my surroundings. Actually it was interesting, firstly because this was my ancestral home, and secondly … my teenage idol was right behind me.

Lincoln Nash seemed to prefer the minimalist approach, but I couldn't help noticing a couple of framed gold records on one of the walls. A reminder of his glory days? I would have read the inscriptions, but, and yes, I know it sounds pretentious and silly, I wanted to pretend I was above all that.

We had reached the rear of the cottage, and Hope started talking about the five young children sleeping end to end in the same bed. Although she made it seem cute, I imagined it was anything but, especially in the stifling heat of those long-ago summer nights. Nonetheless she told a good story, and I was so engrossed in it that it was only when I heard my father call out that I realised he'd finally arrived.

'We're here!'

We? Relief gushed through me in a warm flood. Mum must be home after all! Well of course she was, how could I have been so stupid as to doubt her? She was far too disciplined, too set on doing the 'right' thing, to fail to keep such an important appointment with her sister.

Footsteps were coming up behind us and I was just about to turn when I noticed Hope's face. She had also turned around at the sound of Dad's voice, and in that split second her expression was completely unguarded, and what I saw shocked me. Grief, raw and overwhelming grief.

'Hope?' I whispered, and her gaze slid to me.

Tears sprang into her eyes and her mouth wobbled.

Stunned, I took a step towards her just as she

blinked, and then she was smiling, her mask firmly back in place, leaving me wondering whether I had imagined the whole thing.

'Joe,' she called out. 'So lovely to see you!'

My father's responding smile seemed a little sheepish, but obviously he was pleased to see her. 'Hope, you look as amazing as ever,' he said, and returned her hug with enthusiasm.

I looked beyond him, still believing my mother was about to appear, so it was a bit of a shock when my grandmother trotted up to join us.

'Gran?'

She flicked me a glance but didn't seem to see me, not yet anyway. All of her attention was focused on her youngest daughter.

'Hope,' she said. Just that, just her name.

She was wearing one of her favourite outfits, dark trousers and a mauve blouse, and a straw sun hat decorated with fake flowers. If I hadn't known her so well I wouldn't have noticed the strong emotion she was hiding behind her tight smile, or the way her hands were clenching and unclenching on her handbag.

'Mum?' My aunt was horrified. Of course, I remembered, for some reason she hadn't wanted Gran to be here. 'But I thought … I said …' She stammered to a stop. I noticed her eyes slid to the camera and back again, and she pulled herself together. 'You weren't well,' she said, voice suddenly full of concern.

'I'm feeling much better, thank you,' Gran replied. She launched into what sounded to me like a prepared speech. 'Perfectly fine, in fact.

Maybe you imagined I was too ill to come today and you were being kind, but there's no need, Hope. No need at all.'

Hope took a deep breath and let it out. 'I'm glad to hear it,' she said quietly.

What on earth was going on? I looked at Dad and he shrugged at me. Prue and the cameraman must have been wondering too, because they had become rather excited. 'Mrs Taylor? Oh, this is wonderful. Can we have you over here? And your other daughter …?'

'Faith couldn't make it so I brought Lily instead,' my father explained, not quite meeting anybody's eye.

'Mum,' Hope repeated, and this time reached to embrace Lily with every sign of joy, but I was close enough to hear her say, 'I didn't want you bothered by all of this nonsense.'

'I'm not gaga, if that was what you were thinking,' was Gran's tart response. 'Don't worry, I won't disgrace you.'

Hope laughed, an 'isn't this just peachy' laugh. 'What a lovely surprise,' she said for the benefit of her audience, 'even though you are very naughty coming here when it really wasn't necessary. I was going to visit you tomorrow and spend the day.'

'I'm busy tomorrow.'

A clash of green eyes. Again I wondered what on earth was going on here. I saw Prue murmuring furiously to the cameraman.

I had been observing the whole thing as if I wasn't part of it, lulled into a false sense of security, and then my grandmother turned her sharp gaze on me and shattered that illusion. 'Sam! You should have changed out of those awful clothes!'

'I was working, Gran,' I said, trying not to mind being told off in front of everyone like a five-year-old. 'I have a living to make.'

'And will anyone who sees you on television want to employ you if you look like a ragbag?' she demanded with her usual lack of diplomacy. 'You didn't even put on a bra!'

There were so many things I could say to that. I wanted to cross my arms over my chest and had to restrain the urge, knowing that would just make it worse. It wasn't as if I had anything to hide; I wasn't voluptuous by any means. The cameraman gave a snort that could have been a laugh, and I was just about to rip into him, when to my surprise Hope came to my rescue.

'I think Samantha would look lovely whatever she wore.'

'Pity I can't say the same about her mother,' was Gran's response.

'Faith should be here.'

Dad shuffled his feet. 'Lily, behave,' he murmured.

Prue zeroed in on my father. 'I'm sorry if I misunderstood, Mr Cantani, but I thought your wife would be here. Can we contact her? Perhaps we can meet her in Golden Gully after we're finished?'

'She's, uh, away at the moment. A break.' The misery in his face told its own story and my heart sank. Dad had never been one for hiding his feelings.

'Oh?' Understandably Prue didn't see this as a valid excuse. 'We have a limited schedule so if we could arrange something …?'

Hope stepped in again when it became clear my father wasn't going to answer. 'She's in Queensland, so I doubt you can speak to her at all, Prue. I've only just learned about it myself.'

Gran butted in. 'She didn't even come around to say goodbye. Not like her at all.'

My father rubbed a hand across his mouth, always a sign of stress. 'There wasn't time,' he said. 'She had to catch a plane and …' He shook his head.

There was a room beside me, with a desk and a chair and a photograph of a sunset on the wall. It wasn't ideal but it would have to do. 'Dad?' I reached for his arm, drawing him inside, and kept my voice low. 'What is going on?' Frowning, Hope followed.

'Can we have some privacy?' I said, meaning her.

'Some privacy please,' she said, turning a glare on Prue and the cameraman, as if daring them to join our little huddle. Gran used the opportunity to begin a long rambling conversation about the old days, to which they listened politely, although I could see Prue's glance flickering to us as if she wished she were a fly on the wall.

'You know, this isn't the time or the place,' Hope whispered. 'If you want to chat, we can do it after we've finished filming.'

'We're not performing seals.' I gave her glare for glare. 'You didn't actually ask us if we wanted to do this. I'm not surprised Mum took off. I wish she'd asked me, I would have gone with her.'

'Sam,' my father murmured a warning. He knew my temper too well. 'Leave it. As Hope says, we can talk later. Let's just get this over with.'

Out in the corridor, Prue spoke in a voice quivering with curiosity. 'Is there a problem? We need to get on.'

Hope's smile was back in place. 'No, no problem. I'll explain later, Prue. Where were we?'

I wondered what her explanation would be. Not that I cared. She could trash us all she wanted to.

Hope took a few steps out of the room and then stopped and glanced back over her shoulder. 'Joe? Are you coming?'

She was expecting him to trot after her, do her bidding, and I looked at him, wanting him to refuse. To tell her … I don't know what. But he was smiling. It was the sort of smile he saved for my mother, and I could tell that despite all of Hope's nonsense he actually admired her. Or maybe it was more than admired.

Hope saw it, too, and she gave a soft laugh. 'I knew you wouldn't let me down, Joe,' she said.

And that was it. I was done with them.

I strode to the front door, slamming it behind me. I was so angry, so upset, that when I heard someone call my name I ignored it. I was seeing my father's face as he watched Hope prancing about for the camera, and now I was wondering something I could hardly believe. Had Joe and Hope once been an item? Was that the reason my mother had left? Could this whole thing be because my father had had an affair with his sister-in-law, and when he'd heard she was going to be telling the entire nation her life story, he'd blurted out the truth?

My steps slowed. Thinking these things hurt me, they really did, so what must my mother have felt? How betrayed had she been?

I had reached the ute when someone cleared their throat behind me, making me jump.

It was Lincoln Nash. He had followed me out and I hadn't even noticed. 'Haven't you forgotten something?'

'What? My manners?' I blazed, turning on my booted heel to face him. He probably thought I was a bitch. Not that it mattered what he thought because I was completely and utterly indifferent to him.

'No. Your dog,' he said mildly, and handed me the lead.

I looked down. Mitch sat at Lincoln's bare feet, watching our interaction with interest. I met his doggy eyes and felt immediately so deflated, all the anger whooshed out of me like a punctured balloon. My temper is like that; the flare-ups are spectacular when they happen but they never last.

'Sorry. I would have come back. Don't worry, I wouldn't have left you holding the dog.'

His mouth quirked. 'I don't think the cat would be terribly impressed if you did. She rules the cottage. Won't even let the grocery delivery man inside without him giving her a treat first.'

I found myself laughing, and the fact that I

could after what had just happened seemed miraculous. This time I tilted my head to look at him properly and he looked back.

'I didn't mean to drag out the dirty family laundry in front of everyone. And after you were kind enough to let Hope film in our cottage.' I waved a hand towards the front of it. '*Your* cottage, I mean.'

He shrugged. 'Families aren't always harmonious. Your aunt has been gone a while?'

'And then she turns up with a camera to record the event,' I said dryly. 'My mother was supposed to be here and … she isn't. Hope wanted a Brady Bunch moment and instead she found herself starring in an episode of *Dallas*.' He laughed.

That was encouraging. I might have said more, just to make him laugh again, but I remembered that my family woes were none of his business.

'I'll let you get back,' I said, uncomfortable beneath his steady gaze.

Obediently he stepped away, and the kelpie jumped into the open door of the ute, making himself comfortable on the passenger seat. Not entirely legal, I knew, but I was beyond caring.

'Buckle up,' I muttered, and heard Lincoln chuckle. I was a laugh a minute. I slid in beside the dog and shut the door.

The last thing I saw as I drove away was him closing the crow festooned gate and walking back to the cottage.

It was time now to feel regret that my temper had let me down and I hadn't handled things as well as I should have. And what did Hope mean about a family discussion later on? What I really wanted was for her to go back to Melbourne and catch the first flight out of here.

My groan earned a concerned look from Mitch.

I didn't feel like going back to the primary school. My work there was done anyway. I just wanted to go home. My thoughts slid again to Lincoln Nash and I realised with surprise that he'd seemed almost human today, certainly nothing like the man I had encountered in the hardware store.

I'd actually liked him. Not that that meant anything. I'd liked him when I was sixteen, too, so maybe this was just an echo of my school-girl crush. Maybe I should get out the old Black Crow album and give it a play? 'Dark Star', that was my all-time favourite song. But it was probably worn out from all of those sessions when I was growing up, all that mooning around and dreaming that one day he would see me and just *know* I was the one for him.

But he had seen me and I wasn't. End of story.

With great resolution, I turned my thoughts to the fence near the horse paddock that needed mending. I told myself that by the time I'd heaved about a few heavy lengths of wood and hammered on some wire, I'd be too exhausted to think about Lincoln.

Or why my father and Hope seemed on such good terms. That expression on Hope's face when my dad walked into the cottage— as if she was going to burst into tears. As if—and try as I might not to let the idea take root in my brain, it was too late.

As if some long-lost love had suddenly reappeared.

13

HOPE

14 January 2000, Willow Tree Bend

THE SLAMMING DOOR was still reverberating in Hope's head. It was as if the memory of her sixteen-year-old self had been superimposed on Sam. She had been running, running through the gate, panting, sobbing, running for the safety of the cottage. And then the old screen door slamming behind her. Her eyes had been blinded by the brilliant sunlight, and coming into the cool, dark interior of the cottage, she couldn't see.

Hope?

Her mother! Confused, she wondered what her mother was doing here, when this was one of the days she worked in town.

Hope, what on earth is the matter?

There was a moment of indecision. Tell her, don't tell her, tell her … And then she'd run straight into Lily's arms.

With a blink the past was gone.

'Sam's upset.' Joe was wearing a worried frown.

'She pretends to be tough … strong, but with Faith going off …'

'She's a big girl, she can take it,' his mother-in-law replied, sounding blithe, but her glance at Hope said otherwise. And more than that, it seemed to be laying the blame squarely at Hope's feet.

Joe sounded exasperated. 'Come on, Lily, you know she's really a softy. When she was a little kid she used to cry if she saw me squash the caterpillars in our veggie patch.' Then, with a sharp look at Ken and his camera he said, 'You're not going to film this, are you? We're having a private discussion, mate.'

Ken gave him a smug look. 'Sorry, *mate*, you can't pick and choose. We're making entertainment here.'

Hope spoke soothingly. 'Technically they can, Joe. That was the contract I signed. I did warn you.'

His frown grew fiercer and he shook his head in strong disagreement. 'Some things are personal, Hope, you should know that. You can't tell them whatever you want, not if it affects my family.'

Okay, time to poor oil on troubled waters. 'I'll talk to Samantha. I promise,' she said gently, but he only looked slightly mollified. She mustn't lose control of the situation. When Samantha had stormed out she'd felt as if things were starting to unravel and that couldn't be allowed to happen.

Prue cleared her throat. 'I've organised some interviews.' She proceeded to tick them off on her fingers. 'The owner of the Golden Gully pub, the bakery, and the milk bar. We were also hoping to talk with your sister at Cantani Desserts,' she said with a look at Joe. 'Not much point now, and I can't reschedule, we're only here for one day, Miss Taylor.'

'That's fine. I don't expect you to.' Hope turned to Joe. 'After we're done in town I'll go and see Samantha. Will you be there?' She sounded vulnerable even to her own ears.

He hesitated. 'I might drop by later. If you're still around,' he added sarcastically. That surprised her—Joe had never been sarcastic.

'Are you still coming to visit me tomorrow?' Lily butted in, eyes bright.

'Weren't you going to be busy?'

'I'll cancel my matchstick bingo. We haven't had a *proper* talk in a long time, Hope. Not since you left home.'

There was an awkward silence. Was that a threat? Hope tried to read her mother's mind and, as always, found it impenetrable.

'I remember,' she said at last, carefully. 'I just don't want to discuss it right now.'

Ken lifted his camera and Joe put his hand over the lens.

'Hey!'

'Wait,' Joe told him sharply. He took Hope's arm and began to lead her away. She turned to look backwards, where Lily was left alone with Ken, not liking that scenario one bit. Who knew what Lily might say on the spur of the moment? She was a loose cannon and not to be trusted, and that was the reason Hope had never wanted her to appear on film.

They had reached the rear of the cottage and there was nowhere else to go, apart from out into the yard, but Joe seemed to think this was far enough away from the camera. She was so close to him that she could smell his aftershave, and see a couple of the dark whiskers he'd missed, on the line of his jaw. Had he shaved especially for her? She had to admit he was looking good, but then he'd always been a handsome man. The Cantani men were known for it.

Once again tears stung the back of her eyes, but she refused to let them fall. She turned her head before Joe could see, staring out through the casement window into the backyard. Various pieces of scrap metal cluttered the space and there was a large shed—a modern improvement since her day.

Okay, she was all right now. The feeling had passed. Everything would be all right and she would get through this unscathed. Nothing else could possibly go wrong.

Why did I agree?

But she knew why. The money. She just hadn't understood quite how much she would be affected by being back here, and how the memories, the ones she'd kept locked away for so long, and had believed would no longer be an issue, could start to take on a life of their own.

She'd been selfish, yes, she admitted it. The image of Samantha's face slipped slyly into her mind, followed by Joe, looking so worried, and then her mother's frail body, shockingly so after ten years' absence. And had Faith really run away because of her?

With a start, she realised that Joe was speaking to her and she'd missed most of it.

'You know what Faith's like. She keeps it all bottled up.' His stare seemed to suggest that in his opinion Faith wasn't the only Taylor who liked to keep her own counsel. 'And now she's gone off chasing ghosts.'

She was shocked as much by the bleak expression on his face as she was by his words. Joe loved her sister; he was devoted to her. How could Faith be so selfish? But then Faith wasn't the only one who was being selfish.

'Joe, please tell me what's going on.'

'If I could I would. I don't know for certain, but when you said she mentioned the Angel in her phone call to you … If you hadn't agreed to do this bloody program none of this would be happening!'

He was shouting and she was afraid Prue and Ken would hear. She moved closer, putting a hand on his arm, letting him see she understood, that she was on his side.

He took a deep breath and this time his voice was quieter and more measured. 'I think she's gone to see someone.' '*Someone?*'

He shook his head.

'Was this the man who rang her at the shop? What was so desperately important that she had to fly all the way up to Queensland? Wait a minute, she mentioned something else when she called me.

An old photograph in a newspaper.'

Joe ran both hands over his face, working to pull himself together. 'Yeah, there was a photo. We had a good laugh about it. It was the one the *Express* took in nineteen seventy-four, just before you left for America. "Local girl off to be a Hollywood star", or something like that. When they heard you were coming home they reprinted it, and next moment it seemed to be everywhere. I suppose you're a lot more famous now.'

'So this man who rang might have seen it? Seen Faith?' her voice sounded husky, tired.

He didn't answer her directly; an annoying habit. 'I should have gone with her. I would have, if she'd told me.'

Hope sighed. 'She made certain you couldn't by waiting until you'd left the house. She thinks that this is something she has to fix on her own. Joe, you know when Faith sets her mind on a thing there's no stopping her.'

'It was the same when she went off that first time. I didn't want her to go. Even back then I loved her, but I knew I had to let her do what she wanted to. I just hoped that eventually she'd realise she belonged here, with me.'

'She did realise it. After she came home it was as if her eyes had been opened. You were her hero, Joe.'

But he looked at her as if he didn't believe her, his face haggard. 'What am I going to do if she doesn't come back?'

'Of course she'll come back!' Hope prayed to her mother's God that she was right. 'And once

Looking Back airs, we'll laugh about all of this.'

She knew immediately it was the completely wrong thing to say. She supposed she was actually speaking to herself, boosting her own flagging spirits. Maybe all Joe had wanted to hear from her was an apology for bringing this down on their heads, and she'd failed him.

His expression was disgusted. He stepped away, shaking his head, before he turned and walked off. She heard Lily's voice raised in complaint—'I don't want to leave yet!'—fading, and then the front door slammed. Again. She was still standing there when Lincoln Nash found her.

He'd vanished after Samantha left, and hadn't reappeared when Joe started demanding Ken stop filming. She didn't blame him for keeping his distance.

'Coffee break?' His voice was pleasant, but his eyes seemed to note her distress.

'Where are Prue and Ken?' she asked, looking about her.

He nodded towards the lounge. 'They're in crisis talks,' he said, with a smile to show it could be a joke if she wanted it to be.

Hope supposed they were wondering whether or not to call management. Breach of contract? That was all she needed. Should she go and pour some more oil or should she stay here and rebuild her shredded conviction that she was doing the right thing?

'Coffee would be nice.' She followed him into the small kitchen.

Apart from the dimensions—and her memory

of them was shaky—the space seemed very different. Not that there had been anything wrong with her mother's kitchen, but there was a charm here now that she certainly didn't recall being aware of before. The kitchen had been a place to cook in and eat in, and the heat from the stove had made both uncomfortable. As she got older, Hope had preferred her bedroom, somewhere to be private and to dream.

'Everything feels very tranquil,' she said, and heard the awkwardness in her voice. Now that the camera wasn't on her, she was struggling to keep up the pretence. She was exhausted, and her head ached, and she was worried about Faith and Joe, about Samantha and Lily, and about the skeletons that were lurking behind closed doors, just waiting to spring out at her.

There were potted herbs on the windowsill, with a gap in the middle for the cat to sit, something it was taking advantage of right now, with its back turned and its twitching tail dangling in the sink. She thought about reaching out to stroke it, except Lincoln's cat didn't seem very approachable, unlike Samantha's dog.

That memory made her smile. Samantha had been terribly embarrassed, but actually it had been quite funny, or it would have been if everyone hadn't been quite so tense.

Lincoln took down some mugs and proceeded to make her an instant coffee. He didn't even ask or say sorry he didn't have a machine—it was as if he didn't think there was a reason to apologise. Despite his New Age musician image, he was an old-fashioned man. She wondered what had made him decide it was a good idea to hide himself away here in the cottage.

'I love your sculptures,' she said, taking a lighter note. 'Do you buy them locally?'

He smiled. 'I make them myself. A hobby. I took it up after I moved here. Sometimes it's good to remember that the reason you started doing a thing was for the sheer joy of creating something from your imagination. Easy to lose sight of that fact when it becomes a source of income.'

Like acting, Hope thought. Anyway, she didn't regret her life's work, and she'd be a hypocrite if she said she did. It had been everything to her at one point, her entire reason for being. She'd wanted to be a Hollywood actress, and to a degree she had achieved her ambition.

Her personal life was another matter.

She had almost married three men and yet she struggled to remember why. Loneliness perhaps, and the need to connect, and in at least one case to further her career, so yes, ambition. But in her heart she knew that no one had ever taken the place of the boy she had fallen in love with when she was sixteen.

Lincoln set down the steaming mug in front of her, and then glanced towards the door. 'Should I …?'

'No, leave them. I think we all need a moment.'

His eyes held hers and then slid away. He took his own mug and stood, silhouetted against the sunshine slanting past the cat in the window, and sipped in silence.

Hope breathed in the smell of the coffee and closed her eyes. This was nice. A bit of calm. Who would have thought she'd find it here, in the cottage where so many turbulent events had taken place? But then she reminded herself that there were plenty of good memories to be had too, it was just that she seemed to be concentrating on the bad.

'I didn't want to come home,' she heard herself say, and then wondered why she should choose this complete stranger to unload to. Perhaps it was the atmosphere in the room, so comfortable and relaxed, and she sensed he was a man who would keep her confidence. Not that it mattered, she wasn't going to tell him anything that could damage her.

'Why not?' he asked curiously, taking another sip.

'When I walked away I told myself I'd never come back. Well I did. I've been back twice. Once when my father died, because I felt I should, and again ten years ago, to move my mother out of this cottage. Then this job turned up. I thought it sounded like a good idea, fly in and fly out, no hassle. Well, you can see how that's working for me.'

'Still,' Lincoln said, 'it must be nice to see your family, and for them to see you. Blood is thicker and all that.'

'Is it? My sister and I were close a long time ago, but the last time I was here she seemed like a stranger. She was strung so tight I thought she might twang if I touched her. And this time …

she's gone off to Queensland on some quest or other, and it's all my fault. Don't tell Joe that,' she added, all at once anxious.

He frowned. 'I won't. Not that I'd expect him to come and ask. That was Joe, was it, the pissed-off guy? He's your sister's husband?'

'Yes. He's not usually like that. He's … well, I always thought they'd end up together. When she was seventeen she thought she wanted more, and she went off to Melbourne to find it. Got in with some dubious people, and when she came home she seemed … damaged. Joe was so good—it was him who healed her and made her whole again. But I'm wondering now if maybe there was someone else all those years ago. Unfinished business.'

'The past has a pull to it. Sometimes it's difficult to escape.' It sounded as if he was speaking from the heart.

'Yes. I'd prefer mine to stay on the dark side of the moon, where it belongs.'

He laughed. 'And yet you're making a program about your past, your life. Aren't you going to tell all? I've seen a few episodes of *Looking Back*. They like to delve in depth.' He grimaced. 'Wouldn't be my choice. Aren't you worried they're going to find out things you've kept hidden for,' he cocked an eyebrow, 'forty years?'

She smiled. 'Thank you, but closer to fifty. And I don't plan to suddenly blurt out the name of the boy who took my virginity.'

He smiled back, but there was nothing flirtatious in it. He wasn't interested in her in that way and she didn't blame him. She rather thought that he'd been attracted to Samantha, which would make for an amusing little side show. Samantha, from what Faith had told her, had been hurt a couple of times and had sworn off men.

'Hope?' It was Prue, standing in the doorway and watching her warily. Her pink hair was a nimbus in the sunlight. 'Are you ready to continue? We need to be in Golden Gully in half an hour.'

Hope beamed a smile. 'Of course. Where do you want me?'

As she walked out she gave Lincoln a wink. She could see he was amused, but then he knew a little about fame himself and how important it was to keep up the illusion.

It didn't take long to finish filming at the cottage, everything went smoothly, and then they drove back to Golden Gully. There were a few people about, nudging each other and watching as Hope stood outside the bakery where she used to have a casual job, trying to look pensive. When it was time to reminisce with the new owner of the pub, she gave her fans a smile and a wave, and there was a cheer. The publican looked barely old enough to have been born when she left, but all the same he was obviously flattered to have been asked—probably keen to see his premises on national television.

There had been plans to have Hope and Faith together in the dessert shop, but Prue had ditched that, so the final cameo was to be in front of the old Cantani milk bar. Not for any particular reason, other than that it looked quaint.

'We'll have a voice-over, obviously,' Prue explained, 'but if Ken can shoot you sitting on the seat there. I believe it was in the Cantani family for many years?' She'd evidently been researching, or someone had.

'Yes, that's right.'

The small crowd had mostly dispersed while she was inside the pub, and Hope took up position by an old horse trough planted with colourful flowers. The sun was warm on her back and she began to feel sleepy. It had been a long day with plenty of drama, and it wasn't over yet. She still had to talk to Samantha and Joe. 'That's perfect,' Prue said, and even Ken managed to look happy—she liked him even less after his run–in with Joe. 'We'll leave it there.'

Relieved, Hope stood up, smoothing her slacks, and that was when she heard the voice.

'Hope? Is that you?'

She turned. There was a middle-aged woman coming towards her, her smile so wide it threatened to split her face in two. As she drew closer Hope could see her skin was tanned from sun exposure, and her hair was home dyed an improbable blonde.

She knew she should probably recognise her, but her mind went stubbornly blank.

The woman had reached her, pushing her sunglasses up onto her head, and still smiling. She was wearing shorts and a thin cotton shirt knotted at the waist, making Hope, in her expensive clothing, feel like an alien from another planet.

'It's Lena,' she said. 'We were at high school together. Don't you remember me?' Her smile had begun to fade now and her eyes had an embarrassed look.

Lena.

Hope did remember, hazily, and was finally able to play the part expected of her. 'Of course!' she gushed. 'Lena!'

Lena hugged her with relief. There followed a conversation about her movies and how Lena never missed one of them, and how excited she was to see her, and how everyone in the town had been so looking forward to her coming back.

'You'll be staying, won't you?' Lena said breathlessly. 'I mean, you have to. Everyone will be wanting to see you. You'll stay and catch up? I'm having a barbecue tomorrow night. It would be wonderful if you came. Everyone would be so excited.'

The thought of a barbecue where she was guest of honour filled her with dread. Hope thought about saying an outright 'no', but it seemed safer to use Prue. She glanced at the girl, and Prue recognised the silent cry for help.

'I'm sorry, Lena, but Miss Taylor has a very tight schedule. We have to get back to Melbourne and do more filming there. I'm sure she can catch up another time if you give her your number.'

Lena's face fell. 'Oh,' she said. 'My number.'

'I'm sorry.' Hope moved closer. 'I would come, but you can see how hard they're working me. And they're paying the bills.' She laughed.

Lena stared at her. *I thought we were friends,* her

eyes seemed to say. 'That's okay,' she said, though her voice was cool now. 'I should have realised you wouldn't want to hang out with me anymore.' Then, with a flash of malice, 'Are you going to tell them about Pete?'

That was the moment when Hope remembered why she had never considered Lena a friend, not a real friend. Because she was a gossip, and a vicious one. It had been Lena, that hot summer's day, driving by with her mother. Lena, who had put two and two together, and proceeded to spread the nasty rumours. It had only taken a day and the story was all over town.

Hope had just told Lincoln Nash she wasn't going to blurt out the name of the boy who had taken her virginity.

Now Lena had.

14

FAITH

August 1969, St Kilda

DETECTIVE INSPECTOR AVERY had been gone for quite some time before Faith felt able to stand up and walk to the door. Even when she opened it, she paused to listen, not quite trusting the silence. The elevator had finally stopped making the journey up to the Penthouse and down again, and she supposed that meant everyone was gone—Kitty, too. To where, she wasn't sure.

The memory of the photograph had refused to go away, that shocking image of the young girl gazing at the camera as though she'd removed herself from her sordid surroundings by sheer force of will. But of course the explanation might be much simpler—that she'd taken a drug to blunt the sharp edges of her world.

Melanie.

Physically, she looked a lot like Faith—and Kitty—and Faith found that deeply disturbing. Imagining herself playing a part in such a scenario made her skin crawl. And then there was Avery. She had read in his face that he wanted justice, and he was prepared to stop at nothing to get it. Even conduct a raid on a nightclub that was supposedly protected by Jared's faceless bosses and their tame policemen.

Faith shivered as she walked along the corridor to the landing. She asked herself what she would do if they'd arrested Kitty. She had never known anyone who had been arrested and the mechanics of getting them freed were a mystery to her. In the police series *Homicide*, which she sometimes watched on the Cantanis' television, there was always a lawyer ready to pull strings, but Faith didn't think that in real life it was quite that easy.

Slowly, she began to make her way down the stairs and into the shadows that lay at the bottom. The Mezzanine was empty and so was the Cocktail Lounge. A car went past outside, its headlights raking through the windows. Faith wasn't sure how late it was, but she knew she should go home to bed.

And yet she hesitated. She felt shaken and jittery, and she knew she would find it difficult to sleep alone in her room. The thought of Kitty was nagging at her—it was only due to her cousin's quick thinking that Faith hadn't been hauled into the Penthouse and questioned too. She wondered if she should ring Kitty's family and tell them what had happened. But she was positive that Kitty would be furious with her if she did that, and more than likely see that she lost her job. With no job and no place to stay, she would have to go home.

And yet, wasn't telling on Kitty the right thing to do?

Her mother had always drummed into them the importance of doing the 'right thing'. Rightness, integrity, these words were all part of her moral code. But now, standing in the darkness of the Angel, she wasn't at all sure what the 'right thing' was.

The broken glass was in a pile on the floor where she'd left it. Perhaps she should sweep it up? She was just looking around for a dustpan and brush when a voice spoke right behind her.

'Hello, luv. Where is everyone? I wondered if I had the right place.'

'Ray!' She spun to face him, and stared at him as if she'd never seen him before. There was an ache in her throat and the terrible urge to cry. She tried to stop it, but it was too powerful, and seeing him after all that had happened was such a relief … With a sob, Faith ran into his arms.

'Hey, what's this?' He tried to see her face, except she only burrowed deeper into his leather jacket. 'Faith, what's wrong? What's happened?'

He'd forgotten his Liverpool accent, only Faith pretended not to notice. The fact that his voice was concerned, and the hand cupping her cheek gentle, that Ray Bartel cared … Well, that was enough for her.

The meltdown only lasted a short time, and reluctantly she extracted herself from his embrace. She took a deep breath, her hand shaking as she wiped away her tears. 'There was a police raid,' she told him in a husky little voice.

Ray's eyes widened. He looked around, as if expecting to see some evidence—broken chairs and bruised bodies. 'Was anyone hurt? Faith?'

'No, I … I don't think so. They were more interested in the Penthouse. There was a party going on up there and they took people away. Kitty and—and Jared. I don't know whether or not they've been arrested. I was just wondering what to do, whether I should call a … a … lawyer or …'

'But *you*'re all right?' Ray asked, watching her, a frown between his brows. Without his sunglasses, he looked tired and his dark eyes were bloodshot.

She wondered whether to tell him about Avery's offer, then immediately decided against it. Why should she, when she had no intention of ever taking him up on it? And anyway, wouldn't Ray tell Jared? She was certain the manager wouldn't be happy to hear one of his staff had been approached by the police, and if what Avery had said was true, and he was just a front man for the Angel's criminal backers … No, better not to mention it to anyone.

From somewhere inside she dredged up a smile. 'Yes, I'm all right.'

He smiled back, straight into her eyes, and then he picked up a strand of her hair, winding it around his finger. 'Poor pet,' he said, and the fake accent was back. 'Why don't you come with me over to the Queens? We're having a late session there, just a few friends, nothing heavy. You can watch us. Relax. What do you say?'

Faith knew she wanted to. Desperately. And she really, really didn't want to go home. What if Kitty wasn't there? And what if she was? Facing her after the scene upstairs, knowing what Kitty was involved in … Faith just didn't know how she was going to do that. Ray's presence was like a balm, a way to set aside her problems for a little while.

'But what about Kitty?' Her voice was a little breathless.

He pulled a face. 'She can look after herself. And she has Jared, hasn't she?'

It was as if he was giving her permission to stop thinking about her cousin's predicament and the Angel and everything that had happened.

'I suppose so.'

'Good. Are you coming, then?'

He must have seen his answer in her face because he grinned and wrapped an arm around her. 'All right,' he said. 'Let's go.'

This wasn't like the Allnights' usual stuff. Faith had grown used to the upbeat songs they belted out in the Cocktail Lounge, songs you could swing your hips to as you served drinks to the customers. This was slow and dreamy, and she curled up on a seat in the corner, half asleep, and watched through the haze of smoke as Ray and his band lost themselves in their music.

There were only a few people left at the Queens, but no one wanted to go home. And Faith was glad to stay on with them, letting the traumatic events of the evening float away as, influenced by the late hour and the number of illicit whiskys the band had consumed, the songs got more and more laid-back. By the time they finished their last set, Faith felt completely relaxed.

It was tiredness that caused her light-headedness as they swayed home, arms around each other, taking up the entire width of the street. Ray was telling a story about their trip away, the others jumping in to add to the tale, each addition making it more and more preposterous. She couldn't stop laughing.

When one of them stumbled, everyone lurched to the side, and it seemed very funny. Their merriment echoed around the silent buildings and Faith was filled with a warm, foggy sense of contentment. She wanted to hold on to it and not think about anything that might intrude on what was beginning to feel very much like happiness.

Ray's digs weren't that far away from her own. Once inside she could see that the place was messy, with stuff scattered everywhere, just as you'd expect from a house full of boys who worked late into the night and slept most of the next day. But Faith didn't care, the chaotic atmosphere suited them, and they treated her like a kid sister, teasing her one moment and asking her if she was okay the next. At last the rest of them went off to bed, and it was just her and Ray, alone in the living room.

For a while he talked about his music, how much he wanted to succeed this time, and how much it meant to him. She listened, enjoying the sound of his voice, and when he leaned in and kissed her it seemed just right. The feel of his lips on hers, and then his arms about her. She cuddled up to him, kissing him back, and gradually the curl of warmth inside her began to heat up, until it was burning fiercely.

'Will you come to bed?' he murmured against her ear.

She knew she could say no and it would be all right. He wouldn't hold it against her. But she didn't want to say no, and when he stood up she put her hand into his, and willingly went with him into his bedroom.

Here, in the privacy of the small room, their kisses grew more passionate. He began to unbutton his shirt, watching her in a way that made her feel beautiful. She slipped off her boots, and then he was wrenching at his shoes, laughing. She unbuttoned her dress while he tugged down his jeans, and it became a race to see who could be naked first.

In the end it was a draw, and they were breathing quickly when they stood facing each other. He was thin, his skin as white as milk, with a dark strip of hair running from his chest to his groin. She didn't want to look, but she had never seen a man like this, aroused. Actually, she had never seen a naked man at all, and she couldn't help staring.

He drew her into his arms again, and his voice was a murmur against her hair. 'Is this your first time?' Faith nodded her head.

'Do you still want to?'

'Yes. I still want to.'

He lifted her chin with a finger and kissed her lips. It felt so nice, and he was so nice. Like the music tonight at the Queens, it was slow and dreamy, at first anyway. Near the end, he was a bit rougher, but he said he was sorry, that he couldn't help it because she was so beautiful.

The act wasn't as she'd imagined. Fireworks didn't go off, and it was even uncomfortable and a little bit painful. But being in Ray's arms, the intimacy of her naked skin against his, felt so incredible that it didn't seem to matter. It was the sense of her being a part of him, and him of her, more than any imaginary fireworks, that won her over.

When she climbed out of his bed and dressed in the half-light of dawn, she couldn't help smiling at his relaxed, sleeping face. She wasn't on the pill. Kitty had said she knew a doctor who would set her up, but after her cousin had mocked her excitement about Ray, she hadn't wanted to broach the subject. Anyway, Ray had used a rubber, and when he'd put it on he'd promised her everything would be all right. She trusted him. Just before he'd fallen asleep he'd told her she was his special girl, and now she hugged the words to herself.

The house was silent as she let herself out into the chilly morning and began the walk home to her own bed. The watery sun might be trying to push through winter grey clouds, but it felt like midsummer. Her heart was almost too full to fit into her chest. She didn't know how she was going to keep her feet on the ground today, or the smile off her face.

Was this how it was for everyone? Love?

She might have been teetering on the verge of it from the moment she'd met him on her first day at the Angel, and tonight had tipped her, dizzily, over the edge.

Her life would never be the same.

It was only when she reached her door and turned the key in her warm summer happiness gave way to this cold reality of winter.

15

SAMANTHA

14 January 2000, Willow Tree Bend

WHEN I ARRIVED home—and I was certainly *not* running away—I found a phone message on my answering machine. Jason Miller, the Melbourne chef who was opening a restaurant just outside Golden Gully, and who had asked for a quote for his garden, was asking to see me as soon as possible.

I replayed the message again, just to be sure; he definitely wanted to see me. In fact, he wanted to know if I was available for a meeting at his future restaurant because he was going to be staying there over the next few days.

He must have liked my initial quote, but I'd made it clear that the price would be dependent upon the final decisions we made for his garden. I liked to work with my clients rather than for them and sometimes that put people off—they wanted it handed to them in a nice little bundle so they didn't have to think at all. His wanting to meet certainly seemed like a good sign.

I knew that after all that had already happened today, I would be too restless and upset to concentrate on my usual tasks. All the way home I'd thought about my parents, and Hope. My emotions still felt very raw, and I couldn't help replaying the scene in the cottage over and over again. Hope and my father. Was it possible? Maybe I was imagining it?

Well maybe, but there was definitely *something*. My mother had run off to Queensland and that was completely out of character. I was becoming more and more convinced that there was a dark underlying thread to this tale that I either wasn't seeing or no one was telling me about.

So the chef's request gave me a chance to occupy my mind, with the bonus that, if he liked me, I would land a plum contract. I rang him back and said I'd be there in an hour, and then I did what I should have done before I went to the cottage to meet Hope. I showered, and dressed in a flowery summer dress I had bought once on impulse for a party that never happened, and then brushed my hair so it swung around my shoulders. A bit of makeup and I thought I looked pretty good.

Jason Miller's restaurant-to-be was sixteen kilometres out of Golden Gully and set amongst farming land. It was an impressive two-storey building of timber and red brick, which had probably originated as a single-storey dwelling back in the time of the gold rush. Golden Gully, like other towns in Victoria, began its growth spurt after gold was discovered in the surrounding hills and creeks. Soon it became a centre for the district and that probably saved it. When the gold was gone and everyone moved on to the next rush, the town had stayed.

The soon-to-be restaurant was on the opposite side of town from Willow Tree Bend, so I wasn't all that familiar with it. I did have a vague memory that the house had some historical significance, but right now the details escaped me. Was it protected? It didn't look like much protecting had been going on lately; the place had become unloved and dilapidated. As I came to a stop in front of the crumbling picket fence, I noticed that the upper verandah had a sag that made me think you'd be taking your life in your hands if you ventured out onto it.

The door was propped open with a brick, but I gave a polite knock and waited until an urbane, greying man in his forties came to meet me.

'Sam Cantani.' I introduced myself, holding out my hand.

He was wearing comfortable jeans and a tee-shirt, but I didn't think either were off the discount rack.

'Jason Miller.' He took my hand and held it a moment while he gave me the once-over. His smile, when it came, was warm and friendly, and relaxed in a way that helped me to relax too. Another good sign.

'Looks like you have your work cut out,' I said dryly, as he showed me inside.

We were in a passageway that ran the length of the house, and now I could see that there were holes in walls and dust inches thick. The piles of rubble might have been the product of the renovations, or maybe the house was like this when he bought it. I wasn't sure whether or not I should ask in case I showed my complete ignorance— I was better at gardens.

Jason grimaced. 'It's a massive undertaking. Luckily my partner loves renos. For now we're living and working in Melbourne, but we hardly see each other. We've been talking about a project like this for a while now, and when we saw this place … everything just came together. It's something we can do as a couple. At least that's the plan.'

He shot me a sideways look that made me wonder if he was as completely sold on the idea as he seemed.

'Sounds like a good one,' I said, trying to be positive.

He offered to walk me around the property. For the next twenty minutes, I listened to him talk while I peered into grotty rooms and tiptoed over spongy floorboards. Most of the windows were broken and boarded up, and Jason explained that the house had been left empty for nearly five years before they bought it.

'The people who owned the place before us had plans, too, but then their marriage imploded. Things ended up in a real mess in court, which was why it was abandoned. Their bad luck was our good luck, in a way. We would never have had the chance to buy it if they'd lived happily ever after.'

But was that a good thing? I could already see that this was the sort of 'project' that might destroy more than one relationship.

'People think we're insane,' he went on, and I wondered if he was reading my mind. I looked into his eyes and thought he might be wondering the same thing himself. 'We aim to prove the nay-sayers wrong,' he added in a more confident voice.

'I like your spirit,' I said.

'Speaking of spirits,' he replied with a waggle of his eyebrows. 'There's a fair bit of history involved with this place, and quite a lot of scandal. If you're interested we could grab a latte before I show you the garden?'

I was quick to agree, and he led me into the kitchen.

It didn't sparkle as I imagined his professional kitchen in Melbourne did, but there had been more headway made here than anywhere else in the building. It was clean, too, which made a difference.

I sat down at a scrubbed table while he made me a coffee, and then opened a tin of the most delicious homemade carrot cake I'd ever eaten. And this from someone who considered herself a carrot cake connoisseur.

'Secret recipe,' he said with a wink. 'Derek's that is—my partner—not mine. He's a country boy originally, and he's wanted to get out of the city for over a year now. He found this house on one of his "breaks" and brought me to see it. I have to say I wasn't as enthusiastic as him to start with, but now I think we can make it work. Well, we have to, don't we? This project is a big risk for us, financially and emotionally.'

Oops, his insecurities were showing again. Time to put my positive face back on because *I* wanted him to make it work too.

'I imagine you'll have loyal customers following you up here, Jason.' 'I hope so.' He still looked a bit fragile.

'You know, Golden Gully can be a springboard for great things. My mother started her business here, and now she's selling all over the country, and overseas.'

'Your mother is Faith Cantani, yes? I've heard of her. Maybe we can meet up?'

I felt my stomach do a little dip. I opened my mouth to tell him she'd flown the coop, and then closed it again.

Time to move on.

'What was the scandal you were talking about?' I asked, biting into the cake and trying not to moan. I must learn to cook, I told myself, although I doubted anything I could put together would taste like this.

'Oh the scandal! This house belonged to the Dalzell family. Have you heard of them, Sam?'

I had. A memory was struggling to surface. 'I think it was before my time.'

'As soon as we bought the house Derek was hunting around in the archives, trying to find out about it. Now, I think I have this right. The Dalzells arrived during the gold rush, and the original Dalzell was something to do with the cattle trade—he made his fortune selling meat to the miners. Derek tells me most of the wealthy families made their money that way, rather than actually doing the hard work of scratching for gold.'

'Makes sense.'

'So, to show how important they now were, the Dalzells built this house, although I think most of their time was spent in Melbourne.'

'I remember now.' It was coming back to me. We'd had a lesson at school about important locals and the Dalzells were mentioned. 'Wasn't there something about race horses? And one of them was a politician?'

'Not sure about the race horses, but a couple of them were politicians. Father and son. The son is the one everyone remembers. Hubert Dalzell was around in the nineteen fifties and sixties, and there was a big scandal involving him and a nightclub in the city. Criminals and corruption, that sort of thing. He lost his job and his reputation, and when the government of the day began to talk about a far-reaching inquiry … there was nothing left for him to do but disappear. The rumour is he went north.'

I hesitated with my cup halfway to my mouth.

'What was the name of the nightclub?'

'The Angel. It was pretty infamous in its day. Here, I have a photo taken inside it.'

He stood up and opened a drawer, lifting out a plastic envelope containing a sheet of thin cardboard.

'The Angel,' I repeated, wondering why it

struck a chord, as he set the photograph in front of me. It was torn and tattered about the edges, and had an unpleasant stain across one half.

'Found it under a pile of fallen masonry. And look, someone's written the name underneath.'

The faded colour photograph had been taken in a swanky-looking dining room. There were people in the background, but the focus was a table where a smiling man sat, with a black woman in a sequined dress leaning over his shoulder. She looked very much like Aretha Franklin. Scrawled across the bottom was 'The Angel 1969'.

'High-flier, do you think?' Jason was saying, tapping the man. 'Look at that sharp jacket. And the Wyatt Earp moustache!'

I smiled, but something else had caught my eye. The man wasn't alone at the table. A woman was sitting beside him, and although the stain had obliterated most of her face, I could still see some of it. Enough. My heart gave a little stutter.

'Who's this?' I said aloud, hoping I didn't sound as fraught as I felt.

Jason leaned closer. 'Don't know. Why, do you know her?'

He was staring at me with interest, but I didn't want to tell him what I was thinking, and anyway I hardly believed it myself. So I shrugged my shoulders.

'Probably just a companion for the night, to make him look good,' Jason said dismissively. 'We thought we might get it restored and blown up.'

He went on to speculate about why the photograph had been preserved. 'Maybe Dalzell had a gallery of himself brushing shoulders with various celebrities.' His words barely registered with me.

The woman sitting beside Dalzell looked very much like a young version of my mother, and although I knew it couldn't be, my gaze kept returning to her. Because I'd remembered now where I'd heard the Angel mentioned before. Hadn't Mum and Dad been talking about the club the night I went around to watch *Looking Back* with them?

I glanced at Jason, but he didn't seem to notice my abstraction. My thoughts took a wilder turn. Was it a coincidence that my mother was in Queensland and this politician from the same place and around the same era had run off there, too?

'So, they never found him?' I reached for another piece of cake and then wondered how many slices I'd already had and changed my mind.

Jason noticed and hid his smile. 'Ah, no, they never did. From what we've been told he had oodles of people after him. Police and government, as well as some underworld criminals, so I think it was in his best interests to stay well hidden. I believe there was a bit of a search but they soon gave it up.'

'I thought you were going to tell me his ghost haunts the house.'

'Derek says there is a ghost, but I haven't seen it. Apparently, I'm not very receptive to the spirit world. Too much of a sceptic.' Jason cleared his throat. 'All right, I'm sure you don't want to hear any more of my ramblings. You're here to see the garden so come this way.'

This was what I was here for, I reminded myself, and shut my crazier thoughts down as I followed him out the back door.

Jason's garden was more like a wilderness, where weeds and overgrown shrubs competed for air and light. But as I walked about, pushing aside a branch here, peering into a clump there, I began to recognise some of the shrubs. They were of the old-fashioned variety, now run sadly amok, and I could probably save a few—cut them back, reshape them—but there were others that were at the end of their lives anyway and would need to be removed.

A huge old rosebush had grown in a clump at the very back of the yard. It was covering some sort of structure, which was all but invisible beneath the thick, twisting branches and mass of dead twigs. That it was flowering was a remarkable feat considering the hot, dry summer, and I stood and admired the pale-gold blossoms.

'Safrano?' I thought I recognised it.

He gave me a grin. 'You're good. Yes, that's it. Derek tells me it's an old tea rose. Gold-rush era.'

'Or a bit before. It suits the climate here. They were called tea roses because they were imported to Australia in tea chests from China. What's that underneath it?'

'Derek was trying to find out. A summer house? Pergola? It's difficult to see without cutting the rose down and we didn't want to do that until an expert had seen it. He's been spending long hours at the State Library, so maybe he'll know more when he gets up here.'

'Hmm.' The rose would probably have to go, but I was hoping I could save it, or grow another bush from cuttings. After all this time, I thought it deserved to be preserved in some form or another.

The Dalzells had probably started planting their garden from the day the house was built, and once upon a time someone had loved it. I hoped they would again. It was certainly a big job, but if I could pull it off then I knew it would be a turning point for Green Dreams.

My excitement was rising, as Jason's voice meandered on. He was keen to share his own thoughts on what needed to be done, particularly in regard to a kitchen garden that would be part of the attraction for the restaurant. The food would be grown right on site—green and wholesome and pesticide free.

'I thought we could take up one whole side of the yard. Derek wants to build a wall around it, as protection from the gales that roar through here when there's a westerly blowing. Make it into a proper French potager. Herbs and veggies and fruit trees, too, if there's room. It would give him something to do once the house is finished, and I'm looking after the restaurant and the business side of things full-time.'

It sounded like a fun idea, but I'd have to do some research, and maybe Jason—or Derek—was being slightly too ambitious. Nothing worse than a disappointed client. As for the rest of the yard, it could be a real showpiece—a restored colonial goldfields garden. The customers could dine out here, if Jason wanted to go down that path.

'What do you think?' His voice interrupted my thoughts, and I realised I had not spoken for some time while he had continued to ramble on.

'I think it's my dream come true,' I blurted out before I thought better of it.

He chuckled. 'That's the exact opposite of what I thought when I first saw it,' he admitted, pulling a face. 'I loved the house—still do—but the garden … not my area of expertise, I'm afraid.'

'But you said your partner would be willing? I'm thinking you may not want anything that requires too much maintenance?'

'Oh, Derek would be up for anything. Not immediately though, he's still got the house to do. I'm not sure he isn't taking on too much, but it's no use telling him that. When we decided to buy this place and renovate, he started doing courses on carpentry, brick-laying, you name it. The man wants to do this entire project single-handed, but we still have a business in Melbourne and we'll be dividing our time between the two for a bit longer yet. Then, if things work out here, we'll sell the Melbourne side of things, and live here permanently. So, to answer your question, if everything goes to plan, then yes, I can see him needing something to keep him occupied. Derek has far too much energy.'

'Gardens can be a form of relaxation, too,' I assured him, in case he was imagining this was just more weight on his already overloaded shoulders. 'Were you planning to have animals? Goats, sheep, pigs?'

The expression of horror on his face was answer enough.

'A dog, then?' I said, trying not to laugh.

'I have a cat,' he offered. 'But she's lived a pampered life indoors.'

It sounded a bit like Lincoln's cat, I thought, remembering the way the tortoiseshell had blocked our entry to the cottage. And then I told myself I shouldn't be thinking about Lincoln Nash when I needed to concentrate on my job.

I looked about again and hoped that Jason and Derek would be able to have all of the things they were hoping for. So often in these situations I'd seen people over-extend themselves, and next thing you knew the property was back on the market with some of the gloss taken off it, and at a reduced price.

'We really love it here.' Jason stood, staring beyond the weeds to the distant hills and the blue sky. Was he trying to convince himself?

'It's amazing what love and hard work can do,' I said. 'But what do you need from me? I mean, I can draw some plans for you, or just some ideas on paper. I imagine you have other people to interview before you can make a decision?'

He cocked his head and gave me a look. 'No, no one else. Just you. I had a look at some of the other jobs you've been involved in, and I knew you were the right person for this job. I tend to make snap judgements, Sam, hope that's okay?'

'Oh yes … of course.' I wondered if I looked

as amazed as I felt. Didn't he even want to talk budget? This really was a dream come true.

'Draw me up some plans, and give me your thoughts on how you see our garden. I want this to be a cooperative thing, so then I'll sit down with Derek and we'll have a chat and get back to you. I should warn you though, Derek isn't like me. He's a bit of a control freak, and he'll want to meddle, but I'll make sure he doesn't drive you crazy. How does all of that sound, Sam?'

I gave him a lopsided smile. 'It sounds wonderful.'

By now we'd reached the ute and I opened the door.

'Things been tough?' Jason asked me quietly, and I worried that my smile had given away a little too much.

'I shouldn't complain. I'm doing okay. But Golden Gully is a small place and if it wasn't for the green-changers, and people like you, I'd be out of work in no time.'

'Well, we're hoping the restaurant will bring in a few more people like us,' he reassured me. 'Oh, hang on, forgot!'

He went back inside, leaving me with one foot in the ute. When he returned he had a box with him, which he handed to me with ceremony. 'Carrot cake,' he said. 'Enjoy.'

'Oh. Thank you!'

That was embarrassing. He must have noticed how I couldn't keep my hands off it. Still, I wasn't going to refuse him.

He shook my hand again, his eyes warm, and

I found myself liking him much more than I'd ever thought I would like a celebrity chef from Melbourne.

I climbed into the ute and backed out, giving him a wave. I forced myself to contain my emotions until I was out of sight, but once I'd turned the corner, I let fly, thumping the steering wheel and singing out, 'Yes!' in a voice that would have sent Mitch running for his life, if he'd been in his usual spot beside me.

What I had said was true, this job really was my dream come true, and I was already starting to visualise the garden as it would look when finished. I tried unsuccessfully to rein myself in, with the reminder that I couldn't just go at it gung-ho. I would have to consider Jason and Derek, as well as their business.

It had been a long and emotionally charged day, and I thought it was appropriate I buy a bottle of wine and some chocolate to celebrate. I stopped off at the supermarket and found what I wanted. I also decided to add a few treats for my animal friends—it seemed only fair we should all participate in my good fortune.

'You look nice!' My friend Suzy manning the checkout sounded surprised, and I broke into a smile. 'You know what I mean, Sam.'

'Thanks.'

'Have you seen Lincoln Nash? You used to be his biggest fan, didn't you?' she teased. 'I expected you to be stalking him.'

'I wasn't that big a fan, Suzy.'

'Oh come on! What was that song you were

mad about? It was all you ever played for an entire year.'

I laughed it off, and carried my purchases out to the vehicle. The interior was hot, the afternoon sun barely waning, although it must be getting on for five. Despite what Suzy had said about Lincoln, her flattery had made me feel good. I rarely dressed up around home, so everyone was far more used to seeing me as I'd been this morning at the cottage, in my daggy jeans and dirty boots, with my hair like a bird's nest.

Maybe I should try dressing up more often.

Just for a moment my thoughts went down a strange and unfamiliar path, as I pictured myself bumping into Lincoln Nash in the hardware store, only this time I was wearing my flowery dress with five-inch stilettos, with my hair shining like a shampoo commercial. And instead of dismissing me, Lincoln would be gazing at me with that stunned mullet sort of expression that men were prone to when confronted by super-models.

I snorted in disgust at myself and men in general. 'And that's going to happen,' I muttered as I turned into the driveway that led to my gate. 'Anyway, why are you suddenly so interested in what Lincoln Nash thinks of you?'

Yes, his manner had surprised me this morning, but that didn't mean he wouldn't revert to his uncharming self the next time we met. I wasn't a fan of unpredictable men, the sort who used their moods to manipulate people into doing what they wanted. I'd been there, done that, and it hadn't made me a happy girl. No, I decided, I much preferred the steady types. Someone you could depend on being there for you, for picking up any pieces that needed picking up without being asked.

Had my father spoiled me for anyone else?

He wasn't perfect, I knew that, and perhaps because he was my father I was seeing him through slightly rose-tinted glasses, but I thought he was a pretty good role model.

Just then I noticed that the gate was slightly open. Had I closed it properly? But I was sure I had. I was aware that there were people who stole from properties like mine, waiting for the opportunity when the occupants were out, and then taking anything that wasn't tied down. As awful as that would be, my main concern was always for my animals.

But as I swept my gaze over the yard to the front of the house, I realised someone was sitting on a chair on my verandah. The chair with the wonky leg that I'd been meaning to replace.

All of my high spirits curdled like milk left too long on the hotplate, because there was no mistaking that straight back and expensive ensemble. It was Hope and I knew she'd seen me, so it was too late to turn the ute around and drive off in a cloud of dust.

Time to face the music.

16

HOPE

14 of January 2000, Willow Tree Bend

HOPE HEARD THE motor rumbling down the driveway and looked up as the ute came to a stop beyond the gate. She'd been waiting for over an hour, but it was her own fault. She'd insisted Prue drop her off here at Sam's place, despite there being no one home. Prue would have been happy to take her back to Melbourne, or to a hotel, but Hope hadn't wanted that. So, Prue had left her water bottle for Hope, to make sure she didn't dehydrate, despite the pretty obvious water tap near the steps.

City girls, Hope thought with a touch of amusement, and then wondered when she'd decided she wasn't one. She'd been a city girl for almost thirty years, hadn't she? And now, after spending one day back in her old home town, she was a country girl again.

Sam's kelpie had kept a close watch on her as she'd stepped up onto the verandah, but he hadn't barked or threatened her. Instead he'd kept her company, sitting by her side with a comically important air. A couple of times he'd trotted off on his own business, only to return to his post a short while later. He'd let her pat his head and stroke his soft velvety ears, and then panted quietly while she stared into the distance, wondering if Sam was coming home at all.

Sam had a real menagerie here. Hope had seen the chooks in the pen, and what might have been a turkey, as well as the horses and donkeys. There might even be wombats and kangaroos hidden away somewhere, she wouldn't be surprised. Faith had always said that her daughter preferred animals to people, but until now Hope had imagined it was just one of those throwaway lines.

Some of Sam's chooks—chickens, she corrected herself— appeared to be a bit mangy, and she wondered if they'd been rescued from a battery farm. She could imagine Sam doing that— railing against the cruelty of the animal world, scaling a fence with a chicken under each arm and running off into the night.

The image made Hope chuckle and the kelpie stare.

At least such silliness gave her a respite from brooding about Lena Marshall. Ever since Lena had uttered those words outside the old milk bar, she'd been unable to stop thinking about them. What if Prue had overheard? What would that mean for *Looking Back*? She could just imagine the voice-over on the promo: *Young love, Hope's first sweetheart* ... and the rest. She was well aware that they could spin it several ways, and Hope didn't want them to spin it at all. Because Pete was none of their business and she was going to do everything in her power to keep it that way.

Pete was gone, and if Joe looked exactly like he might have looked if he had reached the same age, and if seeing Joe had filled her with such pain that she could hardly breathe … Well, these were things she was keeping very much to herself …

Pete's lips on hers, his arms tight around her, and the sudden shift in consciousness, so that she didn't really know where she was and what was happening outside the magic of this, their kiss. Although he'd taken her by surprise, she wouldn't have refused him. Pete had a reputation as a flirt, but she knew he was different with her. This was different. Then the tooting of the car horn and Lena grinning out of the window beside her mother's disapproving face, as they sped past …

The next time he'd kissed her, however, no one had disturbed them, nor the time after that. She'd fallen in love with him. Deeply, irrevocably, completely. First love was sometimes all of those things, and it was a love she still treasured to this day. She certainly wasn't going to let *Looking Back* get their grubby paws on it.

The arrival of the ute stopped her thoughts right there.

Even from the verandah she could see Sam sitting in the cabin, staring at her through the window, and she wondered whether her niece was going to turn around and drive off again.

She stood up, so there could be no mistake, and slowly Sam climbed out of her vehicle and went to swing open the gate. Then she drove through and returned to close it securely. That all took time, and Hope didn't think her niece was in any hurry.

At last the ute was parked and Sam walked towards her, and the kelpie abandoned Hope for his true love, dancing around her niece, wriggling so hard she couldn't help but smile. Sam knelt down to pat him, cupping his face in her hands so that she could look into his eyes and tell him how clever he was.

That gave Hope plenty of time to take in the pretty dress and the care Sam had taken with her hair and makeup. And to ask herself why in God's name she hadn't looked like this earlier? She wanted to shout it out, but she bit her lip. There wasn't much point in starting an argument. Usually she was able to remain calm in the face of pressure, but since she'd arrived home there was a ripple in that smooth surface, an undertow that constantly threatened to bring her undone.

'Hello, Samantha,' she said, when the girl finally reached her.

'I didn't realise you'd be dropping by.' Sam's gaze went to her suitcase and narrowed. 'And you didn't tell me you were staying.

Uh, wouldn't you be happier in a hotel?' That wasn't a good start, was it?

'I didn't mention it because … well, we didn't really talk, did we? It was more awkward at the cottage than I'd imagined it was going to be.'

'That's one way of putting it,' Sam muttered.

'Speaking of awkward.' Hope looked about her. 'Where is your grandmother?'

Sam shrugged. 'Dad must have taken her home. Maybe she needed a rest. Since Mum left … well, she's been here with me a lot of the time, and as much as I love Gran it was beginning to feel a bit claustrophobic.'

Hope wondered if Lily thought she was keeping an eye on things, and that was why she was staying with Sam. She would have to have that talk with her tomorrow—Lily wouldn't let her forget about it even if she wanted to—and it wasn't going to be easy.

She pushed her hair back out of her face, wishing it wasn't so damn hot. 'Look, is this really a problem for you, Samantha? If it is you can drive me into town and we can talk on the way.' Hope made herself smile.

She could see her niece's mind turning over all of the possibilities, and she waited with a mixture of amusement and irritation to see what Sam might come up with next. Was she really that unpleasant a person? She suspected Sam saw her as the stranger who had sent her mother fleeing and her father into a downward spin, not to mention what she had done to her grandmother.

But surely, they could use these moments together to remedy any misunderstandings and heal any old wounds?

Sam made up her mind and unlocked the door, holding it wide. 'All right,' she said, and for a moment they were face to face.

They were much the same height, and they both had Lily's blonde hair and long legs. Hope's eyes might be green, whereas Samantha's were blue, but the resemblance must be pretty obvious. She and Sam were cut from the same cloth, they were Taylor girls, and Taylor girls should stick together.

'Go ahead,' Sam invited her. 'I just have to get some groceries from the ute.'

Hope saw immediately how bare the place was. Almost as if it was still being furnished. Also, there was an unlived air to it. She knew Sam wasn't lazy, far from it, so she assumed this was because her niece was far too busy with other matters.

'Did you finish filming at the cottage?' Sam had arrived, carrying the bag of groceries, including a bottle of wine. She set them down on the bench and began busily filling the kettle.

Hope opened her mouth to say something clever about drinking alone and then changed her mind. Best to tread carefully. Just because they shared the same genes did not mean they had the same sense of humour.

Hope dropped her own bag on the floor, keeping an eye on the kelpie, who had followed them inside, in case he decided to make off with it.

'Yes. They were happy with the cottage scenes. I'll see them when I get back to Melbourne in a day or so, but that's it for now.'

Sam looked surprised at her obvious relief. 'Didn't you enjoy it? I thought it was what you wanted.'

Hope laughed, a belly laugh rather than the polite laughter that was her stock-in-trade. She surprised herself to hear it, and Sam's eyes widened, and then she grinned in delight.

'You sound just like Mum,' she said. And then her face closed down and she turned away. There was an uncomfortable silence as she set up the mugs. 'So, you didn't enjoy it?' She wanted an answer, evidently.

'No, I did it for the money,' Hope replied evenly. 'I'm broke, and I'm trusting that this will kick my career out of the doldrums.'

Her niece gave her a curious glance, but some of her antagonism seemed to have dissipated, so Hope was encouraged to explain further.

'It's a job, Sam, the same as any other. I'm a good actress, and I'm not flattering myself by saying it. I've worked hard to become a good actress and I want to stay in work. I figure I'm old enough now to be getting some of those juicy roles that Helen Mirren always seems to land.'

Sam poured boiling water onto the coffee. Like Lincoln Nash, she was an instant girl. 'If you'd told me you were coming to visit then I could have—'

'Could have what? Gone all out to impress me? I didn't want that. And I didn't want you to stress.'

'Oh, and you don't think this is stressing me?'

'Why should it? After this morning, I wouldn't have thought you cared a jot for what I thought.'

Damn! She'd said it, and she'd been trying so hard not to.

Sam looked at her sharply, opened her mouth, and then closed it again. She seemed to be trying to behave. It would be nice, Hope thought, if they could spend the evening together without the conversation stammering to a halt or turning into a blazing row.

She understood her niece was angry about the show, and she had a temper, she'd proved that. Faith was a more of a sulker, if she remembered correctly, while Joe had a typical Cantani temperament. Slow to ignite, but when it did … She had never forgotten that argument in the milk bar years ago. Pete and Joe, toe to toe, their faces white with rage. Hope might have laughed if it hadn't been so frightening.

It had been about her.

She's just a kid, Joe had said to Pete, and Pete had replied, *You're worried about what Faith will say, that's all you care about.* From there it had escalated, the two boys going head to head, their voices so loud Hope was sure the whole town could hear. Mrs Cantani certainly heard. She came hurrying from the back of the shop and began slapping at them as if they were little boys again.

The air had simmered between them for days, like the heat from an open oven, until they finally came to some sort of truce.

She cleared her throat, once again resigning the past to where it belonged.

'Where were you just now?' she asked airily. 'Surely you don't work in that pretty dress?'

'I was seeing a client,' Sam said, and then she took a breath. 'Actually, I should be celebrating. I've just landed my biggest client ever, or at least I think I have. I don't want to get ahead of myself, but he seemed to like me, and … It's Jason Miller, have you heard of him?'

'Should I have?'

'No, I suppose not. He's a chef, he owns a restaurant in Melbourne, and now he's setting up here in Golden Gully. He and his partner have bought an old place they're going to renovate, and they want me to create the garden.'

Hope sat down and crossed her legs. 'Tell me all about it.' She smiled encouragingly.

For an instant, seeing the eager expression on Sam's face, she thought she was going to do just that. But then she seemed to change her mind. 'Isn't that a line from your last movie?' she asked sarcastically.

Hope chuckled. 'Could be. I didn't mean it like that though. I'm genuinely interested.'

'Maybe another time.' The words had a finality to them as Sam served up the coffee from the other side of the bench, effectively creating a barrier between them.

Hope sipped. 'He was nice, wasn't he?' she tried again. 'Lincoln Nash, I mean. I was glad. The cottage should have someone living in it who appreciates it.'

Sam didn't answer her and the silence grew. The kelpie seemed to feel the awkwardness and came to put his paws on Sam's leg, and she smiled and bent to pat him.

Hope longed to launch into questions about Faith and her continued absence, but the words jammed in her throat like a pileup on a freeway, and she heard herself saying instead, 'Perhaps we should have that celebration now. Do you want to go out to dinner? My treat.'

Sam gave her a droll look. 'There aren't many

Michelin Star restaurants around here. Even the pizza man doesn't deliver this far out.'

'Well, that's okay.' Hope got to her feet and went to look in the fridge. 'I'll cook while you open the wine.' 'If you like.' Sam sounded doubtful.

Hope tried not to feel cast down by the state of the refrigerator. There were eggs and some spring onions and tomatoes, and a piece of cheese that looked in reasonable condition, if you sliced off the mouldy corner. Milk and butter. Yes, she could make omelettes. She had always been a good plain cook—her mother had seen to that. Faith had more of a flair, and that was why she'd made such a success of her dessert idea. Lily had never had much time to cook, although when she did, she liked to bake biscuits and cakes. She wondered about Sam, and who had taught her. Joe's family perhaps, or maybe her niece had never had to learn. There would always be someone willing to push an overloaded plate in front of her. If Hope remembered rightly, it was trying to stop the Cantanis from feeding one that was the issue.

'When do you think Joe will be coming over?' Hope asked, taking the ingredients from the fridge and placing them on the counter.

Sam's face darkened. 'I don't know if he is. If that's why you're here then you're wasting your time.'

The angry words were a little shocking. Hope took a moment to consider them. 'Samantha, what is it? I know you must be worried about your mother, but—'

'Was there ever anything between you and my

dad?' The words burst out of her, as if she could no longer hold them in.

'Y—your dad?' So that was it. Sam had got the entirely wrong end of the stick. She met her niece's blue eyes, trying not to be offended by the furious resentment being directed at her.

'No.' She shook her head for emphasis. 'Definitely not. Joe has loved Faith forever. No one else stood a chance.'

'So, you tried!'

'No!' Hope gave an exasperated sigh. 'I was never interested, and neither was he. Was that why you walked out on us at the cottage? Did you think …?' She tried not to smile, but Sam must have caught the gleam in her eyes, because her own narrowed.

'You could say whatever you wanted to and I'd believe you. You're an actress after all.'

Hope glanced at the bottle and wished she could pour a large glass. Intense conversations like this were always easier when combined with alcohol.

'I can't force you to believe me, Samantha,' she said seriously, 'but I can assure you I'm telling the truth. Faith running away to Queensland has nothing to do with Joe and me.'

Silence.

'Do you have an omelette pan?' she asked, becoming a little desperate.

'I have a pan. To your left, bottom shelf.' The resentful note was still there, but at least she answered.

As well as a pan, Hope found a bowl and the

utensils she needed. She began to break eggs.

Sam didn't offer to help. She stood watching her, as if she was trying to work out what was going on.

'Wine?' Hope suggested, looking up.

Sam unwrapped the bottle and, after rattling around in a drawer, found a cork screw. She removed the cork with a satisfyingly pop, and set what looked like a nice bottle of red in front of Hope while she found glasses.

'I'm going to change and sort out the animals before I eat,' her niece announced. 'You go ahead if you're hungry.'

Hope nodded, pretending to be busy reading the label until she was alone.

What the hell am I doing here?

Sam hated her, Joe blamed her for Faith's disappearance, and she felt as if she was walking on eggshells most of the time.

She poured a glass of wine and took a sip. It would be all right, she tried to convince herself. Even Lena's comment could be made to look innocent, if necessary, but she doubted Prue had heard anyway. She was imagining the worst and she must stop.

By the time Sam returned, dressed in her old jeans and a faded shirt, a hat pulled down over her hair, and smelling of sweat and the farmyard, Hope had everything ready on the work surface. Sam poured herself a long glass of water from the tap, drinking it down before pouring another.

'All done?' Hope asked her with a smile.

Sam came closer, the glass of water still in

her hand, and cast her eye over the ingredients Hope had set out. She gave a breathless laugh. 'Mum does that,' she said. 'Lines everything up. Sometimes I think she even arranges them in alphabetical order. At least that's what Dad tells her.'

Her smooth brow wrinkled into a frown. 'Hope, what you said before … I believe you. At least I think I do. It's just … There's too much going on that I don't understand. I'm sure Dad knows why Mum has gone off, but he won't say. Do you …?'

Hope gave her a sympathetic look. 'I wish I did, but no. I've been away a long time, Samantha. I'm in the same boat as you.'

'Oh.'

'So,' she said, shaking off any lingering unease, eager to change the subject. 'What is this big job you've just landed?'

Sam began to talk about Jason Miller and his plans for the restaurant, and Hope half listened while she heated up the pan and began to cook. The kelpie—Mitch was his name—had returned to sit at her feet, watching proceedings with an interested eye. Unlike some other dogs she'd known, he didn't seem overly territorial, or maybe he considered Hope his business, too, after their lengthy conversation on the verandah.

'They're lucky to have found you,' she said, meaning it.

'You think?'

Hope laughed softly. 'What's the worst that can happen? They like you and want you to draw up some plans, and even if they change their minds they'll remember you. They'll talk about you. Someone else will come along.'

She served the omelette and they sat down to eat. It wasn't one of her best, but she thought it was a reasonable effort in the circumstances.

The silence closed over them, although now it was more of a companionable one. Eventually she heard herself saying, 'Do you see much of Joe's family these days?' She held her glass in both hands and breathed in the heady scent of fermented grapes.

'Off and on. You know Nonna died a few years back? Since then we've all drifted a little. She was keeping everyone together. There was always the big turnout every Christmas. Now there doesn't seem to be any point and it's all too hard.'

'I remember.' Mrs Cantani had ruled her family with a rod of iron and Hope could recall several run-ins with her, including the argument in the cafe. The old woman seemed to have the ability to read minds, and she'd suspected something was going on between Pete and Hope, and done her best to put a spoke in it.

The Taylor girls were bad news, or that was the word around town once Faith left home and went to work at the Angel.

More than that, Hope remembered Mrs Cantani had disapproved of Faith even before she left, refusing to countenance any relationship between her and Joe. Then, once she'd gone, it was as if Faith had broken Joe's heart and was never to be forgiven. According to Mrs C anyway.

And as for Pete … Hope still felt a wave of heat wash over her as she recalled the afternoon she'd knocked on the door.

'I won't have you drag his name through the mud,' Pete's mother had said, her blue eyes as hard as ice, her mouth tightly pursed. Mrs Cantani had been carrying on a one-woman vendetta against anyone she thought might tarnish her eldest son's reputation. In her eyes he was perfect.

'I don't know if Dad is coming over,' said Sam, interrupting her thoughts, and answering an earlier question. 'He might wait until tomorrow. When are you going back? I could ring him?'

Hope set down her glass. 'That's kind of you. Would you? I feel like I need to talk to him.' She glanced at Sam's suspicious face.

'Maybe he'll tell me where Faith is.'

He wouldn't, and even if he did she doubted she'd tell Sam, but she needed to talk to Joe about Pete, and if lying was the only way she could persuade her niece to contact him, then so be it. All in a good cause, she told herself, and pushed away the doubts.

Sam went to the telephone, which was just outside the kitchen door. Hope could only hear the murmur of her voice. The wine was relaxing her and she closed her eyes.

'He says he'll try but he has things to do.'

Hope opened her eyes and thought her niece didn't look happy.

'I don't understand any of this. Mum and Dad … I mean they're the couple every other couple wants to be. They always seem so happy. Of course they have fights, who doesn't, and Mum can be hard to please … But they always make up, always. In fact, when I was a kid it was sometimes a bit embarrassing.'

Hope thought about that. 'So, this just came out of the blue?'

'That's what I've been saying, Hope.' Sam rolled her eyes. 'She was looking forward to you coming and talking about the filming, and then she was gone.'

'She told me about an old photo printed in the newspaper.'

Sam smiled. 'Oh yeah. All of us together. Mum looked so young.' Her face clouded. 'I have a copy here somewhere.' But she made no move to get up and find it.

'It was something to do with the Angel.' Hope spoke before she could stop herself, and then wondered if she should have stayed silent. Too much wine was clouding her thinking and Joe wouldn't be happy with her, but damn it, the girl wasn't a child anymore. 'At least that was what she said the night she rang me.'

'The Angel,' Sam murmured to herself. 'This can't be a coincidence.' Then, sitting up straighter, she explained. 'A few weeks ago, I was around at their house and they were talking. I didn't mean to listen, but … Dad said something about the Angel, and Mum said that was over and done with, in the past, and to leave it there. It's a nightclub, isn't it?'

'Yes, it was a nightclub in Melbourne. She never spoke about it to me, but I did hear from someone else ... Joe's brother. He thought it was a cool thing for Faith to do. She worked there in nineteen sixty-nine, before she came home and married your father. She was only seventeen, but she lied about her age, took a job as a waitress in the bar. The Angel ... well, it had an unsavoury reputation.'

Sam looked as if she was going to say something else and then she changed her mind. 'Is it still there?' she said instead.

'Actually yes. Yesterday when I was in Melbourne, I just happened to be passing, and I asked the cab driver to stop. Horribly run down.' She pulled a face. 'There was a homeless man sitting on the pavement outside and I got into a conversation with him.'

Sam laughed. 'I cannot picture that.'

'I often talk to the homeless,' Hope lied. 'They're so honest it's refreshing. Anyway, I asked him about Faith, I thought it couldn't hurt ... just in case.'

Sam sat forward, suddenly eager. 'What did he say, this homeless guy?'

'Not much. I think he did remember her though. He said he used to work there around the same time. He wouldn't give me much, but he did mention someone called Jared Shaw who was the manager. He's still alive, evidently, and living in a retirement home.'

'Maybe we should go and see him. What did Mum say to you when she rang? Tell me everything.'

Hope tried not to smile at her niece's peremptory tone of voice. She sounded so much like Faith. After a pause to search her memory, she repeated the conversation word for word. 'If it hadn't been the middle of the night I might have asked her to explain herself, but then she hung up so quickly.'

'I just wish she'd call me again,' Sam whispered. 'I was horrible to her and now I keep thinking … What if she doesn't come home?'

Hope realised with a jolt that Sam was crying. Reaching out, she gathered Sam into her arms, something she couldn't remember doing since her niece was a baby.

'I know, I know,' she murmured, rocking her, aware of the strangeness of the situation. 'I wish I could turn back time, too.'

Sam gave a watery chuckle. 'Oh God, yes.' And then she snuggled closer, saying something unfathomable about a hardware store.

'Everything will work out, you'll see.' Hope spoke reassuringly, and then wondered who she was talking to—Samantha or herself.

17

FAITH

August 1969, St Kilda

THE POLICE RAID quietened things down at the Angel. On the night immediately afterwards, Faith was sent home early because the place was empty. Word had got out that it was not safe to be seen there, not if you had something to hide, and most of the regular patrons did.

Kitty had been subdued, too.

When Faith arrived home on a cloud of happiness, after spending the night—or was it the early morning?—with Ray, she found Kitty huddled on her bed. Her face was pale and sullen as she smoked one cigarette after another.

The look she gave Faith was such a blend of anger, misery and defiance that Faith bit back her flood of questions. Her friendship with her cousin was important to her and she didn't want to lose it. She was grateful to Kitty, but somehow their relationship had tilted off its original axis—she no longer idolised the older girl. She was concerned for her, and if anything happened to her and she could have done something about it, she'd never forgive herself. But there were other issues at stake here, issues she was still wrestling with. 'Are you all right?' she asked, setting aside her bag and leaning against the doorjamb. She wanted to go and open the window, but she thought if she did that Kitty, touchy as she was, might jump up and leave.

'They didn't charge me,' Kitty replied. 'I haven't done anything wrong,' she added with a long stare. 'They arrested Lenny for possession of drugs.'

'Oh. Poor Lenny,' she said, thinking he deserved it. 'What about Jared?'

'What about him?' Kitty snapped.

Faith hesitated and then shrugged. 'I'm going to make a cuppa.

Do you want one?'

It seemed that she did. Downstairs, Faith took her time, spooning in the tea and then filling the old china pot with hot water. She added two sugars to Kitty's mug, thinking she might be in shock, and then two to her own. For a moment her thoughts strayed to Ray, but she pushed them firmly away. There would be time to daydream later.

She had a feeling Kitty was never going to blame Jared for any of this mess. She was in love with him and he could do no wrong. No point in trying to blacken him in her cousin's eyes, but Faith was worried. If Detective Inspector Avery was correct, then Kitty was mixed up with some very bad people.

Eventually she took a deep breath, pushed aside her own weariness, and carried the mugs back to the bedroom.

Kitty sat with her tea tightly clasped in her hands, as if she needed its comfort and warmth. Despite her effort to appear tough, Faith thought she looked very young.

'Those women I saw in the Penthouse … Do you pay them to be there? I mean they're not guests, are they.'

Kitty's lip curled, but she couldn't quite pull off her usual show of contempt at her cousin's ignorance. 'They're professionals. Jared sends me out to … I mean, *I* go and find them, and pay them. None of them refuse. It's good money, easy money compared to what they usually do. And they get fed and then there's the booze.' She closed her mouth, probably not wanting to mention the drugs Faith was already well aware of.

Faith supposed it *was* easy money. Was that what had tempted Melanie to the Angel, and put an end to her life? Kitty had known the name, but did she know what had happened to the girl? She had been a police informant, so that may have been the real reason for her death.

She took a breath and plunged in.

'When you took me to meet Jared the first time … he thought I looked like someone else. Some other girl. Do you remember that?'

Kitty gave her a look that was a mixture of disdain and alarm. 'There have been a lot of other girls. Maybe he thought you looked like me.'

'Maybe. Gaz said something about it, too, and

you told him to shut up.'

Kitty's mouth tightened. 'I don't remember,' she said. 'Why are you asking, anyway?'

Faith didn't want to make her suspicious and she didn't want to have to tell her about Avery. 'I don't know. I wondered if it was … important.'

'Well it isn't.'

Her refusal to answer was answer enough. Kitty knew about Melanie.

Kitty was watching her. 'What happened to you after I saw you outside the Penthouse? Was there anyone else with you?'

Faith didn't even think twice. 'No. After you told me to go I did. I went down to the Cocktail Lounge and … Ray was there. He took me out with him to the Queens.'

Kitty's face hardened. 'Don't make a fool of yourself with Ray Bartel,' she said. 'He only cares about himself. Anyway, Jared has big plans for him. He won't be around much longer.'

What did she mean? Faith longed to ask, but just then a tear rolled down Kitty's cheek. She came closer to the bed, wanting to wrap her arms around the other girl but not quite daring.

'Will you be all right? I mean, the cops could charge you with something, couldn't they? If they wanted to make an issue of it?' 'Jared knows people.' Surreptitiously she wiped her eyes, as if she was ashamed of her emotions. 'He'll make sure I'm all right.'

'What sort of people?'

'*Important* people. The sort of people who don't want their names spread around town and have enough clout to stop it happening.'

It occurred to her that if Avery got his way, then the Angel might not be open for much longer. Her life had taken an exciting turn since she'd started working at the nightclub, and not all of it for good, but at least Ray was there. She didn't want to lose him, she wanted to spend as much time as possible with him, and if that made her sound as pathetic as Kitty then she told herself she didn't care.

'Why do you stay at the Angel?' she asked suddenly, and it came out blunter than she'd meant it to. 'I mean … Gaz was right, wasn't he? It's risky, what you do.'

Kitty tossed her head. 'The money's good.' She shot Faith a doubtful glance, as if wondering what she was thinking. Faith felt baffled. When had Kitty ever cared about that? 'People come there for a good time, and Jared makes sure they get one. You know that movie star from America? He said it was the best night of his life.'

Kitty was proud of it, but Faith was remembering the photograph Avery had shown her.

'Maybe he did have the best night of his life, but these people, the important people you say look after Jared, they don't really care about us, do they? They don't care who gets hurt for their entertainment?'

Kitty shrugged a shoulder as if it didn't bother her. 'If you mean the women, they know what they're getting into. They're not little Miss Innocents like you, Faith.'

Less and less Miss Innocent these days, Faith

thought with a grimace, but she let the comment
pass.

'You don't, uh … do you?'

Kitty gave a soft laugh. 'I could if I wanted to.
I've had plenty of offers.'

'But you haven't?'

'Once, only once.' She wouldn't meet Faith's
eyes. 'Jared didn't like it, even though I did it
as a favour for him. He's never asked me again.'
Upstairs they could hear movement as their
housemates began to wake. Kitty must have
heard it, too, because she looked at the door. She
wouldn't talk for much longer, and Faith sensed
her cousin may never be this vulnerable again.

'The police wouldn't be raiding the Angel if
there wasn't something illegal going on,' she suggested tentatively.

Kitty snorted. 'Even if there was they couldn't
do anything about it. Jared knows too many people. I told you. Some of his customers run the
country.'

Faith's heart was beating fast. She wanted to ask
for a name, even though she'd told herself she
wasn't going to agree to Avery's request.

Kitty continued, 'You'd be surprised who
they are. Men you look at on television or in
the newspaper and think butter wouldn't melt in
their mouths. It's an eye-opener, Faith.'

Faith had seen a few of the politicians from
Spring Street in the Cocktail Lounge. She wasn't
aware they went up to the Penthouse, but of
course they must. How naive of her to think they
wouldn't! And then there was the Melbourne

snob set, old money, who considered themselves so much better than the rest. Now and again one or two of them would come slumming it at the Angel, and no doubt they'd want the full experience.

Kitty smiled, watching the thoughts flit across her face. 'Come on, then,' she said softly. 'Ask me. You know you want to.'

'Ask you what?' Faith hedged. Because suddenly she wasn't at all sure if it was a good idea to know.

'One of the names. Come on, Faith. Ask me.'

She hesitated, but Kitty seemed to *want* to tell her.

'All right, then. Who?'

'Bert Dalzell,' Kitty said quickly. Her smile turned mocking when she saw Faith's shocked expression. 'Yes, him. Don't believe everything you read, little cousin.'

Her comment related to something that had happened a few weeks ago, when Faith was scanning the newspaper over tea and toast. There had been an article in it about the Honourable Hubert Dalzell, Minister for Planning and Development in the Victorian state government. She remembered reading it aloud and telling Kitty in a respectful voice that the Dalzells owned a house outside Golden Gully. Sometimes she saw the Honourable Bert driving past the milk bar with his family or waiting in his car while the youngest ones ran in for a bag of lollies and a milkshake. No doubt it gave them a thrill to come down from their ivory tower and experience something so ordinary.

At the time Kitty had sneered, saying that anyone could play a part, but that didn't mean it was
real. Faith hadn't thought much more about it.
Kitty tended to spoil things for the sake of it,
especially if she was in one of her moods. But
now she remembered, and she could see from the
expression on Kitty's face that she had remembered too.

'Do you mean he goes up to the Penthouse?'
Faith whispered. Bert Dalzell was like royalty in
Golden Gully and it was unthinkable that he had
feet of clay.

'Of course he does.' Kitty had crossed her legs
and was swinging the top one in an agitated
manner. 'Look, forget I said it, okay? Don't mention it to anyone.'

'Certainly not.'

'I mean it.' Kitty stared into her eyes.

Faith didn't like the way Kitty was turning her
into an accomplice. These secrets would set her
apart from the others, forcing her to watch her
every word.

She itched to talk to Ray about it. She'd discovered that being in love meant she wanted
to share her every thought and feeling, except
now she couldn't. It wasn't that she didn't trust
Ray, no, it wasn't that. It was just that he might
let something slip after a long night behind the
microphone.

'I won't say anything,' she said at last.

Satisfied, Kitty got wearily to her feet. 'I'm
going for a bath.'

Ray had been away for a week, and Faith hadn't seen him at work. The other girls were jealous of Ray's partiality for her, and they enjoyed teasing her.

'Maybe he's shacked up with some model,' one of them speculated. 'He must know loads of them. I heard he has a girl at the Queens.'

Faith shrugged as if she didn't care, but the words worried her. It was true, Ray must have slept with plenty of girls, and to him their night together was probably no big deal. Except to her it was a very big deal.

They'd run out of tomato juice in the Cocktail Lounge and as there'd been an order for bloody marys and no one else had offered, Faith said she'd go up to the Mezzanine bar for them. She was standing, waiting, when Ray came right up behind her and wrapped his arms around her.

'Hey there, lovely,' he whispered in her ear, ignoring the amused stares of some of the patrons. 'Missed you.'

'Where were you?' she blurted out, and felt her face warming. She wanted to ask him if he'd *really* missed her, but she stopped herself in time—she didn't want to sound pathetic.

'I had to go home for my grandfather's funeral.'

'Oh, Ray, I'm sorry—'

'Didn't Kitty give you my message?' He looked surprised.

'She must have forgotten,' Faith lied, knowing that Kitty had chosen not to pass it on.

Ray shrugged as if it didn't really matter. 'Well, I'm here now,' he said. His gaze lingered on her lips. 'Can we meet up later? The boys are going out so we'll have the place to ourselves.'

Her heart gave a stutter, and she had to remind herself to be cool.

Pretend to be Kitty. Only she didn't want to be like Kitty, not anymore.

'Ray?'

Jared's voice interrupted them, and when she and Ray turned, he didn't look very pleased by what he was seeing.

Reluctantly Ray let her go. 'See you later,' he murmured before he turned away.

Surreptitiously, still waiting at the bar, Faith watched the interaction between the two men. Jared was speaking, and although his voice was too low for Faith to hear, she could see by the intense expression on his face that it wasn't light-hearted banter. Ray's arms were folded tight across his chest, and he obviously wasn't happy.

A short time later both men went out through the staff door, and before it swung shut, she saw them climbing the stairs to Jared's office.

'Uh-oh,' the girl behind the bar said as she passed her the tray of drinks. 'Trouble in paradise.'

Faith laughed as if she didn't care, but inside she was asking herself if Jared had been warning Ray off her. Had Jared found out about Avery's chat on the night of the raid? He seemed to know everything—if Kitty was to be believed he had informants everywhere, even in the police force.

When her shift ended, Ray was nowhere to be seen, and she walked home, her hands dug deep into the pockets of her coat, her boots striking the footpath and sending up echoes around the silent street. It was a still night and swathes of mist lay in the hollows. She was nearly home when she heard Ray call out behind her.

He was running towards her and when he reached her, he laughed breathlessly, catching her hand and swinging her around into his arms. She squealed. Then his lips were on hers, warm and tasting of cigarettes and whisky.

'Will you come for a drink with me?' he asked, reluctantly breaking off their kiss.

She hesitated. She wanted to, but something made her pause. At the same time, someone up ahead began shouting, and Ray jumped. He turned to stare. When he realised it was just some kids mucking around, he relaxed again and reached into his pocket for cigarettes.

'Are you all right?' she asked, feeling a tingle of unease.

'Yeah, 'course.' He glanced up at her as he flicked the lighter and she saw that he looked exhausted.

'I'd better get home,' she told him. 'I'm tired. We can go for a drink another night, okay?'

He sighed and then nodded, and taking her hand in his began to walk slowly towards her house.

'What did Jared say?'

'Not a lot.' He frowned, as if he was pissed off about something, and although she wanted to push for an answer it didn't seem such a good idea.

'I thought he might have wanted you to work

tonight,' she said instead.

'Nah. He was still worried about that raid. Wondered if I'd heard anything.'

'Heard anything?'

He looked at her with his eyes narrowed against the smoke, and she had the uncomfortable impression that he was sizing her up, wondering if he could trust her. Just as she was him.

'Jared pays people a lot of money to keep the cops away from the Angel. He's puzzled as to why the raid happened at all.'

'Oh.'

'He thought I might have said something to someone, but I told him I hadn't. I mean, what could I have said that would bring the cops down on him? I thought we were friends … well, we *are* pals. I suppose my feelings were a bit hurt, if you want to know the truth. I'm wondering if old Jared is losing his touch, and I'm not the only one.'

Faith caught his glance, and then his smile as he leaned in to kiss her cheek. 'Probably better if you don't mention this, hey?'

'No, I won't.' She snuggled against him, loving the feel of him and yet her thoughts were elsewhere.

Ray hadn't even been there when the raid happened, so why would Jared suspect he had anything to do with it? And then she questioned if that was precisely the reason. If Jared was casting around among his friends for the culprit, he might think Ray being away was a clever alibi. But Faith knew it had been Avery who'd organised the raid, because he'd told her so.

Suddenly she didn't want to go home. She knew she wouldn't be able to sleep. She looked up at Ray. 'Can I change my mind about that drink?'

He laughed softly, and perhaps with some relief. Maybe he would have trouble sleeping too.

'I'd like that,' he murmured, cupping her face with warm hands and leaning in to kiss her properly. 'I'd like that very much.'

18

SAMANTHA

15 January 2000, Willow Tree Bend

I SLEPT WELL, CONSIDERING. The emotion of last night, and the day before, must have worn me out. I hadn't meant to weep in Hope's arms like that, but she had been nice about it, making sure I was all right, and pouring me another glass of red. After that we'd sat on the verandah in the darkness, with the sky awash with stars, and enjoyed the cooling air after the heat of the day. We didn't say much, and yet it was … nice.

She did tell me some funny stories about her life in the spotlight, and then one about her fall from grace after her film *The Document* flopped.

'Someone began a rumour that I was dead,' she said in that dry way of hers, which I secretly thought very Australian. 'I had to appear as a special guest on a couple of sitcoms, just to prove I was still alive. You know the sort of thing, there's a knock and the door opens and the crowd gasps and there you are.'

Her laugh reminded me so much of my mother

it caused a sharp ache inside me. I felt everything welling up again. Where she was, who she was with, and was she ever coming home?

My father didn't turn up, but then I hadn't thought he would. I could tell from his voice on the phone that he wasn't keen to have an intimate family meal. I made excuses for him to Hope, saying he must be feeling tired, and how full on it must be for him, trying to keep tabs on everything without Mum there. But I think we both knew he just didn't want to talk about what was happening.

Hope had shrugged it off, and then said she was going to see Gran tomorrow and would I drop her there.

'We can catch up for dinner, what do you think? Maybe Joe will visit tomorrow instead. I'll invite your grandmother, too.' 'The more the merrier.' I'd tried to sound enthusiastic.

'I'll cook,' she'd added, and I saw the gleam of her smile in the starlight. 'I can shop in town.'

'I have plenty of carrot cake.' By then I'd remembered the box Jason Miller had given me. As for the photo I had seen at Dalzell's house … I didn't even want to talk about that. Not yet. I was still thinking it over.

The following morning, I dropped off my famous aunt at my grandmother's unit in the heart of Golden Gully. Lily was in, and I left them to it, turning the ute for home.

Estelle had left a message on my answering machine last night, while I was outside on the verandah bonding with Hope. My friend wasn't someone who got to the point in a hurry, and as usual she used up several minutes of tape meandering on about the weather and the animals, and asking how Gobble was. I waited patiently until she finally let me know why she was calling.

We need money, Sam. I never realised how expensive all of this was going to be. And people keep giving us animals. It never stops. So, I've been thinking. What about a fundraiser? You know the sort of thing. Raise some money by trotting out a few celebs, nice food— nibbles probably, well more than likely because I'm not the greatest cook. Drink— or maybe they can bring their own? Music, we have to have music. Give people a reason to turn out and then put them in a mellow mood so they'll feel the urge to dig deep. Umm … someone told me your aunt was in town. Just a thought. Talk tomorrow.

I had to laugh.

Would Hope agree to something like that? I wasn't sure, but I supposed I could ask her. Well, I *would* ask her—Estelle's shelter was a worthy cause and one I believed in. It would have to be tonight because Hope was supposed to be going back to Melbourne the next day, but surely she could hang around for Estelle's big event before she flew off to the US?

And it had occurred to me that there was also another celebrity who might fit the bill. If he agreed.

Would Lincoln Nash be willing to sing one of his songs for Estelle? One of the old songs would be my preference, but I couldn't really say that to his face. And if I told him that Hope was going to be appearing as well, and there'd sure to be publicity ... He'd shown he was willing to do almost anything to get his songs heard, so how could he say no?

It might even be something *Looking Back* itself would be interested in. Famous actress with a heart of gold? And then there was Jason. With his move up here, and his high profile, surely it would be good publicity for him, too? I could see all sorts of reasons for him to want to take part.

Whoa, steady girl. I wasn't even certain that any of these people would agree to my plans—probably they wouldn't—but it seemed too good an opportunity not to try. Estelle needed the money, and this would also highlight the good work she was doing, so I was going to do my darndest to help her.

My original plan for the day had been to start working on my ideas for Jason's garden, but I told myself I could do that a bit later. It was still early. Why not make an approach on Estelle's behalf to one of those celebrities right now?

So I climbed into my rust bucket again, and turned right, humming along with the wind in my hair until I reached the long narrow road that led to the cottage on Willow Tree Bend.

What if he isn't home?

I told myself I wouldn't be disappointed if he wasn't. I'd just turn around and go home again. It wasn't a big deal and I wouldn't burst into tears or anything like that, I mean I could be philosophical about it ...

He was home.

I was nearly at the cottage now, and I could see him standing by the old willow tree. My mother used to talk about that tree, how it was a special place for her and Hope. The spot where all their secrets were shared, during the years when they still shared secrets. Clearly, they didn't share *all* their secrets or Hope would know what was going on with her sister now.

I slowed the ute and drew up opposite him.

He was frowning in a way that would scare away most visitors. I almost spun my tyres and drove off again, but then he recognised me through the windscreen. And smiled.

Well, that was a good sign, wasn't it?

I waited as he walked over to the vehicle, and I looked up at him through the open window, narrowing my eyes against the brilliance of the sun in the cloudless blue sky.

'Samantha,' he said.

'Lincoln.'

'Creek is almost completely dry,' he said tersely, as if to explain what he was doing. 'Even the few pools of water I saw a couple of days ago are nearly gone. We need rain.'

I couldn't disagree with that.

'Do you think the tree will survive without water?' he asked, turning back to inspect the willow.

'It's old and it's lived this long, and there have been quite a few droughts. Willows are good at finding water, that's why they're considered bad for the environment. They're an introduced species and they compromise native plants. Although this one has been here ever since I can remember, and my grandmother said it was here when my grandfather was a boy, too, so I think it deserves some respect.'

He nodded, admiring the lush green foliage. Despite the heat and the drought, the willow appeared to be thriving. After a moment his shoulders relaxed. 'You run a gardening business,' he said, turning back to me and fastening me with those fascinating grey eyes. 'Green Dreams, is that right?'

So, had he been checking up on me, or gossiping with the locals? I wouldn't have put it past Suzy to have filled him in.

'That's right. I'm available if you need any help with the garden, although,' and I smiled in what I hoped was an encouraging manner, 'you seem to be doing pretty well. I've never seen it look so good.'

'Ah. I've had a lot of spare time over the past year.' He hesitated, staring back down the dusty road with its narrow strip of bitumen, and then the words just seemed to pour out of him. 'My last album didn't sell so well. For a while the record company was hedging its bets so I hoped …' He shrugged. 'Anyway. About six months ago they finally dumped me. That was when I turned to gardening and welding scrap metal.'

'Oh.' I wondered if that might explain the incident in the hardware store. Not that I was forgiving him entirely, but if he'd just had some bad news then I could sympathise.

There was an awkward silence, and I wasn't

sure whether to ask questions and offer support, or simply skip over it.

He gave me a sideways glance, and I realised he wasn't feeling too comfortable either. He was probably wondering if he'd revealed too much, or been too vulnerable. Or maybe he just didn't share all that often.

'I, uh, didn't realise,' I said. 'I hear your new stuff quite a bit, so I'd assumed it was doing well.'

'I think everyone wanted me to write songs like I used to in the old days with Black Crow. But I'm older and I've changed, so naturally my music has changed. I can't pretend to be the same, and I think if I tried it would come across as phoney.' He was looking directly at me now.

I really hoped Suzy hadn't told him that I was his greatest fan, and if she had I might just have to kill her.

'I was one of the ones who liked your old stuff,' I admitted, not quite meeting his eyes. 'But I can understand why you might want to move on.'

He shrugged, seeming to relax a bit. 'Anyway. The gardening helped. I'm no expert as you can probably tell, but I enjoyed it. The bad things don't seem so overwhelming when you're out in the fresh air, your hands in the earth, and the birds singing. Now I just have to keep everything alive until this summer is over.'

'It's been hard on everyone. I see you, sometimes, from my place.' I pointed vaguely in that direction. 'If I'm in the right spot at the right time.'

Oh God, that sounded awful. As if I was purposely training a telescope on him, watching his every move. I waited for him to tell me to leave his property and never return.

Instead he nodded. 'Is that your house over there? I hear the donkeys if the wind's blowing my way.'

I smiled, not sure what else to say. I certainly didn't know how I was going to ask for that favour for Estelle, not now.

'Would you like a coffee?'

I looked at him, trying to decide whether he was being polite, but as far as I could tell he seemed to genuinely want company.

'Okay. Thanks.'

I turned off the engine. He opened the door of the ute, and I climbed out and followed him up to the cottage. Once again his feet were bare, and the hems of his jeans were ragged. Not that he didn't fit them nicely, but neither did he look anything like my teenage version of Lincoln Nash. This man had been through hard times as well as reached the heights. He was complicated and complex, far more like a real person than the faded fantasy I had been hanging on to.

At least I was scrubbed and neat this time, in my shorts and the faded blue shirt that I used to think matched my eyes. Maybe I'd turn his pre-conceptions on their head, too.

'Did you say you made this yourself?' I paused at the gate, admiring the dancing crows. 'It's pretty good. I'm surprised people haven't been pestering you for their own copies.'

He smiled. 'They have. Don't laugh, but recently

I've made more money from my metal work than my songs.'

Up on the verandah Lincoln's cat was waiting to give me a dirty look, and I was glad I hadn't brought Mitch with me this time. As he showed me inside the cottage it followed at our heels, obviously keeping a close eye on me, and I tried not to feel as if I was under review.

'I wanted to apologise about the other day,' I began hastily, glancing sideways at the cat, but if I'd expected it to be nodding with approval I was wrong. It had jumped onto the kitchen windowsill and was cleaning its paws. 'It was all a bit much, but that was no excuse for the family meltdown.'

He looked surprised. 'You don't need to apologise. That scene was nothing, believe me.' He didn't elaborate—evidently he was finished confiding. 'Anyway, your aunt seems like a nice person.'

I bit back my initial reaction. She *was* a nice person. I'd discovered that for myself. It was just that I didn't quite trust her, not yet. Oh, I believed her when she said there was nothing between her and my father, but that didn't mean she was telling me the whole truth about every single thing. But then neither was I.

'She's staying with me,' I volunteered. 'I hardly know her, but maybe I know her a bit better now.'

He turned, a teaspoon and a coffee jar in his hand. 'Ah, I think I have to apologise to you. I think you were the girl I was a jerk to in the hardware store.'

I met his eyes and he must have seen his answer there.

'Just had some bad news about the album,' he said, 'although that's no excuse. You were being polite.'

'I didn't think you'd remembered me.' I was surprised and rather impressed. 'Maybe you recognised the boots,' I added with a smile, trying to lighten the mood. 'They *are* pretty disreputable.'

'No, not the boots,' he said, and his gaze slid over me before he turned away. Was he blushing? I thought about asking why and then decided it might be better not to know.

There was a faint beeping sound, and I noticed the handset was off the phone on the wall. 'Your phone—' I began, but he'd reached across and put it back in place.

'Someone called me last night. It was late and I was asleep. She woke me up to ask me to sing for some charity thing, at least I think that was what she wanted. I stood here yawning and she took ages to get to the point. I was on the verge of hanging up several times. She seemed like the sort of person who might ring back. I've had a few like that.'

He looked so annoyed that my heart sank. And yet I had promised myself that I would help Estelle, and I wasn't a coward. At least, not all the time.

'Um, actually, I think that was Estelle.'

He set down my coffee mug on the table in front of me and gave me a direct look. The pieces seemed to connect in his brain and I heard him sigh. 'That's why you're here, isn't it?'

'Partly.'

He leaned back against the sink, holding his own coffee, and I wondered if he was deciding whether or not to throw me out. 'Go on, then,' he said at last, to my relief, 'tell me what it's about. I didn't know she was a friend of yours, she didn't mention it. I might have been a bit short with her.'

Estelle probably didn't even notice, but I wasn't going to tell him that. A bit of guilt might work in my favour.

As I launched into an explanation of Estelle's situation, he listened, and then eventually sat down opposite me, still listening. He didn't interrupt, and when I'd finished I played around with the teaspoon in the sugar bowl, not wanting to meet his eyes.

'I'm not sure I'd be much of a draw card for her,' he said. 'As I said, most people have forgotten me, or they're happy to tell me they don't like what I'm doing now.'

'You could sing some of your new stuff *and* your old stuff,' I suggested. 'I mean, how could it hurt? I know you won't get paid, but Hope has agreed to it, too. Well, I expect she will. I haven't asked her yet.'

Why was I always so honest? And why was he laughing at me? I pretended not to notice, sitting up straighter and giving my voice the firm, professional note I used on clients who couldn't make up their minds.

'I'm anticipating I can get someone else on

board, too. He's a chef, and he's opening up a restaurant outside Golden Gully.' 'Jason Miller?' he said, and chuckled.

He knew him, I realised with surprise, although I shouldn't be.

It was a small world.

'You have been busy. So, it's going to be big, then?'

The laughter seemed to be leaking out of his eyes and the corners of his mouth, and for a moment I was too captivated to reply. Which was not good. Not good at all.

'I hope so. She needs my help. Estelle has a heart of gold, but she's not the most practical of people. Doug, her husband, is working away most of the week through necessity, not because he wants to. If he could give up his job and stay home, I think it would be so much better for them. There are a few dedicated volunteers and she's been trying to turn the place into a commercial enterprise, balance the books, but it's tricky to do that when people keep handing over more animals in need, and she doesn't have the heart to refuse.'

'I can see that.' There was that gleam in his eyes again, as if he found me a laugh a minute. 'Do you volunteer?'

'I … well, not as such, but I do have a few animals of my own.' I said it awkwardly, pretending not to see his amusement.

'The donkeys?'

'Yes. And I'll have you know I am the proud owner of a young turkey called Gobble. Don't you dare laugh.'

He bit his lip, cleared his throat, and made his face sober again. But his smiling eyes gave him away.

'Okay. It sounds like a worthy cause, just give me some time to think it over.'

'Of course. And just so you know, she's planning it for February fourteenth, Valentine's Day.' I rose to my feet. He looked surprised, as if he hadn't expected me to leave quite so soon, but he'd said he would consider it. I thought that was probably as good as it was going to get.

'How do you know Jason?' I asked, just for something to say, as he walked me back to my vehicle.

'A couple of years ago he did some catering for a promotion the record company had arranged.'

'What do you think of the house he and Derek have bought?

Have you seen it?'

'Yes. I'm not sure I'd want to take it on.'

He dug his hands into his jeans pockets. 'I think it's a test of some sort. They broke up once before. This is a way of them spending more time together and trying to sort out their problems.'

'Yep.'

He looked at me and grimaced. 'You don't think it's going to work?'

'Honestly? I don't know. I don't know Jason that well, we've only just met, but I thought I detected a few doubts. I … well, I can't talk. I've never been able to keep a relationship together for longer than five minutes. It just feels like a lot of stress if they aren't both on the same page.'

'Yes,' he agreed. He gave me a look that was almost shy, and quite unexpectedly it occurred to me that the image he'd projected all those years ago, the wild party boy up for anything, was completely wrong.

I'd had no intention of asking him, really I hadn't, but somehow the words just happened.

'Hope is arranging dinner tonight. An old-fashioned family barbecue. Would you like to come? I'm sure she wouldn't mind.'

He seemed to be considering the invitation, as if he was afraid it might bite him, or maybe he was like a child, contemplating taking some nasty medicine because he knew it would do him good in the long run. 'Okay. I suppose I … Thanks. What time?'

'Oh … six, I guess.' I started to give him directions and then stopped. 'You know where it is. Over there,' I said, pointing.

He waited while I climbed into the ute and then stood, his hand on the roof, looking down at me through the open window.

Something about his stillness made me wonder once more what he was thinking, but he had one of those faces that was difficult to read if he didn't want you to.

'Any requests?' he said.

'Requests?'

'For this fundraiser.'

'So, you're saying yes?' I couldn't help the happiness that bubbled up inside me. Wait until I told Estelle! But I was lying to myself. It wasn't Estelle who was going to be over the moon about this, it was me.

'I guess I am. Why not? What else have I got to do? And there's something I've been working on that I'd like to try out. Just to see what people think. With any luck they won't hate it too much.'

'Could you sing "Dark Star"?' I spoke the words before I could stop myself, and then felt my face heat up.

His gaze slid over me, amused, interested. 'I don't usually sing it these days. It's been so overdone. But …' He seemed to be make up his mind. 'Sure. For you.'

'Thank you.' I still couldn't look at him, but as I drove away I could see him in my rear-view mirror, standing and watching me. And then he turned and walked back to the cottage. And all the time my heart was pounding and I was breathing hard, and I knew I was in trouble.

Stupid, I told myself. I wasn't a teenager anymore, I was a grown woman with responsibilities. This was just … stupid. I mustn't allow myself to be drawn into a dead-end relationship, not again. I had too much going on right now, and this was just, well, completely and totally inappropriate.

No, definitely not, Samantha!

And yet … Lincoln Nash wasn't the man I'd thought he was. He was a long way from that teenage vision I'd had of him. This Lincoln was a real person. Not loud or full of his own importance. He was someone I would have to work hard to get to know.

But instead of putting me off, that made me want to know him all the more.

19

HOPE

15 January 2000, Golden Gully

HOPE STRODE DOWN the path that was bordered by garden beds of pink and green succulents—surely Sam had been at work here?—coming to a halt only as she reached the gate. The sun felt all the hotter after sitting in Lily's air-conditioned rooms. Her mother had already closed her front door, and was probably returning to her comfortable armchair. Or was she looking out of her window, thinking the worst?

'It's as if you ran away and now you've forgotten. But we're still here and we can't forget.'

Hope looked over her shoulder, but the glare on the glass panes made it impossible to see anything apart from her own reflection. She hadn't expected their 'talk' to turn into an exhausting rummage through the past, much of which she had been trying to hide from for years.

'I used to go to church … well you know that. You and your sister thought it was silly for a grown woman to believe in something you couldn't see. God was a

part of my life and I miss him. I still go, and sit in a pew at the back. Not often but sometimes. It doesn't help though, it just makes me feel worse.'

'Mum, what do you mean you sit at the back?'

'I don't feel part of the congregation because I can't take communion. And I can't take communion because I'm not in a state of grace.'

'Why aren't you in a state of grace, Mum? You're one of the best people in this town!'

Lily choked on something between a laugh and a sob. 'Because I can't confess. I haven't been able to confess for thirty years!'

Hope hadn't known what to say, but as she desperately searched around for something to make things better, Lily kept talking.

'The priest isn't supposed to repeat anything you tell him, but I don't trust him. When all's said and done he's still a man.'

Her green eyes had been swimming with tears and Hope had been close to them herself. Her mother, always so strong, so indomitable. Her mother, who until today she'd thought would live forever, was crumbling under the strain.

She told herself she hadn't meant for this to happen. She'd tried to steer *Looking Back* away from Lily, as a precaution, although in her heart she wasn't entirely sure if it was necessary. But instead of being grateful, Lily had seen her interference as an insult and a judgement on her trustworthiness. And now … it felt to Hope as if everything had shifted.

She rested her fingers on the top of the gate. The seniors' units occupied a quiet side street, which was empty at the moment—she thought it was probably empty most of the time. She could hear some traffic ahead, where Golden Gully's main drag offered shops and entertainment. She remembered Faith saying when they moved their mother in here that it was a good position, a little enclave for the elderly.

'The cottage was just too much for her, but she wouldn't admit it, not until that fall.'

Hope remembered the fall, too. Lily had tripped over something or other and tumbled down the back stairs. Sprained her ankle and was lucky not to break it. As it was she was bruised and sore for weeks. The biggest drama had been that she hadn't been found for a full day and night—Faith was always so busy. Hope cringed now at what she'd said, accusing Faith of neglect. Well, near enough.

'Maybe you should come and walk in my shoes for a while,' her sister had said quietly, furiously, and hung *up.*

Of course Hope had rung back later and apologised. She'd been upset, not thinking, but it had enabled her to better understand how easy it was to lose perspective when you were an ocean away. Was that what she had done with *Looking Back?* Let her own immediate concerns take precedence over her family?

Inside Lily's unit, the small sitting room had been scattered with half-familiar objects from the cottage. Hope had been directed to a newish sofa, heavy with cushions, and once she was seated, her mother had taken the shabby old armchair.

Pompom was lying at her feet, an eye half open in case one of them dropped crumbs. There was a low table between them, set with tea cups and a floral plate for the shortbread biscuits.

Her mother always made shortbreads. They were for special occasions, and Hope knew her visit today was considered one—in fact, she admitted to herself that she would have been hurt if there *hadn't* been any shortbreads in evidence. When her mother had proudly produced them upon her arrival, she'd boasted that she was still a good cook.

'Dulcie next door forgets her own name sometimes,' she chattered on, as they'd made their way into the sitting room. 'But my memory is as sharp as it ever was.'

'I'm sure it is, Mum.'

'Then why didn't you let those people from the television talk to me?'

Her voice was so accusatory that Hope was taken by surprise and had to search for an answer. 'It wasn't because I didn't trust you. I just didn't want you put through all of that nonsense. If I hadn't put my foot down and said no interviews, they would have pestered you forever.'

'Maybe I wouldn't have minded being "pestered",' she retorted.

'Oh no, you'd have hated it. Really.'

Lily hesitated a moment, but Hope knew with a sinking heart that there was more, and she'd probably been bottling it up for this moment. Possibly for years.

'What about Pete? You're not going to tell them

about him, are you?'

Her mother's gaze was intense and Hope stared back at her, struggling to speak. They *never* mentioned Pete, not even when they were alone like this. The fact that her mother had done so now, broken the unwritten law, was quite shocking.

'Of course not! Mum, you know there's no question of that, you must know? We agreed never to mention it. Have you forgotten?'

Lily looked confused, and then she shrugged in irritation. 'No, I haven't forgotten!'

Hope wondered if she should say more, but watching her mother sitting there with an injured air, she decided it was best to let it lie. She waited while Lily poured the tea, her gaze drifting to the photograph on the wall behind her. It was the cottage, taken in the evening, with the shadows long and the sun low. It was a beautiful scene and Hope remembered Faith saying something about getting the picture taken a few years ago.

Did Lily regret leaving her home? She'd never shed tears, not that Hope knew about, but it must have been a wrench. It was the place she'd come to when she'd first married, and where she'd brought up her girls and made her life through all the shifts and changes. She must have so many memories.

'Do you miss being at the cottage?' she asked, nodding towards the photograph.

Lily twisted around to look and when she turned back once again her eyes were bright with tears. 'I miss your father,' she said. 'I know it will surprise you to hear that. Rex wasn't a good man, or a kind one.'

'He made your life a misery!'

'Well … yes, I suppose he did. But he was a charmer in the early days. Got me to marry him and live in the middle of nowhere, which took some doing I can tell you. That was how I thought of Willow Tree Bend then. The Middle of Nowhere.'

Hope laughed, causing Pompom to lift his woolly head. 'It still is.'

'I always went for the charmers. Maybe that's something you inherited, Hope. Men who can talk the birds down out of the trees. But they're useless when it comes to the practical things, like putting food on the table, or being there when you need them. Or being faithful.'

'It wasn't like that for me,' Hope said, her voice stony.

'How do you know it wouldn't have been?'

'I know.'

'You were barely more than a child.' 'Mum, can we not talk about this?'

Lily sighed. 'I miss being young,' she said.

'You're still young,' Hope retorted.

Lily laughed softly, and they sipped their tea. Hope's was far too milky, the sort of tea she'd had as a child, but she didn't complain. She was just glad that her mother had stopped dragging up memories. Although Hope had come here to talk, she wondered now if that was a good idea. Wouldn't all this delving into the past only make things worse? Wasn't it better just to forget?

The clock on the sideboard was ticking heavily, like an old man's heart struggling to beat. It almost drowned out the voices of children playing next door. Or maybe it was a television she could hear, if Dulcie was as ancient as her mother said.

'Eat a biscuit,' Lily ordered, holding out the plate.

It would be fine, Hope told herself. She was worrying about nothing. Her mother had done okay so far and she wasn't going to say anything now. Why would she? Soon the show's production team would be finished and move on to their next victim.

She chose a shortbread—one of the browner ones, she had always preferred them on the burnt side—and bit into it.

Salty. Overwhelmingly. She tried to hide her dismay, but Lily was watching her face for her reaction and saw immediately that there was something wrong.

'What, what?' she cried.

'Nothing, it's nothing, Mum …'

But by now Lily had bitten into her own biscuit. Her face fell and she spat the crumbs into her hand. 'I don't understand it,' she whispered, staring at the plate. 'I've made this recipe hundreds of times. Thousands. That's never happened before.'

'Mum …' To Hope the cause was obvious: her mother had mistaken salt for sugar. And yet Lily couldn't seem to process it at all. She just kept saying she didn't understand it and staring down at the biscuits and then up at her daughter. That she was completely confused about what she had done, in denial even, was concerning. And when Hope thought of the secrets her mother was the keeper of … Her anxiety returned full force.

It took a little while to calm Lily down, and after they'd disposed of the salty shortbreads, Hope had helped her to open a packet of shop-bought biscuits.

'I'm sorry,' she said more than once. 'I don't know what's wrong with me.'

'There's nothing wrong with you.'

'I've been so worried ever since I knew you were coming home.'

'Mum, I didn't want you to worry. That's why I told them you weren't coming to the cottage yesterday.'

Lily's green eyes looked childlike in her wrinkled face. Her voice barely more than a terrified whisper, she said, 'Hope, what if they find out?'

She reached for Lily's hands. 'Don't. You know we don't talk about that. Ever. If we don't talk about it then they won't find out, how can they? No one can find out.'

Her mother blinked at her, her emotions leaping from fear to belief and back again. 'I know that's true, but sometimes the words swell up inside me and I'm frightened.'

'Frightened of what?' Hope found she was whispering too.

'Frightened they'll slip out.'

After that she began to talk about church and confession, and her sense of no longer being able to participate in the service the way she once had. About her sense of isolation. Which, as Hope explained to her, was silly when she had her family and friends all around her. She wasn't alone, was she? She just had to pick up the phone.

Now, standing on the path, the sun was so hot that a trickle of sweat rolled down Hope's back. She opened the gate and went through, carefully latching it behind her—one wouldn't want Pompom to escape.

She had asked her mother to the dinner tonight, but that was before she had her outburst. Now she couldn't help wondering if it was such a good idea. What if, despite all her promises, Lily let something slip? Could Hope spend the entire evening keeping an eye on her mother, as well as playing the hostess? And how selfish did that make her, even thinking such a thing?

She narrowed her eyes against the glare and slipped on her sunglasses. Had the sun been this hot when she was a child? It had been a hot day when she and Pete rode in the black-and-chrome car, but she'd been young and in love, and the heat hadn't bothered her then. In fact, she'd revelled in it. That and the man's eyes, watching her.

Afterwards, she'd wondered if she could have prevented what had happened. If she had told him she didn't like being gawped at … Asked him to stop the car and let them out. But the uncomfortable truth was that she'd enjoyed it. The way he'd stared at her in the rear-view mirror, as she'd laughed and flirted with Pete. She'd felt strangely excited by the man's voyeurism. It was excusable in one so young, and she'd always had a tendency to perform for an audience, but even so …

There were times, especially now, when she asked herself whether it had all been her fault.

She was walking along the footpath, hardly noticing where she was going because her head was so full of the past. When she reached the corner she turned into the main street, relieved to find there was a lunchtime crowd here, talking and going about their business. A group of schoolchildren filed past in their uniforms, faces red from the heat, while the teacher tried to keep them in order.

The smells of fried food and melting tar made her eyes water and she quickened her pace. She was supposed to be heading to the Cantani Desserts shop—her instructions from Sam—and they would either give her a lift or call her niece to come and collect her. But first she wanted to go to the supermarket on the edge of town, to collect the food she needed for tonight's barbecue. She was ticking the items off on her mental list when the voice called out to her.

'Hope! I thought you said you were leaving town?'

Hope stopped. She didn't want to turn around and she wondered if she could pretend she hadn't heard and break into a fast trot. But Lena was just the sort of person likely to chase after her and make a scene. If only Prue was here to run interference!

Only she wasn't, so there was nothing for it but to plaster a brave smile on her face and turn around.

Lena was standing a few paces away, watching her warily, her smile even less genuine than Hope's. She had a little girl by her side with her hair in a scrunchy, and the child was staring up at her wide-eyed. A grandchild, or had Lena started her family late?

'Lena!' she said, trying to inject warmth and pleasure into her voice, and walked over to give her a couple of air kisses. Lena felt hot and sweaty, but then so did she. 'There was a change of plans. I stayed the night with my niece.' And then, not putting it past the other woman to invite herself over, 'But I'm leaving soon.'

Oh God, that had sounded so obvious! She kept the smile on her face, but she knew she looked strained and perhaps even afraid.

Lena shot her a glance and paused, as if making up her mind about something, before she went on with a rush. 'I wanted to tell you. That girl who was with you yesterday? With the pink hair?'

'Prue?'

'Yeah, that was her. Prue. She came back after you left. She came back and wanted to talk to me.'

Instantly Hope felt sick. She stared back at Lena, seeing the guilt mixed with secret pleasure in the other woman's expression. She remembered how Lena liked to feel important, and she must be feeling pretty damned important right now.

'What did you tell her?' she asked, trying to keep her voice steady and failing.

Lena shrugged. 'I said we were friends, that's all.'

'You didn't say anything about Pete Cantani?'

His name was there between them, heavy with portent.

Lena smiled, and Hope knew she was perfectly aware of how rattled she was. 'She did say something about him, but she already seemed to know most of it. Did you tell her? I thought you must have.'

Hope could just imagine it. Prue would have played Lena like a professional, fooling her into believing she knew the story, and then getting Lena to tell it to her.

Oh God, oh God.

She mustn't panic. What did Prue know after all? Just that she and Pete were girlfriend and boyfriend. She might drag it up, cobble together some maudlin story to fit in with the whole, but apart from embarrassing Hope and her family, it wouldn't mean anything to anyone else. They couldn't possibly know everything. Could they? Unless Prue had spoken to Lily, too? Why hadn't she asked her mother what she'd been chatting about with Prue at the cottage while Joe had insisted on that private conversation?

'Are you all right?' Lena asked. 'Hope? I'm sorry if I've upset you. I didn't mean to. That Prue, she just kept on and on. Anyway, it's been nice to see you. Say goodbye to Hope, sweetie.' The little girl waved shyly.

Hope clenched her hands by her sides, just in case she slapped someone. Somehow she managed to smile as if she meant it, said goodbye, and turned around. She didn't have a clue where she was going, not until she noticed the supermarket in the distance.

Tonight's barbecue.

Maybe she could call it off? Catch the next flight out of here? But she knew that wasn't going to happen. They'd sue her if she broke the contract, or else they'd get the scent of a better story than they'd realised they had. No, she had to face it out and pretend everything was fine. Surely to God she could do that? She'd inhabited plenty of roles in her life, what was so difficult about this one?

The sun was so hot and she'd lost her hat. She put a hand to her lips and tasted blood. She was trembling.

'What are we going to do?' Her voice sounded young and frightened, and her throat hurt. 'Pete?'

And Pete, tall and straight, with his eyes as blue as the sky. 'It'll be all right, Hope.' His arms warm and strong as she buried her face into his bare chest. 'Don't worry. I'll make sure everything is all right.'

Somehow they had managed to get through the nightmare, burying it deep, until it was as if it had never happened.

'*Don't worry, Hope.*' Pete was long gone, but his voice still echoed inside her head.

Well, she was worrying now.

20

FAITH

September 1969, St Kilda

SLOWLY KITTY REGAINED her usual cockiness. Lenny came back, not even slightly chastened, and resumed his role as doorman and seller of little white pills. Once or twice Faith had seen men in suits coming and going from Jared's office, and he'd looked worried and less dapper than usual. One of the girls told her that they were the owners of the Angel, and he was being called upon to explain himself.

They didn't look like criminals, but maybe she was naive when it came to the underworld. She remembered hearing once that Al Capone hadn't looked like a criminal either, until you got on the wrong side of him.

Whatever Jared's bosses thought of him, Kitty was sticking by her man. She and Jared were as close as ever, and Kitty continued to stay out all night. There'd been a couple of private parties in the Penthouse over the past weeks, and now Faith no longer needed to guess what was going on up there.

The truth made her uncomfortable.

According to Kitty, Jared had never asked her to participate again. 'Never' was a long time. Faith wondered how her cousin could be sure that he wouldn't, one day. If he was put under pressure for another favour? Kitty might end up like Melanie, dead in a packing crate.

Faith worried at the situation like a dog with a bone.

Not that there weren't still plenty of good times. She and Kitty could have a good laugh, and when Kitty asked her over to her parents' house for her younger brother's birthday, it had been almost like old times. Although it made Faith feel homesick for Willow Tree Bend.

'I bet you'll go back to the country,' Kitty said, as they sat in the tram on their way back to their digs. 'A lot of girls come into the city thinking it's going to be so exciting, and when they find out it's not for them, they can't wait to get home again.' *Melanie didn't.*

Faith bit her lip to stop herself saying the words. The wind blowing through the tram was freezing. The warmer, enclosed section was full of passengers, and they'd had to make do with the seats near the open doors, gritting their teeth in the arctic conditions. She dug her chin into her scarf and longed for a hot cocoa.

'Mum says that Aunty Lily shouldn't have divorced your father. She thinks marriage is for keeps.'

Faith snorted. 'She might have changed her

mind if *she*'d been married to him. He had that many other women around town, I think he must have had a roster so he could remember whose turn it was!'

'Do you ever see him now?'

'No, and I don't want to. He came to visit once a few years ago and Mum had the shotgun out. I thought I was in an episode of the *Beverley Hillbillies*, seriously.'

Kitty was laughing, her breath white in the freezing air. 'Jared hasn't asked me to marry him,' she admitted, with a glance that was almost shy. 'But he will. I know it.'

'And are you going to say yes?' Faith asked her, holding on to the seat as they turned a corner, the wheels squealing on the tracks.

'Maybe.'

She'd say yes, of course she would. Faith sighed inwardly. 'There are plenty of other fish in the sea,' she said. 'Jared's a bit old for you, isn't he?'

'He's a mature man,' Kitty snapped. 'I'm over boys.'

It began to rain, the misty sheets gusting into their carriage, so that they both shrieked and shifted further along the seat.

'What you were saying before, about country girls,' Faith went on at last, more soberly. 'I do miss Mum. And Hope.' 'And Joe,' Kitty murmured knowingly.

But that wasn't something Faith was prepared to admit to.

Gaz was serving up one of his huge breakfasts to the two girls. They were laughing over some silly story—a customer from last night— and Gaz was smiling back as he sipped his huge mug of milky tea.

'He tried to climb over the bar, did you see him?' Kitty was in full swing. 'He poured more bourbon over himself than in the glass, before he dropped the bottle.'

'He wanted ice,' Faith put in. 'He said we didn't do it properly.'

'Lenny had to drag him out by his feet. They left him in the lane at the back to sober up. He's gone now. I had a look first thing.'

Faith smiled. 'Probably went home wondering why on earth he stank of bourbon.'

'He was lucky,' Gaz said, and something in his voice had changed. His smile didn't reach his eyes. 'Last guy who tried to do that … Jared took him out the back himself and punched the shit out of him. Haven't seen him since.'

A sudden silence lay between them, thick and uncomfortable. Kitty swallowed her mouthful of food, but her face was flushed and when she lifted her gaze to Gaz it was bright with anger.

'You don't know anything about it,' she hissed. 'You're just repeating gossip.'

Gaz leaned back in his chair, his massive chest and shoulders covered in a clean white tee-shirt. His fleshy face reminded Faith of a bloodhound, and his eyes were so bloodshot they only added to the image. And yet there was something about being in Gaz's presence that always made her feel safe. She liked him, and she didn't want to see him on the end of one of Kitty's tongue lashings.

'Kitty, I was here,' Gaz reminded her, suddenly serious. 'I *know* what happened. When he'd finished, Jared put the bloke in a car and someone drove him to the hospital. Dumped him near the doors. I've heard him laughing about it a few times and I'm sure you have too.'

'It's a joke. He likes to make people laugh so he exaggerates. He gets carried away.'

'It happened.'

Faith thought Kitty was going to start accusing him of lying, but she didn't. Instead, she pushed her plate violently away, food spilling onto the table. Shoving her chair back, she stood up.

'Jared wouldn't do that,' she said, her voice tight. 'He took him to hospital because he was worried about him. He didn't have anything to do with hurting him.'

Gaz nodded slowly, watching her. 'You tell yourself that,' he said quietly. 'If it makes you feel better.'

For a moment Faith thought her cousin was going to hit him— her hands were clenched by her sides and she was obviously fuming—but then she spun on her heel and was gone.

Faith set down her knife and fork neatly on her own plate. 'You shouldn't have said that.'

Gaz laughed roughly. 'Why? Because it's true?'

'You upset her.'

'If she wants to hide her head in the sand like an ostrich, then that's her problem.'

'She won't listen to you. She wants to believe Jared is a good man.'

'I keep remembering her as she was when she

first came here, Faith. Sweet and innocent. Like you. Well, maybe not quite as sweet or as innocent,' he teased. 'But the Angel has changed her. Jared has changed her. She got swept up in it all and now she's in a fast car on a single-lane highway, and God knows where she'll end up.'

'You make it sound as if …'

'Jared's been in a bit of trouble since the raid. I'm not saying he doesn't care for Kitty, I think he does, but he may not be able to protect her for much longer.'

Faith stood up, and all the emotions she'd been trying to suppress fizzed in her head. Kitty was in love, Faith reminded herself bleakly. She was under Jared's spell, and although Faith wasn't sure how to release her from it, she doubted Gaz's heavy-handed approach was going to work.

'You're right, she needs to get away from here.' She was talking to herself. 'Maybe if she had some time away she'd be able to see things more clearly.'

Gaz nodded. 'So, tell me Faith, how are we going to do that, any ideas? Know anyone who can help us out?'

It seemed as clear as day that Gaz knew about Detective Inspector Avery—maybe because he himself was one of Avery's informers. Looking into his tired bloodhound eyes, she could see the solution to her problem. She had to talk to the policeman, find him the information that would put Jared in prison and help him solve Melanie's murder, and set Kitty free.

'I can't,' she whispered. 'How can I?'

Gaz's eyes wouldn't release her. 'Only you can answer that one, Faith.'

Faith was working in the Cocktail Lounge, when the Honourable Hubert Dalzell sat down at a table in the alcove and ordered a whisky.

Someone else had taken the order, passing it on to Faith, and she only recognised him as she was bringing it over. He looked more like his photograph in the newspaper than the man she had seen in Golden Gully with his family, where he was usually out of his suit and more relaxed.

Bert Dalzell was in his late forties or early fifties, only a little taller than her and solidly built. His dark hair was greying at the sides in that distinguished way some dark-haired men manage to achieve, and he had a thick moustache. He reminded Faith of one of those politicians of old—his was the sort of face you might see in a history book, or on a bank note.

She knew he had married a Melbourne heiress, and they had three children—two girls and a boy—who went to a posh school. Sometimes in the holidays she'd see the kids slumming it at the milk bar, the girls giggling at Pete and Joe in the way that girls do when boys are good-looking.

Faith knew he wouldn't recognise her, so she wasn't worried he'd try to make conversation. At home, they thought Bert Dalzell was a 'good bloke' and called him a local. Even Lily admired him, and she wasn't a pushover when it came to politicians. Until Kitty had told her about Dalzell's criminal activities, Faith had admired him, too.

She was bringing the whisky over to him when Jared appeared. 'Faith,' he said, and took hold of her arm. She didn't like him so close, but she knew she couldn't pull away without spilling the whisky, which meant she'd have to pay for it.

'What is it, Mr Shaw?'

His voice was low in her ear and he was wearing a smile that never reached his eyes. 'Mr Dalzell will have his drinks on the house tonight. To show our appreciation.'

Appreciation of what? wondered Faith, but she nodded and tried to move away.

'And Faith.' He held her, trapped. 'Kitty says you're giving her a hard time. Stop it.'

Faith opened her mouth and then closed it again. What could she say?

If I'm giving her a hard time it's because I want her to leave here and get away from you, Jared.

He finally let her go, and Faith continued on her way to the alcove and Bert Dalzell.

'Thank you.' Dalzell took the glass off the tray, at the same time reading the name badge pinned to the front of her tight black sweater. His gaze went back to her face and seemed to linger, as if he was enjoying the view. 'Thank you, Faith.'

Her skin prickled with unease. Like him or not, she had to admit he was an attractive man. Charisma, that was what it was called. He had a way of captivating his quarry—she'd seen him doing that during news interviews or up on the Mezzanine when he was having dinner with other people nearly as important as himself. Always the centre of attention, the one everyone else was looking at and wanting to be. And now he was focusing that charisma on her and she felt distinctly unsafe.

'Where's the delectable Kitty?' he asked, looking past her shoulder, and it was only then that she realised Jared had followed her over.

'Sleeping in,' Jared said, his voice low and syrupy. 'I thought she deserved it.'

Dalzell laughed softly, and something passed between them.

'You're a lucky man,' he said. 'Kitty is a girl in a million. I hope you appreciate her.'

'Of course.' Something about Jared made Faith think he was no longer quite so relaxed.

'I'll never forget that night. The special surprise for my birthday. Do you remember?'

Jared smiled, but again his eyes remained cold. Whatever he was remembering didn't make him happy. 'Special surprises like that don't happen very often, Mr Dalzell.'

'Well obviously not. Otherwise they wouldn't be special, would they? Special surprises for special customers, eh? All the same, I hope I will prevail upon her for a repeat.'

Jared looked even more uncomfortable. Then he glanced sideways, as if he'd forgotten Faith was there, and his eyes narrowed. He seemed to be making up his mind about something, and to her astonishment he gave her an awkward pat on the shoulder. 'Faith is Kitty's cousin, Mr Dalzell. Can you see the resemblance?' 'Really?' Dalzell's eyes widened, and he gave her a slow smile. 'Well I can, now that you mention it.'

'Enjoy your evening, won't you?' Jared spoke affably, and with a final look at Faith, walked away.

Why did she feel as if Jared had just used her to bait his hook, and now he was waiting for Dalzell to bite? Faith set down the whisky.

'You're a pretty girl, Faith.' Dalzell's voice brought her back to the moment. 'Jared always finds the prettiest girls for the Cocktail Lounge. He prides himself on it.'

'I'm quite good at serving drinks, too, Mr Dalzell.'

He sat up straighter and she realised she should have giggled and pretended to enjoy the flattery. By standing up for herself, making him see her as a person, she had increased his interest.

'Do you know where I've been today, Faith? In Spring Street making laws. It's a tiring business.'

'Is it, Mr Dalzell?'

'Oh yes, very. I need a diversion. Do you think you might be able to divert me for an hour or two?'

Faith wondered if she could say no and that would be an end to it. She had a feeling it wouldn't be, that he would see 'no' as a challenge. She decided it was far better to try to turn his thoughts elsewhere.

'Haven't I seen your photo in the newspaper?'

He liked that. He straightened his tie as if she had stroked him. 'I could tell you all about it, Faith, but we need somewhere quieter than this.'

Faith looked about her helplessly. She didn't want to say no, she really didn't. She knew Jared wouldn't be happy with her and she might lose her job, but at the same time there was no way she was going anywhere 'private' with Bert Dalzell.

'Mr Dalzell!'

It was Kitty, looking smashing in a stinging yellow sweater and white miniskirt, her fair hair smooth and shiny, and her mouth outlined in pale-pink lipstick. Faith watched her approach, feeling like a prisoner who had just been pardoned.

'Jared should have said you were here,' Kitty scolded, smile firmly in place.

'He said you were sleeping.' Dalzell smiled into her eyes. 'I didn't want to disturb you, Kitty. And your cousin was passing the time with me. We were just about to find somewhere quieter so I could fill her in on the mechanics of governing the country.' Kitty shot Faith a look.

'Actually, I have someone I've been saving for you, Bert,' she said, turning her attention back to the politician. 'She'd love to meet you. Come with me and I'll fetch her.'

She held out her hand, still smiling, and after a moment he stood up and tucked Kitty's hand into the crook of his elbow. She snuggled close and said something that made him laugh. As they walked away he slid a sideways glance at Faith that turned her blood cold.

It felt like a promise, or a warning, that he wouldn't forget her.

And then Kitty looked back, too.

She wasn't angry, Faith realised, and neither was she annoyed. She was worried, and quite a bit frightened. She'd diverted Dalzell's attention away because she didn't want Faith to be alone with him.

She was protecting her, just as she had on the night of the raid.

But who was protecting Kitty?

Faith made up her mind at that moment. There was no longer any question. She was going to agree to do what Avery wanted.

21

SAMANTHA

15 January 2000, Willow Tree Bend

HOPE SEEMED RATHER subdued when she came back from her visit with my grandmother. One of the girls from Cantani Desserts had picked her up from the supermarket and then dropped her home, so I hadn't had to break off from my own work. I thought she might want a cuppa and a chat, but she said she was tired and, after she put the groceries away, went to lie down.

I spent most of my day working on the plans for Jason and Derek's garden, and was happy with the result, although it needed more. I had a vision, as the quote goes, but it wasn't quite there yet. There was a garden-design computer program I knew about, but I still preferred the old-fashioned method, with pen and paper. I had a desk in my spare room, all set up, and Mitch and I spent a lot of time in there with the fan going and music playing. Not Black Crow, well not often anyway, although I still loved the songs from my teen years.

At one point, I thought I heard Hope talking on her mobile phone. By the time I got back from feeding and watering my animals, she had showered and was bustling about in the kitchen. I told her about my spur-of-the-moment invitation to Lincoln and she didn't seem fazed.

'Well done,' she said, with a little smile, but I wasn't brave enough to ask her what that meant. Instead, I launched into the details of Estelle's fundraiser, and finished with a request that she show up—

'Just for a few minutes. You don't have to be there for very long.' I felt my heart bumping as I waited. I just knew she'd say no. She was probably trying to think of some excuse, or maybe she had several of them she kept on hand and right now she was choosing the best one.

Hope was busy marinating some meat and she didn't even glance up. 'Sure. I'll see what I can do.' She re-read the recipe she had propped up on the bench. 'I asked *Looking Back* if I could stay on for a few more days, but they want me back in Melbourne tomorrow. They're even sending a car.' She grimaced. 'But after they're done with me, I'll come home. No hurry to get back to the States.'

So 'home' was here now, was it? Interesting. And interesting that she didn't even seem to realise that she'd said it.

'Oh, okay. Thank you so much, I didn't … well, I wondered if you'd want to do it.'

'The fundraiser? Of course I want to do it. No, it's your grandmother who worries me. And

Faith.' She stopped and gave me a look. 'Have you heard from her? Has Joe heard from her?' I shook my head.

'If we haven't heard from her in the next few days I think Joe should report her missing.'

My eyes got bigger. 'Is that a good idea? Dad won't want to and … I mean, he says he knows where she is and why, so she's not really missing, is she?'

Hope frowned. 'She could be in some sort of trouble,' she retorted.

'Mum can look after herself.'

'Yes, that's a common misconception.'

What did she mean? I watched her pouring oil into a measuring spoon and wondered: Should I tell her about my odd idea? I'd been mulling over it all day while I was drawing up the plans, remembering the photo and what Jason had said, and then rerunning it over and over in my head.

'When I was at Jason's to look at his garden, he was talking about the family who used to own his property. Their name was Dalzell.'

She dropped the spoon. 'Damn it,' she hissed, and began to mop up the mess. She went to the sink to wash out the cloth, and spoke to me over her shoulder. 'You didn't tell me your gardening job was at the old Dalzell house.'

'Do you know it?'

'Doesn't everyone?'

I always found it very annoying when someone answered a question with a question.

'You know who they were … are? I suppose some of them are still about.'

Her smile was tight as she returned to her task. Carefully, she tipped more oil into the spoon. 'They were local celebrities, well known in political circles. Bert Dalzell started off in the family law firm, but then he went into politics, like his father. For a time it looked as if he might do well, but it turned out he couldn't keep his sticky fingers out of the wrong pies. There was a scandal.'

'Yes! In nineteen sixty-nine. Jason said it was to do with the Angel nightclub.' I waited for her reaction.

She was observing me in a way that made me think she was playing a scientist and I was an interesting specimen of insect.

'He had an old photograph he found while they were renovating. It was a bit wrecked. Dalzell was in it with some famous singer or other, but that isn't the point. There was a girl sitting next to him and … I mean, it was pretty badly damaged, but it looked like Mum.'

'And you think …?'

'Maybe it's a crazy idea, but Jason also told me that Bert Dalzell disappeared after the scandal, and went to Queensland. The photo … He and Mum must have known each other, mustn't they? What if he saw her in the paper and contacted her all these years later, and she took off for an impromptu visit? Or maybe it wasn't the first time. Maybe they were …'

She looked at me with a raised eyebrow. 'Friends? Lovers? Faith and Bert Dalzell. Your mother *was* very pretty.' Hope was standing very still, her voice oddly dreamy. Then she shook her head and snapped back into her normal, practical self. 'I can't see it. I mean, *why?*'

'Because you were coming home and she didn't want you to find out where he was hiding?'

Hope laughed. 'If she didn't want me to find out where he was hiding then she hasn't been very subtle about it, has she? And anyway, why would I care?'

She was right, of course she was. I changed tack. 'Did she ever mention him to you? Dalzell?'

'The days when your mother and I told each other everything ended when she went to Melbourne.'

'It seems such an odd coincidence.'

'I think you're jumping at straws.' 'Can one jump at a straw?' She gave me a look.

'Okay.' I shrugged. 'Don't say anything to Dad,' I said hastily.

She forced a smile and patted my arm as if I was five. 'I won't. Now help me with the salad.'

By the time people began to arrive we had things well under control, which was a first for me. Hope was using the barbecue on the back verandah, and had set up the table. She'd also lit candles and strung some lanterns I'd had since the Christmas I moved in. It looked beautiful, and actually it was quite simple if you had the knack. What that woman could do in a few hours made me marvel—clearly the trait had bypassed me. Mitch kept looking at the reflected colours as if he couldn't believe it either.

Lincoln arrived first, and just seeing him walking through the door in his black jeans and white button-down shirt was even better than I'd expected it to be. Although he did seem a bit edgy. I almost said, 'I promise not to ask you to sing,' thinking that might be the problem, but stopped myself at the last moment.

Dad had brought Gran with him, but she'd left Pompom at home in the comfort of the air conditioning. She was wearing her dark slacks and lavender-coloured blouse, and a pearl choker. The pearls were a family heirloom, destined for me, although I wasn't sure I would ever find an occasion to wear them. As she looked about she was smiling, and I could see she appreciated the effort Hope had gone to.

'You always were a clever girl,' she said, accepting a glass of chardonnay.

Hope grinned. 'Glad you finally noticed.'

The last rays of the setting sun were beaming in under the verandah roof, and Lily took out some sunglasses and slid them on. 'They're new,' she explained. 'I found them in the magic aisle at the supermarket.'

Hope was obviously nonplussed by the comment, so while Gran wandered off to find some nibbles, I explained. 'She means the medical aisle. You know, painkillers and vitamins and personal hygiene. Her words get tangled up sometimes.'

'Ah.' Hope smiled, but there was a frown there, too.

Lincoln chuckled. 'I like it,' he said. 'Magical aisle. There's a song in there somewhere.'

Was there? I almost said I'd like to hear it, but again I bit my tongue. I was being very careful—I really didn't want to muck this up.

Hope and Lincoln had begun a conversation about someone they both knew, showbiz talk, so I drifted over to my father. He was bending down to give Mitch a pat, and although he'd shaved and dressed up in tan slacks and a blue shirt that matched his eyes, he looked exhausted. Handsome but haggard.

'Hey, kiddo,' he said, looking up at me. His blue eyes were bloodshot and he hadn't called me kiddo since I was a little girl. For a moment I didn't know what to say. Honestly, I was rather shocked.

I went with, 'Hope's done marvels,' waving a hand around us. 'For some reason, I thought she would just sit back and order us around, but she jumped straight in and got her hands dirty.'

'Don't let the fame fool you. Underneath all of that stardust she's a Taylor girl through and through, just like your mother. They work harder than anybody else, and never complain.'

'Never?' I raised a sceptical eyebrow.

He managed a lopsided smile. 'Well, hardly ever.'

I sipped my drink. My hands were looking callused and rough, and one of my nails was chipped. I was wearing my pretty floral dress and my hair was shiny and loose about my shoulders. I'd even smoothed on lip gloss and brushed my lashes with mascara, but I hadn't noticed the state of my hands until they were beside Hope's in the salad bowl. The comparison wasn't complimentary, and I knew I should take more care, but our professions were very different. Not many movie stars looked like gardeners, and vice versa. I'd just have to accept that I was never going to make the front page of *Woman's Day* in all my dirt-and sweat-streaked glory.

And why was I worrying about it anyway? This wasn't something I usually indulged in. Normally, I was perfectly satisfied with my place in the world.

But I knew why.

Lincoln.

I was worrying about what he might think, seeing me beside my glamorous aunt. Would I measure up? I told myself that if I started off by approaching our friendship like that then I might as well pack it in right now. He'd have to accept me as I was or it was never going to work.

'How's Mum's business going?' I asked my father. 'You know if you need me, I can always help out. I don't mind.'

He was still patting Mitch, who was looking at him adoringly. 'I'm a bit concerned about the launch,' he admitted. 'Do I cancel it? People will need to know soon, so I have to make a decision. But if I cancel and then … I wish I knew when she was coming home …'

His voice trailed off and I wondered if he was thinking the same as me: *If* she was coming home.

I looked away and saw that Lincoln was sitting with Gran, listening intently to what she was saying. I liked him a lot for that—in my experience not many men would make the effort. Hope was fussing around the food table, checking the coverings that she'd thrown over everything as protection from flies. The insect zapper on the wall was going like crazy, but still they kept coming.

'Hope thinks you should report her missing.'

I hadn't meant to blurt it out like that and, startled, Dad straightened up. Mitch, sensing the sudden tension, shuffled closer to my bare legs.

'No! Definitely not.' He said it so loudly that everyone turned to look. As soon as he was aware of it, he lowered his voice. 'She just needs some space, that's all. She'll be back soon.'

But how could he know? I asked myself uncomfortably. Was he indulging in wishful thinking? I knew I couldn't hurt him by suggesting such a thing.

'Okay, Dad. We'll wait.'

'We just have to be patient, Sam.'

I nodded, but I could feel my eyes stinging. He sounded as if he had made a decision to let my mother go in the hope that she would come back to him, but he couldn't really *know*. Not for certain. 'I'm here if you need me.' He nodded.

Hope had filled a plate with dry biscuits and cheese and various other toppings and now she carried it over to Dad and me. 'Eat up,' she said with a smile. 'There's plenty to be had.' She turned a questioning glance at me, and I felt as if I could read her mind.

What's going on?

While my father helped himself, murmuring a thank you, I answered Hope's unspoken question with a little shake of my head. I was worried Dad would say something about reporting Mum missing, but he didn't. The silence became awkward.

'This is the first party I've had in a while,' I ventured. 'I think the last one was the house warming.'

'Didn't I send you something?' Hope was making an effort, too.

Had she? I couldn't for the life of me remember what it was, and I was glad when Dad interrupted us.

'It was a front doormat,' he said. 'You gave Faith and me the same thing when we moved into our first house.' He was holding Hope's gaze. 'Do you remember?'

'I didn't realise I was so predictable.'

She was smiling as if she was perfectly at ease, but I sensed there was something wrong. When I looked down I noticed that her hand was shaking. In case she dropped the plate, I took it off her, but she didn't even seem to notice.

'There were that many people crammed inside we all had to turn around at the same time.' Dad chuckled softly at the memory. 'It was in May, and Faith and I had been married three months.'

Hope nodded, but she still didn't seem herself. She glanced back towards the glass doors that led into the house, and I knew she was thinking of making an excuse so that she could escape.

Dad's voice went on. 'And then there was that knock on the door.'

'Joe …' she whispered. 'Don't.'

I looked from one to the other, because there was something going on. They may as well have been all alone, the past had such a grip on them.

'I went to answer it. There was the poor guy from the post office with a telegram. People say they know, but I didn't. I thought it might be someone sending some house-warming congratulations. Instead, when I opened it, it said that Pete had been killed in action, in Vietnam. I stood there and I couldn't take it in.'

'Oh, Dad!' I stepped closer to grasp his arm, and pressed my cheek to his shoulder. Words seemed inadequate. 'You've never spoken about that before. I knew your brother died in Vietnam, but not how you found out. That's horrible.'

Hope had folded her arms around herself as if she was cold, despite the hot summer's evening. 'Your mother started screaming,' she whispered.

'Yeah. We had to call the doctor to come and sedate her. People were sorry, but they just wanted out of there. Faith was great, she stood at the door and thanked them, and promised to let them know if there was anything they could do.'

Hope nodded and now there were tears in her eyes. 'She *was* great. I remember. Everyone said so.'

I'd seen old photos of my uncle in his uniform, but no one really spoke about him. I suppose it hadn't occurred to me to wonder why, not until now. How painful that time must have been, and how heartbroken everybody must have felt. That was why they didn't speak about it, not because they didn't care but because the pain was still so raw.

'I might … excuse me.'

I was watching my father, but I turned as Hope

spoke. She was walking quickly, and by the time she slipped through the door and inside the house she was almost running.

'Is she all right?' I asked my father.

His face was even more haggard. 'It was a bad night for us all. I shouldn't have mentioned it.'

'Was Hope close to your brother?' I asked tentatively. 'I mean …'

'We were all friends,' he said, and then shook his head. 'I shouldn't have come tonight. Now she's upset. I'm upset. You're upset.'

'That's okay. Why shouldn't you talk about it? He was your brother.'

'Yeah,' he nodded and managed a smile. 'He was. My mother desperately wanted more kids, but she ended up with just the two of us. Pete was the one who made everyone laugh, especially the girls. The girls always loved Pete best. He had a way with them …' He shook his head, smiling. 'Sometimes I'd wonder: how does he do that? But even when I tried to be angry with him, it was hard to stay angry with Pete. Mum thought he was her perfect son. When he was dead we couldn't say anything bad about him. It was as if he had been raised to some sort of super-saint status.'

'Poor Nonna.'

'Pete was twenty when he got called up. His number was pulled out of that lottery barrel, but his prize wasn't a bucketload of cash, it was a one-way ticket to Vietnam.'

'Lottery?' I murmured. This was news to me.

'It was called the Birthday Lottery and they ran

it twice a year,' my father explained. 'They based it on the date of your twentieth birthday and if that date came up then you were conscripted into National Service. Down in Melbourne they used an old Tattersall's sweep barrel and wooden balls. It was all hush-hush because of the rising stink about the whole thing. Anyway, if you won the lottery then you got a letter telling you to turn up for your medical, and if you passed that, and a couple of other checks, then you had a month before you had to present yourself for training at Puckapunyal. Three months of that, and you were ready to be shipped out to join your fellow soldiers fighting in Vietnam.'

'And Pete passed the medical?'

He made a sound that might have been a laugh. 'Yeah, he passed it in December nineteen sixty-nine. He was a fine specimen of young manhood, tall and strong and fit. He was shipped out beginning of May and he was dead within two weeks. Some sort of offensive, thrown in at the deep end. We thought he'd come back—I mean we couldn't imagine it any other way—and then when he didn't … It left a hole, Sam. More than a hole, a bloody big crater.'

He was looking at me as if he was fighting tears. I reached out and gave him a hug. His arms wrapped around me and he hung on tight.

'Sorry,' I murmured into the warmth of his skin, not knowing what I was apologising for.

'Hey, guys?'

It was Lincoln, standing behind us, clearly not wanting to butt in.

'Don't mean to worry you or anything, but … Lily said she was going to get something to show me and she hasn't come back. I can't find her anywhere.'

'She must be here,' I said, thinking the toilet.

I made my way to the little room and opened the door—it was empty, and when I turned around Lincoln was behind me.

'This isn't that big a house,' I told him. 'She can't just disappear.'

We looked all over the house. It was near enough to dark now, and we even searched the yard, using a flashlight for the more out of-the-way corners, just in case. But we couldn't find her.

My grandmother was missing.

22

HOPE

15 January 2000, Willow Tree Bend

HOPE TOOK ONE shaky breath, and then she took another. The tears were rolling down her cheeks even before she shut the bedroom door behind her. Her emotions were in tumult. She felt like one of the strawberry milkshakes Pete used to make for her, only she was the frothy milk, spinning and gyrating in the silver metal container. When it was mixed to perfection, he'd toss in a pretty pink straw, and then smile as he slid it over the counter.

A smile she knew he saved just for her.

If his mother was there she'd give Hope a dirty look and she'd have to pay, but if not, well then it was free. She'd suck up the creamy strawberry milk through the pink straw, her eyes on him as he went about his work—wiping down the counter, cleaning the milkshake machine, serving other customers.

Now and again he'd glance at her. 'Good?' he'd ask, nodding at the shake.

'Best yet.'

He was a charmer, just like Lily said, and the love of her life. She realised it now, perhaps she had always known it, but as time went on, and new experiences crowded out the old, she'd let his memory slip. Too painful to hold on to. And now, suddenly, it was as if everything that happened post-Pete had melted away, and all that was left was him.

The knock on her door brought her thoughts abruptly back to the barbecue that she was supposed to be hosting. This was the second time she'd been interrupted in her misery.

'Go away,' she croaked, and then bit her lip. She was aware she couldn't hide in here forever; she'd have to face them all eventually. Hastily she wiped her face, taking a deep breath, and went to open her bedroom door. The light was off, so with luck the worst of the ravages would be hidden. She could always fall back on the excuse of a bad headache, an oldie but a goodie.

Joe stood there, his face pale and tense. 'Lily is missing. She wouldn't happen to be in here, would she?'

'Samantha already knocked and asked me that.' She frowned. 'What do you mean "missing"? Samantha said she was looking for her, not that she was *missing*.'

'What else would you call it? She's searched the house and yard and no sign of her.' Joe's gaze slid away from her face.

'Where could she have gone?'

'As you might have gathered, your mother gets

a little bit confused sometimes. Faith says it's just because she's old, nothing serious, but lately she seems to be getting worse.'

Once again she wondered what would happen if Lily, the holder of so many secrets, forgot that they *were* secrets? Hope tried to concentrate on what needed to be done. Her elderly mother was missing somewhere out in the dark. 'She can't have gone far, Joe.'

'Sam said she was down by the creek the other day, so I think we should look there. Do you want to come?'

'Of course I do!'

She found some walking shoes and quickly put them on while Joe waited. 'Down by the creek' sounded ominous, despite the current lack of water. Even if she couldn't drown she might fall, hurt herself, get lost in the scrub that ran along the bank. She imagined her mother alone and frightened, and felt sick.

When she was ready she went to walk past him, but he took her arm to stop her.

'I'm sorry. About before. I don't know why I said those things.'

Hope's smile was wane. 'Joe, he was your brother. You're allowed to remember him. It was just … it's been a long time since anybody spoke about that night. I try not to …' She shrugged, but he understood.

'The pain never goes away, does it? It fades, but when you dig a little, there it is, still hurting.'

This time Hope managed a proper smile. 'Exactly. It takes you by surprise.'

When they reached the door to the outside area, Hope could see the light of torches beyond the enclosed barbecue area and verandah.

'I miss Faith,' Joe said, his voice heavy and quiet.

She turned to look at him. 'I wish you'd tell me who she's gone to see, Joe. I think you know, don't you?'

'After she went to Melbourne in sixty-nine, I used to drive by her place in St Kilda, just in case I saw her. It was risky because if she spotted me, well you can imagine what she'd have to say. Sometimes I'd drop in at her place, pretend I was passing. At first it was okay, but then she started avoiding me.'

'Why was she avoiding you?'

'Because there was someone else.'

'Who?' she demanded, thinking, *Was it Dalzell after all? Was Samantha right about that?* 'Did she ever tell you?'

'I never met him.' He waited for her to walk out of the door, not meeting her eyes. 'I wanted to pick her up and take her home with me, but I knew if I suggested it I'd only push her further away. I had to let her go, and pray that in the end she'd choose me.'

Faith had been a mess when she'd returned to Willow Tree Bend, but she hadn't shared her troubles with her sister. It had been an awful Christmas, with Faith locked in her room, and Pete knowing he only had a month before he had to start Nasho training. Hope felt a spurt of anger towards her sister. Who was this other man? How could she put them through this? She'd been happily married to Joe for thirty years and then this other man had come back into her life, and Faith had been unable to resist him.

'After we were married,' Joe said, 'I could have talked to her about him. A couple of times she made the offer, but I chose not to. No, that's not right. I didn't want to, Hope. We were happy and I was looking to the future and it seemed unnecessarily reckless to stir up the past.' And then he shook his head, as if to erase the memory. 'She'll be back. I have to hang on to that.'

Sam's Christmas lanterns were still throwing their coloured lights around the back deck, and the food on the table, that Hope had spent so much time getting ready, remained mostly uneaten. This was supposed to be a celebration, a getting together of the only family she had, and instead it was turning into a nightmare.

She noticed Sam standing close to Lincoln. He was speaking to her softly, maybe offering reassurance, and Hope thought they looked quite at home together. And then Sam glanced up, her eyes wide and anxious, and hurried across. She was talking before she reached them.

'The gate from the backyard to the paddock is open. She must have gone that way. Down to the creek. Mitch is gone too, so he must be with her. At least that's one good thing. If I call he should come, or bark if he can't leave her.'

'Perhaps she's just gone for a walk,' Hope suggested.

'A walk in the dark?' Sam retorted.

Hope realised how silly it sounded. True, Lily

was reasonably fit and didn't need the aid of a walking stick or frame, but what about her mind? Was there more going on than ageing? Putting salt into your biscuit mix instead of sugar wasn't a crime, and in a younger person you could laugh and call it a momentary lapse of concentration. And yet it bothered Hope.

'I think we should split up.' Sam was organising them into two groups—herself and Joe, Hope and Lincoln—and then they set off through the gate and out into the paddock. Sam was calling for Mitch, but they couldn't hear him.

Hope called at intervals, while Lincoln swept the light around them, trying to see anything that might possibly be an old woman. He was concentrating on the ground, and she thought they must both be thinking the same thing—that Lily had fallen and was unable to respond. The beam caught a fox hurrying along on its own sly business, and then an owl swooped on some unlucky creature, carrying its dinner off to the trees by the creek.

Hope wondered if this was all her fault. Her mother had told her how she was feeling, that the past was weighing on her so heavily she could hardly bear it, and yet she had done nothing. After all these years Hope was still trying to protect a dead man.

The warm darkness swirled around her and with it the astringent scent of eucalyptus. Beneath her feet the earth was stony and hard, and her breath quickened with her heartbeat.

And then there it was, in her mind, the black

car with its shiny chrome headlamps, slipping through that long-ago January day. *Dalzell.* Samantha had said she was working on the garden at the old Dalzell house, and that it was going to be a restaurant now. People would come and eat there, enjoy themselves, wander into the garden and smell the roses.

She shivered.

Was it still the same? Last night she'd dreamed again about the garden, that big sweep of lawn that against all the odds Dalzell, or more likely his minions, kept alive. The grass was soft under bare feet as you walked towards the old sprawling rosebush. Green leaves and the frothy creamy yellow flowers, and the sweet fresh rose scent.

'What are we going to do!' She'd cried, the blood pounding in her ears, her breathing ragged, and her voice not like hers at all.

And then Pete. *'It'll be all right. I'll make it all right.'*

She remembered thinking that they were so young, and it wasn't fair that this had happened. That the rest of their lives could turn on this single event. But then Pete wrapped his arms around her, and she'd told herself it *would* be all right. That Pete really could make it so.

'Hope?'

Lincoln was looking at her as if he'd called more than once. In the beam of the torch his face looked bleached of colour.

She really had to pull herself together. She couldn't disappear into the past when she was needed here in the present. It occurred to her that her mother wasn't the only Taylor woman who might be going crazy.

'Sorry, I was … Have you found her?'

'No, but I heard a dog barking, and then Sam called out. That way.'

Hope looked in the direction he was pointing, towards an area closer to the creek. There was a swathe of light, as if a torch was moving, but she couldn't see what they were looking at. What had happened to the stars? She looked up and saw that the sky was clouding over.

Lincoln was waiting with a degree of patience she had to admire. Many other men would be jumping up and down by now and telling her to get a move on.

'All right. Lead on, MacDuff.'

And he did just that, walking slowly and carefully at her side, probably thinking she was old and infirm, or she'd lost her marbles. Then she reminded herself that he seemed like a very nice man and perhaps he was just being kind.

Ahead Sam and Joe, at first mere silhouettes backlit by a torch beam, began to take shape and form. Hope could see that there was someone sitting in front of them on a convenient log, and Mitch was beside them.

'Mum?'

Hope started forward and her mother looked up. The shadows had filled in her eye sockets and etched the wrinkles deeper in her cheeks, and her hair was matted and tangled on one side, as if she'd been picked up from a fall.

'Hope?'

'Are you all right?' She knelt down as she spoke, reaching to take the hand her mother held out to her. It was icy despite the balmy night. Her other hand was tucked in against her waist, and she was holding herself stiffly, as if she was in pain. Feeling a stickiness against her fingers, Hope noticed scratches on Lily's palm and wrist.

'She fell over,' said Sam. 'She says she knocked herself out for a little while, and I think she might have broken her arm. We need to get her to the hospital so they can check her out.' *Old people have brittle bones.*

'Mum? What on earth were you thinking, coming down here alone in the dark?' Despite herself her voice sounded angry. She tried to be calm. 'Where were you going?' she added, more evenly.

Lily was staring back at her and for a moment it didn't seem as if she was going to answer, and then she did, her voice trembling.

'I'm going to hell.'

Hope's heart gave a savage thud.

'Lily, you're the last person I can imagine in hell!' Joe sounded shocked. 'You've got a gold pass straight to the pearly gates.'

'Gran, can you walk?' Sam leaned towards Lily, gaining her attention. 'Can you walk back to the house or do you want me to bring down the ute?'

Thank God Samantha was here, Hope thought. The girl was so practical, and now she was taking charge. Just like Faith would have done if she was here.

Lily turned back and forth between them, obviously confused. 'I can walk,' she announced, but when they tried to help her to stand up she cried out and sat down again. 'I feel dizzy,' she said, 'and my arm hurts.'

Hope watched as Sam lifted the sleeve on Lily's blouse, while Lincoln held the torch. It wasn't pleasant. Lily's forearm was swollen and bent at an angle that didn't look right at all. They needed to get her to hospital as soon as possible.

Sam straightened and wiped her palms on her skirt. The air was stirring, warm and humid, as if it might be going to rain. She looked up at the sky and sighed, and it was as if Hope could read her thoughts. Everyone had been praying for rain for months and months, and now that it was threatening Sam was wishing it away. At least until Lily was safe.

'Gran?' Sam touched the elderly woman gently on the shoulder. 'I won't be long.' A glance to Hope and her father, and she was gone, moving swiftly back towards her house, Mitch at her heels.

'I'll come with you!' Lincoln started after her at a run, and Hope, Joe and Lily were alone.

Hope sat down beside her mother on the log, gently stroking her uninjured hand. 'Don't worry. They won't be long. I wish I had some water,' she added to herself. 'You must be thirsty.'

'Faith?' Lily murmured, peering at her in the light from Joe's torch, which he'd set down on the ground at their feet.

Hope tried not to be worried. Lily was hurt, possibly in shock, and it was normal to be confused in the circumstances. 'It's Hope, Mum. Your other daughter.'

'Hope ran away to America,' Lily said matter-of-factly. 'She ran away and I'm going to hell.'

Guilt and dismay rippled through her, and briefly Hope closed her eyes. When she opened them she glanced up at Joe, who was still standing on Lily's other side, and tried to gauge his reaction. He seemed to be busy looking in the direction of the others.

'I'm sorry,' she whispered. 'This is my fault and I'll put it right as soon as I can. I promise.'

She didn't know if her mother heard her or not. She didn't give any sign, simply staring off into the distance as the glow of Sam's flashlight grew fainter.

Another gust of wind stirred the air and she could really smell the rain now, although none was falling. A rumble sounded in the distance. Great, she thought wryly, not just rain but lightning and thunder, too.

'Why did you leave the party, Mum?' she asked softly, leaning closer. 'Weren't you enjoying yourself?'

Her mother smelled of Joy, and Hope wondered if it was the same perfume bottle she had bought her years ago. It would be just like Lily to eke it out, using it only on very special occasions. And that she should consider Hope's barbecue a special occasion was both touching and painful.

'I wanted to see the cottage,' her mother chided, as if the answer should be obvious. 'I haven't seen it for so long.'

'But you were there the other day, remember?

With me and the others? For the show I'm filming?'

Had she really forgotten? The shock of the fall perhaps.

'Oh. Yes, of course,' Lily murmured, her eyes closing. 'I'd forgotten. I'm very tired, Hope. I haven't been sleeping. I keep thinking about …' Her voice trailed off.

Hope peered anxiously into her face. Lily had slumped against her and instantly she thought Lily had lost consciousness, or worse, but then she realised her mother was taking a nap.

'I can hear the ute,' Joe said, and now Hope could hear it, too. The rumble of the engine and the bright headlights were drawing closer as the vehicle made its way over the uneven ground towards them. Thunder growled again, and it seemed closer.

'Over here!' Joe called, and lifted his torch, waving back and forth so Sam could see them.

Lily woke up with a start. 'My arm,' she groaned.

'It's all right, Mum. They're nearly here. Won't be long.'

The ute came to a halt, and Lincoln and Sam jumped out. 'Come on, Gran,' Sam said. 'Let's get you back to the house so we can get a proper look at you.'

This time they didn't ask Lily to walk; Joe lifted her in his arms. 'Okay?' he asked her, as she blinked up at him. 'You're as light as a feather, Lily.'

She giggled, and Hope bit her lip on her own reaction. Laughter or tears, she wasn't sure.

Joe carried her slowly and carefully to the vehicle, and they eased her into the passenger seat, using the cushions Sam had thought to bring to make her comfortable. It was clear Lily was in a lot of pain, but she didn't make a sound. Hope thought she might have fallen asleep again, tucked up with a woolen blanket covering her, and went to close the door.

That was when Lily looked up at her, her face pale and drawn in the interior light. Her voice was as firm and determined as it had ever been. 'I'm going to hell, but it's all right. I've made my choice.'

'Oh, Mum,' Hope gasped, a lump forming in her throat. 'Of course you're not going to *hell*.'

A short time later Sam was at the wheel, carefully turning the vehicle around and then heading back towards her house.

Hope stood staring after the fading red tail-lights, barely aware of the approaching storm, or the voices of the others. Perhaps she really was going crazy, she and Lily, because the hairs had lifted on the back of her neck, and just for an instant, she thought she heard a whisper.

A voice from the past. Pete's voice.

It'll be all right. You're safe, Hope. I promise I'll look after you.

So many promises. Only it wasn't safe, not any longer, and all at once Hope was looking bleakly into a future that she had never imagined she would have to face.

23

FAITH

September 1969, St Kilda

THE POLICE STATION was built of red brick, and the hand rail felt greasy as Faith climbed the stairs to the public entrance. At the desk she asked for Detective Inspector Avery, and received some scrutiny from the uniformed officer behind it. He told her she'd have to wait. There were a couple of others also waiting—one man who was obviously very drunk and a woman with a bruised eye and a dog.

It was morning, and early for Faith, but she'd decided early was better than after work. She'd been prepared to come back later if necessary, but now it seemed there was no need. She'd hardly slept last night, and she knew she wouldn't sleep again tonight if she didn't get this over with.

The wait seemed to take forever, and to pass the time Faith examined the notices on a board attached to a grubby white wall. Mug shots of the missing and wanted, and those in between. Underneath her coat she was wearing a black skirt with her white sweater, and every time she turned around the drunk was staring at her legs. He kept trying to strike up a conversation, despite her ignoring him, and she was relieved when the officer told him to 'pipe down, mate'.

And then Avery appeared.

He stood by the desk, leaning over to talk to his colleague, who nodded towards her. Avery obviously recognised her. He was wearing his grey suit, or maybe he had several of them, and as he came over to where she was standing she found herself examining his face.

He looked older, the lines etched deeper, and the pouches more pronounced beneath his eyes. His skin still had that unhealthy tinge of grey, and she remembered him saying he was retiring at the end of the year. Maybe he didn't have a choice.

It wasn't her business.

Avery reached her and stood a moment, just looking at her, and there was a certain amount of satisfaction in his face.

'I'll buy you a coffee,' he said. 'It's just around the corner,' he added, when she gave him a doubtful look.

She followed him out the door, where he paused to light a cigarette, tossing the spent match on the footpath. He seemed in an expansive mood.

'I was down in Russell Street until a few months ago,' he said, referring to the police head-quarters. 'When I said I was retiring they dumped me out here. Hoped I wouldn't cause any more trouble.' He showed her his teeth in what might have been a smile, and which seemed to suggest he was planning to cause plenty of trouble.

'It' was a narrow cafe jammed in between a pawn broker and a betting shop. There was barely enough room for the tables and chairs let alone customers, but it didn't matter anyway because Avery led her straight to a door at the back, and through to where there was a private room with a fireplace.

The calendar might say it was spring, but it still felt like the dark heart of winter. Faith held out her gloved hands to the red embers, almost moaning with pleasure. It was cold in Kitty's house and not much better in Ray's, although at least there she had the option of cuddling up to him to get warm. The memory made her smile fleetingly.

She hadn't told Ray or Kitty or anyone else about this, but that was the way it had to be. It was something she had to see through on her own. Taking a steadying breath, Faith turned to face him.

Avery looked even more unwell in the light from the fire. His face, his hair and his shirt, all grey. Maybe he'd been up all night. Maybe he never slept. In that little room on the third floor of the Angel, she'd imagined him to be a man who believed in the triumph of right over wrong. But was he?

Yes, he was obsessed with Melanie, and yes, he was determined to find her killer and bring him to justice, and for that he would probably do anything within the law to get the job done. Perhaps he would also be willing to go outside it.

He was waiting, letting her play this her way,

but when she didn't speak he grew impatient. He nodded at a chair opposite in what she guessed was an invitation for her to sit down. 'I've heard things are back to normal at the Angel. If you'd call it normal to sleep with rich men to please your boss. How is your cousin?'

Her cousin? So he knew. Well of course he did, he would have made it his business to find out all he could about her.

Faith opened her mouth to tell him that wasn't true, that Kitty didn't do things like that, and then found she couldn't say the words. Because she was no longer sure, not after that incident in the Cocktail Lounge with Bert Dalzell, and the look that had passed between Bert and Jared. Her boss had all but offered him Faith instead.

Next time she'd quit. She'd have to. There were other jobs, and Faith no longer doubted her ability to find one, but leaving would mean abandoning Kitty to a situation she now knew to be dangerous in the extreme.

'What do you want from me?' she said at last, and those watchful eyes finally showed a gleam of warmth.

Before he could answer, the door banged open and the waitress brought in their coffees. She clattered them onto the table, and then plonked down some teaspoons and a grubby sugar bowl, too, at the same time giving Avery the evil eye. Faith could tell that she knew him, and didn't like him. Or was she one of his informers? He probably had dozens all over town, spies everywhere.

So why hadn't he closed down the Angel

already? Why did he need her?

Faith sat on a chair with a squishy vinyl seat and sipped her coffee. The beverage was hot and surprisingly good, and at least it occupied her while she sat there awaiting Avery's answer.

'I want you to be my spy, Faith. My eyes and ears inside the Angel. Tell me who comes and goes, and how important they are to Jared. Who he takes upstairs to the Penthouse, because that's where the real action is. I know Lenny was selling drugs—he probably still is—and I know Kitty lets the street girls stay in the lounge for a percentage of their profit. That's small fry, so don't try to fob me off with that stuff. I need information that will give me a solid-gold reason to arrest Jared, because once I have him in custody I can make him talk.'

'Talk about what?'

He leaned towards her and she could smell the stale cigarettes on his breath.

'He knows who killed Melanie, and I want him to tell me.' Back to Melanie again.

Faith took another sip. 'Mr Dalzell's been in the Penthouse,' she said. 'Something special. He told Jared he wants another night like that one, but I don't think Jared is too keen. Are you interested in Mr Dalzell?'

Something flared in his eyes. 'Oh yeah,' he said quietly. His gaze slid over her and a frown cut a line between his brows. 'You're his sort, aren't you? Pretty and blonde. Young. Has he noticed you yet, Faith?'

She considered his question and then shook

her head. 'Not yet.' She knew Dalzell was more interested in Kitty.

Avery gave her a sour smile and glanced at his watch. He picked up the cup and drank his coffee down in one long swallow. It was a wonder he didn't burn a hole in his throat, but maybe he was used to drinking on the run.

'If he hasn't noticed you yet then he will,' he said with a certainty that chilled her, despite the hot cup in her hands. 'How often does he come into the Cocktail Lounge?'

Faith lifted her chin defiantly, so he wouldn't know how she was really feeling. 'Surely it's not against the law to sit in the Angel and drink whisky? That's all I've seen him do so far.'

'No, but it *is* against the law to use your influence to protect a place that's selling drugs and sex. He and Jared are like that.' He twisted one finger around the other, an expression of disgust on his face.

Carefully Faith set down her coffee. 'The girl in the photograph? Melanie.'

'What about her?'

'Did she know Mr Dalzell?'

He rubbed a hand over his mouth and she sensed he was taking care with his words. Because he didn't want to frighten her?

'Probably. She was his type, too.' His hard eyes stared into hers. 'Be careful, Faith,' he said quietly. 'These people don't care what happens to you, as long as they don't get caught.'

'But this whole thing is risky, isn't it?'

'Yes, it is. Worth it though. Jared and his mates

can't go on doing what they're doing. As well as the protection they get from Dalzell, they have some of my colleagues in their pockets. That's one of the reasons I've been shunted away from Russell Street—for asking questions they didn't want to answer. I'm not expecting to see any of them suspended, but if I can shut down the Angel and see Melanie's killer punished … I think that will be enough for me.'

It sounded like a final request. Again, it was on the tip of her tongue to ask him if he was ill, but again she didn't. If she knew then she might begin to feel sorry for him.

'And if I do what you ask … You won't involve Kitty?'

'She might get caught up in the net, but I'll see that she's released. Might be better if she does get hauled in, otherwise they'll be thinking *she's* the informant.' *Instead of me.*

'Look, I have to go, but if you need to see me then send a message that you'll be here, waiting. I'll make it my priority.'

He meant it, she could see that, and although she should feel comforted by the importance he was assigning to her safety, it only made her more anxious.

Just for an instant Faith considered changing her mind. But what then? Find herself alone with Dalzell, or come home and find Kitty had vanished, her body turning up in a packing crate?

'All right?' Avery was waiting. She could hear the rasp of his breathing above the crackle of the fire. 'Are we on the same page, Faith? I need to know.' He held out his hand.

Slowly, she did the same and felt her fingers swallowed by his big, warm palm. He didn't crush them, something she'd been expecting. He held her gently, lightly, as if she was a fragile bird.

'Thank you,' Avery said, and nodded his head. 'You're a brave girl, Faith, and I won't forget it.'

The street was quieter now, although there were still people about. There were always people. The Angel was long closed, but Faith had been walking, thinking, wanting time on her own. She walked confidently these days, as if she belonged to this place, even if she was no longer sure she did. There was a tight feeling in her stomach tonight, after her earlier meeting with Avery.

At one point as she'd walked through the rainy darkness, she'd thought someone was following her. And when she'd looked back, just for a second, she'd thought she saw the shape of a man against the blur of streetlights. She should have been afraid, but instead she'd felt something else altogether, because he reminded her of Joe Cantani.

Faith told herself not to be silly. Joe was at home, in bed, ready for an early start in the milk bar. Or else he was out in his car with a girl, his music forming a soundtrack to whatever they were doing. The thought of Joe and another girl—his hands on her body, her mouth on his—made her steps slow and almost stop. But then she told herself again not to be silly. Joe had never been anything more than a friend, and besides … She had Ray now.

A tram rumbled past a few streets away, and Faith quickened her steps, relieved to see that her house was close. Someone had left the light on over the front door—probably because they'd forgotten to turn it off—but otherwise the place was in darkness.

'Faith?'

She jumped, thinking *Joe?* But it was Ray who stepped out from a newsagent's doorway. She realised he'd been sitting on a thick pile of newspapers, delivered ready for the morning. He laughed when he saw her reaction.

'I've been waiting for ages,' he complained, giving her a kiss. 'Wondered if you were ever coming home, luv.'

The Liverpool accent was there in spades tonight and suddenly she was sick of it. Why couldn't he just speak in his normal voice? Why pretend to her? And then her irritation faded, and she excused him in her own mind, telling herself he was just so used to doing it that he didn't notice. Ray was like a method actor who had to remain in his role day and night, or lose focus.

'Faith?'

She hadn't heard what he said and had to ask him to repeat himself, while she dug out her key and unlocked the door. Inside the house smelled of stale toast and damp washing.

'I said did you want to come out for a drink? I looked for you at work, but Kitty said you'd left already, and the girls here said you hadn't come home.'

Was he checking up on her? She glanced at

him sideways, but Ray was Ray, and she told herself not to be ridiculous. Ray wouldn't hurt a fly.

'I went for a walk,' she offered. 'I wanted some fresh air after all the smoke.'

He laughed. 'Gets like that, don't it. It's worse at the Queens.'

Ray had been playing at the other venue for a few nights, but he'd be back at the Angel next week. Then there was a gig in Sydney, and a meeting with a record company that he was hoping would open doors for him up there. The only problem, in Faith's eyes, was that Jared had arranged it through his contacts and that meant Ray would be indebted to him even more than he was already. Faith had made an effort to warn him off Jared, but Ray had only laughed and said he needed all the help he could get.

The house felt empty. By now the other girls were either in bed or unlikely to be coming home. She hesitated, but then asked herself what did it matter? She wanted Ray here with her tonight. She loved him, and she wanted him to stay. Kitty wouldn't be home before dawn, she never was these days, and even if she did turn up it would be like the pot calling the kettle black, as her mother was fond of saying.

'Ray?'

He was reaching into his jacket pocket for a cigarette, and looked up with a smile. 'Babe?'

Something about his inner sweetness, the warmth in his dark eyes, tugged at her heart so hard that nothing else mattered. 'Come on,' she said, holding out her hand.

With the bedroom door closed, he wrapped her in his arms, his mouth finding hers. They undressed each other and fell onto the unmade bed, and she felt a desperation in the familiar movements. Perhaps it was her meeting with Avery, her determination to see the Angel closed and Jared in jail, but it was as if a timer had been set.

'You all right, Faith?' he asked her, tucking her hair behind her ear and smoothing her cheek with his thumb.

She looked up at him, the urge to tell him the truth on the tip of her tongue. But Ray, innocent that he was, would tell Jared, and then Ray would be in danger, too.

'I'm fine,' she said, stretching up her arms to draw him down to her. 'Everything is just fine.'

24

SAMANTHA

16 January 2000, Willow Tree Bend

THE HOSPITAL INSISTED on keeping Gran in. Her arm was broken, quite a serious break they said, and it needed to be set under anesthetic. But that would have to wait until the morning. They weren't too happy about her elevated blood pressure either, oh and by the way, what was she doing wandering around alone in the dark like that?

That was the sixty-five-thousand-dollar question, and none of us could answer satisfactorily, not even Gran. The fall had shaken her, and she was having trouble remembering much at all about her evening stroll.

After I drove home through the rain—there wasn't much, but I was grateful for every drop—I fell into bed, exhausted. And when I woke in the morning Hope was sipping a cup of black tea and waiting for her car. She gave me a sombre greeting. She'd tidied up the house and back verandah, and all signs of the party were gone.

Well, almost.

When I opened the fridge door I found that the shelves were groaning with uneaten food. But that was okay—leftovers meant I wouldn't have to cook for days and days, always a good thing in my opinion.

'I'll ring from the hotel to find out what's happening,' Hope was saying as she carried her cup and saucer to the sink. 'I'd wriggle out of this if I could, Samantha, but I suppose it's best just to get it done. I'll be back as soon as I can.'

'I'm sure Gran'll be okay.'

Hope nodded, but I could see how worried she was. She put the crockery down to drain and turned to face me. We were the same height.

'One good thing might come out of this. I'm hoping it will bring Faith home. Make sure Joe passes it on to her, won't you? *If* she happens to call him,' she added under her breath.

'Okay.' I would have thought there was no way my mother wouldn't come home when she heard about Gran, but then this whole situation was peculiar.

Hope had spent some time on her makeup and clothing. She looked very elegant and professional, and her shoes looked expensive. I wondered how she did it, but maybe it was just practice. My mother always said Hope was better at dressing up than she was, but I thought Mum was pretty good at it, too. I remembered her telling me once that someone had told her that the trick was to make the most of what you had, play up your best features and play down your worst.

And never try to look like someone else.

'Why do you think Gran went off like that?' I asked Hope. 'She wasn't making much sense last night.'

'I don't think she knew herself. At least she'll be safe in hospital.' She looked to the front windows, and I saw that a shiny red car had pulled up outside the gate. I moved to go out but she stopped me.

'Don't worry. I have everything. I'll leave now.'

'All right. Goodbye.'

We hesitated and it felt a little awkward, and then she reached to give me a hug. I was enveloped in Shalimar, and I immediately felt a bit teary, which was ridiculous. But the brief time she'd been here seemed to have brought us closer together, and perhaps that was one good thing I could take away from all of this.

'See ya later,' she said, putting on an Australian drawl, and pausing only to give Mitch a pat.

I watched as she picked her way across the yard to the gate, where a man in a suit helped her open and close it, took her bag, and then held the car door for her. I was still standing there when he turned his car around and drove her away.

The house was quiet, but I told myself I'd soon get used to it again. I'd just begun preparing food for my many and varied animals when I heard the sound of another car arriving. Had Hope forgotten something? But when I went to the window it wasn't my aunt returning, but a newish station wagon. It stopped, engine running, while the driver climbed out to open the gate, and I recognised Lincoln.

That was a surprise.

Maybe he'd come to see Hope? More likely he was here to ask how Gran was doing. I looked down at myself and groaned. I was still in my pyjamas and no doubt my hair looked, in Gran's words, like I'd been dragged through a bush backwards.

In the time it took him to open the gate, drive through and close it again, I'd pulled on jeans and a tee-shirt and brushed my hair. He knocked on the door and I let him in.

'How is Lily?' He hadn't shaved, or maybe that was just the rumpled rockstar look. It certainly suited him, I thought, and then reminded myself to behave.

'She's getting operated on today. I'll drop in and see her a bit later this morning.'

'You don't know why …?'

'No, I don't. It's really weird.' I hesitated, not sure whether to say more, but he seemed like a good listener and it might be helpful to talk through some of my ideas. 'You know my mother has gone off to Queensland?'

He nodded, watching my face.

'Right. I suppose you do. Well, when she rings Dad's going to let her know about Gran. We're hoping that will bring her home.'

'I take it this isn't normal behaviour for your mother?'

'God no! She's the most responsible, well-organised person I know. To just take off like this … I don't understand it at all. It's worrying. The other thing …' I told him about the old Dalzell house and the photo Jason found. 'The woman looked so much like my mother. I'm not sure what was going on exactly.' Was I rambling? I thought he looked as if he was still interested, even sympathetic. 'It could be a coincidence, I suppose, it seems like a stretch—Hope thinks it's ridiculous—and yet for some reason I get the feeling that the two things are connected.'

'You think your mother and this Dalzell guy were close?'

'I'm assuming so. I wish I could talk to someone who worked with her, but only she would know who they were. I thought there might be something in the local newspapers about Dalzell at least. I could have a look in the archive at the library, they have old issues.' He nodded. 'Do you need some help?' he asked casually.

I tried to read his expression. Did he mean it? He seemed to. Maybe he was bored and this offered him some distraction? Or perhaps he was just lonely. Whatever his reason, it might be good to have someone else to bounce ideas off.

'We could go to the library after I visit Gran. Unless you're busy today?'

'Apart from basking in my past glories,' he murmured, and then grimaced. 'Sorry. No, I'm not busy. I seem to have run into a brick wall with my new material, and that's the time when I start to wonder why I'm bothering to write at all.'

'It must be tough,' I said sympathetically.

He screwed up his face. 'Sometimes. I tell myself I may as well move into metal sculptures full-time, at least that gives me an income, but I still have dreams … Never mind, forget about that. Are you ready to go now?'

'I have to feed and water the animals.'

'I can help with that,' he offered and then, seeing my startled face, he said, 'Only if you'd like me to, of course. Maybe you prefer to do things your own way.'

Honestly? I didn't know what to make of him. He seemed to be my new best friend, and while it was nice, it was also slightly disconcerting. It was a long time since any man was this keen to spend time with me, and as it was this man in particular … Hadn't he had a thing with a model? I was hardly in that class. And then I thought, what the hell, let him get his hands dirty if he wants to. If he never came near me again I'd know, right?

'Thanks, I could use some help.'

We headed out together, me leading and him following. And actually, he turned out to be rather handy. He said he hadn't had much to do with horses, and nothing at all with donkeys, but unlike some people, he wasn't afraid of them. He had a gentle but firm touch—and no, I wasn't going there. We finished up in record time, with Mitch supervising, and then I went inside to tart myself up while he washed his hands.

We took his car—it was a bit more presentable than the ute— and I didn't say much. Thoughts about my family were occupying me, so that I mostly stared out of the window at the parched landscape—the brief rain storm hadn't done much to quench its thirst—until we reached

Golden Gully.

Our hospital was small, but it had a good reputation. Needless to say, the more serious cases were taken to Melbourne, but for Gran's arm it was perfect. They could operate here and she'd be closer to home and family. Last night after they'd checked her out, they'd cleaned up her cuts and scrapes—the bump on her head wasn't serious. According to the nurse on duty, my grandmother was a tough old bird.

When we walked into her room she was propped up in bed, pale but bright-eyed. She smiled when she saw me, and I bent to kiss her cheek.

'Hope,' she said.

Now that was slightly worrying. Had she forgotten who I was?

'Sam. Faith's daughter, Gran, remember?'

'Of course I do! I'm not senile yet,' she retorted, green eyes flashing. 'I meant … has Hope gone?'

'Oh. Yes, she left this morning, but she says she'll be back as soon as she can. I'll ring and let her know how you're doing.'

I had already been told that the operation would go ahead as planned this morning, and I could visit again this afternoon to check on her. I'd also been warned that sometimes when someone of my grandmother's age had an accident it could have repercussions—in other words her mind might be affected.

'It was just a silly error of judgement,' Gran said, as if reading my thoughts. 'I wanted to walk along the creek and see the cottage in the moonlight.

I'd forgotten what an old chook I am now,' and she gave a disparaging chuckle.

'But, Gran if you wanted to see the cottage you could have asked one of us to drive you there! Lincoln wouldn't mind if you visited. Would you?' I looked at Lincoln with raised eyebrows and he took the cue.

'It would be a pleasure,' he said, giving my grandmother a charming smile. 'You could tell me some more about the history of the place. In fact, it'd be a good idea to write it down. I've been thinking about those five boys head to toe in the one bed.'

His eyes had a slightly unfocused look, and I wondered if that meant he was thinking up lyrics for a song. It was probably the sort of expression I got when I was planning a new garden in my head, before I put pencil to paper. A creative look.

Gran was sleepy, and they had medications to give her in preparation for the surgery, so we left. The hospital had my number, I reminded myself, and apart from a few minor issues, Gran was fit for her age.

My stomach gave a growl and I remembered I hadn't eaten breakfast. I might have ignored that inconvenient fact, but Lincoln must have heard, because he suggested we sit down in the old milk bar for a while. 'We can discuss our research,' he said.

I wasn't sure looking up a few newspapers deserved a discussion, but I didn't want to seem ungrateful. Anyway I was starved, and once we were seated I barely hesitated over the menu before ordering the full breakfast. Lincoln asked for a coffee and toast. Then he tried not to stare as I devoured my huge plateful.

The Cantanis had sold the milk bar not long after I was born, so I never knew it as it was back then. Once the new owner had moved on, the place had been sold a few more times, and remodelled until it was unrecognisable, or so my parents had told me. Ironically, the latest purchaser had gone for the retro look, and stripped it right back. They'd made much of the vintage features, and I noticed the old metal milkshake containers were lined up in a row on a shelf above the counter, like the relics from the past that they were.

I tried to imagine my mother working here, and my father and his brother, Pete. The thought of Pete sent me down a side alley for a moment, remembering last night and the realisation that I knew very little about the uncle who had died so young. I'd seen photos of him, and I knew he was very like my father. There had been one at Nonny's, in pride of place, with him in his uniform, and forever smiling. I wondered where it was now that she was gone.

It wasn't until I finished my meal and set aside the plate that I realised Lincoln was no longer pretending not to watch me. He was even wearing a little smile, as if I amused him, and I wasn't at all sure that was a good thing.

'What?'

'Nothing. I like a girl with a healthy appetite.' He must have realised how that sounded because he tried to backtrack. 'Not that you ate a lot. And even if you did then you'd probably burn it off with all the work you … oh God, unfortunate choice of words.'

Was he having a go? I'd been all ready to take him on, but now I wondered if he was just lacking in some of the conversational skills.

'I don't always have a breakfast like this,' I said warily. 'Usually I don't have time.'

'I have a sister with an eating disorder,' he blurted out, and instantly that changed everything. 'Seeing you tucking in so unself-consciously was a revelation. And a relief.'

I didn't know what to say, but he didn't seem to mind.

'I'm not much of a breakfast person myself,' he went on, sounding much more relaxed. 'Too many late nights. Although I'm working on getting up earlier these days.'

'Best time of the day, those first few minutes when the sun peeps over the horizon,' I informed him, relieved to move on.

He didn't look entirely convinced and I hid a smile. Was there any chance of us ever getting together, with him up all night and me an early bird? Our body clocks would ensure that like the protagonists in the movie *Ladyhawke*, we only ever saw each other for a few fleeting moments of every day.

After the milk bar, we headed over to the library. I knew the older issues of the *Express* had been photographed and put onto reels of tape, which were kept on metal scrolls. I'd seen people using the machines when I exchanged my books, and

I'd heard the reason that they were placed right at the back of the library was so no one could hear the profanities when the tapes jammed.

The *Gold Country Express* was the full name of the local paper, and we'd worked our way through quite a few issues before we found anything. The Dalzell family was mentioned several times— it was the most 'important' family in the district—and its members and their doings were always of interest. Hubert 'Bert' Dalzell had a wife and three children, and when I found a photograph of them outside their house, smiling for the photographer, I was intrigued. This family had owned and lived in what was now Jason's house. The children had played in his garden. It gave me a feeling of responsibility, and I knew I had to tread carefully in my garden restoration if I didn't want to undermine the integrity of this historic place.

Bert was of medium height, and very well dressed. Suave was a word that came to mind. His wife was tall and thin, and she had a stressed look in her eyes, as if right up until the photographer pushed the shutter she was saying she didn't have time for this. The three children looked like typical bored rich kids.

News of the scandal started about three issues later, but it was tactfully reported. I imagined that no one at the *Express* would want to upset the local bigwig. There were hints that Bert had been 'caught up' in a criminal investigation in Melbourne, and the police were 'looking into it'. When he unexpectedly stepped down from his position in the government, the reporter said it was only 'temporary', and as soon as his name was cleared he'd resume his role. And then when he arrived home in Golden Gully it was 'for a break' from the stresses of such a high-profile position.

But when his wife started divorce proceedings, the *Express* could no longer pretend everything was rosy. She went home to her parents in Melbourne and took the children, while Bert hid out in his house, refusing to talk to anyone. There were still valiant attempts to pretend that soon everything would be over, with Bert's name cleared, but I got the feeling that no one really believed it.

'Here it is!' Lincoln pointed out the paragraph. I tried not to smile at his excited tone, and anyway I was no better. We were like two kids in a lolly shop.

Mr Dalzell has not been seen at his home for the past three days. His car is also gone and a friend of the family told this reporter that Mr Dalzell has interests in Northern Queensland and has often expressed the wish to visit there, perhaps even to make a permanent home. The Police responded to our questions with the official comment: Inquiries are continuing.

I tried to work out what this meant. Maybe I was imagining the link between Faith and Dalzell, and her leaving was nothing to do with him, and yet … There was something, and I was sure of it.

Several issues later there was more news, although Bert had slipped to a smaller paragraph on an inner page.

Dalzell car found! The vehicle belonging to the Honourable Hubert Dalzell, who went missing earlier this month, has been found. It was discovered parked at a train station in the north of the state, and it appears that the missing man may have caught an interstate train. Police are of the opinion Mr Dalzell is presently somewhere in Queensland.

Well that was pretty cut and dried, I thought. Case closed.

'Look at this.'

Lincoln had scrolled back a page or two to an earlier issue, and another photograph. This one was taken in Melbourne, and I leaned forward to peer at the fuzzy image.

'The Angel? That's the nightclub where Mum worked in nineteen sixty-nine!'

Although the newsprint was grainy, and the photo not so great, I could see Dalzell standing in the centre of the group. There were about a dozen people in all, crammed in together. I could imagine the photographer telling them to 'squish up'. My eye skipped over the faces, searching for my mother. And there she was.

'Oh my God.'

Lincoln caught on fast. 'Your mother?'

'Yes. Not sure about the guy beside her in the dark glasses, but the woman on the other side is Mum's cousin, Kitty.'

'Did you know she worked there, too?'

I thought about it but I couldn't remember. 'We don't see her much. I think the last time was when I was about eighteen. We went down to the funeral for Mum's aunt, that was Kitty's mother.

I remember in the car Mum and Dad had a massive argument.'

Lincoln looked interested. 'And what was that about, did you know?'

'Dad didn't want to go. He didn't want Mum anywhere near Kitty.' I glanced at him, as the pieces swiftly clicked into place.

'Maybe it was really about the Angel.'

Was I getting closer to the truth? Maybe, and yet it still felt like a story in a novel with half the pages missing.

'Kitty lives in Melbourne. I don't know where. I don't really know anything about her except what I've told you. Hope might remember more.'

But even if she did, would she tell me?

'I wish …' I began, and bit my lip.

Lincoln seemed to know what I was feeling. He put an arm around me, which was a bit of a surprise, but a nice one.

'Let's have a coffee before you go back to see your grandmother,' he suggested. 'But first, I'll ask if we can get printed copies of this stuff about Dalzell and the Angel.'

I watched him make his way to the counter, where the bored woman slumped behind it suddenly sat up straighter. I frowned again at the grainy photo—at my mother's young face and her happy smile. Was it her in the photo Jason had shown me? I was no longer sure. The guy next to her, the one in the sunglasses, was leaning close, as if he was murmuring something only she could hear.

His hair was cut in a shaggy style—I supposed

it was the era. Kitty wasn't smiling at all, staring straight ahead as if she just wished it was over. Dalzell was right next to her. My mother and Kitty were, I realised, very alike.

There was a caption underneath the photograph and I leaned even closer to read it, until my nose was all but pressed to the screen. I didn't know Lincoln had returned and was standing behind me until he touched my shoulder and made me jump.

His mouth twitched. 'Sorry. I was just going to tell you they can copy it for us. What are you looking at?'

'The caption. It's smudged or something. I think it says: "The Honourable Hubert Dalzell takes time …"'

Lincoln leaned in beside me. '"… takes time out from his busy … job", is it?'

'Sounds about right. What does "takes time out" mean? I'm not sure every politician of the day would think it a good idea to be hanging around the Angel.'

Lincoln frowned. 'Maybe he didn't care. He might have thought he was untouchable.'

I looked again at the faces. Dalzell knew my mother, and she knew him. Even if I disregarded the old photo, there was no denying this was a definite connection. Now I just had to find out if it meant what I thought it did.

25

HOPE

16 January 2000, Melbourne

HOPE FRETTED ALL the way from Willow Tree Bend to the outskirts of Melbourne, wishing she didn't have to leave like this, and yet knowing there was nothing she could do if she stayed. Sam had things under control and Lily was only a phone call away.

By the time they hit the suburbs she had convinced herself she was doing the right thing, and had set her mind to playing her part for the television program. She could do it, she was an actress for God's sake!

As long as there weren't any nasty surprises.

And that brought her thoughts around to Prue and Lena, something she'd put aside while Pete and her mother took precedence.

How much did Prue know that she wasn't telling her, and should she call her on it? But if she did, and Prue revealed whatever it was, what then? There was always the chance she could do what she'd always done, and lie her way out of trouble. Perhaps if she said nothing it would all blow over, and anyway, how did she know Prue was going to use whatever information Lena had given her in the program?

Or I can just pull out and walk away.

The idea was very tempting. But from experience Hope knew that telling the producers she was withdrawing would probably cause more ructions than proceeding. They could take her to court, but even if they didn't there would be questions asked and bad publicity—and despite what some people believed, not *all* publicity was good. She supposed she could blame her mother's accident, but it was only a broken arm and they'd be sure to point that out.

No, she would just have to grit her teeth and get through it the best way she could. On the plus side, she had to admit, the money would be welcome, as would be the possible future media appearances.

She'd lain awake last night thinking about the irony of Sam's job at the old Dalzell house. Who could have foreseen such a thing all those years ago? What were the chances of Sam becoming a garden designer and the Dalzell place being sold and the new owners hiring her?

Problems kept piling up. Sam and the Dalzell garden, Lily with her injuries and looking so confused … Maybe someone was trying to tell her something? Was it time to face the dilemma she'd been avoiding most of her life?

But one thing she did know, she couldn't speak up without consulting Faith. Perhaps it was yet another way of procrastinating, but Hope clung to the decision like a lifeline. She told herself she wouldn't do anything, come to any determination, until her sister was back home. Then they could talk about it face to face and reach a solution together. It was something they should have done a long time ago.

And that presented her with another problem. Finding out why her sister had run off, and bringing her back home.

Hope opened her Gucci purse and took out her notebook. Flicking through it, she found the page where she'd written down the name the homeless man had given her. *Jared Shaw*. Beside it was written the street in which the nursing home was situated. *Acland Street*.

Good. She told herself that after she'd finished with the *Looking Back* team she'd visit Jared Shaw. He must remember Faith, he'd worked with her, and she had to believe he could help her understand what was going on.

The car took her directly to the suburbs and the apricot-coloured building she remembered from last time. With a smile, she greeted the receptionist and followed her into the lift. Hope was aware she was looking good—something that increased her confidence. Classy, elegant, understated. The more approachable Grace Kelly.

'Miss Taylor.' There were smiles and nods, followed by murmurs of sympathy for Lily. She noticed that Prue wasn't there.

'I'll need to get back as soon as possible,' she said firmly, taking the opportunity while they seemed amenable. 'How much more filming is there left to do?'

Glances were exchanged. 'Uh, Prue will be here soon. She has the schedule.'

'Is Prue ...?' someone murmured, and then stopped when a head was shaken.

Someone else piped up. 'You are coming to the dinner tonight? We'd certainly appreciate it.'

Suddenly Hope wished she could read minds, because these people were pretty good at hiding their thoughts.

At that moment Prue arrived, looking flustered, and Hope wondered if the girl had been crying. Obviously there were more things going on in her life than taking care of Hope, and she felt a momentary pang of sympathy. And then she remembered how Prue had been poking around and spying on her, and her heart hardened.

'They want you to go to the theatre where you had your first big break,' she explained, when they were heading downstairs to the car. 'Ken was meant to do it first thing, but he stuffed up. Sorry, I shouldn't have told you that, but it's true.' Her mouth went hard and tight, and Hope twigged to the fact that whatever was going wrong in Prue's life then Ken the cameraman was at the centre of it.

'We have a new guy, much more reliable,' she added, as she walked past Hope to open the passenger door, but her shoulders were rigid, as though she was keeping a careful hold on her emotions.

Hope decided against asking. A cool distance

was required. The girl's life wasn't her business, and after her behaviour with Lena, it would be impossible to trust anything she said.

The theatre was even shabbier than she'd remembered, although it held many fond memories. Hope was happy to wander about for an hour while the new guy took photographs and filmed her looking pensive. Those days had been good days, she admitted, and it was nice to revisit them—a little bit of an escape from her current reality.

Afterwards, Prue had arranged a lunch with some of the current actors and staff, and Hope found that pleasant, too. They were very interested in her and appreciative of her time, and she was flattered. Even when someone asked her about *The Document* it wasn't awkward and she was able to smile and move on to something more agreeable.

'Okay,' Prue said at last, when they were done. 'Thank you. That was fab.'

Even though the girl was trying hard to be positive and bubbly, Hope could see she was feeling miserable. Again, despite her resolution, she was tempted to ask her what was wrong, or offer some sympathy, until Prue turned away and the moment was lost.

'I'll stay here,' Hope said, not moving from the footpath outside the restaurant. 'I have something else to do.' She'd looked up the address of the nursing home and it was only a short taxi ride away.

Prue peered at her, shading her eyes against the

glare of the sun off the asphalt. For a moment, she seemed to be about to ask what that 'something' was and then she forced a smile instead. 'Okay,' she said, 'I'll see you later at the dinner. I'll pick you up.'

'No need. I'll get a taxi. Seven, wasn't it?'

Meeting the sponsors and doing her best to charm them was probably a small price to pay, and it might be a good idea to end her time with *Looking Back* on a high. Although, being nice to people didn't always mean they would be nice back, she thought wryly, as she watched Prue climb into her car and drive away.

The nursing home was old, but it had been nicely renovated. It certainly looked more presentable than Hope had been expecting, although the hospital odours of tasteless food and disinfectant hung about in the corridors. A glance into the sitting room showed a number of people on walking frames staring at a television screen while an American soap star strutted his stuff.

Jared was in his room and one of the nursing staff showed her the way. As they walked, she gave Hope a couple of sideways glances, as if she recognised her.

'Lung cancer,' she explained, when Hope asked what was wrong with him. 'Heavy smoker.'

'Is he bedridden?'

'No. He just prefers his own company. He doesn't mingle well with the others.'

'He's able to communicate, then?' She hadn't considered that until this moment, but the nurse put her mind at ease.

'Oh yes. He'll talk to you. It's just that sometimes he doesn't want to.'

She didn't sound terribly impressed by Jared, and Hope didn't know what to expect when she entered the room. There were only a few pieces of furniture in the small space—a chest of drawers, a bed and an armchair on which Jared was slouched. He was staring at nothing, while on the wall above and behind him was an old photo of a building she immediately recognised as the Angel in its heyday.

An oxygen canister had been placed beside his chair, but it wasn't in use right now.

'Mr Shaw?'

He looked up at her, his sunken eyes sliding down her body and then up again. 'Who are you?' he asked without the slightest attempt at manners.

'I'm Hope Taylor. I've come to ask you about my sister.'

He looked hard into her face, and then he smiled. She didn't like his smile and she didn't like him, but she made herself smile back. There was only the one chair, so after an initial hesitation, and seeing she had no choice, she perched carefully on the side of the bed so that she was facing him.

'You're Faith's sister,' he said.

The fact that he knew her and remembered Faith was a little surprising, but she was relieved that she wouldn't have to spend time explaining to him who she was. They could cut to the chase and— with a glance at her watch—she didn't have that long to do it.

'Got to be somewhere else?' he asked her with a nasty look. He didn't miss a thing. She wondered why he was in here. He didn't seem to be suffering from dementia, so perhaps it was just that he could no longer manage his illness on his own, or he didn't have any family to care for him. Or, more likely, Hope decided, if he did have family they had long ago washed their hands of him.

'I'm afraid I don't have long, Mr Shaw. Please, can you tell me anything about the time Faith worked for you at the Angel? It's important.'

He grunted. 'Not much to tell,' he said, and sank lower in his armchair. He was wearing tan trousers, a beige button-up shirt and slippers in a tartan pattern.

There was a pause while he considered whether or not to answer her, and she realised she could hear him breathing. A raspy sound, as if he was having difficulty drawing the air deep enough into his lungs.

'Was there someone Faith was particularly close to?' She tried again. 'It's just …' Hope paused, asking herself if she really wanted to tell him what had happened to her sister. And yet, if he could help, if it persuaded him to say something that would put the pieces together, then surely it was worth it?

'Just what?' Jared seemed interested despite his pretence at indifference.

'Faith has run away.'

For a moment he stared at her, and then he began to laugh.

Hope bit her lip, waiting for him to finish, and then tried again. 'When I say that she's run away I mean she's gone off to Queensland and we're not sure where. Everyone is very worried, Mr Shaw, and it seems to have something to do with her time at the Angel.'

The laughter had turned into a cough, and he reached for the oxygen mask. The canister hissed as he turned a valve and his gaze slid to her face over the top of the clear plastic, as if he was trying to read her thoughts. Or decide whether or not to help her.

'I visited the Angel the other day. It's certainly not looking as swish as in your photo.' She nodded at the wall behind him. 'Broken windows, trash everywhere. There was a homeless man. He said he used to work there. It was he who suggested I talk to you.'

That had captured his interest. He removed the mask. 'Lenny,' he said in a hoarse voice. 'Used to be our doorman. He visits sometimes, when they let him.'

'I see. Was he telling the truth? Are you able to tell me more about Faith?'

He shrugged. 'Not much to tell. She worked as a waitress in the Cocktail Lounge, downstairs. Sometimes, if they were busy, she'd help out in the Mezzanine, too. As a waitress she was okay, a bit too serious for the clientele, but she did her job. I had no complaints at the time. It was only later that I realised ...' But whatever it was he realised he wasn't telling her.

'Was there anyone she was close to? I mean,

anyone she might wish to meet up with again after all these years?'

'Doubt it,' he said. 'Everything went tits up around the time she left. She went home and I was glad to see the back of her. After the Angel closed, things were never the same.'

'I heard that the Angel was forced to close. Was there financial trouble?'

He looked at her with dislike. 'You really know bugger all, don't you?' he said with a shake of his head. 'The cops closed us down. That bastard Avery. I went to jail for five years.'

Hope felt as if the ground was moving under her feet. Why hadn't she known this? Why hadn't Faith opened up to her when she came home?

'Faith …?'

'What, you don't think she had anything to do with it?' His tone was bitter and angry, his eyes hard. 'She was Little Miss Innocence. Too bloody good to be true. I never trusted women like that and now I know why. I would have sacked her earlier if not for a friend of mine fancying her and wanting her to stay. I did him a favour there. Come to think of it, they deserved each other, those two.'

'Who? Who fancied her, Mr Shaw?'

But he'd put the oxygen back on and closed his eyes. She waited in case he would have more to say, but Jared Shaw was asleep, or pretending to be. She supposed she could sit here, see what happened, but she knew there wasn't enough time.

Reluctantly Hope got up and left the room.

Outside in the corridor it was quiet, the murmur of voices muted by closed doors. She was so deep in her own thoughts, she was halfway down the stairs that led to the reception area before she saw the woman standing there.

Faith!

Overjoyed, Hope almost cried out. Just for an instant their eyes met, and then the woman turned and was hurrying towards the entrance. The doors whooshed shut behind her.

She'd thought it was Faith! With her fair hair and delicate features, she looked so much like her sister … But now she had a chance to consider, she knew it wasn't Faith. Hope floundered, trying to connect the pieces, and then another name rose up from the past. *Kitty.* She hadn't been in contact with her cousin for a long time, and they'd never been close, but she was sure now that the woman she had just seen was Kitty.

What was she doing here?

Belatedly, Hope began to descend the final set of stairs, thinking if she hurried she might be able to catch up with her cousin. Then her steps slowed as she conceded there was no point. Kitty would be long gone.

Her thoughts returned to her conversation with Jared Shaw. Who was the man Faith had made such an impression on? It must be the same man who had rung her at Cantani Desserts and sent all of their lives into freefall. Someone at the Angel, someone she knew well.

Little Miss Innocent.

Hope supposed Faith could play that role, but she also knew that her sister was no fool. Far from it. Jared Shaw had gone to jail, which meant that something criminal had been going on. Faith would have known about it. So, what had her sister done to make Jared hate her? Because it was obvious he did.

Even after all these years.

26

FAITH

October 1969, St Kilda

SHE SAT UP, ready to leave, but Ray rolled over and pulled her down again. Faith laughed quietly as he smiled at her. 'Do you have to go yet?' he asked.

He would be in Sydney tomorrow night, and for two weeks after that. This was their last chance to be together until he got back.

She snuggled closer. 'I wish I didn't have to, but I need to wash some clothes or I'll have nothing to wear.'

'Hmm, interesting thought.'

He kissed her and it went on for quite a while. Faith wished she didn't have to get up, as she sighed and snuggled even closer against his bare skin.

'Weren't you telling me about the record deal? Before you got distracted,' she added, reminding him of their earlier conversation.

He rolled onto his back, tucking his arms beneath his head, and grinned at the ceiling. 'Yep,' he said. 'The people Jared knows in the business are very interested in doing a deal. We just need to show them our stuff.'

'Sounds exciting,' she said softly. She was pleased, she told herself. Ray deserved to return to the dizzy heights of a year ago, before he and the band lost their focus. He had talent and she wanted him to succeed.

Selfishly, on the other hand, she couldn't help wondering, if he did succeed, what it would mean for them. Faith was under no illusions about the music world; it was full of women who had no scruples when it came to throwing themselves at men like Ray. She'd seen what went on at the Angel. She wasn't sure she could hold him, and if he got bored with her and turned elsewhere, whether she would want to.

'Do you really need Jared to help you?' she said, running a finger down his chest. She could feel his ribs. He didn't eat enough.

'Why not? What do you know?' He turned his head to look at her, but she avoided his eyes.

'No reason. It's just …' she shrugged. 'I don't trust him, Ray. I don't think he has your best interests at heart. I think Jared is only looking out for Jared.'

A frown creased his brow. He caught her hand and seemed to be concentrating on their linked fingers, yet she knew he was considering her words. 'I owe Jared a lot. Without him …' he didn't finish, but she got the general idea. 'You know how things were after that hit last year.' He glanced sideways at her. 'Or maybe you don't. A hit and then a flop. They were calling us one-hit wonders, and that stung. So, we set out to do the hard work, playing in clubs and pubs, showing people that actually we were pretty bloody good at what we were doing. Now we have a following and it's time to try again.' 'But do you need Jared for that?'

He sat up, and now he was looking at her properly and she wondered if she had said the wrong thing.

'Faith, you need to know that Jared is willing to finance these new songs. He's paying for the tapes we've produced for the record company.'

'And what's in it for him?'

Why couldn't she just shut up? But she knew why. He didn't know what Avery was planning and she couldn't tell Ray, and she wouldn't be able to live with herself if she didn't at least make an effort to wean him away from Jared.

Ray said nothing for a heartbeat, and then he chuckled and fell back onto the bed. 'You're right,' he said. 'He doesn't do anything unless there's something in it for him.'

'And Mr Dalzell? Is he helping you, too?'

'Bert Dalzell? What's he got to do with it?' He sounded surprised.

She shook her head. 'I don't know. I don't like him, that's all. The way he looks at me.'

Dalzell had been in again yesterday, sitting at his usual table, sipping his whisky and watching as she served other customers. She'd thought maybe he was waiting for someone—perhaps Kitty— but when she'd mentioned Kitty was in the office, he'd smiled and said he wasn't here for Kitty.

What did that mean? she'd asked herself nervously, trying not to stare at him, pretending he wasn't there.

Eventually she'd looked up and he was gone, and it wasn't until then, as relief washed over her, that she'd realised how much he affected her.

Now Ray seemed to think it was funny. 'Dalzell? He's a character all right, but don't worry, he prefers to look. That's what I've heard anyway. He won't touch. Not if you don't want him to.' He met her eyes again, and she could see he was still amused. 'Do you? Want him to touch, I mean?'

'No, I do not.'

Faith got up at last, searching around for her clothes. She pulled on her skirt and zipped it up, and then tugged on her sweater. Her tights were bunched up and she pushed them into her handbag, and then sat down to pull on her boots.

He watched her lazily, but she liked it when Ray watched her. It was different from Dalzell. She wasn't afraid of Ray. Dalzell, on the other hand, frightened her.

'See you before I leave tomorrow night?' he asked her at last. 'The plane takes off at eight.'

'I'm not sure if I can change my shift.' Kitty always said it was best to keep men guessing, they respected you and were more inclined to stay interested longer. Games. Faith didn't like playing them, but Ray seemed to expect her to.

'Hey.' He sat up and reached for her hand, lifting it to his lips. 'Smile, gorgeous. Everything will be fine, you'll see.'

'Will it, Ray?'

His face fell. 'Ah, Faith.' He pulled her to him and wrapped her in his arms again, and she immediately felt better. 'Look, I've got an idea,' he began. And then, in a rush, as if he wasn't sure he was saying the right thing or even if she would want him to, 'Come with me to Sydney. You can say it's a holiday. Or just tell them to stick the job. What do you say, luv?'

His sudden offer was a surprise. Faith had been so anxious about him going, and she knew she should be over the moon and agree immediately. What was wrong with her? She wanted to be with him, didn't she? But the thought of being dependent on Ray, of following him around like one of the girls she despised, wasn't what she wanted either.

She pulled back slightly and found him watching her with a look that was at once hopeful and full of doubt. Oddly, it comforted her to know she wasn't the only one feeling like this.

'Ray … I can't leave, not just like that. What if your record deal doesn't work out? I'd have no home and no job.'

He forced a laugh, but she could see he was thrown even more off kilter. Perhaps he hadn't meant to ask her and was now regretting it. 'Not as if I'm asking you to marry me, babe,' he protested, making it into a joke, yet she could see he was hurt by her reaction.

'Anyway,' he went on, 'of course it'll work out. Jared says they already love us. We'll probably be relocating to Sydney. What then? Are you going to hitchhike whenever you want to see me?'

She leaned in to kiss him, and then hugged him tightly. 'If you go to Sydney then I will too,' she reassured him, feeling guilty now.

'Glad to hear it.' He was smiling again. 'Come and say goodbye at least? Wish us luck?'

Faith agreed, and their kiss lingered until she wondered if she could bear to go. Then Ray flopped back onto the bed with a yawn, wondering aloud what the room would be like in the hotel Jared had booked for them in Sydney. He was like an excited child, she thought with a wry smile, but then who could blame him? This was his big chance to show everyone that the All-nights were finally here to stay.

Outside, it was raining, and the street was shiny and wet in the glow of the lights from the buildings and the passing vehicles. A tram rattled by as she hurried along, head down against the cold, hands jammed into her pockets. She wasn't aware of her surroundings, too deep in her own thoughts, and it was only when she was approaching her house that she looked up.

There was a car parked out the front, under the streetlight, and she recognised it.

Joe.

Faith slowed and then stopped, not knowing what to do. His image popped into her mind—his smile and his eyes—and the thought of him was a joyful bubble inside her. But as much as she wanted to see him she knew she couldn't walk in there, not now. Joe knew her too well, and he'd know at once that she was hiding something from him. And once he knew he'd try to get her to tell him, and she couldn't tell him. He'd want her to come home, and she couldn't do that either.

Ray.

No, she couldn't see Joe. Not now. It was impossible.

Faith turned on her heel and had barely reached the corner when she heard the door to her house open. Voices. Joe and Kitty. They were talking, and then Kitty laughed. Faith hesitated, almost revealed herself, but then decided to stay put.

Joe started up his car and she heard him drive away. The door closed. She waited another beat before she set off back to the house. By now she was aching with weariness and a dark cloud of depression had settled over her. The thought of Sydney and Ray's big chance, and a new life for them both, should have filled her with excitement, but it just seemed too much to deal with right now.

She was inside and on her way upstairs to the bedroom when Kitty's voice stopped her.

'There you are!'

Kitty was looking up at her from the kitchen doorway. Her cousin's gaze swept over her, taking in her rumpled hair and bare legs, and she smirked.

'Your Joe was here,' she said, and turned back into the kitchen, adding, 'There's tea if you want some.'

What Faith wanted was a bath and to fall into bed and let oblivion take her. But she couldn't walk away from that comment. *Your Joe.* Slowly, reluctantly, she retreated down the stairs again.

Kitty was boiling the kettle, and Faith sat, setting her bag carefully on the floor beside her. Her head ached and she rubbed her temples, eyes closed. When she opened them, Kitty was watching her.

'I didn't think you'd be home,' Faith said automatically, feeling she had to make excuses for her own absence.

'I needed a night off,' Kitty replied evenly, although her eyes remained observant. 'I thought you'd be in by now. Joe waited for over two hours. Not that it mattered to me whether you were here or not. He was good company.'

Faith sat up straighter, making the other woman laugh in scornful amusement.

'Jealous? Come on, Faith, you can't have your cake and eat it, too.'

'I'm not jealous,' Faith mumbled. 'Joe is … well, he's nice.'

Kitty nodded. 'He is, isn't he? Joe is a rock. I get the feeling you could lean on him and he'd never give way.' She laughed again. 'I'm sounding very philosophical tonight, aren't I? Bert says I'm the voice of the common people. He thinks he's flattering me. He thinks he's anything but common.'

Faith wanted to say how much she disliked the man, but Kitty didn't let her.

'You should go home,' she said bluntly, and finally turned her back.

Faith heard her pouring the boiling water from the kettle into the teapot, and then she was rinsing mugs. The silence stretched out until she couldn't stand it any longer.

'I don't want to go home.' Her voice was husky with weariness.

'Why? Because of Ray?' Kitty sneered, as she carried everything over. 'Do you really think that's going to last? Once Jared gets him that record deal he'll be on the rise. He'll want a girlfriend who'll make him look good, not a kid from the country. It's what happens.'

She said it as if she knew from experience, and perhaps she did. There had been plenty of famous people who came through the Angel.

'Ray isn't like that,' she protested, but her voice sounded small.

Kitty began to pour the tea. It was barely drawn—weak and watery—and Faith looked at it with distaste. 'You've only known him five minutes,' her cousin said.

'He's asked me to go and live with him in Sydney. If he gets this deal.'

That made her stare, Faith thought—she hadn't been expecting that. And then she felt guilty for using Ray's offer in this tug of war with her cousin.

'And what? You've said yes? What about when he decides he's over you and dumps you? Don't expect to get your job back. It won't happen.'

'Ray loves me,' she said stubbornly, and she knew he did, right now. But what about in a month or a year? She wanted desperately to trust him and believe in him, but at this point she felt as if things were moving far too quickly for them both.

Kitty looked at her and sighed. 'Joe loves you,' she said. 'He's willing to wait until you get this … whatever it is, out of your system. You should go home with him. Ray can be nice enough, but he's only ever going to do what's best for Ray.'

'How can you say that?' Faith demanded, her voice rising. 'Why are you trying to send me away? I don't understand you!'

Kitty smiled without a trace of humour. 'I don't understand myself. I think I'm trying to save you, Faith. You remind me of me. It's not safe at the Angel. I can't always protect you.' She looked directly at Faith. It was like looking into a mirror. 'There are things going on and it's so easy to get drawn into doing things you'd never imagined you'd do.' Kitty shrugged irritably. 'I don't have to spell it out, do I?'

'What about you?'

Kitty drew pictures on the table with some spilt sugar, running her fingertip through the grains. 'Too late for me.' She spoke in a wooden voice. 'Anyway, I don't want to go. My life is here, and Jared … He needs me. You have no idea. He probably wouldn't let me go anyway because I know all the secrets.'

'What secrets?'

'What do you think? Things about Jared's partners in the business, the men who think they own him. Can't be too careful. Some people only listen to threats, and Jared knows their darkest secrets and has dates and places to back himself up.' She grinned. 'He has a book.'

Faith's head was spinning. Kitty knew exactly

what was going on at the Angel. What if she told Avery that, then what would happen? Would he offer Kitty a deal in return for information?

But she already knew Kitty would never betray Jared, and she would never leave him either. It was up to Faith to save her cousin whether she wanted to be saved or not.

'The police … wouldn't they have found the book when they raided the Angel?' She remembered seeing Jared's office, papers scattered everywhere.

'He doesn't keep it there. He keeps it somewhere safe, with someone he can trust.'

Faith tried to think—she was tired and her brain was sluggish. 'You mean Mr Dalzell?'

Kitty looked furious. 'Him? I'm the only one Jared trusts! I'm sorry I said anything, Faith. Go away and leave me alone.' Faith got up and dragged herself to bed.

27

SAMANTHA

16 January 2000

LINCOLN HAD NEEDED to talk to someone who was interested in marketing his sculptures, and while he went off to have a chat, I took Dad with me to the hospital. Gran was okay, a bit sleepy from the drugs, but her arm was finally in the cast.

She was pretty dopey so we left her to rest, promising to return later.

Dad had been feeding Pompom, but I offered to bring the ugly little dog back with me to Willow Tree Bend, just until Gran was home again. Mitch would hate it, but we all had to make sacrifices.

I questioned Dad about Mum on the drive home.

'I can't ring her,' he said with studied patience, which I recognised as him feeling the opposite. 'It's a private number and she hasn't shared it.'

'So a private house?'

'I'm not sure if it's a house.'

'What, then?'

'Sam, I don't know!'

I considered telling him about the photo, and what Lincoln and I had found at the library, but I didn't think it was a good idea. He knew Mum had had a phone call from a man, and that she had travelled a very long way to see him—they were the facts. All I had was speculation.

'Have you changed your mind about reporting her missing? Maybe the Queensland cops could make some discreet inquiries?'

He gave me a look. 'I tried interfering years ago, and it didn't get me anywhere. Don't you think I'd like to take off after her? Drag her home by her hair?' He took a breath and unclenched his hands from the steering wheel. 'She didn't tell me for a reason, Sam. She has something to deal with, and when it's over we'll hear all about it.'

What more could I say? I promised myself that if her new dessert release came and went, and Hope came and went, and she still wasn't home, then I was going to go up there myself and find her.

Once home, Pompom sprawled on the floor in the kitchen and gave a satisfied groan. I tried to get Mitch to join him, but he sat out on the verandah and gave me wistful doggy looks which I read as: *How could you?*

'I had to, mate. Poor Pompom, come on, he's not so bad.' Mitch didn't agree.

Hope rang as I was considering returning to my plans for the Dalzell garden, and we spoke about Gran for a while. I wondered aloud why it had been necessary for me to see a social worker, sitting in his cramped little office, the walls covered in posters about eating right and washing your hands, as he shuffled forms and frowned.

'What did he say? When he'd finished shuffling?'

'Only that sometimes, when an elderly relative has an accident, it may not be possible for the relative to return to their home. That was it, more or less.'

'Ridiculous! Lily will have a thing or two to say about that.'

Hope sounded tired, or distracted. I could hear the traffic in the background, so maybe she was out to lunch. Then I looked at the clock and realised it was well past that time and I hadn't thought to eat.

'Has she mentioned going to hell again?' Hope asked.

'I think she was too sleepy. Maybe she's forgotten about it.'

'Hmm.'

'She's had quite a few visitors. Friends and some of the other seniors from the units. I left her to it. I'll go back tonight.'

'Give her my love, then. I'll be back sometime tomorrow, all being well. Maybe Faith will have turned up by then.' But she didn't sound as if she believed it, and neither did I.

I'd stuck the photograph from the *Express* on the fridge, and now when I looked at it, the grainy face of my mother seemed to be staring out at me.

'Do you remember your cousin Kitty?' I asked. 'I was wondering if she might know what this is all about. I found out today that she and Mum worked together at the Angel.'

Hope gave a wry chuckle. 'You are a clever girl. And strange you should mention Kitty. She's been on my mind, too. Do you have any idea where she lives these days?'

'I think Mum had an address somewhere. They exchange Christmas cards, but that's about it.'

'Oh? I thought they were good friends? They used to be, anyway. I remember Faith thought Kitty was it and a bit. I was quite jealous for a time there.'

'Did she?' I tried to imagine my mother idolising her older cousin and supposed it was possible. 'Maybe they *were* friends once, but not recently. In fact, not for years.'

Hope murmured something in the background, an address, and I realised she was getting into a taxi. 'Have to go,' she said breathlessly. 'Duty calls.'

Reluctantly I said goodbye and hung up. I had a suspicion that my famous aunt was up to something and wasn't telling me. She'd been going to see that Jared person at the nursing home, but she hadn't mentioned it. Well, I told myself, there would be plenty of time to ask her about it tomorrow.

Pompom thumped his tail on the floor as I passed, completely at home, and completely indifferent to Mitch's misery.

In my work room, I spent a moment perusing the plans for Jason's garden. They were coming

along, but I would need to take some measurements if I was to do this job properly. And I was
keen to present him and Derek with something
that was as close to perfect as possible.

Taking a chance that he was there, I rang the
number. He answered after a couple of rings, and
to my relief said he was happy for me to come
out to his house. 'Derek's here, too,' he added.
'He arrived last night. He's keen to have a chat.' I
hoped that was a good sign.

Mitch came with me this time—honestly, I
couldn't keep him away—and we drove in the
afternoon heat, through Golden Gully and out
the other side. I noticed that Cantani Desserts
was open, with the sign out, and there were a
couple of cars out the front. Probably tourists or
prospective customers. Dad or one of the staff
would be in there, giving them the spiel, lying
about my mother's whereabouts.

How much longer could this go on?

I was hoping the visit to Jason and Derek would
take my mind off my worries, for a little while at
least.

Derek turned out to be younger than Jason,
with a narrow, tanned face and brown hair tied
back in a ponytail. As soon as I saw him I pegged
him as your typical alternative type, but his accent
was private school and then some. A rich boy
rebelling against family expectations? Maybe.

Mitch seemed to like him, anyway, which I
always thought was a good sign.

'We decided to put in a big week here at the
house,' Jason was saying, with a sideways glance at

Derek, as he led the way outside to the garden. 'We're aiming to open at Easter.'

I thought that might be pushing it, but smiled and nodded.

Derek snorted. 'She thinks you're insane,' he declared. 'And so do I. We need more time, Jas.'

Jason frowned. 'If we can't manage Easter then we shouldn't be in the business. It's perfect timing. Any longer and it'll be winter and no one will be making the trip up the highway. And we can't afford to wait until spring.'

Derek said nothing, even though he still didn't look convinced.

'We may need to find a tradey to help with the tricky bits,' Jason carried on smoothly, as if he had won that round. 'I'm sure Sam can help us find one.'

'We were going to do this on our own and take our time,' Derek reminded him with barely suppressed annoyance. 'A project to do together. Not something that must, definitely, no arguments, be completed by Easter!'

This was starting to turn nasty.

'Look,' I said, 'I can come back later if you're both busy.'

They looked at me, having completely forgotten I was there, and then Derek's shoulders slumped and he shook his head. 'No, it's okay. Don't mind us. We argue all the time.'

'Not all the time,' Jason muttered under his breath, 'just most of the time.'

Derek ignored him. 'Jas said you needed to take some measurements? Want to do that now?

I'd be interested in your thoughts. Jason tried to explain it to me, but it didn't make much sense.' He shrugged.

Jason gave me a long-suffering look. 'I'll be upstairs,' he announced, 'peeling off wallpaper.'

After he'd gone Derek continued on towards the back of the house. 'He's pretending to enjoy all of this, but I know it's for me, really,' he said over his shoulder. 'I thought it would be a good idea for the two of us to take some time out. Totally forgot Jason was a control freak and a workaholic.'

I couldn't help laughing at his droll tone. 'Good combination.'

The garden was wilting in the heat. We walked over to the side where the vegetable garden was to be, or the potager, as Derek called it.

'I saw one in the south of France when I was on holiday once. Loved it. I know it can't be quite the same, but I thought we could do an Aussie version.'

'Well, the climate is very similar, so you never know. What sort of plants were you thinking of?'

Derek had obviously given it a lot of thought, and we had a meaningful chat. I took my measurements and then we talked about the walled aspect of the garden, and he explained how he wanted to use some of the stone from the paddocks outside the fence. Evidently, when they bought the house they'd bought the land, too, but at the moment they weren't planning to do anything other than lease it out for agistment.

I told him about my own idea for a goldfields

garden, in keeping with the house and the area, and he was into that, too. He said he had a book that contained lists of plants that were in existence in the 1850s and 1860s, around the time the house had been built.

'Although it's been through some changes since then,' he admitted with a grimace. 'I think the original place was more or less a wooden hut with a verandah. As the Dalzells climbed the social ladder, they wanted something a tad more up-market.'

I shaded my eyes. We were standing in the middle of the yard, and I could see the big clump of the rosebush, and whatever it was that was under it. Last time I'd thought a pergola, but now it looked bigger than that, and was an odd shape. Mitch was gallivanting about like a kelpie half his age, probably eager to show me how much better he was than Pompom, who just slept all day.

'What is that thing?' I asked, pointing.

Derek looked over and grinned. 'I know, I've been wondering too. I had to ring up the local historical society and talk to someone who sounded about a hundred.'

'But they knew what it is?'

He smiled. 'You'll like this, Sam. The Dalzells were mad on horse racing back in the early nineteen hundreds. They bred a few winners in their time and one famous one was called Zanzibar. When Zanzibar died they wanted something suitable to commemorate him, and that's it.'

'So ... there's an entire horse under there?'

My face must have been a picture because

Derek doubled up laughing. 'Yes,' he said, when he could speak, 'an *entire* horse. That's a tribute to Zanzibar, or it was before Safrano took over. I'm not sure what can be done with it because, like the house, the memorial is heritage listed. We can't knock it down. Maybe, after we've finished the potager, we could take out the rose, although it seems a shame.'

I looked at the pale golden blooms glowing in the sunlight and thought, yes, it would be a shame.

'No hurry,' I told him. 'You should never be in a hurry to take anything out of your garden, or even to change what you have— unless it's weeds of course—especially in an old garden like this one. Take your time and see what happens during the year. Sometimes bulbs pop up in the spring or something that looks like a boring shrub will suddenly burst into stunning summer colour.'

He smiled, and although he probably thought he knew all of that, I could see he liked my attitude.

'Bert Dalzell,' I said tentatively. 'He was a bit of a character.' 'You could say that.' Derek looked at me.

'Jason showed me the photo he found. Dalzell seems to have walked out, left everything, and headed off to Queensland.'

'Yes. They say he went to ground up there, as far away from here as he could get. He left his wife and kids, too. A real charmer.'

'There was a place in St Kilda he had some involvement with. The Angel?'

His eyes lit up. 'Yes, I know about that. How do you?'

So, time to fess up. 'My mother worked there at the same time he was there.' *I think she's in the photograph.* But something stopped me going that far.

'Really?' His thin face cracked into a smile. 'Strange how coincidences happen—if they are coincidences and not the hand of fate. You know, after we'd bought the house, we were so full of enthusiasm that we told everyone what we were planning. And then one day Mrs Dalzell came into Jason's restaurant. We didn't know it was her, but she'd heard about our venture—"adventure" Jason calls it—and introduced herself.'

'What was she like?'

'Nice. Rich of course. I think her family had money, or maybe Bert squirrelled some away for her. She said she remembered the house with immense fondness. Not sure whether or not she was just being polite, but she seemed genuine.'

'You didn't ask her where Bert had got to?'

Derek shook his head. 'I thought about it, but Jason changed the subject before I could be a sticky beak.'

'The police searched the house?'

'Naturally. They searched the house and the garden. For a while they thought Dalzell was dead, so they had dogs, shovels, whatever was at their disposal in those days. They didn't find him. Don't worry, Sam, you're not going to turn over his mouldering bones when you start work here.'

After that the conversation moved on, and

Derek took me back to the house to show me the book he'd mentioned, although I already thought I knew the one he meant. Upstairs, I could hear a radio playing and the sound of the steamer as Jason dealt with the wallpaper.

'We're trying to get it down to the original layers,' Derek explained, as we sat at the table in the kitchen. 'See if there's anything worth saving. Jason wants the whole place painted white, but I'd like to keep some of the earlier paper. Gives the place character. And you never know, there might be a clue to Bert's whereabouts under there.'

'A map with X marks the spot?' I ventured, and made him laugh again.

We took some time looking through the plant listings, and I ticked off the ones I knew were still available. Specialist nurseries carried old-fashioned perennials and roses, or if necessary I could use newer versions with the same growing habits.

'I'm loving your ideas,' Derek said, although I thought a lot of them were his.

And that was fair enough, this was obviously Derek's baby, and even if Jason fell by the wayside, I thought he might carry on here alone. Hopefully though, it wouldn't come to that.

Mitch was lying panting on the floor and I was refilling his water bowl when Jason came down, dripping with sweat and covered in dust. He filled a glass with water and sculled it, and at the same time cast a look over the gardening books.

'Everything okay?' he asked, filling the glass again.

'Great,' Derek replied, smiling at me. 'I think

we're on to a winner here.'

Which was very flattering, and I told Mitch so after we left.

It was early evening by now, but the day still had a long way to run. At this time of day the heat was only just starting to wane, while the sun continued to blaze as it slid towards the horizon. Making sure we all remembered it.

I rolled down the windows and Mitch stuck his head out and lolled his tongue.

My thoughts turned to Bert Dalzell. Derek had said something about his car, a big black Rover, which he used to drive around the district.

'Like a lord of the manor who couldn't afford a Rolls Royce,' Derek had said.

'There's a ghost here, so I've been told,' Derek had added, ignoring the way Jason had rolled his eyes. 'But it can't be Bert, as he's up north somewhere. A man though. I haven't seen him myself, but a friend has. Youngish with blonde hair. Sounds a bit of a dish, actually.'

Definitely not Bert. When my mother came home I planned on asking her about Dalzell, among other things.

Golden Gully was quiet, the shops mostly closed, but the supermarket still had a few hours before Suzy could go home. She assured me that the bunches of flowers were fresh, and I bought one for Gran. I needed to wash and change—it was almost visiting hours. Dad had said he would be there, and I was looking forward to seeing him. Perhaps he had some news?

Perhaps my mother was on her way home and

had rung and … oh, I hoped so, I really did.

We needed her, and I hadn't realised how much until she was gone. And then I remembered that Hope was just a few hours away, and she'd said she wasn't going anywhere. The sense of relief was surprising. I'd never felt close to my aunt, never thought of her as someone I could look to for support or comfort. But now something had changed, and for the better.

28

HOPE

16 January 2000, Melbourne

THE DINNER DRAGGED on. Hope did what was expected of her, smiling and being charming, winning over the program's sponsors. It was all part of the game, and she knew that. She was earning her pay packet.

But behind her smile, where her real thoughts resided, Hope was in another place.

Sam hadn't known where Kitty lived, and Hope didn't insist she look it up in Faith's address book. There were many reasons she didn't want to let Sam know that she thought Kitty might be a key player in all of this, another of them being this mysterious man.

Although her niece already seemed to have an inkling.

Clever girl, Samantha.

She'd rung Jared Shaw's nursing home and charmed them into telling her where Kitty lived. She'd guessed her cousin must be a regular visitor and they'd have her address. It wasn't that difficult. And it helped that the girl on reception remembered Hope and, if she wasn't a fan, then her mother was.

It turned out that Kitty was Jared's primary contact. Now that was interesting. She'd like to ask Kitty why she was so concerned with the life of a man she had worked for thirty years ago.

But first she had to get away from this interminable dinner.

Finally, she felt able to make her excuses and venture out into the lobby. She chose a time when someone had told a particularly amusing joke and everyone was busy laughing. And Prue, who had been clinging close, had been called away to the phone. She hadn't come back.

Possibly, thought Hope, another argument with Ken the cameraman. Poor Prue. She certainly wasn't the bright and chirpy girl she'd been when Hope first met her. Just went to show, she told herself, slipping on her lightweight jacket, and then wondered what it *did* show.

That love was a waste of time and you were better off without it? Did she really believe that?

Pete's face came into her head, smiling, his blue eyes half closed against the brilliance of that long-ago summer sun. The best summer of their lives, and the worst. His memory shone brightly, his mother had made certain of that, but Hope had colluded. Was she really going to tear down the shrine Mrs Cantani had built to him?

And what choice did she have?

'Hope?'

Prue's voice was right behind her and made her

jump. She turned with a breathless laugh, hand to her throat.

'There you are,' she lied. 'I was looking for you.'

Prue gave her a knowing look. 'Were you?'

'Anyway, I have to go,' Hope went on, fastening the buttons of her jacket. The garment was a little old now, but so well made, and it never dated. She loved it. She tended to hang on to clothes rather than always go for the latest trends. Class had nothing to do with what was 'in' this season and everything to do with clothing that suited you and presented you in the way you wanted to be seen.

Had Faith told her that? She couldn't remember.

With a wave she set off for the door.

'I'll come with you,' Prue said, falling into step beside her. 'Are you going back to the hotel? I did want to have a little chat with you, Hope, if you don't mind.'

So it was *Hope* now, was it? When had she ceased to be Miss Taylor?

'Sounds ominous.'

'Not really.'

Abruptly, the last of Prue's happy, smiley face vanished and she gave a big sigh, wrapping her silk scarf around her throat as if she wanted to throttle someone.

'Actually, I was going to see my … a friend,' Hope spoke as they reached the door. 'I'll take a cab.'

Prue was adamant she would drive. 'Where does your friend live? We can talk on the way.'

Hope hesitated. If she told Prue and then Prue followed it up and used Kitty in the program, what then? But if she dillydallied much longer she would only further spark Prue's curiosity. Resigned, she searched for the address in her purse and smoothed it out, squinting in the poor light outside the hotel door. Why hadn't she brought her glasses with her? In the end she gave up, and casually handed it over to Prue, who flicked an uninterested glance over it.

'Okay, I know where that is. More or less,' she said.

As the car was brought around, Hope put a hand on Prue's arm. 'You don't have to do this,' she said quietly. 'She may not even be in. We can talk tomorrow. I'm not leaving until after lunch.'

'I *want* to take you,' Prue insisted. 'Really, it's no trouble.'

Hope sank back into the passenger seat, and Prue drove them carefully out onto the street. The traffic was busy and it seemed natural to remain quiet and allow the other woman to concentrate. Whatever it was Prue wanted to talk about, Hope thought it could wait. She had a hunch it was something to do with Ken and she really, really didn't want to be the recipient of her PA's romantic woes. Surely she didn't expect sympathy from someone she barely knew?

'Ken left me.'

Hope tried not to groan. 'I'm sorry to hear that, Prue. But he didn't seem all that … well, he was rather beneath you, I would have thought.'

Prue looked at her, wide-eyed, and then she

smiled. 'Thank you!' she said. 'Everyone else I've told has said how sorry they are and that perhaps I can win him back. As if I'd want to!'

'God no,' Hope assured her, keeping an eye on the road, something Prue didn't seem to be doing. 'Have a break off men altogether and then, if you still want to dive into the ocean, find a much, much nicer fish than Ken. And preferably someone who isn't in the same job as you. I find that never really helps. You just end up competing.'

She was speaking from experience, and Prue seemed to appreciate it. 'Thank you,' she whispered, blinking back tears.

'Is that what you wanted to talk to me about?'

Prue's pink hair was glowing in the lights from the passing cars, and she seemed so young and fragile. Maybe, Hope thought, she had got her wrong after all.

'No, that just came out. Sorry. I wanted to tell you about what Ken overheard when we were in Golden Gully.'

It turned out that it was Ken who had suspected Lena knew something about Hope's past. He had insisted they go back and get some film of Lena, and then Lena had told them all about Pete, and how she had seen Pete and Hope kissing.

'She made it seem rather nasty,' Prue said. 'Like a blue movie. Which I'm sure it wasn't. I had no intention of using it, or of mentioning it to anyone. I swear to you, Hope. But Ken did. And now that they know, they want to pursue it. I'm so sorry.'

Hope was sorry, too. Very sorry. This was the very thing she'd been afraid of when she spoke to Lena, but she told herself that at least now she was prepared.

'I really don't want Pete's family bothered with this,' she said softly, struggling with her words. 'When he was killed … it was a nightmare, really. I don't think his mother ever got over it. Truly awful and very sad. Well, none of us escaped unscathed.'

'He was my son,' Mrs Cantani had said, her voice icy as she stood squarely in the doorway. *'I won't have you drag his name through the mud.'*

Prue took a moment to answer. 'I thought it was something like that. Listen, I like *Looking Back*, and I think they do an amazing job, but I also believe that sometimes they can go too far. The public don't always have the right to know, not in my opinion.' She looked away.

'But they *are* going to talk about Pete in the show?'

'I think so. They've teed up an interview with your brother-inlaw, Joe. I don't think he knows what it's about, but you could give him a heads-up on that, maybe?'

'Oh God, poor Joe, that's all he needs.' She bit her lip, glancing at Prue, but the girl was staring ahead at the road. 'Thank you, Prue, I do appreciate this. And I'm sorry about Ken, but you're better off without him. He's too much in love with his own career to care about you.'

Prue smiled wanly. She began to slow the car. 'This is it, I think,' she said, peering out of the driver's side window. It had begun to rain. 'Yes, number forty-one. Are you sure you want me to leave you here, Hope? I could wait.'

'Under no circumstances. You go home. Or better yet go and have a drink somewhere, and a dance. Look, the lights are on, and I can see a shadow. I'll knock and when I'm done I'll call a cab back to the hotel.'

Hope didn't want Prue nosing around Kitty. She might seem nice and genuine, and she probably was, but if the chance came to leapfrog over Ken, who knew? Hope decided it was best not to put temptation in her way.

As the car drove away, Hope turned towards the modest-looking, single-storey house. The rain splattered about her as she hurried to the gate, unlatching it, and walked swiftly up the path to the front porch. The door had frosted glass panels on either side, and the glow coming through them was muted. She could hear a television.

She took a breath, and then put her finger on the white button.

The sound of the bell echoed inside, followed by footsteps coming towards her. She took another breath, realising she wasn't even sure what she was going to say. With Prue in the car she hadn't had time to prepare.

But then Kitty had seen her today at the nursing home and she would probably guess why she was here. Maybe she was even expecting her.

As long as her cousin didn't slam the door in her face.

29

FAITH

November 1969, St Kilda

GAZ HAD GIVEN her a note. Faith was pulling on her coat and preparing to leave the Angel, when he'd appeared. 'Faith,' he said, 'how are things?'

Which seemed odd as she'd only seen him a short while ago, when she went to the kitchen to collect a customer's order. And odder still was the piece of paper he slid into her coat pocket when he reached her, disguising the movement by putting his hands on her waist.

Surprised, she pulled out of his grasp and went to reach into her pocket. 'Best not,' he said, his voice too low for anyone else to hear. 'It's a message from our mutual friend. Wait till you get home.'

The look in his eyes persuaded her to do as he said. She glanced anxiously about and noticed Jared was at the door of his office, but silhouetted as he was against the interior light she couldn't tell if he was watching. All the same she forced a smile for Gaz as she said goodnight.

'And, Faith.'

She looked back at him.

'Be careful.'

All the way home it was as if the paper burned a hole in her pocket, but she resisted stopping to read it. Once she was inside her door, she ran upstairs to the bedroom and shut herself in. She sat down on the bed, not even removing her coat, and took out Gaz's note. It was creased, and she smoothed it out and held it up to the lamp until she was able to read the hasty scrawl.

Meet me at the same place at 11 tomorrow.

A chill ran through her, whether from fear or excitement she wasn't sure. She'd suspected Gaz was part of Avery's spider web of informants— either willingly or unwillingly—and this proved it. But that wasn't what was worrying her now.

She knew Avery would want to know what she'd found out and all she had to tell him was Kitty's revelation. Would that be enough for him? And once he'd learned about the secret book, what would he want her to do?

Faith was tired—it had been a long and busy night at work—but when she tried to sleep she found herself tossing and turning in her bed. By the time she eventually dozed off it was morning, and moments later she was awoken abruptly by one of the other girls slamming the front door.

Bleary-eyed, aching with weariness, she pushed aside the covers and went to the window. The sun was trying to shine, making her eyes water as it reflected off the wet street outside. Ray would be returning from Sydney later today, and he'd promised to call in on her tonight, when she was doing her shift at the Angel. The thought cheered her up, and all at once she noticed that the clouds seemed to have dispersed. Perhaps today wouldn't be so bad after all.

Faith dressed in a new frock she'd bought at Circe—black velvet with short sleeves and a white collar. She thought she looked a bit like Lulu in *To Sir, With Love*, although she didn't say that to Leanne, in case she got the lecture about the importance of being yourself. Maybe, she thought, feeling petulant, she was tired of being herself. Lately, being herself just seemed to get her into trouble.

To her surprise, Kitty was up too and scrubbing furiously at the stove. Her hair was tied back in a scarf, out of the way, and she was wearing some old jeans and a baggy sweater.

'Rent's going up,' her cousin sent her a frown over her shoulder.

'It'll go up even more if they see how filthy the place is.' Maybe that explained the slamming door earlier on.

'It wasn't my turn to clean,' Faith protested. She would have liked to make herself some toast, but she didn't fancy it with Kitty in this mood.

'Not mine either.' Kitty straightened her back and glared at her.

'Where are you off to this early?'

Faith was ready for her. 'We need milk. It's my turn to buy it.'

Kitty opened the fridge and looked in, then

grunted. Faith waited a moment, and when she didn't say anything more, she went out and closed the door.

The cafe was empty, and the girl behind the counter was halfheartedly drying some glasses. She looked up hopefully as Faith came in, and then scowled when she recognised her. 'He's out the back,' she said.

Avery was standing by the fireplace, although there were no cheery flames today. He had a small cylinder in his hand, the sort of clear container you get from a doctor or a chemist. He popped some pills into his mouth and tucked the cylinder back into his trouser pocket.

Since she'd last seen him he'd deteriorated. His face was very drawn and he'd lost weight— so much so that his suit looked too big for him. Avery was obviously ill and getting worse. He came over to the table, where there were two coffee mugs waiting, and picked one up.

'Am I late?' she asked, knowing she was.

'You're fine,' Avery said, taking a gulp of his coffee. He swallowed with difficulty, it seemed.

Faith told herself she wasn't worried about him. She barely knew him.

'You wanted to see me?' she asked, trying to keep the disquiet out of her voice.

He watched her as she sat down opposite him, drawing the other mug towards her. 'Wondered how you were getting on.'

'Jared doesn't like me. It's difficult to ask him things without him getting suspicious.' The truth was she couldn't ask him anything and hadn't even tried.

Avery sighed and admitted what she'd long suspected. 'It's Dalzell I'm interested in, Faith. He's the organ grinder, Jared is just the monkey.'

The room was cold and Faith wrapped her hands around the mug, feeling its warmth seep into her flesh.

'Ray says Dalzell doesn't touch the women in the Penthouse,' she said. 'He likes to watch.'

'Ray Bartel?' he asked sharply, and when she nodded, his mouth quirked into a smile. 'Young love,' he muttered, and shook his head.

'Ray's not involved. I haven't told him anything.'

Avery's face hardened. 'Best not to. He and Jared are good mates. He'd feel obliged to tell him about me. And you.'

She wanted to protest but stopped herself. She'd already decided not to tell Ray for similar reasons. At least if Jared was arrested now it wouldn't affect Ray's career. She'd had one phone call from him, just after he'd arrived, and he'd said it was all great and he had high hopes. He didn't leave a number so she couldn't ring him back, and anyway she told herself he could tell her all about it tonight.

Avery was leaning towards her, claiming her attention, and she forced her tired brain to concentrate.

'Maybe Ray's right and Dalzell does like to watch, but that's just at first. He watches until he's ready to participate, and then he likes to hurt. He puts his hands around the woman's neck and squeezes slowly, and all the while he's—'

Listening intently, Faith hadn't taken a breath, and she was glad when he stopped. Her imagination could finish what he'd started. 'Did Melanie tell you that?'

'He did it to her twice, maybe three times that I know of. It gives him a kick, and I can't see it being something his wife lets him do at home. She's a lady in every sense of the word and Dalzell likes young girls like Melanie, with the bloom of innocence not quite worn off. So, he asks his friend Jared to find them for him. Trouble is, this time, he squeezed too hard. Then he called on Jared to help get rid of the evidence. I reckon he promised it wouldn't ever happen again, and maybe he meant it when he said it, but I think he *will* do it again, Faith.'

Shocked, Faith gawped at him. 'Jared wouldn't let him hurt Kitty!'

'Jared might be a crook and a thug, but he doesn't believe in killing young girls for the sake of it. And maybe you're right, and he'd protect Kitty while he can. But even if he can hang on to his job and his girl, that won't stop Dalzell. If he can't have Kitty, he'll only set his sights on someone else.'

She didn't want to believe it was true, but she knew in her heart it was. Faith remembered the last time the politician had come into the Angel, and the way he'd watched her. The way Jared had encouraged him. Being Dalzell's 'type' made Faith's situation all the more dangerous.

In a moment of total clarity, Faith knew she

had only one choice, and being the girl she was, she made it.

'Jared has a book, a special book. He doesn't trust anyone, apart from Kitty, so he writes down names and dates, and amounts paid. In case he ever needs to use it to save his own skin. Kitty told me about it. She says the book isn't at the Angel, but she knows where it is.'

She felt an immediate sense of euphoria. She'd burned her bridges and there was no going back.

Opposite her Avery set down his coffee with a thump. 'A book?' he said softly. 'Oh, you're a good girl, Faith. I knew it the first time I saw you. You're worth your weight in gold.'

Faith's throat was sore from talking, and she felt queasy. The anxiety seemed to have gone to her stomach. She just wanted him to stop, but now that she'd told him about the book he went on and on. It was as if he could see his goal in sight and he was running at it full tilt.

'Right, I need to get my hands on that book, Faith. Can you think of a way to do that?'

'No. I don't know where it is. If it was in the house I would have seen it. Kitty and I share a bedroom and there's barely enough room to swing a cat. It must be somewhere else.'

'Would she be willing to bring the book to me if it meant saving Jared? He'll go to jail, I can't prevent that, but I might be able to see he gets an easier ride. Cut his jail time in half. If the book helps me to get Dalzell I'd be happy to kick Jared out of Pentridge after five years.'

'But Kitty will know it's me who told you!'

He held her gaze, and it was as if there was a flame in his eyes. 'I promise I'll do my best to keep you out of it, Faith, but there's a decision to be made. Yours as well as mine. If I don't get that book then Jared will keep running the Angel, and Kitty will stay with him, and even if you leave, she'll still be there. And even if Jared manages to hang on in his current position, one day he will owe Dalzell a big favour, and the payment for that favour will be Kitty.'

'Stop it,' she whispered. He was manipulating her, and yet what he was saying was very close to what she herself had feared might happen.

'Where's Kitty now?' he asked.

'At the house. She's cleaning the stove.'

'I'll send someone to pick Jared up, take him in for questioning, and then I'll go and have a bit of a chat with Kitty. Impress upon her the seriousness of the situation. I think you underestimate her, Faith. Your cousin is a clever girl. She'll come round to my way of thinking.'

'What about me?'

'You keep your head down. No one is going to know it was you. I'll look after you.'

She wanted to believe him, but a little voice in her head said, *Like you looked after Melanie?*

30

SAMANTHA

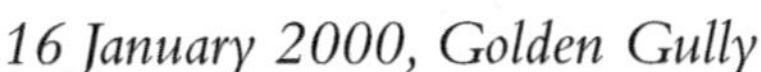

16 January 2000, Golden Gully

THE EVENING STILL had plenty of heat in it as I drove to the hospital. Dad would be there by now—I was late—but by the time I'd showered and daydreamed about Jason and Derek's garden, I'd barely had time to dress and feed the animals. The donkeys were giving me mournful looks, and the horses needed a good gallop rather than just frisking about in their paddock. Even my poor old chooks and Gobble ran after me as I securely closed their pens. I felt guilty I'd been neglecting them, and promised myself that after Gran was out of hospital, and Hope had left our shores, and Mum was home … Well, I would try to do better.

Mitch gave me worried looks while Pompom slept on, but I explained to him that the hospital wasn't the place for dogs, and I'd be back soon. He was sitting at the gate, watching me, as I drove away.

The hospital was busy, and it took me a while

to find a place in the small carpark. Walking towards the entrance, I noticed some clouds on the horizon, playing peekaboo with the glare of the dying evening sun. Maybe we were going to get another storm, but one with a bit more rain to it. I really hoped so. I might be able to pick up some more business if people actually thought there was a chance of their gardens thriving instead of crumbling to dust.

As I entered Gran's room, both she and Dad looked up at me with sparkly eyes, as if they had a secret they were bursting to tell me. Dad gave me a hug. He definitely had a spring to his step that had been missing earlier.

'Here she is,' he said, as if they'd been wondering when I would turn up. Which meant I had to apologise and make excuses.

My grandmother was looking alert despite her pallor.

'I'm trying to persuade your father to sign my cast,' she said to me, as I bent to kiss her cheek. 'There's an old chap in the next room whose cast is covered in jokes and smiley faces.'

'And you want to do better than him?' I teased her. 'Perhaps you should wait until you get home. What about all your friends in the units?'

'*Your* friend was here just now,' Dad said, a teasing note in his voice that caught my attention. Was this the surprise they had been bursting to tell me?

'My friend?'

'He means Lincoln,' Gran explained with a knowing smile. 'He's come to visit me.'

'I'm sure that must be it.' Dad's mouth kinked up into a halfsmile. 'It wouldn't be to impress Sam now, would it?'

I ignored him, for the simple reason that I wasn't sure what to say. It was too soon to talk about this, far too soon.

'He's just gone out to get us some jelly babies,' Lily went on, sounding cheerier than I'd heard her for ages. 'Much nicer than grapes, I always think.'

I couldn't help laughing. The thought popped into my head: *I'm glad I changed into my new blouse and skirt.* But why should it matter whether I turned up in this outfit or my daggy work clothes? And in fact, I had the distinct impression that Lincoln *liked* my daggy work clothes.

'Hadn't you better tell her?' Gran was looking at Dad expectantly, and I could see that, just like Mitch when he smelled lasagne, she was quivering with excitement. 'Go on then, tell her, Joe!'

I laughed. 'Tell me what?'

I could see by Dad's face that he was trying to hold in a variety of emotions and not doing a very good job of it.

'Your mother's coming home. She rang me this afternoon and I told her about Lily, and Hope, and … She's coming home.'

I felt a huge sense of relief, followed by anger, and concern, and then a mixture of all three. I waited for my father to say more, to explain to me what was going on, but he didn't.

'And?' I prompted him, hands on my hips.

His gaze slid to Gran and back, as if he was

implying that he wasn't going to tell me in front of her, but I knew it was an excuse. He just didn't want to tell me full stop. I accepted that possibly he didn't know the whole story, but he knew some of it.

Apologetically he reached out to touch my hand with his. 'Sam, she'll explain it to you when she gets home. I keep telling you it's not my story. She did say she was held up, that it hadn't turned out the way she'd thought it would, and that's why she couldn't leave in time to meet Hope at the cottage. But it's all okay now.'

Couldn't leave? Did that mean Dalzell had begged her to stay, or had she wanted to stay? And if that was the case then why was she coming home?

'Dear me, all of this mystery,' Lily spoke tartly, and I could see she was as annoyed as I was, but maybe not for the same reasons. 'Makes me hungry. Ah, just in time!'

Lincoln had arrived with his hands full of bags of lollies. He caught my stare as he dumped them on the table over Lily's bed, and his face was a bit flushed. Overkill, I thought, not sure whether to laugh or frown. What was he trying to do, send Gran into a sugar coma?

'Couldn't find jelly babies,' he said, 'but there must be something here you like, Lily.'

Lily was already using her free hand to work through the stash. 'Snakes, strawberries and cream … liquorice all sorts!'

'I didn't realise you'd be here,' I said to Lincoln, and then thought I sounded suspicious and ungrateful. I was neither, just floundering. 'I mean, I thought you'd be busy. Not that I didn't want to … Uh, how did that meeting go anyway?'

My father made a sound suspiciously like a snort. Or was it a laugh? I ignored him.

'Good. And when I got back to the cottage I finished *two* of my new songs,' Lincoln said, with another quick glance in my direction. 'Amazing. Really amazing. Must have been … the change of scene. So, I thought I'd try it again, see what happens, and here I am.'

'Two songs,' I repeated, and found myself grinning back at him. 'Wow. Do we get to hear them?'

He shuffled a bit. 'Maybe. Not yet. I have more work to do on them.'

Gran was soon tired, her eyes fluttering as she tried to keep them open, and we left her to sleep. Dad took most of the sweets with him for safe-keeping—'I'll give them back to her when she gets home,' he said.

Together we walked to our cars.

'I'm so glad Mum's coming home,' I said, smiling at Dad, and meaning it. 'I'll probably give her a hard time when I see her, but she deserves it.'

Dad laughed. He looked years younger suddenly, as if a tremendous strain had been lifted from him. 'Don't worry, she won't be getting an easy time from me either,' he joked.

I thought, *Oh yeah*. Dad was a big softy and he'd soon be completely under Mum's spell again. And actually, that would be nice, too. Everything back to normal.

'Okay, I'd better go,' he said, and I caught his

glance at Lincoln. 'You all right to get home?'

'I drove,' I informed him a little stiffly. 'I'm fine.'

As he turned away I was sure he was grinning to himself, but I didn't want to know. And the fact that he tooted his horn as he drove off was annoying, yet it was also rather endearing. My father hadn't been this childishly exuberant in a while.

'Good news. That your mother is coming home.' Lincoln had walked me to my ute—not that I'd asked him to—and seemed in no hurry to leave.

'Yes, very good news. I should ring Hope.'

And yet I made no move either. I told myself I was waiting for Lincoln to leave first, but the truth was I didn't want to go anywhere. I'd forgotten how nice it was to be in his company.

'Do you want to stop somewhere for a coffee?' he said, leaning his hand on the roof of the cabin as if he had all the time in the world. And then, with his eyes narrowing, 'Have you had dinner, Sam?'

I smiled. 'Can you hear my stomach rumbling again? No, I haven't. I was running late. I decided at the last minute to go out to see Jason, and it turned out Derek was there, too, so we had a talk about the garden. He's very enthusiastic. Time got away from me.'

Lincoln was smiling as I spoke, as if he could imagine the scenario all too well. 'Come on,' he said, 'why don't I take you to the hotel and we can have a counter meal?'

'Are they still serving?' I glanced at my watch.

'They'll serve me,' Lincoln replied with a certain arrogance, and I found myself laughing.

'Listen to you,' I teased him. 'Do you always get what you want, Mr Nash?'

He reached out and took my hand in his, and I was too surprised to do anything about it, and then I didn't want to.

'Not always,' he said, examining my fingers, 'but that doesn't stop me trying.'

Lincoln was right, they did serve us despite the kitchen being on the verge of closing. Although it turned out our star status wasn't all to do with him. The manager came into the empty dining room to confirm that I was Hope Taylor's niece, and then to tell me in a slightly boastful voice about being on camera with her.

'I'll be on *Looking Back*,' he said with satisfaction. 'Good publicity,' he added quickly, in case we thought it was all about him.

I was trying not to laugh, not looking at Lincoln, but when we were alone again I couldn't resist saying, 'My aunt seems to have eclipsed you, Mr Nash.'

'I'll rise again,' he retorted. 'You wait and see.'

The meals arrived and I asked him if he was still going to sing his new songs at Estelle's Valentine's Day charity event, and he said he was, with an enthusiasm I couldn't doubt.

'I feel as if I've broken through a brick wall,' he said, pausing with a forkful of steak halfway to his mouth. 'I've been struggling, but that's just the way it is. And then, out of the blue, along comes someone who turns out to be your muse, and everything is flowing again like magic.'

'My grandmother will be thrilled.'

He glanced at me, opened his mouth as if to refute that, and then changed his mind. 'The cottage is helping,' he went on after a moment. 'I think living amongst all of that history is good for the imagination. The five boys lying in one bed … great stuff.'

'So, these are folky songs?' I said, trying to sound happy about it.

He seemed to read my mind, and his eyes gleamed. 'Sort of,' he answered, and then a smile broke through. 'I said I'd sing "Dark Star" and I will. It won't be the same because it won't have a backing band. But you might like a stripped-down version, you never know.'

'Of course I'll like it!' I scoffed, although I was secretly worried I wouldn't.

He was still watching me. 'The girl at the supermarket—Suzy, is it?'

I waited for him to go on. I knew my face was warm so I was probably turning pink. What had Suzy said? I hated her, I was never going to help her out with her garden again.

'What about Suzy?' I demanded, when it was clear he wasn't going to tell me without some response from me. 'And by the way, we went to school together, and I grew up and she didn't. She still thinks it's funny to drag up nonsense from years ago.'

I thought that had about covered all bases, so why was he laughing softly to himself? He wiped his eyes and sighed, leaning back in his chair and looking at me. Just looking.

'Lincoln?' I murmured, wondering what on earth was going on.

'Sorry,' he said, and sat forward. 'You're just so … Everything you feel is right there on your face. You're totally transparent.'

'I am not,' I protested. 'Am I?'

He nodded. 'You are.'

Sade was playing in the background, her mellow voice a perfect accompaniment to the evening and our intimate meal. I half listened to her, lost in contemplation. If I was so easy to read then maybe I should work at changing that? How embarrassing. Did that mean he'd recognised my fan-girl feelings from the beginning? Everything, laid bare?

Lincoln seemed to realise I was rather over-whelmed by this news because he changed the subject and began to ask me, quite gently, about my mother.

So, I told him about Mum, how she had come home from the Angel all those years ago, fallen in love with Dad and married him. After I was born, she began to think about what else she was going to do with her life. It wasn't that she didn't love being a mother, just that she was the sort of woman who had to have several irons in the fire. So Cantani Desserts was born and had gone from strength to strength. From a niche market to a local icon to a worldwide phenomenon, or at least I believed, if my mother had her way, it soon would be.

'That was why it was so unlike her to go off

like that. She's always there, for me and Dad, for Gran, and for the business.'

'It must have been something very important,' Lincoln said. 'Something that couldn't wait. She seems the sort of person who sets priorities, and for this to take precedence over everyone and everything else …'

Of course he was right. My mother had given this journey to Queensland top priority in her busy life. She hadn't gone on a whim—how could I have thought such a thing!—and nor was it some midlife journey of discovery.

I still wished she'd told me what was going on. I didn't think it was fair or right that she hadn't.

'Maybe she didn't expect to be away this long,' Lincoln replied, when I spoke aloud. 'She might have thought it would be all over by the time your aunt arrived, and she'd have plenty of time to talk to you about it. Your father said she was held up, didn't he? Something must have happened up there that meant she couldn't get home again, not until now.'

'I still think it has a lot to do with Bert Dalzell. Those photographs and the Queensland connection … There are too many coincidences.'

'They could be just that, coincidences,' he said, playing devil's advocate.

'Hope thinks there's a connection, too. I can tell. She's busy nosing around in Melbourne right now. She wanted to know cousin Kitty's address, and Kitty was at the Angel with Mum.'

'Have you asked Hope what she knows?'

'Of course I have! She won't tell me, or at least

she slides around the subject. She's very good at it actually.' I gave a big grumpy sigh. 'I want to *know*.'

'Sam, sometimes waiting for a thing makes it all the more special.'

I had the feeling he was saying a lot more than the words seemed to suggest. I struggled to work it out, or maybe I was afraid to believe what my own ears were hearing.

'Come on,' he said. 'We'd better go before they throw us out.'

I wanted to tease him and say that no one would dare throw Lincoln Nash out, but I was feeling a little bit out of my depth. Together we walked to the hospital carpark, where we'd left our cars. No holding hands this time, but we were close, shoulders brushing, and I could feel the warmth of his body and smell his aftershave. It felt as if we were on the verge of something, but I wasn't sure what and I didn't want to jinx it by pushing too hard. 'How did you end up in Willow Tree Bend?' I asked him, realising I had never asked this particular question, and right now it seemed important.

'Derek told me about it,' he said, and I could tell by the tone of his voice that he was smiling. 'After he and Jason bought their place, he did some exploring in the district and came across your cottage. Thought it would be just the thing for a failed singer and song writer to regain his muse.'

'Another coincidence,' I murmured.

'Yes, they keep cropping up.'

We'd reached the ute. Time to say goodbye, although it wasn't really a forever sort of goodbye. I reminded myself that Lincoln would be playing for Estelle, and then there was Gran, who seemed to have developed a crush on him, or was it vice versa?

Lincoln, I told myself with relief, wasn't going anywhere.

'I didn't finish telling you what Suzy said,' he spoke softly. I felt his breath stir my hair. 'Or the question I asked her.'

'No,' I sighed. 'Come on, then, what was it? I bet she told you about the poster of you I had on my wall, didn't she? In my defence there were others. I liked INXS, too.'

He looked a bit startled. 'No, it wasn't that,' he said, 'although I'm a bit miffed to hear you had Michael up there as well as me. I would have thought I deserved top billing on your bedroom wall.'

I laughed, I couldn't help it.

'No, I asked her if you had any men in your life, anyone special at the moment, and she said you don't.'

'Oh.'

We were close enough so that, when his lips brushed against mine, we didn't have to move much at all. I just leaned into him and he slid his arms around my waist, and we let our mouths do the rest.

'Thank you, Suzy,' I whispered, when I came up for breath.

He muffled his laughter in the angle of my

neck, sending tingles up and down my spine.

I would have liked to take him home with me, but it was too soon. Seriously, I couldn't do that to my heart.

'Lincoln,' I began, but he was ahead of me.

'We'll take it slow,' he said, tucking a strand of my hair behind my ear. 'Slow is always best, something I've learned over the years. As long as you want …'

Was that doubt I saw in his eyes? Well, what did you know. 'Oh yes, I want,' I said. 'Very much. But slow is good.'

He nodded, hesitated as if he wanted to kiss me again, and then stepped back. And then again, until we had a good distance between us.

'Goodnight, Sam,' he said.

I watched him walk away. Everything was tingling and spinning, and my heart was thumping, and I felt as if I might be able to fly. I knew the signs. I told myself I should force my feelings back into their box and lock it up tight, but the truth was I didn't want to.

Lincoln Nash wanted to be my man, and I sure as hell wanted to be his woman.

31

HOPE

16 January 2000, Melbourne

KITTY'S HOUSE WAS reasonably clean, Hope decided, but with the sort of untidiness that comes of someone not having enough time to put things away. Her cousin hadn't slammed the door in her face, or even looked very surprised. She'd simply stood back and let her inside.

In the lounge, magazines and books were scattered about on the furnishings, along with quite a few cups and plates from the day's meals. Hope wasn't judging her; she imagined she'd be the same if she didn't have room service. Anyway, the place felt comfortable, as if the person who inhabited it was at peace with herself.

Kitty had said she was divorced and lived on her own, and that she had no desire to share again. Having her own space suited her. Her two daughters had grown up long ago and left home, and one was studying and one was overseas. Shown some photographs of the girls smiling at the camera, Hope thought they looked a lot like

Kitty.

'They do their own thing and I do mine,' Kitty said, returning the frames to their position on top of the television. She'd been watching a movie, but now she switched it off and nodded to the sofa. 'Sit down.'

Hope had had plenty of time to observe her cousin by now. She was the same and yet different, older certainly, although her face still retained much of the pretty girl she had been. That was one thing you could say about Lily's family, they aged well.

'This *is* a blast from the past,' Kitty said, flopping down on a chair and crossing her legs. 'Not often I have a famous Hollywood actress in my house.'

'Not so famous now.' Hope took the sofa. That was when she noticed there was a distinct odour of dog in the air, although she couldn't see one.

Her cousin was watching her. Waiting, thought Hope, for her to confess to spotting her at Jared Shaw's nursing home. Apart from that moment when she opened the door, when her eyes gave her away, Kitty had said nothing about this afternoon. Clearly she wasn't going to make this easy.

Hope had never had as much to do with Kitty as her sister. Kitty was nearer to Faith's age, and Hope was aware that her sister idolised her cousin. There were times when she'd been jealous of that— how they'd whispered together as teenagers whenever Kitty was visiting, and then fallen silent when Hope entered the room. She'd always been relieved to see Kitty go home again, so that she could have Faith all to herself.

She glanced around at the room and knew she didn't have anything to be jealous of now. Kitty's life had been relatively pedestrian compared to hers. She told herself to stop it. This wasn't about silly past resentments. This was about her concern for her sister and, she hoped, Kitty's, too.

Time to cut to the chase.

Hope leaned forward and fixed Kitty with a direct look. 'I saw you today.'

Kitty smiled and raised an eyebrow as if she was at perfect ease, but her upper leg was jiggling up and down. 'You may have. I do go out most days. I have a part-time job at a cafe.'

'I was at a nursing home, visiting a man called Jared Shaw, and I saw you there. The receptionist gave me your name, but even before that I knew it was you, Kitty.'

Kitty frowned and Hope thought she was going to lie, prevaricate, or waste time with silly games.

'I came because I want you to talk to me,' Hope said quietly, trying to impress her cousin with the gravity of the situation. 'I need your help.'

Kitty looked surprised, but she was biding her time, picking at a hole in the stretchy material of her black leggings. Hope waited her out and eventually the other woman began to speak.

'Look, you obviously know who Jared is or you wouldn't have been visiting him. What sort of help can I give you? We haven't seen each other for over thirty years, and even then we weren't that close. You never liked me, Hope.'

She thought about denying it, but there seemed

no point. Kitty was right, she hadn't liked her then and she probably didn't like her now.

'This isn't about you and me. It's about Faith. She's gone AWOL and I think it's to do with her time at the Angel. I wanted to ask Mr Shaw about her, but he wasn't very forthcoming. And he wasn't very complimentary about her either.'

Kitty gave a snort of laughter. 'No, I don't suppose he was.' She fiddled with the loose blouse she was wearing over the leggings. It was green, like her eyes. She looked good, but as Hope remembered she always did have a certain flair.

'Where has she gone?' Kitty asked abruptly.

'Queensland. The top part, I think. She had a phone call and a few hours later she was in the air. There was a man … someone she knew from the Angel. Joe thinks it's Faith's story to tell, but I can see he's worried. Samantha, too. And now Lily is in hospital. What is it all about, Kitty?'

'How should I know?' Her eyes narrowed.

'You worked with her, she lived with you, and after she came home there was a rift between you. Something happened. Just a guess,' she added wryly.

Kitty fiddled with her blouse again, pleating the hem. 'Is she still happy with Joe?' This time she looked up directly into Hope's eyes. 'I used to think there was nothing that could put a wedge between them. Nothing except for the Angel, that is, and back then Joe was willing to overlook that.'

'Overlook what?'

But Kitty wasn't prepared to answer that question.

'Did you know it was Faith who closed down the Angel?' she went on. 'Oh, the police took the credit, but she did their work for them. Jared went to jail. They dragged Dalzell down from his dizzy heights. Not that I minded—he wasn't a … nice man. He scared me and plenty of others. No one was willing to make him stop, until Faith did it.'

Hope felt the shock trickle through her like ice water. It took her a moment to find her voice and she hoped her face didn't betray her. 'Bert Dalzell was involved?'

'Of course. Don't you know anything?' she said with a scornful glance. Jared had said much the same thing. Treating Hope like a fool who hadn't done her research.

'He had a house in Golden Gully,' Hope went on, not sure why she said it, not sure why she was prodding at this particular sore.

'Yes, Faith told me. She thought he was some sort of local hero until I put her right.'

Hope wasn't warming to her cousin. In fact, she was beginning to remember just why she had never liked her. 'Samantha said there was an old photograph found in the house. Dalzell and a woman she thought was Faith. Was it you?'

Kitty shrugged. 'Probably.' She paused. 'I was worried about Faith, if you want the truth. I was sorry I'd offered to find her a job, and especially there. But by then it was too late. I had no idea that she—'

She bit her lip.

'Honestly? In the beginning I thought life at

the Angel was exciting, on the edge, you know. It didn't seem real half the time. Faith made me see how real it was, and when she changed towards me—looked at me differently—I understood just what it was doing to me. I needed to get out and she gave me that opportunity.'

Hope tried to imagine her sister riding to war like some Joan of Arc figure. Faith had only been seventeen. True, she was strong and she had a propensity for standing up for those weaker than herself, but to bring down a gang of underworld criminals? It seemed a little too incredible.

Kitty was still talking.

'Afterwards I was let off with a suspended sentence. Avery made sure of that; it was one of the last things he did while he was in the job, poor bastard. I found work and forgot about the past, and soon I met a man and we had a family. I'm not saying everything was perfect—what is?—but if I'd stayed where I was, with Jared, I'm pretty sure I wouldn't be alive today. I remember Faith telling me that, and the annoying thing was she was right.'

The corners of her mouth lifted in a smile that made her look twenty-one again.

Hope let that sink in. There were questions, and she was certain Kitty was leaving out whole chapters from her story, but at least she was beginning to get somewhere. The pieces were falling together even if they weren't quite in order.

'I don't understand why you visit him? Jared.'

Kitty shrugged. 'It just sort of *happened*. I'd lost touch when he went to jail, put him out of my mind, but then I heard he was there from someone who had a relative in the same facility. It wasn't an easy decision. There were some good memories between the two of us, as well as some bad, but I wasn't looking to rekindle our romance,' she said with a wry look. 'In the end, I think it was picturing him all alone in that place that did it. I felt sorry for him.'

'And maybe the fact that he's dying?' Hope murmured.

Kitty sighed. 'That, too. I went the once, thinking that should be enough, but he was so glad to see me. And I enjoyed the visit more than I'd thought I would. I'd forgotten. I used to love him, really love him, and I'm pretty sure he loved me. We still had that connection. I know he did some bad things, but he looked after me, kept me safe from the likes of bloody Bert Dalzell. Lately he's told me a bit about all of that, things I didn't know at the time. Once Jared was arrested Avery went at him hard, but it wasn't him he was after, it was Dalzell.'

Hope waited a beat. 'And yet Dalzell got away,' she said quietly.

'His friends got him bail and he went up to his place in Golden Gully to escape the press. By then he must have known it was only a matter of time before he went to jail, too. Avery had it all set to go. And then Dalzell was gone, just vanished. That finished him, I think. Avery, I mean. He gave up after that. Dalzell was the only reason he was hanging on.'

Hope was trying to integrate this story with

her own, and meshing the pieces together made her feel quite dizzy. She wiped her palms on her jacket.

'Did Dalzell know it was Faith who helped the police? Was he ever told?'

Kitty looked away, chewing her lip, and that was enough for Hope. Quite suddenly, everything about that hot summer's day, everything she'd believed to be the truth, was turned on its head.

'What?' Kitty's gaze was back on her face. 'What have you thought of?'

Hope said the first thing that came into her head. 'Sam thinks Faith has gone up north to meet up with Dalzell.'

Kitty gave her a disbelieving look. 'No way. Never in a million years. Do you know he tried to strangle me once? Dalzell. Had to wear a scarf for weeks until the bruises faded. It was supposed to be for his birthday, and Jared caved in—Dalzell must have had something over him—and asked me if I'd do it. For a favour. Only it wasn't just sex, he wanted a bit more than that. I've thought about it since and maybe it was the only way he could get off. Ejaculate, you know?'

Hope's hands were shaking and she squeezed them hard together, trying to calm herself.

'Shocked you, did I, Hope?' Kitty asked, looking pleased.

'Not in the least.'

Kitty smiled, and then seemed to come to a decision.

'You were asking a minute ago why I would

want to see Jared again, and I told you there was a connection. We share a past. Maybe that's what Faith is doing up north. Maybe she's still got a connection.'

'That's not enough,' Hope retorted. She was feeling angry now. Kitty knew the truth and Hope was damned if she was going to let her get away with fobbing her off with this philosophical crap. She needed answers, for the sake of Sam and Joe, but more than that. She needed to know for her own peace of mind.

'Tell me who this "connection" is. Who could have such a hold over my sister that she'd drop everything and fly from one end of Australia to the other, all for a single phone call?'

She really didn't think Kitty was going to answer. The room was quiet, apart from the passing traffic, and then a dog finally wandered in. It was an old golden labrador, and he slumped down by Kitty's feet, awkwardly arranging his arthritic paws. Automatically, she reached to gently stroke his head and he closed his eyes.

'I always wondered,' she said to herself, 'whether that particular problem would come back to haunt her. I hoped not, I really did. Joe was perfect for her, and only Faith couldn't see it. I used to get a bit jealous when he came down to Melbourne to visit her. Not that Joe thought much of me. After she went home, she stopped phoning me. That was Joe, I reckon. He blamed me, but I only wanted to help her. That's all I ever wanted to do.'

'Maybe they just needed to put the past behind

them,' Hope said, using her sympathetic voice, yearning for it to persuade her cousin to confide.

The dog sighed and lay down and almost immediately began to softly snore.

Kitty made her decision.

'All right. I'll tell you what you want to know, Hope. But don't blame me if you end up wishing you'd never asked.'

32

FAITH

November 1969

AVERY SAID SHE was to behave as normal, so Faith went and bought some milk to take back to the house. The queasiness was worse than ever and she wondered if she'd caught the tummy bug that some of the staff had complained of. Or was this the consequence of playing God with people's lives? Anxiety always did go straight to her stomach.

She could hear the radio before she opened the door—'La La' by the Flying Circus—and Kitty singing along. She wasn't keeping in tune, but she was enjoying herself. Faith bit her lip, feeling a hysterical laugh welling up. It would be all right—she had to believe that—and then she strode into the kitchen when all she really wanted to do was go up the stairs and climb into bed and pull the covers over her head.

'Milk,' she said, opening the fridge to put it in.

Kitty looked up, her face sweaty and dirty. She was working in the oven now. 'You took your time.'

'I had a chat with the boy in the shop.'

'Nice for some,' her cousin muttered. 'When's Ray coming back?' She opened her mouth to say today, just as someone started pounding on the door.

Kitty stood up, clutching at the stove top to keep her balance. 'Who the hell is that?' she demanded, startled.

'Do you want me to get it?' Faith moved in that direction, but Kitty was brushing past her.

'No, I'll do it.'

She heard her cousin's bare feet on the wooden floorboards, and then the sound of the door opening. There was silence while Faith held her breath, and then …

'Get out of here!' It was a screech. Kitty was running, going for the phone, but Avery was behind her. Faith huddled into the corner, out of the way, as they careered into the kitchen. Avery got there first.

Straight away, Kitty turned around, making for the open door, but he caught her arm and held her, slamming her back against the fridge hard enough to make her breath *oomph* out. The recipe books that had been resting on the top thumped down onto the floor, scattering around their feet.

'You're hurting her!' Faith cried. 'Let her go.'

She wasn't sure he was hurting her. Kitty looked red-faced and furious rather than injured, but Avery was crowding her, intimidating her.

'Jared's in custody,' he growled. 'Are you listening? Lover boy has been arrested.'

Kitty went still, her eyes on his. 'What?' she seemed confused. 'He hasn't done anything! You can't just—'

Avery sounded annoyed and very weary. 'Oh come on, love, we both know that's not true. He helped Bert Dalzell dump Melanie's body. And then he helped him cover it up.'

'What are you talking about?' Kitty was shouting, and the radio was still blaring. Avery went over and turned it off. The silence was a relief, but only temporarily. The detective was leaning against the doorjamb, blocking the way out, but Faith doubted that would stop Kitty. This wasn't what Faith had thought it would be like, this violent confrontation. She'd thought they would talk in a civilised manner. Persuade her cousin with words and argument, not this hostility. She might as well not even be here. She was a ghost and Avery hadn't looked at her once.

'I know you have information,' he was saying. 'You can help Jared. At the moment, your boyfriend is going to be charged with Melanie's murder because Dalzell will say Jared killed her. You know he will. He'll expect Jared to take the blame for him.'

Was that true? Faith didn't know. Kitty was shaking her head, not wanting to believe it either, but she didn't seem quite as full of conviction as before.

'Jared wouldn't take the—' she began, her voice shaking with fury and frustration.

'Oh, but he would. Dalzell has friends who'll back him up. Jared knows this. That's why he has his little book of secrets, isn't it? Just in case?'

'How do you know—'

'If Jared goes down, you know what will happen, don't you, Kitty? You'll be all alone and unprotected, won't you? With Dalzell.'

Kitty was staring at him as if he was a snake and she was the rabbit. Faith was staring at him, too, because she'd only just realised just how much Avery actually knew. She'd thought herself so clever, feeding him little bits and pieces, protecting her cousin, and all along he had known everything.

For the first time he looked at her, swinging his eyes towards Kitty and back again. Faith knew what he wanted and she felt like refusing, but it was too late. They had come too far. And besides, she knew Avery was right, despite the way he was going about it. Without Jared to protect her, Kitty could end up dead.

She extracted herself from the corner. Her head was spinning and that sick feeling was still twisting her stomach, but she couldn't worry about that now.

'Kitty,' she said, and slid an arm around her cousin's waist. She fully expected to be shoved aside, hard, but Kitty stood stiffly at her side as if she wasn't even aware of her. 'Maybe he's right,' she went on, with a glance at Avery and then away again. 'I mean, without Jared there … You told me that was the only reason you were safe, remember? So, if Jared goes to jail …'

Kitty gave a shudder—it seemed to be coming from deep inside her. She ripped off the scarf she'd used to bind up her hair, and the fair locks came tumbling down around her face. 'You want the book,' she said matter-of-factly.

Avery nodded. 'I want the book.'

'Who told you about it?'

He shrugged. 'Jared isn't very smart, he lets these things slip out. People he thinks are friends, people he trusts. It's a wonder Dalzell hasn't heard about it and come looking for it. Although he wouldn't dirty his hands, would he? He'd send someone else.'

'There's stuff in it about Dalzell. Dates and payments and to who, girls he wanted and who we had to persuade to spend the night with him in the Penthouse. Sometimes that wasn't easy. His idea of pleasure isn't everyone's.'

'What about you? Have you spent some time with Dalzell, Kitty?'

Her jaw tightened, the corded muscles of her throat standing out, as if she was fighting the urge to scream.

'I thought so,' Avery said in a quiet voice that was sympathetic enough to reach through Kitty's hostility.

Faith felt the tension go out of her cousin's body, felt her weight resting against her.

'All right,' she whispered. 'You win.'

Kitty insisted on washing her face and changing her clothes first. Halfway up the stairs, Avery said, 'Don't climb out of the window.'

Kitty made a sound that could have been a laugh. 'That's not my style,' she said, as Faith hurried after her.

'I think you're doing the right thing,' she said, as her cousin scrubbed the filth from the oven off her hands, and splashed water onto her sweaty face. 'I've seen Dalzell look at you.'

Kitty reached for the towel, and Faith handed it to her. She dried her face slowly, deep in thought.

'I'm trying to remember who I told about the book. Not many people. Lenny, probably, and you.'

'But who did Jared tell?' The words were out before she could stop them, and with them any thoughts she might have had about confessing the truth. Right now, the truth wasn't going to help either of them. 'Kitty, you're scared of Dalzell, I've seen how scared you are. And if Jared is going to jail anyway, whatever you do, then why not try to help him and yourself?'

'You sound like Avery. He'd say anything to get what he wants. The Angel is my life, it's all I have.'

Faith followed her into the bedroom, where Kitty began to undress. 'It isn't all you have,' she insisted. 'You have me.'

She was feeling dizzy again, her head spinning worse than ever. Hot bile rose into her throat and she put a hand to her mouth, as if to keep it down. She reached out for the dressing table and nearly missed it, stumbling sideways. Kitty caught her arm and held her upright.

'What is it?'

Black shapes were flapping around the edges of her vision, and she thought in surprise, *I'm going to faint!* And then slowly the sensation began to fade, leaving her shaken and white-faced. At some point, Kitty had helped her onto the bed and she sat with her head down, breathing deeply.

'You're up the duff.' Kitty's voice was harsh. 'You idiot. I told you, I *warned* you.'

Tears sprang into Faith's eyes as she shook her head, denying it, even as she knew it was true. 'I didn't have any breakfast, that's all.'

'It's Ray, isn't it?' Kitty had dropped her voice, remembering Avery was listening in the room beneath them.

'He loves me,' was all that Faith could think to say.

Kitty snorted. 'So he'll what? Marry you and buy a sweet little cottage for you and the baby to live in? Don't be so stupid. He's aiming for a career, and he won't want a brat hanging around. How do you think the fans will feel about him being married and a father? Those screaming, squealing girls? The record company will put you away, out of sight. Ray will want to forget you exist.'

'You're wrong!' She was angry and upset, with herself as well as Kitty. She had been stupid. She should have been more careful, she should have seen that Ray was more careful, but in the heady rush of love she hadn't wanted to be practical and cautious.

Kitty smoothed her sleeves and reached for her handbag. She was wearing a black skirt with a pale-blue cardigan, and black shoes with court heels. She looked as pretty as ever, but older and more serious. Her face was almost as pale as Faith's, although with less of the sickly green tinge.

'When's Ray coming back?'

Faith took another breath, finally starting to feel better. 'Today,' she said. 'I'm not sure exactly when. He left a message for me with Gaz.'

'Good old Gaz,' Kitty muttered. 'Okay, well here's my advice, for what it's worth. If you want to hold on to him then don't tell him about the baby. Get rid of it and don't ever tell him.' Faith stared at her, speechless.

'You can go on as before and maybe you're right and he does love you, and it will last, and one day he'll marry you. Then you can have another one. But this one,' and her eyes flickered down to Faith's flat stomach and up again. 'Let it go.'

Kitty moved to the door. 'And go in to work. If you stay away they'll think you had something to do with all of this. Do your shift and keep your head down, and I'll see you when I get home. We can talk about this then.'

Was that regret she saw in her cousin's face? Sorrow? Maybe. And other emotions Faith didn't have time to read before the door began to close. She sat, staring at it, and then carefully rose to her feet. She was still a bit shaky but better now. When Kitty was gone she'd eat some toast …

She went out to the top of the stairs just as the front door clicked shut, leaving her with the maelstrom of her thoughts.

33

SAMANTHA

17 January 2000

I FELT RIDICULOUSLY HAPPY.

I know, I know. Why should a kiss mean so much? And yet it did. Despite all of the turmoil in my life, here was something really, really good, and I wanted to indulge myself by replaying it over and over in my mind.

A video on rewind.

Like when I decided I loved the movie *To Sir, With Love* so much I had to watch it every afternoon when I got home from school. It was made before I was born, and I'm not sure why I found it so endlessly fascinating, but I did. I think Mum finally hid it. From this distance I didn't blame her, but at the time I was pretty upset.

'Come on, forget about that.' I remember Dad coming to fetch me from my room. 'Help me with the garden.'

So, grudgingly, I did. Was that where my love of plants had come from? Maybe.

I'd rung Hope last night, but there was no reply.

Now, when the phone rang, somehow I just knew it was her.

'Sorry,' she said. 'It was late last night and I had things to do. How's Mum?'

I told her about Lincoln and the jelly babies, and heard her soft laughter.

'I'm going to collect her a bit later.'

'Good news, then.'

'And Hope … more good news. Dad has heard from Mum and she's on her way home. She was delayed or something very mysterious, and she will tell us all about it when she gets here.'

I'd meant her to laugh again, only she didn't. There was quite a long pause and I wondered what she was thinking. I wished I could see her face, so that I could read her expression, but then I'd never found my famous aunt easy to read.

'That *is* good,' she said with a sigh. 'Really good, Samantha.'

'Are—'

'I spoke with Kitty last night. There are things I'll need to discuss with Faith. I wish I could tell you what they are, but I don't think it's fair, not without her permission. You'll understand soon.'

'Not again!'

'I know, I know. I'm sorry.'

'Just tell me one thing. Was I right? Was Bert Dalzell involved?'

I thought she wasn't going to answer me and then she said, 'I'm afraid to say he was.'

'So, it *was* him Mum went to see!'

'I didn't say that, Samantha! You're jumping to conclusions. I'm sorry, but I really can't tell you anything more until I see Faith. I promise that I will do all in my power to persuade your mother to share this with you. I *promise*. And if she won't then … I will.'

I wanted to be cross with her, and yet I found my anger draining away. I believed her, and oddly enough, I trusted her.

'By the way,' Hope went on. 'That photo left in Dalzell's house. It isn't Faith. It's Kitty.'

'I think I was beginning to realise that.'

'And I have some more bad news.' She sounded tired, as if her energy was at a low ebb.

'You're flying back to New York,' I blurted out, and then wondered where that had come from, and when had her leaving become bad news?

'Well, actually, no. I was aiming to come back to Willow Tree Bend today, but something else has come up. Out of my control, I'm afraid, so it will have to be tomorrow. I'm glad Lily's okay. It means I can hang around that little bit longer and try to sort out this problem I'm having with the producers.'

'Right.'

'We'll talk soon, I promise,' she repeated, and because it seemed so important to her, I said I was looking forward to it. I wasn't sure that I was, really. It sounded as if we were going to have some long and intense conversations.

'Oh, I almost forgot the most important thing! Tell Joe not to talk with *Looking Back*,' she went on hurriedly. 'I believe they've arranged for an interview with him. It's about Pete. He'll know what I mean. They shouldn't even be going there—Pete is really none of their business.'

Was that anger I heard in her voice? I'd noticed before that when she was under the influence of strong emotion her vowels became much more Australian.

'Right. I'll tell him.'

What was the big deal with talking about Dad's brother? Or maybe Hope just didn't want him upset—I'd seen how painful the subject of his brother was on the night of the barbecue.

There was another pause while we both gathered our thoughts.

'How's Lincoln?' she said in a more relaxed voice.

'Ah. Good. Really good. He's written some new songs and he plans to sing them at Estelle's.'

'Does he now? I'm looking forward to that.'

'Estelle is very excited. I couldn't get a word in when I told her. She's already sold more tickets than she thought possible. I think she's going to need a caterer.'

'Might be a job for Cantani Desserts. Didn't Faith have a new pudding she was launching? Maybe she'd consider combining the two?'

It was a good idea. I thought I might suggest it when I had a chance. After we'd had that long, intense discussion.

'I have to go,' Hope said. 'Prue will be here to pick me up and I'm not dressed yet. I'll see you soon.' And she was gone.

I tried to ring Dad, but he wasn't home, and the girls at Cantani Desserts hadn't seen him. Then the hospital called to let me know Gran would be ready to go home after lunch, so I decided to spend some time working on my favourite garden design.

Of course that meant I forgot all about Hope's message for Dad.

I'd been thinking about the memorial to Zanzibar, and wondering whether I could make more of a feature of it. Maybe move it into a prominent position? But then that would mean digging up the horse and moving him, too—if there was anything left. Being heritage listed meant nothing would be simple, and no doubt I would have to fill in endless forms explaining myself, as well as appearing before groups of earnest people who are the guardians of our past. I was glad they were there, really, they did a fabulous job, but … Any grand ideas I had might just be a complete waste of time.

As for the rest of the garden, that seemed to be falling into place just as I wanted it. The potager and the old goldfields section were taking shape. The wall, too, although Derek wanted to do most of that himself. I was of the opinion that building a wall from scratch might take longer than he thought and hold up the rest of the work, but what did it matter anyway? They had time. Even if the restaurant opened for Easter as Jason wanted it to, they didn't need to have the garden one hundred percent completed.

I heard a car pull up out the front and for a moment my heart went pitter-patter, thinking it was Lincoln. I hadn't forgotten about the kiss last night—how could I? I still had that breathless, dizzy feeling. So I rushed out of my work room, over to the window, to see if it was him.

It wasn't. It was Dad, and as he jumped out of his dusty four wheel drive to open the gate, I noticed two things. One, he was dressed in a suit, which seemed very strange in the rising heat of the morning, and two, there was another car coming up the road behind him, a low-slung car I didn't recognise at all.

He drove through and then kept coming, leaving the gate open for the other car. By the time I got out of the door, he was already on the verandah, with Mitch dancing around him. Even Pompom, woken from his slumber on the kitchen floor, had waddled over to see what was going on.

Dad looked flushed and flustered. 'Sorry, Sam, didn't have time to ring. I'm supposed to be doing an interview for *Looking Back*, something Hope teed up, evidently. They wanted to meet me here.'

I looked at him in bewilderment. 'I spoke to Hope on the phone. She said to tell you not to do the interview! I tried ringing, but you weren't there. It's about Pete and she said you'd know what she meant.'

He stopped and stared at me. All sorts of emotions seemed to be fighting for supremacy on his face. Anger won.

'They can't do that! Not without her permission,' he growled.

Why would they need Hope's permission to talk about Pete? I wondered, but had no time to get the question out.

'Where *is* Hope?' he demanded.

'She said she was staying in town another night, to try to sort things out. Dad—'

The second vehicle—I could see now that it was a well-loved Porsche—had pulled up behind Dad's four-wheel drive. A man and a woman were visible through the windscreen, but it wasn't until they got out that I recognised the camera guy from that memorable day at the cottage.

Camera guy was smiling—annoyingly I couldn't recall his name—and I didn't remember him doing much of that last time I saw him. The woman with him wasn't the one with the pink hair—this was an older, sleeker person, her hair dark and straight, and wearing a very nice outfit that was totally inappropriate for my place. She picked her way towards us in her spiky heels, reaching out a hand and plastering on a smile.

'Mr Cantani? Miss Cantani?'

'Yes,' Dad answered for both us, frowning down at them as they reached the verandah.

They'd been about to mount the stairs, only now they didn't. My father had broad shoulders and when he wanted to he could look very intimidating.

I could see the woman considering her next move, but she must have decided that whatever it was she was after was worth the aggravation.

'So pleased to meet you both,' she said, ignoring the waves of hostility. 'I'm Frances Durant from *Looking Back*, and I think you know Ken. We're here to talk to you about Hope Taylor.'

'Hope just rang to say not to do the interview,'

I said.

The two of them exchanged glances before Frances took the lead again. 'Look, do you mind if we come in and talk about this? The sun is awfully hot out here.'

Dad was still frowning, or was it a scowl? 'First tell me what this interview is about.'

So, no air conditioning until they came clean.

'It's about your brother, Mr Cantani. He and Ms Taylor had an affair, didn't they?'

Whoa! I looked at Dad to see if he was as shocked as me, but he wasn't. That was the moment I realised that this piece of amazing information wasn't news to him, and that actually it was probably true.

Although, 'affair' seemed a pretty big word. Hope must have been a teenager and Pete was only twenty-one when he died. Surely it was a fling, a first love, or maybe a one-off in the backseat of Pete's car?

I didn't like where this was heading.

Frances had also noted Dad's expression—was his face as easy to read as mine?—and a smug note crept into her voice. 'Now that's out of the way, please can we come in and talk? If you've been speaking to Hope then she should have told you that she's also being interviewed on the same subject. In Melbourne.' She glanced at her watch. 'Around about now, I should think.'

I could see Dad was wavering. He didn't know what was going on, and although he didn't like what he was hearing, he was also aware that Hope had signed a contract to tell her story, and maybe this was just part of it.

'I don't think this is fair,' I spoke up. 'Hope said not to do the interview, and until we hear from her … This seems awfully personal. My father's brother has been dead for a long time, he died in Vietnam, and now you're dragging his memory into this. Sorry, but no.'

They must have seen they were losing us. After another exchanged glance Frances appeared to make an executive decision. She nodded at Ken and he put his camera on his shoulder and a red light came on. He moved closer and instinctively I stepped back. Dad stepped in front of me.

'Stop right now,' he said. 'Or I'm calling the police.'

'Sam?' Startled, I looked up.

At some point during all the madness Lincoln had arrived and I hadn't even noticed. Relief flooded me as he came striding towards us, looking as if he was prepared to rescue me from something far more dangerous than a camera.

'What's going on?' he asked, giving the show's duo a dirty look.

'They want to talk to us about Dad's brother,' I said. 'According to them he and Hope had an affair when she was …?' I gave Dad a questioning glance.

'Sixteen,' he muttered.

Lincoln shook his head, nonplussed. 'What, when they were kids?' he said. 'Experimental sex, was it? Wow, guys, that will up the ratings.'

Frances's perfectly made-up cheeks turned pink.

Lincoln jumped up onto the verandah without using the steps, and Mitch, thinking this was fun, jumped too. 'Come on, guys,' he said. 'Go home. There's nothing for you here.' But they weren't going home.

'Samantha,' Frances reclaimed my attention. She continued to talk, but Dad had raised his voice over hers and I could hardly hear her. Something about a private hospital.

Ken had that camera on my face, and Lincoln leaned down and gave him a push. Ken staggered but straightened up again, determined to carry on. Things were getting seriously out of hand.

'Did you know … October nineteen seventy, Hope Taylor gave birth … baby … private hospital … Curtis House, and the father … Peter Cantani?'

She was shouting and this time I heard some of what she said. Enough.

'W—what?' I gasped, almost laughing, because it was ridiculous. Wasn't it? I looked to Dad to confirm just how ridiculous this was, and for the second time I saw affirmation. It was true. My famous aunt had a secret love child. And, oh God, *Looking Back* were planning to make it public knowledge.

'This is so unfair,' I whispered. And then louder, into her face, no longer caring about the camera, 'This is unfair! She didn't give you permission to talk about this. She wouldn't want—'

'She signed a contract,' Ken retorted, still filming. 'This was the deal. She was happy to take the money.'

I shook my head.

'A baby *girl*, Samantha,' Frances spoke over him. 'What have you to say to that?'

'Get her inside.' My father's voice was low and rough, and Lincoln took my arm and began to hustle me through the door. I wasn't putting up much of a fight, I admit. I was in shock.

The dogs were wildly overexcited, Mitch barking, and then Pompom deciding it was time to make his own claim to fame. As Frances came up the stairs, chasing after me I suppose, he nipped her on her neat ankle and made a hole in her stocking. She shrieked. 'That animal bit me!' Just as Lincoln closed the door.

I could still hear Dad reading them the riot act. We went to the window, peering out from behind the curtain like spies. Ken had decided he'd had enough and was packing up his camera and putting it in the car. Frances limped over to him, her arms waving furiously. Making threats to sue or wanting him to carry on?

I wasn't sure which. Mitch and Pompom were still barking, but as they were the victors they didn't feel the need to leave the safety of the verandah.

I sat down on a chair. I found my legs wouldn't hold me up. Dad opened the door for the dogs and they shot inside, Pompom flopping down on one side of me and Mitch on the other. They were like Praetorian guards, and I would have thanked them, if I'd been able to think at all. I stared up at Lincoln.

'You all right?' he asked me with a worried

frown.

'Hope had a child,' I whispered.

Outside, the Porsche was on the move. They must have been backing out of the yard, because a moment later I heard a metallic thump, and then a tinkle of glass as the rear light hit my gate post. Lincoln went to the window again and I heard him laugh softly under his breath. He was enjoying this. I was glad someone was.

Hope Taylor had had a baby girl in October nineteen seventy, the daughter of Pete Cantani. I was born on the fifth of October nineteen seventy, and I was the daughter of Faith Taylor and Joe Cantani.

According to my parents I was born prematurely, a month before my due date. They were married in February. I'd always accepted what they said. Why wouldn't I?

Now there was another girl born in October of the same year, and it was a coincidence, it must be. Because what I was thinking was completely and utterly impossible.

When you were born I held you in my arms and I felt as if I'd been given a miracle.

My mother's voice replayed in my head. A miracle? Suddenly, the word held all sorts of connotations.

The phone started to ring. It was Lincoln who went to pick up. I could hear the murmur of his voice outside the kitchen door, but I wasn't listening. I seemed to have removed myself so that there was a wall between me and the world. Mitch butted my hand and automatically I patted him, and then Pompom whined and I ruffled his head.

'Sam?'

Lincoln was back and I looked up at him, wanting him to tell me this was all a nightmare.

'That was Hope,' he said, and his voice was coming from far away. 'She wanted to let us know that *Looking Back* were coming here and under no circumstances were we to let them in.'

From somewhere inside I felt a bubble, and then it turned into a laugh. I put my hand to my mouth to stop it.

Too late, *Aunt* Hope. The secret was out.

34

HOPE

17 January 2000, Melbourne

HOPE STOOD IN front of the mirror as she buttoned her silk blouse. She looked composed and professional—although, she hoped, still approachable. But if *Looking Back* was going to ask her about Pete, then definitely not *too* approachable.

She stepped back and carefully inspected herself, making certain she was as perfect as she could be, from the top of her glossy hair to the tips of her Miu Miu sandals. The woman staring back at her was an accurate example of the old saying: looks can be deceiving. Because beneath her calm exterior, Hope had a deep, simmering anger that she was struggling to keep under control.

Pete was off limits. Anything to do with him was a cruel invasion of her privacy and that of his family. Pete was one of the secrets that should never have been dug up and laid out for public view. And Hope had sacrificed so much to keep that from happening.

Don't you dare drag my son's name through the mud.

And she hadn't. She had kept their shared past locked up in its little box so that Pete, smiling charmingly on his mother's wall, forever the brave young soldier, could remain pristine and perfect.

And now the show's producers were going to take all of her sacrifice away from her as if it was nothing.

It had been very late when she left Kitty's house, and even when she fell into bed in her hotel room, her cousin's revelations had kept her awake off and on throughout the night.

Hope asked herself: why she hadn't known at the time? There was irony in there somewhere, if it wasn't so tragic. Faith was her sister and she'd needed Hope, and Hope had gone missing. It seemed all the worse when she remembered that when she had needed Faith, her big sister had been there with bells on.

So much was making sense now. So much was falling into place. The driver of the big black car and his cold eyes, watching her so intently in the rear-view mirror. Faith's joy when she'd held Sam in her arms. *It's like a miracle*, she'd said. And that phone call from a man in her past, drawing her back to a place she had thought she had left far behind.

Hope knew who it was. She understood.

One thing was certain, when she'd sorted out *Looking Back*, Hope and Faith were going to have a long heart-to-heart, and she wasn't going to allow her sister to go all silent on her. It was time to bring their secrets out into the open.

Nervously, Hope twitched the collar of her blouse.

She wondered what Pete would have thought of all this, and as if on cue his face came to her. Smiling, his teeth so white and his eyes so blue against his tanned skin—he was better looking than any movie star. It had been a long hot summer that year and Pete always browned up. No freckles, not like Hope, just warm brown skin.

He had a reputation around town, but that hadn't bothered her. He'd told her she was special, and she'd believed him. From the first time he'd kissed her she'd known this was for keeps. From the second time there was no going back for either of them. The unkind thing was that they never had a chance to show everyone else, all the many doubters, that their relationship could endure.

The end had come much too soon.

After Pete's call-up, they'd had a month. A whole month. It wasn't long enough, but they'd tried to stretch it out. And then he was gone, reporting to Puckapunyal for three months' training. He wrote to her, his letters going to Joe first, who didn't entirely agree with what was going on, but was too busy being in love himself to put up much of an argument. Hope's letters were sent back the same way, under cover of Joe's.

Miss you more than I can say. I'll be getting some leave soon. Joe says he'll make sure we get to see each other, and without Mum getting all upset. You know what she's like.

Mrs Cantani did not want Pete and Hope getting too serious. Bad enough in her eyes that Joe and Faith were marrying in February, but Joe had never been her favourite. Pete was her eldest and the apple of her eye, and after Mr Cantani died she had become even more possessive of his time and affection.

There was a cousin she wanted Pete to marry. A Cantani girl who visited regularly and was always thrown into Pete's company—a girl too timid to stand up to the older woman. Pete was kind, but he told Hope he didn't want to marry his cousin and he didn't love her.

Give it time. Everything will turn out, you'll see. Mum just has to get used to you. Once I've done my two years' National Service, and I'm home again, I'll tell her it's you or no one.

Mrs Cantani wasn't the only one who objected to her child being involved with someone she'd deemed unsuitable. Lily didn't like Pete. She didn't trust him, and she didn't think he was good enough for her daughter. She didn't object to Joe, but he was well known for being a steady, trustworthy boy, and everyone was well aware of how he felt about Faith. But Pete had had lots of girlfriends and had been the source of plenty of jealousy when he'd encroached on the girlfriends of other men. There'd even been talk of a fling with a married woman.

Pete was home from Pucka for a weekend in March, and Hope thought he looked tanned but skinny, as if he wasn't eating enough. Pete said he was eating like a horse, but they were working them hard. He shared a hut with sixteen other men, and he was learning the basics of being a soldier. He seemed to be enjoying the life a great deal more than anyone had expected, despite the way the Nashos were treated by the regular army.

Joe and Faith took him out for a meal, and Hope came too. Mrs Cantani wasn't happy when she heard, but it so happened she had a bad cold and was confined to bed. Pete asked Joe to drop them near the creek, and said he and Hope would walk from there.

When they kissed it felt a little bit odd at first, as if they were strangers. So Pete sat down with her and they talked. They talked for hours, and when they kissed again everything was all right.

'Do you ever think of that day?' he asked her afterwards, lying with his arm around her, her naked body curled against his.

'All the time,' she whispered.

'Then you shouldn't,' he said, lifting his head to look down at her. 'What happened … I'm paying for it by going to Vietnam, that's how I look at it anyway. Isn't that what the Bible says? A life for a life.'

'Pete!' she gasped, horrified. 'You have to come back, you have to—'

He'd laughed and hugged her closer. 'I'm not saying I'm going to die for that piece of shit,' he said. 'I meant I'm going to give two years of my life fighting for my country. I think that's a pretty good bargain, don't you?'

Hope hadn't known she was pregnant then. She was tall and lithe, and any changes she noticed she thought were due to her turning from a teenager into a woman. Ironically, it wasn't until Pete left for Vietnam that she realised the truth, and then she didn't know what to do. For a week or two she was in shock.

This time when she wrote to Pete it was privately, without Joe's involvement. She never doubted he would be happy, and that he would marry her. They loved each other, and that's what people in love did. She had never thought for a second that by the time her letter reached him, he would be dead.

When Joe opened the telegram, and they learned that Pete had been killed, everything stopped. She felt cut adrift, alone, her happy future receding into the distance.

Mrs Cantani was screaming in the other room—short, sharp screams that pierced the air. When they realised what was happening, most of the guests started to leave, and Faith—who seemed like a grown-up stranger—stood at the door and thanked them all. Hope had run out into the backyard and sat on the old swing, made of half a tyre, which was tied by rope to the huge peppercorn tree.

A life for a life.

She'd sat there, unable to think, unable even to cry, just frozen. That was where Faith had found her.

By the time Faith had managed to persuade Hope to tell her the truth, she had already guessed it. Perhaps, thought Hope, because she'd experienced these changes for herself, and clothing that was suddenly too tight, and morning queasiness, now made sense to her.

Hope wasn't sure what she had been expecting. Accusations, perhaps, or a family lock-down while they sorted it out. Instead, Faith had wrapped her in her arms so tight she could hardly breathe. And the *relief* of that moment, of knowing that despite Pete being gone she wasn't alone, had been like the dull glow in the dawn sky, when you know the sun is just below the horizon and eventually it will rise up and shine on another day.

It was only later, when Mrs Cantani had received Pete's effects and read her letters, that Hope had learned that the child she was carrying was never going to be acknowledged, not by Pete's mother, and if she had her way, not by any of his other relatives either. Apart from Joe.

Mrs Cantani had begun the beatification of her son, and there was no place for Hope.

Hope blinked. She wasn't sure how long she had been standing, staring in the mirror. The girl she was remembering felt like someone else. Her life had turned out very differently from the one she'd expected, and there was no point in wondering what might have happened if Pete had lived. He hadn't.

One thing she had decided, that day she stood at Mrs Cantani's door, looking into the woman's haggard, grief-stricken face. She would never do what Pete's mother expected her to do, and drag his name through the mud.

There was a knock on the door, and Prue's voice. 'Hope?'

She went to open it, before turning back into

the room. 'Nearly ready,' she said over her shoulder. 'Now where is my handbag …'

'Hope?' Prue spoke again, and there was a note in her voice that stopped Hope in her tracks.

The girl's face was white, and her mascara had smudged under her eyes, as if she'd been crying and had tried to clean herself up in the lift on the way up here. Although not very successfully.

She launched into speech before Hope could say a word. 'I'm so sorry. They know about Curtis House. They've been there, interviewing the staff. They've been digging into the records. Hope, they know.'

Hope felt that sense of being frozen in time, just like the girl on the swing in the Cantanis' backyard. They knew. They *knew!*

Prue hadn't finished.

'They've sent the pit bull to Golden Gully. Her name is Frances Durant and she has no scruples. She's going to talk to your brother-in-law and your niece. Ken's behind this. He's weaselled his way into getting another chance. I told them how w—wrong it was, but they just said,' she hiccupped a sob, 'that they were sorry but they'd have to let me g—go.'

The ice was beginning to thaw, probably because her anger was back. Strangers had taken away the story that should have been hers to tell, that didn't belong them.

What would Joe and Sam think? To be confronted with this news without any preparation, without any *warning*.

There was a cream-coloured telephone by the

bed and she grabbed it up, dialling for an outside line. She remembered Sam's number from her recent call, and her fingers were surprisingly accurate. The anger was helping, clearing her head. *You've coped with worse*, she told herself. Later, she could have her nervous breakdown, but for now she had to remain in control.

It was Lincoln who answered.

That threw her, but only for a second. This wasn't the time for irrelevant questions. She was just glad he was there with Sam. Somehow she managed to get the words out, rapidly and concisely, and luckily he was the sort of man who was good in a crisis. By the time she'd hung up she knew the worst, but there was still time to undo some of the damage. And maybe even to make things right.

At last.

Hope began to pack, throwing her belongings into her case, while Prue stood watching her. Her mascara had run again, and Hope thought unkindly that, with her pink hair, she looked like a sad clown. She'd obviously overheard the telephone conversation, so she knew the pit bull had already arrived and made things worse. If she apologised again, Hope thought, she might just have to strangle her.

'I need to go home,' she said, slamming down the lid and flicking the locks.

'To New York?'

'Home!' Hope snapped, all at once too angry to try to hold it in. 'Willow Tree Bend is home, not—not New York.'

Prue nodded several times. The shouting seemed to galvanise her, and she went to drag the case off the bed. It was heavy and she struggled to get it to the door, despite the wheels on the bottom.

'I'll drive you,' she said. And when Hope began to protest she insisted, 'No, I want to. I need to.'

Arguing was a waste of time, so Hope didn't. Together they wheeled her case to the elevator and pressed the button to take them down to the lobby, where Prue paid with the *Looking Back* credit card, at the same time shooting a smug glance at Hope. A moment later they were in her car.

35

FAITH

November 1969

SLEEP TOOK HER almost at once. No time to think about anything before she fell into a deep, dreamless slumber.

It was when Faith woke that her troubles crowded in on her. She sat up, pushing her hair out of her eyes, and saw that she was still wearing her boots. For what seemed like an age she just stared, and then she laughed. The laughter turned to tears, but afterwards she felt better. She could think more clearly, and as she got up and began to get ready for work, she began to plan.

Whatever Kitty might think, Faith could not accept Ray would reject her so callously. Not the man with the gentle eyes and tender hands. When he arrived at the Angel, she would ask him to meet her later, and after he'd told her his news—and she was sure it would be good news, the record company could not help but love his songs—then she would tell him hers. They would sit together and talk about what they were going to do, how they would balance his career with their new family.

Everything would be all right.

After all, he'd asked her to go with him to Sydney, hadn't he? He loved her and she loved him. Now the time had finally come to make a decision about the rest of her life, and Faith chose Ray and their baby.

As for Jared and Kitty, there was nothing more she could do. She knew Avery was going to use the secret book to charge Dalzell with Melanie's murder, and then Kitty would be free. Whatever happened after that was up to Kitty, but Faith hoped she would cut herself off from the Angel and find a new life.

'Faith?'

She'd been making her way up the back stairs to the staff cloakroom when she heard her name called. Lenny had followed her, and he looked as if he had something on his mind.

'Have you seen Kitty?'

'Why? Isn't she here?' Her ability to deceive was getting easier.

The doorman cracked his knuckles. 'The cops've been here. That bastard Avery. He took Jared away, and Kitty hasn't come in to work. I tried ringing her at home, but there was no answer.'

He was looking at her and Faith gave an apologetic shrug. 'Sorry, I heard it, but I was sleeping. Haven't been feeling so well. That wog that's been doing the rounds.'

Lenny nodded, still watching her. Ever since

he'd been arrested and bailed, he'd been more paranoid than ever. That he was even talking to her seemed unusual—he was Kitty's friend, never hers.

'Gaz's gone too.'

Startled, she said, 'Gone? Gone where?'

'Just … *gone*. Mr Dalzell reckons he's been part of it all along, telling tales to Avery. "A spy in our midst", he says.' And he smiled, pleased with the turn of phrase, and with himself for remembering it.

The name lodged in her heart like a stone. She took a moment to answer him, hoping he wasn't going to tell her that Dalzell was here now. Hoping he wouldn't see her.

'Mr Dalzell …?'

'He's in Jared's office.' Lenny didn't even let her finish. 'Come as soon as I rang to tell him what was happening. He calls me "his man".' Faith could see he liked that.

Faith glanced in the direction of Jared's office and was relieved to see the door was closed. 'I should get to work,' she began edging towards the cloakroom.

Lenny watched her with his suspicious eyes, but she told herself he couldn't know. She just had to act normal until Ray arrived and then …

'How's Ray?'

It was unexpected and there was something in the tone of his voice, as if he was enjoying himself.

'I don't know, I haven't seen him for two weeks,' she said coolly.

'Funny, isn't it, how Ray's always off somewhere whenever the cops come calling. I said to Mr Dalzell—'

'Lenny!'

It was the captain of the Mezzanine, holding the staff door open, and staring straight at them. He didn't look happy.

'You were supposed to help move those tables.'

Lenny hesitated, but in the circumstances he could hardly linger here, talking with her, no matter how much he was enjoying upsetting her. He set off at a half-jog.

Down in the Cocktail Lounge, the girls were huddled together gossiping or speculating, or both. If Kitty had been there she would have torn strips off them. Faith didn't join them. She began clearing away some glasses that had been left out from last night and then the black Bakelite telephone on the bar rang. No else one appeared eager to get it, so she went over and lifted the receiver. 'Cocktail Lounge, the Angel.'

'Faith?' The voice was familiar.

'Who—?'

'It's Gaz. Look, I haven't got long. I need to tell you something.'

'Lenny said you were gone,' she said, dropping her voice and huddling over the handset. 'Where are you?'

He made a breathless sound, like a laugh. 'Never mind that. You said Lenny's been talking about me? He's been saying lots of stuff. Whispering in Dalzell's ear, making himself look good. Maybe he's planning to take over from Jared.'

'Gaz—'

'Listen! I haven't got long. Lenny told Dalzell that it was Ray who was Avery's inside man. He's jealous of Ray, always has been. Until Ray came along he was Jared's best mate.'

The other waitresses had broken up their gossip session and were wandering over to her. Faith huddled even closer to the telephone.

'Lenny told Dalzell that Ray was Avery's informer?'

'Yeah,' Gaz sounded tired. In the background she could hear a voice over a tannoy, calling passengers to board. 'Ray's back, Faith. He called me this morning to leave a message for you. He said he'll be late getting to the Angel tonight, but never mind that. Now things are changed you need to get word to him. Tell him to stay away until you know what's happening with Jared. Ray will need a friend at the Angel if Dalzell turns on him.'

'I thought Dalzell was going to jail,' she said.

There was a silence on the other end. 'That was the plan,' he said gently, 'but you just never know.'

'Faith? Should we open the doors?'

Faith looked past the waitress and saw that the doors were still closed and locked. 'I …' Ray was already home, and when he arrived at the Angel he would be walking into a dangerous situation. Gaz was right, she had to warn him. She had to find him and warn him.

She hung up and turned, heading for the cloakroom. She'd need her handbag and her money. Ray might want to go straight back to Sydney.

And she'd be going with him.

'Faith!' the call echoed after her, but she ignored it. Hardly heard it. She snatched up her handbag from the shelf, and as she turned around, the door to Jared's office opened.

Dalzell didn't see her at first, not until she moved, and then he found her. She wondered if everything was written on her face, because she felt as if it was. Guilt and fear and desperation.

'Hello, Faith,' he said in that low, oily voice of his. 'Would you like to step into my office? I have a few questions I want to put to you.'

She actually took a step towards him, before she stopped herself. She knew she couldn't go in there. She could tell herself he didn't know what she'd done to bring him down, but he had as many spies as Avery. She wouldn't be safe.

Faith turned on her heel and ran back down the stairs to the Cocktail Lounge. She heard Dalzell calling for Lenny, but she was already halfway to the entrance doors. They'd been opened by one of the girls, and in one movement she pushed her way through and ran out onto the street.

The heat rose up from the footpath under her shoes, and with it came the smell of car fumes and unemptied rubbish bins. She gagged but kept going. No time for that. She had to get to Ray's house.

One step at a time, she told herself. One step at a time.

One of the Allnights, bleary-eyed and with his hair on end, opened the door. Obviously he'd been asleep, but he broke into a smile when he saw Faith standing outside.

She didn't give him a chance to start a conversation. 'Is Ray here?'

His smile wavered. 'Ah, Faith, I'm not sure if he wants … Faith!'

She was already pushing past him and he was too slow to stop her. She knew the way, up the stairs, second on the right, and as she opened his door she was already talking.

'Ray, you have to get out. Dalzell thinks you've been talking with the police and—'

It was a moment before she realised Ray wasn't alone. The head that lifted from the pillow next to his was that of a woman, long dark hair tangled around her naked torso, her dark eyes narrowed in annoyance.

'Faith?' Ray was awake now. He was half out of the bed, staring at her in dismay. He stood up, seemed to remember he was naked, and reached for his pants. 'Faith, what are you doing here?' he said. 'I was going to meet you later at the Angel.'

Faith turned away. She had thought she felt shattered earlier, after Avery took Kitty away and she realised she was pregnant, but this was worse. Somehow, she'd convinced herself that Ray loved her and everything would be all right. Now nothing was.

She wasn't sure where she was going, but she'd hardly taken a step before she stopped herself. Whatever Ray had done to her, he was in danger. She had to warn him at least. If she walked out now and something happened to him, it would be her fault. She might tell herself now that he deserved it, but later, when time had cooled her anger and soothed her pain, it would be hard to live with.

'I have to talk to you.' She stood just outside the door, looking away, not wanting to see them in there. 'It's important,' she added, when the woman muttered something about stupid bitches.

Ray's voice was a soothing murmur. 'Come on, babe,' he said, 'just give me a minute.'

The words were so familiar her heart felt as if it had cracked in two. He'd spoken to her like that. They were his words to *her*, *her* memories, and this was all wrong.

The woman brushed past her in a cloud of perfume, a sheet wrapped around her nakedness, her hair hanging down her back. The bathroom door shut loudly and a tap began to run in the bath.

Faith took a step into the room. 'Who is she? What is she doing in your bed?' Her voice went up and down, wobbling like a little girl whose best friend had dumped her. *Stop it*, she told herself. Shouting and screaming, weeping and sobbing, none of that would get her through this. She tried to remember her mother the day her father finally left for good. That white face and tight mouth. 'Good riddance,' she'd said.

Faith understood now. It was either that or collapse in a puddle of grief.

'She works at the record company's office in Sydney,' he said. He was sitting on the bed, pulling on his shoes. She wondered why he was bothering. 'She came back with me. She's nice, actually. This isn't her fault.'

'No, it's your fault.'

He looked at her as if he wished he could think of something to say, something to make everything better. That was the thing about Ray, he wanted to be everyone's friend.

'I need to talk to you,' she said. 'Not about … this.' She swept her hand in repugnance. 'Something has happened.'

'What's happened?' he asked, and there was a thread of irritation in his voice.

Faith took a breath and told herself she had to make this good or he wasn't going to believe her.

'Jared's been arrested. He has a book with details in it about Dalzell. Things that Jared has done for Dalzell. They're going to arrest Dalzell, too, and charge him with murder. Gaz told me to find you and tell you. You can't go to the Angel, it's not safe. Lenny is spreading rumours about you being a police informant. If Dalzell thinks this is all your fault …'

He shook his head at her.

'Ray, you have to get away. Hide. We … you have to hide.'

He laughed, but there was no humour in it. 'Dalzell is a weird one, that's for sure. But he isn't my problem. This isn't my problem, luv.'

'Ray, listen to me!' She was beginning to sound hysterical and she'd promised herself she wouldn't. 'Listen to me,' she said, dropping her voice, taking another breath. 'Gaz has gone, he knows it's not safe. He was talking to the cops. Me, too.' He looked at her, eyes narrowed. 'I wanted to tell you, but I was worried you'd tell someone or …

I didn't want to involve you.'

'I see.' He reached for his shirt and pulled it on, leaving the buttons undone over his thin chest. 'You're a bit of a surprise packet, Faith. Here I was thinking you were hardly more than a schoolgirl, and all the time …' He shook his head, smiled. 'It could be that you'd done me a favour.'

Faith didn't understand. Behind her, in the bathroom, the water stopped running.

'Jared is a good guy, don't get me wrong, but you were right when you told me he was only in this for himself. I've outgrown him. The record company and the tape, and all that, I'm grateful. I could have done it on my own, but he paid the bills and got me there sooner. But I have other friends. Friends of Jared's. They're looking after me now.'

'You mean Dalzell?' she whispered, aghast.

'No. You're obsessed with that man,' he said, chuckling. 'No, not Bert. I mean the men who actually own the Angel and half the other clubs in Melbourne. Bert only thinks he does, and that's because they let him think it. I won't give you any names, Faith.'

'Criminals,' she said in disgust.

'Criminals go to jail—they're too clever for that. They're backing me now.'

There was something confident about him she hadn't seen before, or maybe she'd missed it. She'd come here to save him and he hadn't needed saving.

Ray stood up and began to button his shirt. 'I

have a meeting to go to. I was going to see you afterwards, at the Angel.' He gave her a regretful look. 'You should have waited and then we could still have been friends.'

'I thought we were more than friends. You asked me to go to Sydney with you. What if I'd said yes?'

'I don't know.' He seemed to be trying to imagine that scenario, and then he shook his head. 'Too late now anyway. You're a lovely girl, Faith, but it wouldn't have lasted.'

'Didn't any of it matter to you?' she asked, her throat aching with tears. She wouldn't cry.

Good riddance.

''Course it did. We had fun, and you were … Well, I won't forget you, Faith.'

He was smiling and he appeared to genuinely mean it. Maybe he had loved her for a while, until he forgot about her and moved on.

She almost didn't tell him. A few moments ago she'd decided she wasn't going to. She didn't think he would change his mind, they were beyond that, maybe it was just that she thought he had a right to know.

'I'm pregnant.'

He went still, then something passed over his face. Regret, maybe, and indecision, too, but then his expression closed down. 'Your problem,' he said.

She didn't wait to hear any more. She let herself out of the house just as she'd done many times before and walked the few blocks home. Kitty wasn't there, but she'd come home eventually, and Faith would need her help then. So she sat down on her bed and waited.

36

SAMANTHA

17 January 2000, Golden Gully

IT FELT IMPORTANT to be practical. Being practical was something I was good at, and then I could set aside my anger and my hurt, and feel as if I was in control. I didn't want to think about what that woman had shouted at me, before Pompom bit her. I didn't want to believe that I wasn't who I'd always thought I was, but actually the secret love child of my famous aunt and my dead uncle.

After the Porsche drove off, leaving my gatepost with a serious lean, all the puff went out of the situation. Dad jumped in his four wheel drive and took off after them without even speaking to me. I hoped he wasn't going to try to run them off the road, but he seemed angry enough to do anything.

Lincoln made me a coffee, at the same time telling me how he'd been outside his cottage and noticed the unusual activity going on at my place. He'd come over to see if he could help.

'Do you feel all right?' he asked for the seventh time, setting the mug down in front of me. 'You look shattered.'

'I don't know how I feel. I'm trying to pretend I didn't hear what that woman said, and then I won't have to deal with it.'

'Sam,' he murmured, and I knew he was going to be sympathetic and give me some heartfelt advice, or maybe he was just going to kiss me again. And I knew if he did then I would crumple into a sobbing mess and I couldn't let that happen. I needed to be strong.

I couldn't just go to pieces.

There were people depending on me.

'Gran!' I shouted, making him jump. I looked at my watch and groaned. 'I have to pick her up,' I explained, lowering the volume. 'I should have been there ten minutes ago.'

'I can do that,' he offered.

I tried to smile. 'Yeah I know about you and Gran. She's your muse.'

He shook his head at me. 'No, Sam, as much as I respect your grandmother … *You're* my muse.'

I stared into his eyes and I could tell he wasn't just trying to be nice. *I* was Lincoln Nash's muse. Well, how about that? A bubble of happiness rose out of my whirling emotional soup, and I clung on to it.

'Oh.' I gave him a real smile this time.

He smiled back. 'A bit of a surprise, hey? Probably for you as well as me. When I moved here I wasn't expecting to meet a woman who would be occupying my thoughts night and day. And I didn't expect to feel jealous of Michael Hutchence, just because he was on your bedroom wall, how many years ago?'

'Quite a few,' I admitted. There was a warm sensation in the pit of my stomach. 'We're more or less strangers,' I told him, my practical self reasserting itself. 'And I dumped my last boyfriend because he preferred cars to animals.'

'I like animals, particularly your animals.' That seemed a reasonable start.

'We need to talk,' I said, taking a breath. I felt shaky, and my inner anger hadn't gone away, but I was better than I had been a moment ago. Whatever happened, however this story about my parents panned out, Lincoln Nash was willing to stick by me. 'We need to talk, but not now. I have to go and get Gran.'

He nodded, letting me have my way. That was a good sign, I told myself. Lincoln knew when to be in charge, like the man I'd seen jumping onto the verandah to rescue me, and he knew when to let me be in charge, like now. It boded well for the future.

'I'll see you when you're finished,' he said, as I collected my keys and bag.

'That would be nice.' I sat down to do up the buckles on my sandals, watched closely by the two dogs. They were almost leaning on each other. Frances Durant would be remembered for one good deed—she'd taught Pompom and Mitch the meaning of friendship.

'Come to the cottage.'

That man's eyes! Maybe it was the aftermath of

strong emotion, but the warmth in the pit of my stomach travelled further afield and I struggled to tamp it down. 'Sounds like a plan,' I murmured, as I straightened up.

His breath warmed my lips and then he kissed me, but only lightly. I was simultaneously sorry and relieved. If he kissed me properly I might forget about Gran altogether and that would never do. 'Later,' he said, and it was a promise.

Although Gran was all packed and ready, there was a wait for the doctor to sign her out. The social worker tried to draw me aside for another chat, but Gran took charge, insisting she couldn't wait any longer.

'My mother will be wondering where I am,' she complained.

I couldn't look at the social worker's face. I knew I'd burst out in hysterical laughter. As it was I was barely out of the door before I started to giggle.

'He'll think you're even battier than he already does,' I warned her.

'Why? My mother *could* still be alive.'

I shook my head at her. 'You're incorrigible, Gran.'

At least Lily *was* still my grandmother. At least she hadn't been taken away from me.

'Sam? What is it?'

Something in my expression must have given me away. Gran was looking up at me as she walked out of the front door by my side. It whooshed shut behind us and the hot dry air was a shock after the overly cool air conditioning.

I took her arm, leading her towards my vehicle. I'd been told Gran would need someone with her for the present so she was going to stay at my place.

'Pompom is already there, but you'll need a couple of changes of clothes, so we'll stop by the unit on the way.'

I'd successfully distracted her, and as we drove to the unit I told her that Mitch and Pompom were now friends—although I didn't explain exactly how this incredible event had been achieved. She nodded and smiled, listening without interrupting, and soon we were pulling in to the kerb outside her unit.

Gran was busy collecting her mail, and then she had to sort her catalogues, checking the specials. I went to pack her bag.

The small bedroom was clean and neat, the floral quilt and matching curtains as crisp as ever. I opened her cupboard and then her drawer, taking out what I thought appropriate for the next few days. There was a row of photographs along the windowsill. Lily, Faith, Hope and me. I'd seen them a thousand times before, but it felt as if this was the very first time I had really looked at them.

Our faces were similar, some of the features repeated, some of them not. Green eyes and my blue eyes, and all fair-haired. *The Taylor women*, Dad called us, half joking. And then, if we did something to annoy him, *You Taylor women!*

I moved closer, examining the faces, trying to see something, anything, that would answer my questions. But the more I looked the more I just didn't know.

Back in the car we headed for my place.

I'd left the air conditioning on, and it was nice and cool inside. Gran had been using the third bedroom, and that's where I took her stuff now. 'I'll turn down your bed,' I called to her. 'You're supposed to rest.'

'I've been lying down in hospital,' she called back. 'I'm sick of resting.'

I came out to read her the riot act, and found her sitting on the sofa, Pompom and Mitch at her feet.

'You were right,' she said, eyes sparkling. 'They're friends.'

'Gran,' I sighed, and sat down.

And just like that the barricade of strength and purpose I had built around myself began to fall apart. I felt overwhelmed by it all.

I was aware of her hand on mine, her knuckles swollen with arthritis, and realised she was staring at me with concern. 'What is it, Sam?'

She was an old woman, I reminded myself, and it wasn't fair to dump this problem on her. She may not even know the answer. Hope seemed to have been very successful in keeping her secrets to herself.

'Pete Cantani,' I finally said, more because I was interested in what she had to say, rather than with any expectation she would suddenly cry out: *But he's your father!*

Gran pursed her lips, eyes looking into the past. 'I didn't like Pete. I didn't trust him. He reminded me of Rex.' Then, with a frown, 'Your grandfather.'

Well, I *had* asked. My conception was beginning to feel more and more like a one-off in the backseat of Pete's car.

'Joe's mother, Mrs Cantani, didn't help matters. She wouldn't hear a word against him, especially after he died. I could have told her that no man is perfect, far from it. I probably did.'

'Yes, you probably did.'

Gran sighed, and squeezed my hand. 'Perhaps I will have a little lie down after all, Sam.'

I jumped up. 'Of course. You need to rest.'

'I wish … I wish it was all over.'

A tingle of shock ran through me. 'What do you mean?' Surely she wasn't talking about her life?

'That man,' she murmured, 'that awful man.'

I stared. 'Pete?'

Gran turned to me, looking confused. 'Pete? No, no, not Pete. He was never awful, he was very nice. Too nice when it came to the girls. No, I was talking about Bert Dalzell.' She rubbed her cast and grimaced. 'I think I might need some of the painkillers the doctor prescribed. My arm is aching.'

'Sure.' Confused, I wanted to ask her what she meant—why she was talking about the Honourable Hubert Dalzell—but I could see she was in pain.

I went into the bedroom and found the box of painkillers with directions attached. 'You're only allowed two every six hours,' I said, bringing them with me into the kitchen.

I carried the tablets and a glass of water over to where Gran was standing, looking out of the front window. As she took them from me I saw a car pulling up behind my ute.

'Who's that?' I said, thinking it might be Ken again, and the woman with the hole in her stocking—thank you, Pompom. Maybe they'd hired a new car? I really, really hoped not, because there was no way I was letting them in.

Gran took her tablets and sipped the water. 'It's that nice girl with the pink hair.'

Then I saw Hope climb out of the passenger side.

I thought she looked a little less perfect than usual, but then we'd all been through a rough patch—I was sure I wasn't looking too good myself. She must have far exceeded the speed limit to get here so quickly. What did that mean? She was eager to see me, or was she just desperate to stop the truth from getting out?

'Hope!' Gran said, sounding genuinely pleased.

It was pointless hiding, I knew that, although I was momentarily tempted. But I had always preferred to confront my demons—or in this case my famous aunt, who may in fact be my mother—and I went to the door and opened it.

37

HOPE

17 January 2000

HOPE STARED AHEAD at Sam's house, feeling as nervous as she did at any important audition. She tried to look upon it as a positive—she did some of her best work when she was nervous—but then again it wasn't as if the director could step in and say 'Cut' and give her another take. She knew she only had one chance at this and she wanted to get it right.

Mitch spotted her as she came up the steps onto the verandah, and began running around her legs and wagging his tail. Over at the fence the donkeys were braying.

The door opened and Samantha was standing there. Hope gave a breathless laugh. 'It's like Noah's Ark,' she said.

Sam didn't smile back. She was pale, her eyes wide, a bit like a car-crash victim. Immediately, Hope felt guilty.

Why was she feeling guilty? Hope told herself she had nothing to feel guilty about. She could never have been a successful actress if she was tied down with a baby, and then a toddler, and then a child. Some women did it, she had seen them, but she wasn't one of them. She would have had to give up her dreams, taken a job that offered reasonable hours and security, and her life would have turned out very differently.

'I think we need to have a little talk, Samantha,' she said. 'Can I come in?'

'Hope!' Lily came trotting towards her, looking a great deal better than last time.

She told her so, and at Lily's insistence she examined the pristine cast and promised to auto-graph it, all the while aware of Sam standing watching them. Her daughter—how long since she'd allowed herself to call Samantha that?—was wearing her pretty dress, and with her fair hair down and her blue eyes, she looked so much like Pete that it almost stopped Hope's heart.

'I've been so worried,' her mother was saying, lowering her voice. 'You probably don't under-stand, Hope. You probably don't worry about anything. But I'm not as young as I used to be, you know.'

'Oh, Mum,' Hope whispered, and she put her arms around her mother's frail body and for a moment just held her.

'We might need some advice,' Lily said, her voice muffled against Hope's shoulder. 'Legal advice. What do you think?'

'Legal advice' sounded good, although scary, too. For someone who liked to micromanage every detail of her life, letting others make decisions wasn't going to be easy.

Lily stepped back, a frown drawing familiar wrinkles on her forehead. She glanced at her granddaughter. 'Sam is feeling very upset,' she scolded, 'but she won't talk about it with me. She thinks I'm too old and feeble.'

'I do not think that,' Sam butted in. 'You were going to have a rest, weren't you? I think you should, and then Hope and I can have that "little talk" she mentioned.'

'I'd better stay,' Lily said firmly. 'Where's the girl with the pink hair?' She looked towards the window. 'Will I ask her in?'

'Prue's gone into town for a latte.'

During the car journey Prue had spoken to her from the heart, revealing that she was adopted and still searching for her birth parents. Samantha, she'd informed Hope, was lucky because her biological parents were not a mystery. Prue seemed to think that it was important to tell the truth—a truth Hope had been avoiding for most of her life.

Lily gave her a nudge. 'Go on, then.'

'Samantha,' Hope began in a bracing voice. 'I'm so sorry about what happened. *Looking Back …* well, they're being unbelievably crass. And not just that, so unprofessional. I'll certainly be making complaints. I wonder if I could sue them?'

'Well there's a thought,' Sam murmured, but Hope could see she was unimpressed. 'Just tell me one thing. No prevaricating, no fobbing me off. Are you my mother?'

Direct, straight to the point, just like Faith.

'Well, technically I suppose I am, but in every other way Faith is your mother. From the moment she held you in her arms, you were hers.'

Sam was nodding, but her face looked pale and stony, and there was the glitter of angry tears in her eyes. 'You should have told me. Someone should have told me. Tacked it on to the talk when I was twelve, about boys and periods. "Oh, by the way, Sam, there's something else you need to know …"' She swallowed, trying to gain control of her voice and not quite managing it. 'Why didn't *you* tell me?'

'Samantha …'

But she'd gone; a whirl of her skirt, and she'd taken herself out of the room. Somewhere a door slammed.

Lily raised her eyebrows. 'Good start,' she said.

Hope looked at her mother. 'I think I need to sit down.'

'I'll make the tea,' Lily announced, and her eyes were wise and kind. 'You'd better go after her. She'll be crying her heart out in there.'

Picturing Sam's face, Hope wondered if that was true. And then she remembered the other night, when she had held her daughter in her arms, properly held her, for the first time since she was born. She hadn't thought of her as her daughter then. She was Samantha Cantani, her niece. She hadn't been her daughter since that early October day in nineteen seventy, and surely that was a good thing all round?

What she'd just said to Sam was the absolute truth. Technically she *was* her mother, but in all other ways it was Faith who deserved the title.

Sam was in her bedroom. At least, Hope thought with relief, she hadn't run off across the paddock. She really wasn't up to traipsing down to the creek in her Miu Miu sandals.

'Samantha?' She opened the door.

Sam sat up on the messy bed as if she didn't want to be caught at a disadvantage. Hope didn't think she was 'crying her heart out', as Lily had said, although her reddened eyes and flushed cheeks suggested she was certainly emotional.

Sam glanced up and then away again, as if she couldn't bear to look at her. That hurt. They had, thought Hope, been getting on so well.

'You always call me Samantha,' Sam said in a small wooden voice. It was a statement of fact.

Hope smiled. 'I do, don't I? Faith teases me about that. I don't know why I do it. Maybe a shrink could tell me. I named you, so maybe that's it. To me you will always be that baby called Samantha.'

'My father …?'

'You know who he was. Pete. So, you're still a Taylor and a Cantani, just not the same Taylor and Cantani.'

Sam nodded, and she suspected her daughter found comfort in that. Her family was still her family, her home still her home. The ground might have shifted, but not too much.

'Why did you give me away?' There was no resentment in her voice now, or sorrow, no accusations and drama. Just a genuine curiosity.

Relieved, Hope sat down on the end of the

bed, far enough away that she wasn't encroaching on Sam's space, yet close enough so that she didn't have to raise her voice.

'I was sixteen … seventeen by the time you were born. Pete had been killed in South Vietnam. And Faith and Joe wanted you so much. That was the perfect reason for me to hand you over. I felt safe doing so, and I suppose in a way I was relieved. I had plans for my life and I wasn't ready to be a mother without Pete there to be a father.'

Sam thought about that. 'Did he know?'

'That's the million-dollar question.' She looked into Sam's blue eyes. Pete's blue eyes. 'I wrote to him and told him, but I don't know if he read the letter before he died. His mother told Joe it was unopened, although she *would* say that. Anyway, it doesn't really matter if he read it or not. He was going to marry me as soon as his two years of National Service was up.'

She had her handbag with her, and reached down into it, finding the carefully wrapped parcel.

'I have his letters,' she said. 'His to me. Mine to him were sent home to his mother after his death, and I'm pretty sure she would have destroyed them. I was never part of her plan for her favourite son.'

Sam looked at the small sheaf of letters, tied together with string and wrapped in plastic. Hope knew they didn't look very romantic. No ribbons or bows. But they were exactly how they had been when Pete died—she'd hidden them under her bed in an old school book—and she'd never been able to bring herself to change that.

She held them out. 'Here. You should read them. I know what people say, that he had lots of girlfriends and I wasn't special, that he'd never have married me. Perhaps these will change your mind, but if not …' She shrugged. 'Doesn't matter. I know the truth.'

After a moment Sam took the letters, but she didn't undo the string and read any of them. More questions, thought Hope, and braced herself.

'After he was killed …?'

'Faith found out about … you. She took charge. Faith's good at that, but then you probably know that yourself.'

Sam managed a flicker of a smile, gone in an instant. 'Does Gran know?'

'Yes, she does.'

'God, I feel like I'm surrounded by ASIO spies feeding me false information. Everything I thought was true was a lie!'

'It wasn't like that,' Hope said urgently. 'Really it wasn't.'

Sam took a breath, fighting for control, and then she nodded. 'Go on,' she whispered. 'Faith took charge.'

'She told Mum, who was actually more supportive than I had imagined, once she was over the shock. I knew she believed it was another Rex situation, and that somehow she was to blame by passing on genes that rendered me vulnerable to men who were only after one thing. Faith and I had a good laugh about that. I insisted on telling Mrs Cantani myself, but by then she already knew. She wasn't happy and she refused to believe you were Pete's, so that was the end of that.

'I was booked into a private hospital called Curtis House, and at the same time Faith announced she was pregnant. She pretended to be having "difficulties", and I had to go with her down to Melbourne for a few months. To help. Actually, it was a relief to get away from the gossips and the people who knew me. I enjoyed my time in Melbourne, and it rekindled my dreams of being an actress. It gave me a future to plan for.'

'Well, you wouldn't want to be a mother, would you?' Sam asked, with a surprising lack of sarcasm.

'I doubt I would have made a very good one. Faith was much better at it than me. You dodged a bullet there, Samantha.'

She made a sound that was almost a laugh, and looked down at the letters, but Hope could see she wasn't finished yet. There were more questions to come.

Hope decided to jump in first this time. 'When you were born, Faith and Joe were there, and I handed you over to them. They were … incredibly happy. I believed, and I still believe, it was the best thing I have ever done.'

Sam went to speak when her gaze flickered past Hope to the door. Her face lit up. 'Mum,' she whispered, only for the joy to drain out of her. It was heartbreaking to see.

Hope turned around.

It was Faith. She was standing in the doorway, and she was wearing shorts and a shirt that wouldn't have been out of place in Hawaii. Her fair hair was pulled up into a ponytail beneath a baseball cap and there were bright pink Jellies on her feet. She looked like a seventeen-year-old.

It was only as she blinked the mist from her eyes that Hope could see her sister wasn't a teenager anymore. There were weary lines around her eyes and mouth, and shadows in the hollows of her cheeks. She had obviously been through a difficult time, and yet … Hope noticed there was a soft glow about her. The sort of glow that a deep sense of contentment brings.

'You've made a terrible mess of this, Hope,' she scolded in typical Faith fashion.

Hope managed to laugh. She made her face repentant. 'I know. I needed you to sort it out. You're better at that than me.'

Faith smiled and then her gaze slid past her sister. 'Hello, Sam,' she said, and opened her arms.

Just for an instant Sam held back, but the next moment she had flown off the bed and was hugging her mother as if her life depended upon it.

Hope was certain they didn't even notice as she crept out of the room.

She told herself she wasn't jealous, that she had made her decision long ago. Honestly, she wasn't certain what she was feeling. Perhaps some sadness, and a lot of happiness, and the usual mountain of doubts you get when looking backwards at the choices you'd made. Crossroads. Would you do the same if you had the moment again? What would have happened if you hadn't done this, or done that?

'Sit down, Hope.' Lily was busy pouring tea into a cup with one hand. 'You look done in.'

Hope managed a soft laugh and flopped down onto the chair without her usual elegance. 'Exhausted.'

'But not sorry?'

She thought about it and then shook her head. 'No, not sorry.'

'That's the main thing, then.'

Hope sipped her tea. She thought about the past, and Pete. She thought about Sam. She even thought about Prue and her quest to find her parents, and the sudden decision she had made on the trip up here to help the girl, and those like her. Some sort of charity, perhaps. The silence drew on, but it was comfortable, and she didn't feel the need to fill it. She realised that her mother knew her so well, knew her inside and out, and that was comforting too.

'Do you think they'll be all right?' she asked, hearing the murmur coming from Sam's room.

Lily nodded. 'I'm sure they will.'

'Good.' Hope smiled, and meant it. 'That's good.'

38

FAITH

17 January 2000, Golden Gully

SHE HADN'T PLANNED what she was going to say when she got there. She'd just been so desperate to get home, taking the first available flight into Melbourne, and then the taxi—who cared that it cost a fortune? Faith knew she needed to be here, where she belonged.

Her trip north had taught her that lesson at least. She belonged here, with her family, and not in the past.

Sam was blowing her nose. They'd both had a good cry, but despite what she'd said about Hope making a mess of it, her sister seemed to have laid the groundwork very well. Now it was up to Faith to do the rest.

'I'm sorry I told you not to come home,' was the first thing Sam had said, when she was able to speak.

'Oh, Sam, I knew you didn't mean it! Do you remember what *I* said?'

'When you first held me in your arms it felt

like a miracle.' Her lip wobbled.

'That was true. It did feel like that. It *was* a miracle. Joe and I couldn't have children and then suddenly there you were. There were other emotions, oh lots of them, but that was the biggie.'

'The man you went to see,' Sam said, giving her a sideways glance. 'Was it Bert Dalzell?'

Faith felt shock rippling through her. When she shook her head, she felt the muscles in her neck tense and jerky. 'No, nothing to do with him. Why did you think that?'

Sam tucked her hair behind her ears and cleared her throat. 'A couple of things. There was a story in the *Express*. I was looking at back issues, trying to find out …' She shrugged. 'Anyway, I saw the photograph of you at the Angel, with Kitty, and Dalzell was there. He lived in Golden Gully, too, and …' She paused, seemed to change her mind, and ended with, 'He went to Queensland, too.'

'So, you put three and two together and made twenty-one,' Faith guessed. 'No, it was someone else I went to see. He was also in that photo. Ray Bartel.'

'Let me guess.' Sam closed her eyes, and when she opened them she was smiling with triumph. 'Shaggy hair and dark glasses?'

Faith's laugh was husky, as if she hadn't been laughing much recently. 'That sounds like Ray. He was a singer, a musician, working at the Angel. I fell in love with him, but in hindsight that was probably due to a combination of things. I'd loved his songs and then to meet him in person … And he seemed so nice, genuinely nice. Charming. He broke my heart, or at least I thought so, but in hindsight I'm not so sure he did. He did shake me up, stopped me from making a terrible mistake, and maybe it was just as well.'

Sam was thinking it over. 'Maybe it was the gene Hope was talking about—Lily's Vulnerability to Charming Men gene,' she explained, when Faith looked puzzled. 'Gran believed she'd passed it on.'

'You mean because of my father?' Faith asked. 'Now there's a thought. My advice, stay away from charming musicians, Sam.'

Sam's expression underwent a series of alterations. 'Yeah, well … So why did you go all that way to see Ray? If you never really loved him?'

Faith pulled off her baseball cap and tossed it onto the bed. Without the cap her hair looked greasy, as if she hadn't been able to wash it properly for days.

'Ray rang me. He'd seen that photo they printed when they knew Hope was coming home. Me, Hope, Joe, Mum and you. You were about three at the time. Ray saw it and thought you were *his* daughter.'

Sam searched her eyes. 'Any reason he should have thought that?'

'There was a reason, but that's something for later. Okay?'

She thought Sam might insist on knowing it all right now, and was glad when she appeared to accept that there were details she might need to wait for.

Faith continued on. 'When we broke up he

was focused on his career. He walked away from me, which was a good thing, because your father was waiting, but I was pretty upset at the time. I hadn't thought of him in years, so when he rang it was a bit of a surprise ...'

At first she had been seriously shaken. She'd tried to explain that Sam wasn't his and let him down gently. It was all so long ago, and over the years the pain she had felt had faded. She hadn't thought of him for ages. But it wasn't the same for Ray and she soon realised that for some reason he had fixated on Sam. She was his daughter and he refused to believe otherwise. Instead of being sensible, he'd started making threats.

You can't get away with this. I want to see her and if you stop me then I'm going to the press!

He'd hung up and she'd stood there in her shop, staring at the phone, her happy, ordered life in shreds around her. What would happen if Ray went public? The only way to counteract his story was to tell the truth, and therefore cause pain to all of those she loved. The truth must be told, she knew that now, and she blamed herself for being too complacent to do it before. And what about Joe? Joe, who had always been her rock. She couldn't bear to have Joe hurt by this hand grenade from her past. This was all her fault and she had to fix it.

She'd set off, and all the way north she had been driven by her determination to make Ray accept the truth and agree to leave them alone. It was only when she arrived that she'd understood that not everything was black and white, and not everything could be fixed …

'Life hadn't been kind to Ray. He'd had disappointments. In the last few years he'd ended up alone, and with too much time to think. The crowd he got in with, the ones he thought would look after his interests, they didn't. Well, there was a lot of baggage he wanted to unload. The main reason I couldn't come home straight away was that he'd just had a medical diagnosis and it wasn't good.'

Ray was dying. Despite all that passed between them in nineteen sixty-nine, she had found herself pitying him. For a while after they broke up, she'd hated him, and then forgotten him, although she'd never forgotten that awful trip with Kitty to the 'doctor'. That was the reason—after a serious infection and another operation—she hadn't been able to have any more children. And now, thirty years later, Ray was telling her that he'd seen the photo of Sam, and demanding to be allowed to play a part in her life.

She couldn't forgive his threats, but at least now she understood why he had made them. He was frightened. The trip north that she'd thought would only take a couple of days, maybe a week, had suddenly changed completely.

'It wasn't until I got there that I realised what sort of state Ray was in.'

The grotty little cottage above the inlet, where the mangroves grew, the lack of sanitation, and Ray spending his days drinking booze and eating whatever was left from his weekly foray into the nearby town. Ray Bartel, former pop star, had turned into a cliché.

'But you stayed?'

'He didn't want me to go. Even when I told him you weren't his, he clung to the idea that I wasn't telling him the whole truth. He got quite upset.' Aggressive. Swearing, sobbing, spittle running down his chin.

You're lying! She is mine. You loved me. You wouldn't have done that. Faith, how could you do that?

Conveniently forgetting that he had wanted nothing to do with her or the baby. Ray seemed to have forgotten a lot of his past, and she supposed that various substances had taken their toll. The overworked nurse who visited daily told her that he had some mental issues that weren't helping him to come to terms with his situation. That probably explained the threats.

'Maybe if you can help us persuade him to go into the hospice,' she'd said. 'It's the best place for him. He needs looking after.'

Faith did what she could, talking to him about the past and what was best for his future, and eventually he had agreed. She'd even gone with him, and sat in his room and held his hand. He'd been calmer then, and it was a nice place, with a view from his window of a bright tropical garden.

'I regret a lot in my life,' he'd said, when she'd explained to him she had to go home, that there were people there who needed her. 'But I don't regret you.'

Now Faith cleared her throat. 'There's one more thing I wanted to explain. You probably think we should have told you, and maybe we should, but it was just the way things turned out. At first we didn't want to, we were a family, and Hope was busy with her acting. We thought it could wait. And then when Hope became famous … that threw up bigger problems. It wasn't just our secret, but one that the media would love to get their hands on. With her away so much, we just let it go. It was only when she said she was doing that program that we started to get really worried. If Ray hadn't rung I probably would have told you before Hope arrived.'

'But would you?' Sam said. 'I know the reasons why you waited, but … you should have told me a long time ago.'

Faith nodded, afraid she might start crying again. 'I'm sorry, Sam. I really am.'

After a moment Sam sighed. 'Okay.' Faith thought she was going to say more on the subject, but then she realised she was letting her off the hook. For now, at least.

'I've met someone,' Sam went on. 'He's a musician, too. He was quite well known in the eighties. Now he makes more money out of his hobby, welding metal sculptures. He's a nice man, kind, but I'm not sure you'd call him charming, and after what I've heard, that could be a plus.'

Faith recognised the look on her face. *Oh God* … But she swallowed down her doubts and concerns, telling herself that grabbing Sam and holding her tight and refusing to let her go was probably not the wisest thing to do just now.

'What's his name?'

'Lincoln Nash.'

Faith stared at her. 'You mean the guy who owns our cottage? Well that's convenient! Mum will be over the moon if you marry him, you do know that? The cottage will come back into the family again. She'll be round every five minutes.'

Sam laughed, her face pink. 'Don't be ridiculous,' she scoffed. 'We're taking things slow.'

'Good, I'm glad to hear it.'

'I can second that. She is trying to take things slow, but Lincoln is very keen. He's even sucking up to your mother.'

Faith spun around. *Joe!* She meant to say it aloud but her throat had closed up, and as she flung herself into his arms she was trying hard not to burst into tears.

It didn't work. She hadn't cried when she was away. Now there were the tears streaming down her cheeks.

He was making little murmuring sounds, holding her tight, and she didn't notice Sam leaving them to their privacy.

'I'm so sorry,' she said, kissing his face, burrowing into the warmth of him. 'I thought I could stop him talking to the press, and then when I saw him … how sick he was. Joe, I had to stay. I wanted to come home, I missed you so much, but I had to stay and finish it.'

'You should have told me,' he said, and although his voice was quiet she heard in it the days and days of anguish. 'I know you thought it was your problem, Faith, but it wasn't. It was ours, and if I've ever made you feel differently then I'm sorry.'

'Joe—'

'All the same, you had no right to go off without at least talking to me.'

She ran a shaky finger over his cheek because he was crying too. 'I suppose if I told you he didn't have a phone and I had to go into town, you wouldn't forgive me?'

He wasn't listening. 'Faith, I … I knew this guy had a pull on you, and you'd loved him once. He'd been part of your life at a time in your past when everything seemed to be lit up in technicolour. Didn't it occur to you that I might be feeling a bit insecure?'

Insecure? Could Joe have really believed, even for a second, that she still loved Ray? 'I went because I wanted to protect you and Sam. Hope, too. Because I messed up all those years ago and I wanted to make it right once and for all. It was never about him. *Never.*'

Staring into his so familiar face, she wondered if he believed her, and the thought that her crazy dash to Ray's side might have ruined all she held dear in her life made her feel dizzy and breathless. And then Joe said, 'I'm very glad to hear that,' and it seemed more important to kiss than talk.

It was a while later that Faith asked him, 'Do you remember what happened when I came home from the Angel? You came to see me and I wouldn't let you in. You kept coming, and I kept saying no, and then finally …'

'Was it the tenth time?' Joe asked, a gleam in his eyes.

'Could have been.' She refused to be sidetracked. 'When I finally gave in, we sat under the old willow tree, and everything just came spilling out of me. I couldn't stop, even though I was sure it was going to put you off. I was positive that after what I'd done, I was beyond forgiveness, and beyond loving. I thought I'd tell you and then you'd walk away, and it was exactly what I deserved.'

'I put my arms around you.'

'You held me so tight and told me it didn't matter and you loved me and always would. And after the first shock I started to cry, and then … I felt better.'

'Looked awful though. Red eyes, snot, drool—'

She pushed him, laughing. 'I'm being serious, Joe. Without you I doubt I'd be the woman I am now. You're my hero and my husband and everything in between.'

He leaned forward and kissed her lips, a tribute to her words.

'Are we back to normal now?' he asked her.

'Back to normal,' she agreed.

This was love, true love, and Faith knew that when you'd felt the real thing, you never again mistook it for the cheaper version.

39

LILY AND FAITH AND HOPE

Some days later, Golden Gully

HOPE NOTICED THAT Lily had the old porcelain teapot out on the table in her sitting room—it was one of the mementos she'd brought with her from the cottage to her new unit. Pompom was sprawled on the floor, ears twitching from the sounds of Dulcie's television next door. He'd been missing Mitch, and Lily said it was probably time for a visit.

'I'm not sure how Lincoln's cat will deal him though,' her mother went on thoughtfully. 'Bad enough with Mitch. Sam said she had to separate them the other night. Not a fight, exactly, just a lot of noise.'

'Sam is used to a lot of noise,' Hope murmured, reaching for a shortbread. She paused, glanced at her mother, and then took a bite. Her face relaxed into a smile. 'Delicious,' she said.

'Mum said you wanted to talk about something.' Faith took one, too. 'I'm due at the shop. Will it take long?'

'It might.' Hope brushed the crumbs off her fingers to give herself time to consider her story. She'd had thirty years to think about them, true, but she hadn't tried to put those graphic memories into words since she was sixteen.

Lily gave her elder daughter a stern look. 'You need to hear this, Faith. The desserts can wait.'

Faith hesitated and then, resigned, settled into her corner of the sofa.

'I didn't want to talk about this the other day,' Hope went on. 'There was already so much to tell Samantha and it wouldn't have been fair. It will all come out,' she said with a glance at her mother, 'when the time is right. But you need to know first. Especially after what Kitty said to me.'

'You've seen Kitty?' Faith's voice was sharp.

'Yes. And what she said helped me to make sense of what happened. You see, I'd always believed it was random, or maybe even my own fault, but now I don't think that was the case. What happened to me was just the final link in a chain that connected us all. Bert Dalzell, you and me.'

Faith interrupted again. 'And you knew about this?' she asked Lily with a frown.

'Yes. It's something I needed to keep to myself,' her mother said. 'You'll understand in a bit.'

'Mum is one of the reasons I want to talk,' Hope explained. 'Time to take this particular skeleton out of the cupboard.'

'Dalzell!' The name caused Faith to give a shudder. 'That name. Sam was asking me if that was who I was going to see in Queensland. She'd read about him running away up there. I didn't tell her this, but if Dalzell was heading in one direction I'd be pretty certain to run in the opposite one.'

'He knew you, didn't he?' Hope said. 'Down in Melbourne, I mean, not up here.'

'He was at the Angel a lot. He was sniffing around Kitty, but she was terrified of him, and with good reason.'

'Kitty told me that he tried to strangle her once, during sex. She said he'd killed another girl the same way. She was always scared he was going to kill her, too. Or you.'

Faith was staring at her, green eyes enormous. 'I think you'd better tell me this secret.'

It took Hope a moment to find her words, those words she hadn't spoken for thirty years. 'After you came home, when you and Joe got together, the cottage was empty most of the time. Mum had a part-time job—she's told me that she was enjoying getting out and about, seeing new faces. It wasn't,' she added, raising her voice as her mother began to speak, 'anyone's fault. I'm not blaming anyone. It was just something that happened.

'It was January nineteen seventy, and school holidays. Pete had got his National Service call-up, and he had a month before he had to report to Pucka for training. He used to come around and we'd go down to the creek, talk, and …' Her voice drifted off and she glanced at Lily.

'I think we can skip that bit,' said Faith. 'Tell me about Bert Dalzell.'

Hope nodded. 'That afternoon was a hot one—whenever I think of that summer it always seemed to be hot. We'd been sitting under the willow, drinking Fanta, and we decided to walk into town. Pete had to work and I was going to hang around until he'd finished. We were together as much as we possibly could, and it still wasn't enough.'

The sun was hot on her back and Pete's hand sweaty in hers. They'd made love, and it was getting better every time. At first she hadn't been that keen, but he'd said it would get better, and it had. He'd found some magazine that talked about a woman's fertile time of the month and they'd worked out it would be all right without a rubber. He said he'd have to buy some contraceptives next time he was in Melbourne to see his uncle, because he couldn't buy them in Golden Gully. If he did then everyone would know.

That was the trouble with living in a small town, everyone knew everything.

When she looked up there was a car coming towards them, a stream of dust in its wake, and they moved aside to let it pass. But it slowed down and stopped. The body was black and there were chrome headlamp covers and a chrome bumper bar. She should have recognised it, but she was still floating from having Pete's arms around her, her body moving with his, and it was only when he wound down his window that she realised who the driver was.

Bert Dalzell. Golden Gully's claim to fame.

At the time, it hadn't occurred to her to wonder what he was doing driving up her road, towards her cottage, and later she'd tried not to think of it at all. When he offered them a lift they were quick to agree, climbing into the cushy interior, smiling at each other, as he turned the car around and headed back towards Golden Gully.

'He kept looking at me in the rear-view mirror. His eyes were on me the whole time.'

She admitted to herself that it had felt good. That attention. She'd lit up because of it, flirting with Pete, tossing her hair. She was the star and he was her audience. Later she'd blamed herself for that, too, wondering if what happened next was her fault, if he had believed she was asking for it.

He didn't drop them in town as he'd said he would. He drove right through, and when Pete started asking questions, he said he had to go to his house and would they like to see it.

'I didn't know that he was up here hiding out. I was in a world of my own that summer. I suppose I believed his wife and kids would be there. And then, when they weren't, I thought: "Goodie, it'll be more fun without them." I wasn't frightened or anything, just … excited. Pete was with me, you see, and I thought nothing bad could happen.'

Faith said nothing. Hope noticed she was sitting with her shoulders rigid, and hands clasped tightly together, almost as if she guessed what was coming. The silence stretched on until Lily made an encouraging noise in her throat, and poured more tea.

'He brought out a bottle of whisky, said it was very old and very special. I wasn't going to drink any, but Pete did. He drank quite a lot, and he wasn't used to it. He said he needed to pee, and Dalzell sent him inside the house.

'Did I say we were sitting outside in the garden? There was an area of lawn, and a table and chairs set up near the big rosebush. I was wearing one of his wife's shady hats. It was so quiet out there, so peaceful. I was telling myself that when I was a rich and famous actress, I'd have somewhere just like that garden. Then Dalzell poured me another glass of whisky. He was talking about the sort of things he did in Melbourne, in parliament, but it wasn't boring, not at all. He was making me laugh. He had an amazing voice, so easy to listen to. Smooth …'

'Oily,' Faith retorted.

'I suppose so, but he was interesting. I didn't find him sleazy. I think, if I had, I would never have stayed there drinking with him. Or maybe I'm kidding myself. Maybe I was just too stupid to know what I was doing.'

Faith waited a beat and then said, 'What happened next?'

'He started to come on to me. Touching my hand at first, holding it in his. And then he was smoothing his fingers up and down my arm. I laughed because I still wasn't taking him seriously, and I suppose I was a bit drunk too.'

'A lot drunk,' Lily corrected.

'Probably somewhere between the two. Pete still hadn't come back and I was looking around for him. I started to stand up, saying I needed to find him, but I slipped … lost my footing … At the same moment, Dalzell grabbed me and pulled me down onto the grass. It was nice and soft, and my head was spinning, and I realised he was on top of me.'

She had decided she wouldn't go into detail. There might come a time when she had to—the police would want to know. The images flickered through her brain now, like a worn-out 1920s silent movie. His hands on her breasts, and then down the front of her shorts. The noises he was making, pulling at his own clothes, the pain as he tried to enter her. Once, twice, trying and failing. His frustration turned to anger as his body refused to perform as he wanted it to.

She was aware of what was happening and yet removed from it, so maybe she should thank the whisky for that. The smell of the roses was very strong, overpowering. When his hands closed around her throat she sobered up pretty quickly though. All of a sudden, he was squeezing tighter and tighter, and she could feel how excited he was getting.

'I couldn't breathe,' she said, her voice as matter-of-fact as she could make it. 'I thought I was going to black out. I wouldn't be able to struggle at all then and I could tell he was going to rape me. Choking me was making him hard. Then he let me go and I could breathe again. When I looked up Pete was standing over us, and he was holding a cricket bat.'

Faith whispered, 'Jesus.'

'Faith,' her mother reproved her, but her heart wasn't in it. 'You're taking the Lord's name in vain.'

'I think the Lord was very much on Pete's side that day.' Hope gave a shaky laugh. 'God was wreaking his vengeance on Dalzell.'

'What happened?' Faith said quickly, before their mother could intervene.

'Pete pushed Dalzell off me and got me up. He straightened up my clothes and he was swearing, he was so angry. Not with me, with Dalzell. I was hysterical, coughing and taking big gulps of air. Pete said he'd gone upstairs and lain down on a bed because he felt sick, and then he'd heard me screaming. He got up and went to the window, and he could see what was happening. As he ran out the door, he picked up the first thing that came to hand—the bat.'

'I'm sorry to ask, Hope. But did Dalzell say anything? I mean … while he was …'

'I wasn't paying much attention, but later, when I thought about it, I remembered him calling me his "lovely girl". And then, before Pete hit him, he was calling me a "treacherous bitch".'

Faith chewed on her lip but didn't make any comment. Lily reached out to gently touch Hope's hand, urging her to finish.

'This is the worst part,' Hope said, clearing her throat.

'I can't believe it could get much worse,' Faith murmured. 'My sister was attacked and nearly raped and I didn't even know. She didn't even think to tell me.'

'I couldn't tell you. Do you want to hear this or not?' Hope said, her calm surface beginning to shatter.

'We're listening,' Lily assured her. 'Faith, please, this wasn't to do with whether or not we trusted you. This was about keeping you out of it, and safe.'

Faith looked contrite. 'Sorry.'

Hope tried to smile and failed. 'Pete was saying that we needed to get out of there, and that we didn't want to be around when Dalzell woke up. He said we'd take the car, leave it somewhere. I said I wanted to go to the police, but Pete said no one would believe us. And then in the middle of it all, he *did* wake up.

'He was roaring like a bull. He was so angry. He came at Pete, swinging his fists, and Pete tried to fend him off. Pete was strong, but he wouldn't have hurt him unless he had to.' She stopped, taking her time, telling herself she was nearly finished.

'Pete hit him again,' Faith guessed. 'And this time he didn't get up.'

'Yes,' Hope whispered. She cleared her throat. 'He'd broken the whisky bottle and he was threatening Pete with it, saying he was going to kill him. He tried to slash him with it and cut Pete's stomach. It was bleeding, and although afterwards we could see it wasn't deep, at the time I didn't know that. All I could think was that we were going to die, and I believe Pete thought so, too. And that was why he hit him with the bat the second time.'

Dalzell went down. He made a noise, a horrible croaking sound in the back of his throat, and then there was silence. Pete turned him over and felt for a pulse, but he was dead.

Hope lost it then. Pete carried her inside and ran a

bath for her and washed her clean. He held her until she calmed down. 'We'll go to jail,' she kept saying, because it was Bert Dalzell they'd killed.

But Pete thought of the plan. He went around, gathering up anything that would give away the fact that they'd been there, and then he went outside into the garden and told her to wait inside the house. When he came to get her, he looked pale despite his tan, and he washed his hands with hot water and soap, although Hope couldn't see any marks on them.

He said that Dalzell was in the boot of his car.

'I'll drop you off at the cottage, and then I'll take him somewhere no one will ever find him. You don't have to worry, Hope. Everything will be all right, I promise.'

They took the back roads, avoiding meeting any other traffic, and whenever they hit a bump Hope kept thinking of Dalzell's body, in the boot. After Pete let her out at the cottage, he turned around and drove away again. Hope stood, watching him go, and then she ran. She was crying again, and her throat was hurting, and she burst inside the cottage, the door slamming behind her.

'It was only then I realised Mum was home.'

'She came pelting in through the door like the hounds of hell were after her,' Lily said, a faraway look in her eyes. 'I could tell something had happened, but at first I didn't think she was going to tell me.'

'If I'd been able to calm down, I probably wouldn't have spoken, but seeing Mum like that, and it all so fresh … It all came flooding out.'

Faith looked between the two of them. 'But neither of you ever said anything!' she cried and

Hope saw the hurt in her eyes.

'What was the point?' Hope's voice was resigned. 'Did you really want all of that on your mind? You were getting married, I couldn't do it to you. Pete went off to training and was shipped out to Vietnam, and then he was killed. I found out I was pregnant. Wasn't that enough to be going on with?'

For a while they were silent, and Hope could see that Faith seemed to be deep in thought. 'You said that when he offered you a lift that Dalzell was driving towards the cottage. That doesn't make any sense. Who would he be going to see at the cottage?'

'I didn't know that either, until I spoke to Kitty and she told me that you were involved in bringing Dalzell down. And that he knew about it.'

Faith shivered. Her sister had demons of her own. 'He came looking for me,' she agreed. 'Yes, I can see him doing that. Repaying me for the wrong I'd done him. Perhaps when he saw you on the road and stopped his car, he thought you *were* me. But then he realised you were my sister—he'd know I had a sister. If Kitty hadn't told him then he'd have found out. And you were definitely his type, Hope.'

Hope nodded. 'What Kitty said, about you helping the police. Is it true?' she asked. Faith didn't look like Joan of Arc, sitting on their mother's sofa in her black cargo pants and short green top, with her fair hair loose around her shoulders.

'It was Avery who charged him.' Faith gave a wry half-smile. 'The man was obsessed with the girl who was murdered. He would have done anything to see Dalzell punished.'

'Avery?' Hope frowned, something stirring in her memory. 'I wonder if …?' It was unlikely, probably not relevant, but she decided to tell them.

'Pete told me that last time he was on leave, an ex-policeman had come to see him at the training base. He said it was fine, nothing to worry about, but someone had seen Dalzell's car that day and thought they'd recognised Pete as the driver and me as the passenger. Of course Pete had pretended it was nothing, but he'd needed me to know, in case this ex-policeman wanted to talk to me, too. I'm sure his name was Avery.'

'Did he? Ever talk to you?' Faith asked, a gleam in her eyes.

'No. And neither did the police investigating Dalzell's disappearance.'

'Avery had a way of finding information that others missed,' Faith said.

'I remember Pete saying he kept telling Avery that he wasn't there, it was a mistake, but he thought … he wondered if maybe Avery knew the truth. He wondered if he'd tripped up somehow. There was a moment, a silence, as if Avery had realised the truth. Pete was scared, he said he was sure he was going to arrest him, but the next moment Avery was smiling and patting him on the back. He said something like, "That's fine. I'll just stamp it no further action".'

'All Avery wanted was justice for Melanie, the girl he believed Dalzell had killed.'

'Pete said he didn't look well.'

'If it was Avery,' said Faith, 'then I'm glad he knew about Dalzell before he died. I hope he did.'

Lily adjusted her sling. Their mother's cast was covered in signatures and cartoons. 'Hope is going to tell the police,' she said.

'Hope, are you sure?' Faith half stood up, clearly rattled. 'You know I will never say anything!'

Hope smiled, and reached for her hand. 'I know you won't. It's not that. Mum has had to hold on to this secret for thirty years, and it isn't fair to make her wait any longer. Pete's dead, there's no one they can punish.'

'And if they try I'll have something to say to them,' Lily muttered.

'The media will have a field day,' Faith warned her.

'So what? I'll make use of it, sign some inter-view deals, write a book. Make a movie,' she added softly.

Faith rolled her eyes.

'Sometimes,' Hope felt as if she was far away, 'I wonder if Pete let himself be killed. He spoke about "a life for a life", and said his two years in the army, fighting for his country, was going to be payment for what he did. But maybe, when he got to Vietnam, he changed his mind. Maybe he didn't think two years was enough. He wasn't religious, he used to laugh at the whole concept of it, but his mother was. He'd been brought up to always believe in the sanctity of life.'

Faith put an arm around her, squeezing her

close. 'If he'd wanted to be punished for what he did, why not just turn himself in to the police?' she said, the voice of reason.

Hope let her head drop onto her big sister's shoulder and sighed. She was feeling very tired. 'Because if he did that then they would have known about me. Pete was protecting me, just as he always said he would.'

Just as I have protected him for all these years.

40

SAMANTHA

14 February 2000, St Valentine's Day

THERE WERE MORE people at Estelle's property than I could have imagined a month ago, when she first came up with the idea of her fundraiser. Now she was talking about making it a yearly event.

'They're here because you do such a wonderful job,' I'd told her, but secretly I thought it probably also had a lot to do with Lincoln, and Hope, and my mum's delicious Cantani Desserts.

'Don't forget to take Bonnie and Clyde when you go,' she'd called out to me as she hurried away.

I wondered if Lincoln would notice the two goats in the back of the ute when it came time to leave. Of course he would. He'd laugh himself silly.

Jason Miller hadn't been able to make it. He was back in Melbourne, and very relieved, according to Lincoln. He said he was still planning to open the Golden Gully restaurant; however, the date kept getting pushed further into the future. Derek was staying on at the house, renovating it on his own, but he still wanted me to do the garden.

'No hurry,' he kept telling me, and as he was always adding to or changing my plans, that was just as well. One day, I thought.

I looked down from my seat on the slope above the stage. Estelle had an area on her property that was like a natural amphitheatre, and she was making the most of it. You could sit on the grass on the slope, or there were chairs down on the flat area, closer to the stage.

Gran was down in one of the chairs. I'd seen people signing her cast and shuddered to think what we would find when we took her home. There had already been a few comments that had to be erased, when we explained to her what they meant.

I had chosen the slope because it gave me a better view of Lincoln on the raised stage below. He had his guitar with him, and he was adjusting the microphone, about to start.

He'd been nervous on the drive over, but he said he was always nervous before a performance.

'It doesn't matter if they hate my new stuff,' he'd said, as if he really believed that. 'I got an order for another gate yesterday.'

I'd smiled over at him, pausing before I answered as I made a turn into Estelle's road. 'I love your gates.'

'What about my music?'

'I love your music, too.'

'My new music?'

We'd had this conversation so many times I knew it by heart. He wasn't going to get me to admit I preferred his old stuff, no matter how he tried. '*All* of your music.'

He laughed. That was one thing about Lincoln, he wasn't a sulker. He had some dark moments, sure, and didn't we all, but they didn't linger. He picked himself up and got on with it. Just as he had when his record company dropped him and he started making metal sculptures.

It was still early days, but I thought we got on pretty well. I knew I only had to look at him to feel that slow curl of heat in my stomach. Was that a sign of compatibility? I thought so. There were others: how we could make each other laugh; how he was a softy when it came to animals; how he listened so intently to Gran waffling on; how much Dad and Mum enjoyed his company. I could go on.

Mum had agreed to have another unveiling of her latest Cantani Dessert. She hadn't been able to move the original date, but it didn't matter because the first one was for the buyers and her bigger customers, and this one was for the locals and us.

She'd had to hire a refrigerated truck, and Dad had been busy putting out notices to publicise the event. After I'd seen the way they were together, the day Mum came home, I knew I would never again question just how much they loved each other. I couldn't believe I'd had those weird suspicions about Hope, or Bert Dalzell.

I hadn't asked to hear the rest of her story, or learn more about Ray Bartel. I'd decided that could wait until some other time, or maybe I wouldn't ever want to know. Dad had sat down with me and told me how sorry he was about keeping the secret, and how much he loved me. Even though I thought I should still be feeling hard done by, I was actually feeling pretty special. Life seemed pretty good just the way it was.

I could see Hope over near the stage, saying something to Lincoln, probably offering him encouragement. There hadn't been any more talk about her going back to the States. She'd had some harsh words to say about *Looking Back*. She got an apology out of them for bringing in the pit bull, Frances Durant, and the awful Ken. Eventually, Hope and the producers had come to an agreement about her show. She had brought me in, too, and Mum. We all had to agree, and we all did.

Hope is going to do a one-off interview. She is going to talk about me, and Pete, and Mum and Dad. She is going to let Australia, and the world, into our secret. Prue is arranging everything— that was part of the deal—and Hope is going to use the money to set up a trust for people who are looking for their birth parents and need help finding them. Prue is going to run it.

There's another story, too.

Hope said she wouldn't tell it to me until after I'd read Pete's letters, because she wanted me to know him better first. It took me a while to read them. And when I did, I cried, because he sounded so young and so … well, so nice. He loved her, you could hear it in every word, every sentence.

'Are you going to tell me the other story now?' I'd asked her, when I gave them back.

Hope looked down at the letters and smiled. 'Very soon,' she'd said. 'That is going to be quite complicated and I'll need some advice. Let's get Estelle's fundraiser over first.'

I have a feeling we're in for more drama, but we'll get through it. We always have.

Hope was right when she told me she was only technically my mother. In all the ways that matter, Faith and Joe are my real parents. Still, I get on well with Hope, we have a lot in common, and it's good to know that she's there if I ever need her.

Lincoln ran his fingers over his guitar strings, and people grew quiet. I felt a shiver run up my spine, seeing him down there. It was getting dark now, but they had a light rigged up, and it was shining on him.

He started to sing.

At first I didn't recognise it, and then I realised it was 'Dark Star', *my* song. He was right, it was stripped down and raw, and as I listened I felt my old sense of excitement rising. At the end I was applauding as loudly as everyone else.

I didn't enjoy the new stuff as much, except for the last song. It was one of the ones he'd written recently, about five boys sleeping head to toe in a bed in a cottage, far from home.

Came all the way out here on a sailing ship, Taylor

boys, Taylor boys.

It gave me chills.

When he was finished he made his way up the slope to me. I could have come down to him, but I enjoyed watching everyone patting him on the back and shaking his hand, saying how great he was. By the time he reached me he was flushed and laughing.

'That was so good,' I said. 'The very best.'

'Yeah?' He sat down beside me and gave me a sideways glance. 'What about the last song?'

'You wrote a song about the cottage and my family. No wonder I love you.'

His eyes lit up, and then he wrapped his arms around me. A few onlookers cheered, but I was too busy kissing him to care.

ACKNOWLEDGEMENTS

Firstly, to everyone at Harlequin Mira Australia for making writing my books such a pleasure. Special thanks to Rachael Donovan and Alexandra Nahlous on their very good advice in the editing process.

Gratitude to my agent, Selwa Anthony, who as usual gave me wonderful support while this book took shape, and thanks to Linda for finding the perfect face for the cover. (Australian edition).

My appreciation to the State Library of Victoria and the National Library of Australia, who comprehensively answered my questions on aspects of the social scene in 1960s Melbourne.

I've dedicated this book to Sandy Curtis. Her memories of Melbourne during her time working as a cocktail waitress were invaluable, and she shared them most generously. And no, she isn't in the book, this is a work of fiction.

I'd like to mention the Edgar's Mission Farm Sanctuary, which was an inspiration during the writing of this book. The world needs more kindness.

I couldn't write anything without the support and encouragement of my family, so a huge thank you to them!

And most importantly, to my readers, thank you one and all!

ABOUT THE AUTHOR

Kaye Dobbie has been writing professionally ever since she won the Big River short story contest at the age of eighteen. Her career has undergone many changes, including writing Australian historical fiction under the name Lilly Sommers, to romance written as Sara Bennett and published in the US and Australia. Her books have been translated into many languages. She is currently writing under her 'proper' name, Kaye Dobbie, and is published by Harlequin Mira in Australia and Weltbild in Germany. Kaye lives on the central Victorian goldfields, where she creates her stories and in her spare time researches her family tree.

www.ingramcontent.com/pod-product-compliance
Lightning Source LLC
Chambersburg PA
CBHW070151120726

47909CB00001B/71